Girls From Da Hood 10

Girls From Da Hood 10

Treasure Hernandez,
Blake Karrington,
and
T.C. Littles

www.urbanbooks.net

Urban Books, LLC
97 N18th Street
Wyandanch, NY 11798

ISBN 13: 978-1-62286-763-9
ISBN 10: 1-62286-763-7

First Mass Market Printing August 2016
First Trade Paperback Printing May 2015
Printed in the United States of America

10 9 8 7 6 5 4 3 2 1

This is a work of fiction. Any references or similarities to actual events, real people, living or dead, or to real locales are intended to give the novel a sense of reality. Any similarity in other names, characters, places, and incidents is entirely coincidental.

Distributed by Kensington Publishing Corp.
Submit orders to:
Customer Service
400 Hahn Road
Westminster, MD 21157-4627
Phone: 1-800-733-3000
Fax: 1-800-659-2436

All in the Family

Chapter 1

"Oh my freaking God! Not now of all times!" Unleashed panic quickly filled the room.

"Girl, Jakki, what's wrong?"

"I'll be damned, hell naw, not now! It was all good just a minute ago. This is mad crazy. That ill-bred snake School Boy got us all messed up with his hating ass! I know he did this."

"Jakki! Jakki! What? What's wrong? What is it? What he do? What, tell me!"

It was close to three in the morning as an emotional mixture of confused terror, resentment, anger, and denial took charge of the young women's voices. A warm summer evening that started out with taking shots of Rémy, smoking blunts, and popping a few pills was well on its way being a nightmare turned reality for both females, one they would soon live to regret. Wearing skirts, sandals, and tight-fitting T-shirts, they were ready to hit the local park or some low-key afterhours spot, not what they were unwisely in the middle of doing.

"Wow, I can't believe this!" Without a second thought, Jakki loosened her grip on her newly acquired "come up." The cheap cotton pillowcases filled with several expensive dresses, custom jewelry, and mostly designer purses she was holding dropped to the marble floor. With the last wine-colored leather bag she'd just moments before stuffed inside falling out at her feet, Jakki's palms grew increasingly sweaty as she thought on what to do next. The flashlight she was holding then hit the floor causing the batteries to come out and roll across the room.

"Plea . . . please tell me." Begging, Lena was close to tears seeing her newly chosen mentor visibly upset.

"This right here is some real bullshit! Why fucking me?" Jakki wondered out loud. Normally cold as ice, she was shook and it showed. Her mind traveled in a million different directions at once. She felt this obvious betrayal couldn't be happening. This couldn't be life, but it was. The so-called abruptly planned carefree night of thievery she and her cohorts intended on having had started to unravel. This was just supposed to be fun and not part of the contest. This whole thing was petty anyhow!

"Wha . . . what is it? What's wrong?" Always a follower and never a leader, whatever Jakki said, Lena naïvely took as gospel. She'd never witnessed her get excited and never once thought about questioning the moves Jakki or her cousin School Boy suggested they make. It didn't matter if it was illegal or not, Lena was down for the hustle. Up until this point, Lena trusted her newfound friend. But this caper was different. She might've been slow, but she was far from dumb. Lena could easily tell something was drastically wrong. "Why we stopping? Wh . . . wh . . . why?"

"Look, Lena, fall back and don't ask me nothing right now. Just come on, follow me and hurry!" Feeling another vibration on her breast, the big-boned beauty paused. Frustrated, she read yet another unexpected text message before stuffing her cell back in her lace wired bra. That sneaky backstabber!

"Wha . . . what is? Jakki, what's going on? Tell me!" Lena, past being on the verge of unease stood motionless in the dark wanting answers. "Plea . . . please."

"Look, girl, I'm not playing around with you. Not now. It's about to go down so instead of talking you better get ready!" *Why in the hell did I bring this green chick? Matter of fact why'd I come in the first place?*

"Jakki," Lena argued as if they were at home trying to decide what to cook for dinner not in the middle of a burglary with the high potential of turning into something much worse. "I . . . I'm not playing! What's wrong? Ready for what?"

"Okay, you stupid stutter box in a skirt, how about this? Do you like how handcuffs freaking feel? Do you? Do you wanna be in the cell next to your brother? Do you wanna get killed in this motherfucker tonight?" Jakki's tone was full of intense rage aimed at Lena.

"Nnnnn . . . no."

"All right then shut up with all that stuttering and do what I said," she demanded reaching her arm backward in the almost pitch-black darkness. "Take my hand and come on. These fools are back!"

Lena's heart was beating at least five times its normal rate. Her eyes grew wide and her mouth dry. Swallowing the sudden lump in her throat, the street-naïve seventeen-year-old could barely speak let alone think. "Okay but I . . . I . . ." Her terrified voice trembled as she stumbled into a small-sized display table causing a mannequin to tilt over. "I can't see your hand. Where you . . . you at?"

"I'm right here!" Jakki felt for Lena's extended arms. "Now come on before they come in this building and see us!" Once again she barked out in a low, muffled whisper after doubling back for her still very much green temporary partner in crime. "You wanna get us knocked or what? 'Cause a chick like me ain't trying to go back to jail! Your momma or grandma might bail ya slow, skinny ass out no matter what. But me, I'm hit; my pops still in the hospital. And my so-called loyal family, the bastard who dick you sucking, apparently he on some other type of cutthroat mentality this week!"

Practically dragging a lightweight Lena by the wrist, Jakki found a huge rack of clothing near the rear exit of the exclusive fashion boutique School Boy claimed he'd staked out for days. Receiving two text messages from her older cousin announcing the owners had pulled up in the parking lot and were getting out their cars, Jakki knew she and Lena didn't have time to escape the same way they'd come in: a hole in the side of the building School Boy crashed a stolen pickup truck through. If they did take a chance and tried it, Jakki wasn't brand new to the game and knew they ran the risk of being met with God knows what. At this point, they were trapped. It was bad enough they were taking such a gigantic risk by robbing who School Boy claimed was a retired pimp turned businessman, his bottom bitch's and partner's store, but now here they were, seconds away from possibly being caught red-handed.

"They who?" Obviously confused, Lena's eyes darted from side to side searching the dark showroom hoping to answer her own questions. "Whooooo is coming? I'm scared! Who is back? Jakki, who?"

"There you go with all them irrelevant questions again and that annoying dang gone stuttering! The owner and his woman, stupid, okay! The people who own this spot is back." Jakki was fed up with all the impromptu explanations and laid it on the line. "Now shh, I said be your scary self quiet. School Boy just text saying they got guns in they hands so chill! And right about now, knowing him, he probably gave them the bullets!"

"Guns! Bullets!" She shouted like she hadn't heard Jakki announce the owners were back on the premises and mere moments away from coming inside. "But . . . but I thought you said this was gonna be easy; in and out like the other places," Lena interrupted nervously biting at the skin surrounding her fingernails. "You ain't say nothing a . . . about guns!" She fought to get her words out as the sides of her temples started to pound.

"Listen, dummy, I thought my Master Splinter–minded cousin said it was no pistols involved either. But never mind what I said earlier or him. This is the fuck now and trust, this is serious! So for the last time shut up; besides nobody strong-armed you to come with us anyhow!" *Jesus, please be a gag in this trick's mouth.* Jakki, already positioning herself out of easy sight, roughly snatched Lena down to her knees. Moving the multitudes of hangers just right so the clothes could hopefully conceal their entire bodies, the two huddled close together. Momentarily there was nothing but dead silence inside the store. "Girl, relax and stop breathing so damn hard and loud." Listening to the cylinders of the several dead-bolt locks turn, Jakki put her index finger up to Lena's quivering lips before taking a deep breath herself. "Now shhh, be cool. Here they come."

Both saying private prayers of grace and mercy, the quiet before the storm ended. They abruptly heard infuriated loud voices and the thunderous sounds of heavy-paced footsteps simultaneously burst through the front entrance. From the makeshift clothing cave each girl braced up preparing themselves for what was to come next. Listening to whoever was clicking the light switches up and down, Jakki was relieved to know School Boy hadn't totally double-crossed her when he claimed to cut the electricity to the building, like his convenient misinformation about the guns. She had to believe it had to be nothing more than dumb luck that had brought the storeowners back in the middle of the night interrupting her criminal activities. After all what else could it have been? He had proven to be a snake earlier in the week, but claimed he was over all of that now and wanted to get past the drama.

"This don't make no type of sense. This the third time this year we've got broken into," Maino angrily proclaimed tossing his keys near one of the shattered glass showcases. Holding his cell phone for light in one hand and a gun in the other, he cautiously made his way back near the gaping hole in his otherwise perfect business. "These sick bastards had the nerve to drive a goddamn truck through my wall. Why in the world?" The ex-pimp turned businessman and drug dealer shook his head in disbelief while kicking some of the smaller amounts of debris out his way. "Who does something like this? Only an animal! I swear I wish we would've caught them thieving bum fools violating my property. On everything I love, I wish I would've been here! First the other night at the house, now this!"

"You right, babe. I can't believe how desperate these thirst buckets have become here in Detroit. You can't have anything in this city, not nothing!" his girl, holding her own gun equipped with a laser, agreed, while trying her best to see the damage. Using the popular flashlight app on her phone, his forever loyal moneymaker got a much better look and caught even more of an attitude. "I'm pissed, for real! Look at all my stuff, destroyed, scattered everywhere! I hate all these haters!"

The third person to enter the building had a screw-driver in hand the crooks probably used to start the broken steering wheel columned ignition as well as his gun. "Yo, Maino, whoever work truck they used gonna be pissed come tomorrow. The whole front end of that bad boy just about gone."

"Man, forget them and they problems. I ain't even gonna entertain that conversation! Right about now, I got worse. Look at my wall!" Enraged, Maino was ready to tear something up himself. Used to smacking one of his whores or putting his foot up they backside for being short with his money, the six foot one, slightly overweight older player was out the element of his street game having no "trick to blame" and no choice but to call the law. "If it wasn't for the silent alarm going off and alerting my cell, it ain't no telling how much more damage them sons of bitches could've done. I swear a black man can't make it in the world going legit!"

Waiting for the electric company, a tow truck, and the slow-responding police to all pull up, the disgusted old school trio checked to see if the most expensive jewelry, authentic purses, exclusive leath-ers, and the several minks in the upscale boutique were still there. Deciding to remove a few more things in stock to claim as stolen to the insurance company, they heard a strange movement from the rear of the supposedly empty store. Freezing dead in their tracks, they instinctively reached for their pistols. No words were passed between them as

Maino, still sporting pumped-up finger waves, tilted his head over toward the noise.

Following his lead, his woman and best friend slowly eased in that general direction prepared for battle. Step by step, each one anticipated who or what they'd find. Knowing the outcome would be nothing at all nice if the burglar was still on the premises, Maino tightened up on the rubber handle of his beloved 9 mm as his homeboy eagerly did the same.

Seconds later the ruffling sound was heard once more. Bred with the Detroit courage of two old lions, both men stood tall holding their own. Knowing they had the best hand against whatever came their way; it was on; kill or be killed. However, Maino's woman, gangsta to her heart and normally a hood soldier against any of her former johns who wanted to get a little rough, was not feeling as brave, gun in hand or not. Unsure of herself, she refused to be a coward even after haphazardly tripping over a pillowcase filled with items from the store, breaking one of her extra-long multicolored acrylic nails. Suddenly, out the corner of her squinting eyes, she caught a glimpse of what appeared to be a gray object dart by in the distance. Not knowing if it was just the thick eyelashes she was wearing, the small-frame dark-skinned female didn't want miss an opportunity to prove she was still down for her man. Aiming the crimson red laser beam at what she believed to be the mystery intruder who'd interrupted her peaceful night, her arm raised. Feeling the weight of the pistol in her lower forearm, she got a chill.

Not taking a chance on what the unknown held for her and her people in the dark boutique, her index finger hooked around the hairline trigger. Without further hesitation, she fired off three rounds back to back. At the end of the rapid ear splitting tirade, the store grew silent once more. Praying she'd struck her target, the quick-to-react woman defensively took a few paces backward allowing the men to investigate what, if anything, was hit.

"Hey, girl, what in the heck you was shooting at? What you see?" Maino, having been just caught off-guard and robbed by four lightweight females at his spot wanted to show he wasn't too old to still be in the game. He was ready for combat and to protect what was his as he shrugged her shaky hand off his arm. "I ain't see nothing! What did you see?"

"Over there." She excitedly pointed with the bright beam still illuminating from her pistol. "I seen someone crawling! They was moving real, real fast, on they knees! Right over there!"

What started as a few brief minutes hiding underneath the rack of overpriced clothing soon began to feel like an eternity in hell. Listening to the owners furiously discuss what would've taken place if they would have caught the culprits in the act, Jakki knew she and Lena had to either stay quiet and pray they weren't discovered for God knows how long or wait until they got a chance and made a desperate run for the hole. She was good with that. Lena, however, wasn't as calm as Jakki. Her head started to hurt even more as the grueling moments dragged by.

She tried to control her heavy breathing, but it was a struggle. Knowing one of her full-blown anxiety attacks was only seconds away from taking over her body, the petrified teen tried to warn Jakki, but was immediately met with a swift right elbow to the ribs to shut up.

"Be still, girl, before they hear us," Jakki, ignoring another vibration text alert from undoubtedly School Boy, lowly whispered in her ear after peeking out in between a few pair of blue jeans and a blouse. "That man is pissed off for real about that damage the truck made! Plus they got they guns out. They ain't playing around with our black asses! I swear they ain't!"

Hearing the word "gun" didn't make Lena remain calm; in fact, it did the complete opposite as her heartbeat increased feeling like it was going to jump out her chest. Wishing she was back home in her own bed or even chilling over at School Boy's getting turned up she started to squirm even more. With a numbing sensation flowing through her limbs, she fought to stay movement free. "I . . . I can't breathe." She quietly forced the words out as Jakki's hand quickly reached over grabbing her mouth.

Mad at herself for bringing School Boy's little inexperienced jump off with them in the first place, Jakki had to keep the scary female in line before they both were caught breaking and entering cases and were sent to jail or, worse than that, considering the rage in the owners' voices, found dead somewhere in a ditch. *Dang I think they heard us*. Jakki momentarily paused as the voices stopped talking. Hearing the soft but apparent sound of footsteps coming in their direction, Jakki's eyes widened in anticipation of what was to come next as small beads of sweat formed on her forehead. *This dumb tramp done got us about to be knocked.* Realizing Lena was the weak link Jakki pressed her hand down harder over her now closed mouth praying she'd not panic even more and recklessly yell out that she surrendered.

Lena felt the painful pressure of Jakki's palm pushing her lips against her teeth causing the inside of her top one to split. She already couldn't breathe and this was making matters worse. With the owner's footsteps getting louder, she wanted to faint as tears streamed down her face and over Jakki's powerful hand. *I just wanna go home,* was all she could think when a small beam of red colored light came through the multitudes of clothing finding its bull's-eye directly on her left leg. Not sure of what the light truly was, Lena had seen enough gangster movies in her short time alive and hoped it wasn't what she assumed it to be.

Oh my God! Jakki held Lena even closer after seeing what she knew was a laser beam shine in the confines of the makeshift cave and on the girl's bare leg. In a matter of seconds both their fears were tragically confirmed. Jakki gouged her curved fingernails deeply into Lena's jaw line pressing down even harder over her mouth as three gunshots rang out inside the store. *Fuck! Fuck! Fuck!* was all she could think before, during, and after hearing the gunfire. Feeling Lena's skinny-boned body jerk and her head tilt back, Jakki knew the girl was hit.

Lena suffering from an anxiety attack or even going to jail was now the least of her problems. There was a gaping hole the size of a nickel ripped through the flesh of her skin striking a main artery. In excruciating torment, her mind blacked out. Her short life flashed before her tear-filled eyes. Wanting to yell for help from the very people who she'd victimized, she couldn't as Jakki callously still covered her mouth and now had her much bigger entire body holding hers still. The intense burning sensation, coupled with the heavy amounts of blood now leaking from the wound, was more than the young girl could stand. Traumatized, she felt warm piss run out in between her inner thighs as her body grew limp. Before Lena could ask God to forgive her for all of her sins, just like that it was lights out; her lifeless body slumped over in Jakki's cruel tattoo-covered arms.

Damn, now what? Shit! Where is the police when you need they dirty asses? Jakki, convinced she was also on her way to get called home, closed her eyes waiting for what was gonna ultimately happen after what came next.

Chapter 2

Maino lowered his gun after getting a closer look. "Ahh naw! A stray alley cat! You gotta be kidding me." In spite of the current situation with the electricity being cut, the police who had yet to show up and the tires and front grill of a truck crashed through his rear storeroom, the fact that his girl mistook a burglar for a four-legged feline that must've come through the open hole was hilarious, not only to him but his homeboy as well. "It's a sin and a shame. You done fell all the way off. I thought you was still trained to straight go!"

"Oh my God! Oh my God! It's bleeding to death all over the floor!" she screamed holding both hands to her face as the innocent cat squirmed fighting to live. "I can't believe this. I just can't."

"Well believe it." He laughed sideways at his "always down for whatever" rider who ran toward the front of the store and stood in the open doorway. "Your crazy, pilled-up self done assassinated a cat. You hit him right in his hip." Maino used his cell phone for light as he yelled over his shoulder. "So I guess that solves the big mystery of what the noise was over here huh?"

Not realizing one of the three bullets had struck not only the cat but one of the women who'd caused the late night chaos as well, Maino had his boy grab a few plastic bags, some gloves, and a shovel from the rear of the building. Taking the still very much alive but suffering animal out to the Dumpster, all three of them decided to hit a joint to calm their nerves while leaving the front door wide open.

Appreciative she was spared, at least for the time being, Jakki silently thanked God. Having been through numerous times of being caught up in some wild Detroit street, tonight definitely topped them all. Still holding Lena's deceased body in her arms, a rightfully paranoid Jakki waited until she heard the shovel scoop up the injured cat that saved her from taking the next deadly bullet of the night. She finally exhaled hearing the three voices head toward the alley.

Peeking out from the clothes rack once more, Jakki saw the front door was open and the bright streetlight beamed in. With School Boy continuing to blow up her cell, she knew her grimy-intentions cousin was still close by if nothing else. *Family ain't about nothing. How that asshole gonna play me of all people? Something told me not to do this caper. How he ain't got me?* Of course she wondered why her first cousin hadn't burst through the door, guns blazing to save her from harm's way, especially after hearing gunshots, but now was not the time to figure that part out.

Quickly coming to the realization she was on her own and her life was on the line, Jakki wasted no time getting her mind back right and focused. Allowing Lena to fall over in the still growing puddle of her own blood and urine, she sighed knowing there was nothing more she could do for School Boy's jump off. She was gone. With the eerie feeling of death looming in the air, Jakki knew this was her time to make a move. It was now or never if she wanted to live to see daylight.

Being mindful that one or all of the three could come back inside the building at anytime and change her future for the worse, Jakki silently moved the hangers aside. On her knees, she stuck her head back out making sure the coast was clear. With a blood-soaked skirt and saliva- and mucus-covered hands, she emerged from their hiding place. Cautiously she stood to her feet feeling wetness on her toes as well, which had to be more of Lena's blood. Still hearing the lighthearted teasing of the girl shooting the cat by mistake and one of the men choking on what smelled like the truth, Jakki looked over at the open door judging the distance she had to go to make it to freedom. Acting as if they were giving away free cheese, butter, and honey to the first twenty people in line, Jakki took off running. Only a few yards from making a clean getaway, the frantic female stumbled to the floor tripping over the same pillowcase filled with stolen items she'd dropped earlier. Scrambling desperately to get back on her feet, Jakki heard one of the men yell he'd heard a noise back inside of the store.

Damn I'm about to get killed too! I know I shouldn't have broken into this spot without doing my damn homework! This is so messy. At the same time she heard the sounds of footsteps rush through the back entrance she saw a set of high-beam headlights in the front of the building coming her way. *Lord please let this be School Boy's backstabbing, double-crossing ass! Please!*

Chapter 3

A Week Earlier

Ruben was getting old or, as he called it, a little up in wisdom years. Having been in the game of nickel and dime hustling since he was a youth, the gray-haired man had no problem whatsoever still putting in street work. Never having a steady nine to five without it being demanded by a probation officer, he was the head of household ruling with an iron fist. Teaching his kin nickel and dimes added up to dollars and cents, and dollar and cents added up to power and respect, not only in your own community, but wherever you went; he was proud of the man he was. Encouraging his family members to do the same, never working for anyone outside of their immediate bloodline had become a Crayton Clan badge of honor and a symbol in their prison-drawn code of arms.

Being cursed, as he often voiced to his loyal wife, with two girls and no boys, he spent a lot of time with his deceased brother's son nicknamed School Boy. Ruben took him under his wing at an early age despite resentment from the boy's mother who wanted something better for her son. As the years went by Ruben's intentions were obvious even to Ray Charles. Grooming School Boy to take over his spot at the head of the family and make the major

decisions if need be unfortunately was not going as
planned. Ruben was a man who sat back observing
situations before reacting. Studying School Boy was
no hard task. Being stubborn, vindictive, jealous, and
all in all out for himself instead of the general good
of the family was more than a problem in Ruben's
eyes. On more than several occasions, School Boy
had dropped the ball causing great financial strains
on the Crayton Clan general fund. Ruben didn't mind
paying out medical or legal fees if one of the family
members got injured or locked up, but cashing out
on the sheer stupidity School Boy was becoming
infamous for was more than a problem.

"Look, you young fool!" Ruben shouted across the
crowded street. "Bring your dumb, ignorant self here.
This don't make no type of sense."

Hesitantly, School Boy waited for traffic to clear
before slowly making his way toward the house. He
knew what Uncle Ruben wanted, but wasn't in the
mood to endure another one of his long, drawn-out
speeches in what he was doing wrong. "Yeah, Unc,
what's good this morning?"

"Don't 'what's good this morning' me, you shift-
less idiot. I got a wakeup call at six this morning
informing me that you and some skinny little broad
from around the way was roaming the streets beating
dudes I used to run with out they pension checks."

"Listen, Unc—" School Boy started to take a cop
but was immediately interrupted.

"Shut your smart mouth, boy! I'm talking and you
listening, you dig!" Ruben's chest stuck out daring his

deceased brother's son to grow some real balls and jump bad. "I done told you time and time again, the Craytons don't shit where we sleep. But apparently you like forget me and the family!"

"Naw, fall back some, Unc! It ain't like that!" School Boy, feeling embarrassed of being chastised by his uncle, slightly raised his voice trying to impress a small group of passing females.

Grabbing him by the throat, Ruben rushed his nephew against the concrete wall of the family home. Fed up with his blatant contempt for the rules of the game, Ruben applied more pressure to the boy's neck than he probably should have. "How many times I gotta tell you not to disrespect me, young buck? This right here I'm telling you ain't a joke and neither am I! One day you gonna step in the wrong pile of shit out here in these streets and get your ass handed to you!"

"Ruben, Ruben, don't!" His wife bolted out the front door with his oldest daughter, Jakki, following closely behind. "You're gonna mess around and kill him. Take your hands off that child, please! Don't go to jail for the likes of him!"

As School Boy fought to break free from his uncle's tightening grip, Jakki gave him the "I told you so, dumb nigga" look. Realizing her cousin was near death as his eyes bulged, she too stepped in begging her father to let him go. "Dad! Dad! Stop it! Let his stupid butt go! I keep telling you he ain't ready for what you need him to be!" Her judgmental but justified words rang out on the block they called home. "It ain't in him, it ain't. And we all see it but you!"

Hearing his firstborn's voice and words of wisdom, Ruben reluctantly loosened his chokehold allowing School Boy to fall to the ground like an old rag doll. Towering over him, he watched his wife fake pamper the boy checking his neck for any signs of immediate bruising. "Jakki, you probably right. Matter of fact I know you are, but what choice do I have? It's this idiot's rightful place we talking about."

Jakki had just about enough of her father's biased attitude toward women and their place in the crime-minded Crayton family. Angrily she voiced her opinion loud enough for the entire block to hear. "Look, Dad, no disrespect to you, Uncle Ronni, Uncle Tim, or grand-father's legacy, but ever since I was little, I've been breaking my neck to show y'all that I wasn't like mom or my little sister who chose to go away to college." Glancing over at her mother, Jakki gave her a faint smile reassuring her that the statements she had said and was about to say was nothing personal. "I'm not saying I'm as hard as y'all or even as smart, but I can hold my own out here in these streets and you know it. I make moves all the time to bring money to the table but all you see is School Boy. Female or not, I do's my thang," she proudly announced daring either of her family members to dispute her gangsta or raw street credibility. "It ain't nothing personal against him. I love my li'l cousin like everybody else, but dang, Pops, you not seeing the obvious, the bigger picture. School Boy might be blood, Pops, but you can tell he ain't cut from the same cloth as us. He built to fold. Can't you see that? He's a reckless mess! You gotta see it!"

Catching his breath, Ruben was still heated but knew not at least hearing his opinionated daughter out was not an option. "And, Jakki, what exactly is that? What am I missing?"

School Boy was now on his feet and could easily tell where his cousin's impromptu conversation was headed. Not wanting to be cut off from what he as well as his Uncle Ruben felt was his destiny, he spoke up while rubbing his sore neck. "Yeah, Jakki, you fake hater, what is you saying he missing? You got me all the way messed up! I hold my own too. You bugging!"

"Watch your mouth!" his aunt demanded ironically now ready to choke School Boy out herself. "You know better to address any woman in this family like that, especially out in public!"

"Naw, Auntie, she straight outta line! You hear her on that snake tip!"

"Shut your goddamn mouth; all of you," Ruben inter-jected holding his right hand up to his chest. "I'm tired of all this back and forth bickering. For months you two have been at each other's throats about this, that, and the other thing. Well I'm sick of the bullshit! Jakki, no one is saying you don't do more than your share, sometimes more than I think you should risk doing, but this family . . ."

Before Ruben could finish his statement, he clutched his chest falling toward the handrail.

Rushing to his side, Jakki's mother desperately screamed out for someone to get help for her husband. With complete pandemonium erupting throughout the block, Jakki quickly dialed for an ambulance while School Boy stood back frozen in fear that his beloved uncle, mentor, and family patriarch had taken his last breath. When the medical technicians finally arrived, they did all they could possibly do on scene and ran for the transport gurney. As they roared off, sirens blaring, lights flashing, heading toward the hospital, the likelihood that Ruben would survive the trip seem bleak.

After several medical tests were run, Ruben thankfully was soon resting comfortable in his private hospital room. Having had some of the most respected physicians in metro Detroit examine him, he was easily diagnosed having weak valves in his heart and would require surgery. Doomed to bed rest for at least seven to ten days before the procedure could take place, Ruben knew the beat had to go on with the family enterprise. With his wife and daughter posted at his side, Ruben finally gave in to Jakki's wishes allowing her as well as the proven to be irresponsible School Boy to equally share the responsibility as the potential bread winners for the infamous Crayton Clan. Instructing his wife to relay the terms of the joint hustle partnership to an obviously missing in action School Boy, Ruben closed his eyes hoping for the best, but expecting the worst.

Chapter 4

"From this point on, you get your bread and I'm gonna get mine," Jakki eagerly proclaimed. "And, School Boy, try not to be a hater when I come up on you either."

"You, a backstabbing nothing female, come up on me? Imagine that jumping off."

"Remember, fool, like I told my father, you was built to fold! At the end of the day, that's who you are and who you always gonna be." With both hands planted firmly on her hips, she laughed knowing she was going to end up on the top in the long run.

Going in their separate directions, Jakki's female intuition told her undoubtedly before her dad regained his health and was able to take his rightful place back at the head of the table, her older cousin was going to give her hell to pay. Wasting no more time, the trained to go female dipped into her bedroom grabbing a spiral notebook. Writing down the single number zero beside the date, she vowed to make her family proud.

Calling a few of her homegirls who'd been riding with her ever since second grade, Jakki instructed them to sit down at the picnic table located in a remote area of the park. Promising them a certain uplifting change to their financial situation if they'd help her bring School Boy down, all three were happily on board. With the distant carefree sounds of kids playing tag, Jakki laid out her game plan. Within hours, they were ready to put in work.

Nightfall came. Jakki, always calm, cool, and collected, strangely bit at the side of her fingernails. Wanting nothing more than to prove the point she was ready to stand at the head of the table, she was determined this first caper would go off without so much as a hiccup. "Okay y'all, first things first. I already got word from my boy who drives the UPS truck. He let me know the regular package they get over on McGraw and Third was delivered a few hours ago. So I know they still holding heavy in that son of a bitch."

"Whoa, that's what's up, Jakki." Paulette smiled knowing her girl stayed on point with the 411. "Then the rest is gonna be easy as one, two, three. Shiddd, I got some bills to pay."

Jakki was confident as well but didn't want to be overly cocky. She'd been raised in a family who taught the hard life lesson things could and would go wrong at any given moment when you dealing with the unknown. "Girl, say that shit; from your mouth to the great hustle God's ears. As soon as Faye and Carla get here, we'll be ready to put thang in motion."

No sooner than the crew showed up, they agreed that their choice of clothing was perfect for the game

plan Jakki had in mind. Cutoff shorts, small, fitted
T-shirts, and of course high-top sneakers to give
them that around the way girl look but also double as
a good running shoe if need be; all was well.

"Okay, Carla, like I said earlier, they don't know
you in this neighborhood, so you the point person to
get us through the front door as smooth as possible.
Trust me when I tell y'all my boy knows these thirsty
fools around here like the back of his hand. He told
me the old guys who run this spot is just like that
simple-minded cousin of mine School Boy. As soon
as they see some new kitty cat on the set, they gonna
break they necks to try to front and hit the skins first,
like they gonna get a trophy." Jakki looked her homegirl up and down handing her a small .22-caliber just
in case things went haywire. Sure she wanted to beat
School Boy and prove her father and the rest of the
men in her family wrong, but her friends all seeing
daylight was her first priority.

"Don't worry, sis." Carla tucked the small handgun
in the lower small of her back. Slightly adjusting her
T-shirt with the words 100% FUN written across the
chest in bright neon pink lettering, she grinned with
confidence. "I'm all over my part. I got this. Just
make sure you divas is ready to rock when I send the
text."

Jakki, Paulette, and Faye each made sure their
own pistols were loaded as Carla made her way up
the walkway. Popping her chewing gun, the brazen
beauty took a deep breath before knocking on the

door of the well-known west side trap house. After a few brief seconds she was met at the door by a middle-aged man who was obviously the home-owner.

"Yeah, what you need?" he defensively growled through the semi-closed door until seeing Carla's innocent face and standing at full attention breasts poking out.

"Hey, ummm, I'm looking for Tone? Is he here?" Jakki had wisely chosen one of if not the most common name in the hood knowing full well if a dude named Tone wasn't inside at the moment, and hopefully there'd be none, there damn for sure straight was a Tone someone at the trap house knew. Needless to say, after Carla flashed her bright Colgate smile, any hot-blooded male, young or old, would be disarmed.

"Tone?" The man puzzled opening the door all the way not sensing any real danger. "I'm sorry, baby doll, but it ain't no Tone here."

"Really?" Carla sheepishly tugged at her hair. "I know I'm at the right house. He told me to meet him here."

"Oh yeah?" The man rubbed at his growing bald spot wishing he was ten years younger and his old lady didn't have keys.

"Wow." Carla pouted pulling her cell out from her bra while making sure he got a full view of what she was working with. "That's why I hate these young guys. They always clowning around when they should be about their business! I'm about to erase his tired number from my phone. He don't deserve me anyhow," she flirted as his old eyes stayed glued to her youthful shape. "I'm too good at what I do."

"And just what is it that you do?" His old pimp player curiosity was piqued thinking about where he put his little blue pills.

As Jakki and the others anxiously peered from the porch of an abandoned house located three doors down and across the street, Carla soon sent a text saying, It's on. Then, just as planned, the old man stood to the side as she made her way inside the house.

Phase one of the caper was coming together just as Jakki hoped it would. Making sure the coast was clear the trio eased down the block, bent the corner, and disappeared into the dark debris-covered alley. Having staked out the premises the day before, Jakki led the way into the backyard of the trap house. Paulette and Faye each pulled out the red-colored bandanas they had tucked in their shorts. Tying them tightly around their faces, Jakki made sure she could only see their eyes. Then, just to be on the safe side, they put on clear-lens Ray-Bans. Luckily, none of the girls had easily recognizable tattoos on their arms or legs, so that was all the better in case they were unfortunate to run into one of their soon-to-be victims later on down the line. Everyone knew Detroit was the smallest big city around. It was often said that if you was about that life you didn't have to find trouble in Detroit. Just wake up and brush your teeth; that headache would find you.

With the grace of three panthers, Paulette and Fay guns drawn, crept up on the back porch as Jakki continued on to the side of the front porch. Ensuring her own bandana and glasses were in place, she braced herself waiting for Carla's next text. Hearing what seemed like two different voices, not including her homegirl's, Jakki's heart raced with anticipation. She'd done hundreds of illegal things throughout the years, but this time was different. This time was like she was gambling with a million dollars on the line, all with one roll of the dice or pull of the highest card. Hoping no one came to cop and interrupt what they had going on, Jakki prayed Carla would come on with the come on.

Watching a set of car headlights drive by and keep going, her cell finally buzzed. Reading the text, Jakki's thoughts were confirmed. Carla informed her there were only two dudes inside the house. She also said they were relaxed, hoping to take turns getting their old, limp peckers sucked in exchange for a few dollars for cab fare back to the side of town she'd claimed she'd come from and a few pills. That was all a cold and calculating Jakki needed to know to put the second phase of the plan into full motion. If all went as planned they'd be back on their side of town in no time flat, counting money, popping bottles, and smoking a fat blunt.

Wasting no more time, Jakki texted Faye so they would know the plan was definitely about to go down and to be on point. Raising her hand upward Jakki

used the gun's barrel. Lightly she tapped on the side
glass window like she'd seen a few pill heads do the
night before. Quickly, before anyone could look out
the side window and see who was who, she darted
on the porch. With an attitude, she knocked twice.
Standing over to the far side, Jakki hoped the dude
working the door would be so distracted with Carla
inside tempting them with the possibility of that
good good and the fact he assumed it was one of
their regular customers who knew the knock on the
side window routine, he'd carelessly swing the door
open, no questions asked.

"Yeah, what's up? What you need tonight?" His
voice rang out in a rush to get back to the young girl
inside who promised to suck his balls dry.

"I need everything you got, old timer!" Jakki
bum-rushed the man shoving her gun up to his
throat. With force, the big-boned diva stuck the
barrel deep into his jugular vein letting him know
she was about her business and not one to be played
with. "Now keep it Gucci and make my dreams
come true tonight! I'ma need that package that just
dropped. And if you know what's really good don't
try to short change me either! I know what's up! I
know y'all just got the re-up!"

"Hold up, hold up!" He fought to speak as his blood
pressure leaped to crucial heart attack and stroke
levels. Being caught off-guard, he knew she had him
at a disadvantage but wanted to stall for time hoping
his gun-toting woman or at least a pill-seeking cus-

tomer would show up and save him and his partner from whatever fate they were facing.

"Listen, sir." Jakki, a woman of her word, tried switching up giving the man, seeming to be about her father's age who was still sporting finger waves, a small bit of respect. "I don't wanna hurt nan one of y'all!" She roughly marched him all the way back inside the fully furnished house where Carla had the other man laid out on the floor with his pants down to his ankles undoubtedly interrupted believing he was about to get his hookup sucked. "We just need the pills, the cough syrup, and that cash. You run us that shit and we outta here as quick as we came."

"Yeah," Carla laughed opening the rear door for Paulette and Faye. "We gonna need a little bit more than them few measly nickels and dimes y'all was offering me to get my knees dirty. Matter of fact, if we wasn't in such a hurry, I'd make y'all both suck each other's thang just for fun."

Knowing there wasn't much they could do but hand over the stash if they wanted to survive, the man who opened the door grudgingly gathered several plastic freezer storage bags filled with Oxycontin, Oxycodone, Vicodin, and maybe twelve or so morphine patches. Packing up at least thirty-nine bottles of prescription-strength cough syrup they had perfectly lined up on the living room mantle, along with about $2,900 in cash, Jakki smiled knowing this pay out would be good not only for her cohorts, but the Crayton Clan family pot. Noticing an abnormal amount of designer purses, clothing items with tags on them, and other items you'd find at a store, Jakki assumed not only was this a pill spot, but some sort of booster house as well. But they weren't there to go shopping.

Humiliated, he was still sprawled on the floor with his soft, drawn-up manhood exposed, the distraught victim, who seemed like he used to be that deal back in the day, begged Paulette and Faye to at least allow him to pull his pants up so if he died he could have some sort of dignity when facing his Maker. As both girls giggled from behind their disguises, Jakki, yelling from the other room, callously informed him there would be no negotiations or favors done. The only order of business would be just his boy getting them what they came for and them leaving. "Look, dude, hold tight. We almost done here!"

Using a roll of gray duct tape Faye had on her wrist like a bracelet, they securely attached one man's arms to the steel shower rod in the bathroom and placed his own sock in his mouth to keep him from calling out for help once they'd left. The other man's arms were taped to the leg of the dining room table that was full of empty food containers and a few dirty glasses. With his penis still out for the world to see, Carla cruelly wrapped it with the tape knowing it would hurt like a pain he'd never felt before when he tried to take it off.

After turning the television up loudly, the four brazen females on a mission discretely retreated out the back door of the trap house as sounds of a *Sanford and Son* rerun kept the two older men company. Jumping in the car that was parked one block over, Jakki started the ignition and skirted off heading toward the freeway. No one was really hurt and the men, both criminals themselves, had no alternative whatsoever but to suck the loss up. Of course they couldn't call the police. Jakki's plan had gone off without a hitch.

As the girls joked about what Carla had done to the man's tiny-sized pride and joy, Jakki's mindset was totally focused on the lick they'd just hit. *Let School Boy crazy behind top this!*

Chapter 5

Proud of herself and what newly gained revenue she'd brought to the table, Jakki issued out her girls' cut for their part and of course her boy, the UPS driver, had to be hit off for the initial info. Hand delivering the rest to her uncle who'd always acted as a makeshift treasurer and inventory specialist, she felt satisfied. Having no true ambitions to be anything other than just that was one of if not the main reason Ruben wanted to groom School Boy to move up the family ladder when the time was right.

Dropping the package off at seven o'clock in the morning within sixty short minutes, word spread throughout the entire close-knit tight-lipped family that Jakki had come through with a huge blessing. Getting praise from everyone, she was elated she'd done good. Brushing her hair back into a ponytail and putting on a new pair of leggings, a T-shirt, and sandals, she was almost ready to go. Grabbing her oversized purse and cell phone off the charger, she was on her way out the front door to visit her father when School Boy came from out the kitchen. Knowing her mom or one of the other family members had thrown up in her cousin's face the perfect crime she'd committed, it was easy for Jakki to see he felt some sort of way.

Here we go. "Hey, cuz, what's good with you?"

School Boy, as she thought, was not in the mood for a family love bonding session and cut straight to the chase. "What the entire hell ever," he evilly hissed tugging at his crotch. "Word in the street is you and them slut bucket rats you run with got down last night."

"Dang, you good hating black man! Why they gotta be slut buckets?"

"Later for them nut gobblers and your show off ass!"

"Damn, cuz, you mad or nah?" Jakki laughed antagonizing him further.

"Me mad? Nah never that," he tried playing it off but she saw straight through him. "You think that lightweight in the pockets job you did last night was something, wait 'til you see what I got up later."

"Dawg, whatever!" Jakki brushed past him going into the refrigerator for a glass of juice. "Do you, playboy. Trust, I ain't hating! And while you busy doing you why don't you go visit your sick uncle! Or is that too much like right? At the end of the day, I'm all about family and thought you was too!"

"Suck my dick, Jakki!"

After their brief confrontation, Jakki was out the door knowing she had a few important runs to make in hopes of lining up some more work before visiting her father later at the hospital.

***

"Yo, real talk, guy. I ain't about to let Jakki get away with thinking she did something so untouchable and great!"

"Dude, you is pissed all the way off, like a dog trying to catch his tail."

"Nah, man, I'm not. But that daddy's girl Jakki was talking trash about me to my uncle like I don't be out here getting that paper." School Boy posted up with his friend after buying the last two out of season wool face masks from the corner dollar store. "Well after me and you shoot this move, we gonna see who the family be jocking then! I'm about that life for real! I'm trained to go!"

After stealing a Dodge Magnum from the employee parking lot at the local college, School Boy and his forever loyal comrade hit I-94 heading west. As his friend drove, School Boy went through the owner's glove compartment and center console hoping to find some petty cash or possibly a credit card. Finding nothing of great value, he reclined the seat for the short-distance ride they were taking. After twenty minutes or so, they pulled over at the mall parking the car in far corner of the lot so no one would notice the broken steering wheel column. Going into one of the main entrances, they didn't stop to window shop as they exited at the far end easily finding another vehicle to steal. Back en route to their destination, School Boy followed the same routine in that car as well. Coming up empty-handed again, he was soon consoled as his homeboy slowly turned into the parking lot of an out of the way jewelry store in a not so crowded strip mall. As they drove passed they noticed the showroom was empty of customers.

Momentarily seeing no one was coming in or out of the adjacent stores, the pair inconspicuously slipped on their masks. With hammers in their back pockets, they quickly exited the car leaving it running and the doors unlocked. Within a matter of seconds, the wild, ill-minded pair was inside the normally tranquil confines of the store. As a shocked staff hurried to mash the alarm button, the showcase glass was shattering and School Boy and his friend were grabbing their hearts' desires of rings, chains, and watches, putting them in plastic bags. Just as fast as the masked hooligans had entered the building they were gone. Jumping back in the second stolen car, they roared off and were soon back in the first one on I-94 homebound.

Jakki think she did something last night. She ain't about that life! School Boy thought as he looked through the bag of jewelry. *Wait until my uncle hears about this here!* Using his cell phone he took a picture of the jewelry sprawled across his lap sending it to Jakki.

Having the plug with just about everyone she met, Jakki looked up an old contact of hers who stayed getting jobs at different types of store just to run scams for extra cash. After going by his mother's crib, then one of his baby mommas' houses, Jakki soon found out Roe was working as a sales rep at T-Mobile and thankfully was still popping pills.

Obtaining that valuable information courtesy of his bitter baby momma who she threw a hot twenty to, Jakki happily headed straight over to the store. Hearing the bell ring when someone entered or exited everyone glanced at the door, just because. Roe, thirsty for a for sure come up, saw Jakki walk through the door. Immediately he passed his current customer over to his coworker knowing full well whatever had brought his homegirl Jakki his way was worth far more than the small commission he was gonna make off signing some random hard-working nine-to-five city employee up on a family plan on two inexpensive phones. He'd been hooking folks up with lines using other people's identities for over a month or so now, but knew his time at this job was just about up, so Jakki showing up was right on time.

"Hello, how are you?" Jakki devilishly grinned while winking her eye.

"Hello, miss, is it something I can interest you in today?" Roe caught on to her body language and knew she wanted him to act as if they didn't know one another. "Are you already a T-Mobile customer or are you looking for new service?"

"I really came in just to get a brochure of your different plans for a friend of mine." Jakki waited for

Roe to return with what she'd asked for slipping him her number on the sly. "Thanks for the information. And by the way, is it anywhere around here that I can get lunch at real quick?"

Once again, a streetwise Roe caught on and played the game advising her to go two blocks down to the Burger King. Jakki thanked him and left out the store. Less than five minutes later she received a text from a strange number she knew had to be Roe's saying he'd be there shortly. Jakki ordered a Whopper with cheese and waited.

It was nearing five o'clock in the evening and Jakki was finally finished with her running around setting her traps. Determined to beat her cousin, especially since he was so rude to her earlier, she took pride in knowing what she had planned next with Roe's scandalous ass. School Boy would be livid beyond belief. Driving into the parking garage of the hospital, Jakki used her hands to smooth back any loose hairs from her ponytail. Wanting to gloat to her father about the amount of money her uncle said the pills and cough syrup would bring the family while he was out of commission brought Jakki satisfaction. Placing the green ticket in the upper part of her dashboard, she got out heading toward the lobby. Feeling the vibration of her phone, she took it out her purse. Seeing it was a picture message from none other than School Boy kinda made her blood boil low-key, considering she blamed him for her father even stressing out being in the hospital in the first place. Tossing her cell back in her purse, she decided not to even look at it knowing it was probably more insults or dry mouth threats. *I'm tight on him right now!*

"Yes, hi," the nurse greeted Jakki as she was leaving out Mr. Crayton's room. "Please don't stay too long. Our patient has had visitors all day and needs his rest."

"No problem," Jakki replied to the nurse, heading over to her father's bedside. "Hey, Dad, how you feeling this evening?" Jakki lovingly asked while trying to fix Ruben's pillow. "How long ago did Mom leave?"

"She left about twenty minutes ago. She said she had to go to the grocery store or something." Ruben shook his head laughing. "You know your mother; when she sees a new recipe on one of them cooking shows she has to try it out."

Glad to see her father was in good spirits, Jakki was bursting at the seams for him to praise her for what she'd pulled off the night before. "Dad, I know Mom told you."

"Yes, Jakki, of course. You know she did." Ruben smiled knowing his daughter lived to make him happy. "And your uncle was here too with one of his crazy girlfriends."

Just as the sick but strong-willed head of the Crayton Clan was about to tell his firstborn how proud he was of what he heard she'd done for the family's financial situation, a breaking news report flashed on the television. Like everyone else who watched any broadcast, whenever a breaking story came on, especially at the top of the hour, all eyes were focused on what was deemed so important. Reaching for the remote, Ruben aimed it up at the wall-mounted set.

With the volume now much higher he and his daughter watched the newscaster describe the wild events that'd taken place earlier in the afternoon in a nearby suburban city. Staring at graphic video of two masked men bursting into a jewelry store then smashing showcases with hammers after threatening to harm the workers, Jakki and her father were both speechless. It was like time was standing still and they were frozen. She knew her loudmouth crazy cousin in action when she saw him, mask or not, just as Ruben recognized his nephew.

"Oh my God! Sweet baby Jesus," Jakki finally mumbled under her breath. "No, he didn't!" Reaching back in her purse for her cell, she finally hit the small icon downloading the message School Boy had sent her right before coming upstairs.

"Does that fool realize the amount of heat he could bring to the family doing some crazy garbage like this?" Ruben was ready to snatch the IV out his arm and the heart monitors from his chest. "That slow-thinking idiot! That damn boy is a moron! After all the years I've had him under my wing he turns around and does something this stupid, and in broad daylight! Get your uncle on the phone Jakki, now! We gotta do some damage control before that fool boy brings the whole family to its knees!"

Jakki was stunned. She didn't know what to say let alone do. *So this what he was talking about doing this morning.* She could barely wrap her mind around what her eyes were seeing. Letting her father look at the picture now on her cell phone screen, any doubt or hopeful prayer the star of the local five o'clock newscast wasn't actually School Boy was quickly shot down. "I wonder just how many other people that dummy done sent this incriminating mess to. See, Dad, I told you that boy ain't ready. He's outta control! He trying to get the entire family knocked. He's trying to ruin us!" Jakki rubbed her forehead wishing she could turn back the hands of time and stop School Boy from doing the ridiculous stunt he'd done.

At a loss for words, Ruben's true emotions were noticeably apparent as the nurse on duty rushed back in to check his vitals trying to figure out what suddenly caused the significant spike in the machines' patterns at her desk. With her patient's heart racing twice the normal rate and huge amounts of perspiration leaking from his skin, the trained caregiver asked Jakki to please step out the room after calling for emergency assistance from a doctor.

Chapter 6

"I told you we was gonna come up!" School Boy and his friend sat back in an abandoned house they'd been squatting in ever since the beginning of summer.

"Yeah, Dawg, but my girl just called me asking was that you and me on the news just now."

"Say what now?"

"Yeah, School Boy, she said it's some videotape that's on nearly every channel. She said you can't see the dude's faces, but she knows what I had on this morning."

"Damn, my dude, well we might need to get rid of these clothes." He acted as if being the stars on *Live at Five* was a big joke. "Maybe that's why everybody in my whack all in my business family keeps blowing my shit up like they crazy. Maybe they want a real player's autograph!"

Still not taking it as serious as they should be, they popped a few pills after both sipping from a huge doubled-up Styrofoam cup of purple-colored lean. Putting some loud smoke in the air, each laughed about the looks on the salespeople's faces when their hammers were going wild. Separating their ill-gotten gain, the fact that they were facing double-digit football numbers if and when they got caught seemed not to matter as their high took command.

***

Back on the block, Jakki asked everyone she came in contact with if they'd seen School Boy or knew where he was at. Getting just about the same response from each of her neighbors, she gave up knowing sooner or later her wayward menace of a cousin would show up bragging and boasting about the brazen crime he committed.

Reassuring her mother that her father was doing much better and resting comfortably after his abrupt medical scare, Jakki disappeared into her bedroom. Dropping down to the side of her bed, the usually calm, cold, and calculating female clenched her hands together saying not only a prayer for her dad, but the entire Crayton Clan who was sure to suffer behind School Boy's off-the-hook antics. Glancing over her shoulder at the clock radio on the dresser she took notice it was nearing nine. Even though School Boy had thrown a serious wrench in her disposition about the financial hustle challenge her father had issued between the two, Jakki knew the beat had to go on. Sure her uncle had put the family on high alert to be cautious in case the cops were watching and no one was supposed to speak to anyone about any personal family business until further notice; however, she had to meet up with Roe and hit this last major lick before falling back.

"Hey, my baby, I'm down the block at that same Burger King we met at." Jakki looked around the parking lot feeling like she was being watched. "You about ready to put in this work or what?"

Roe had already gathered his few personal items from the T-Mobile store placing them in the side door dented rust bucket he was driving. Promised a small plastic baggie of hard to come by prescription only drugs and a bottle of potent cough syrup, the struggling pill head swiftly replied: he was born ready.

Driving around the rear exit of the building, Jakki parked two stores down, turned off her headlights and killed the engine. Popping the trunk, she stepped outside the car waiting for Roe. Leaning back in the shadows Jakki checked her cell phone seeing no one had called. And right about now in her world, no news was good news. Moments later Roe emerged from the back door of the T-Mobile store with a medium-sized garbage can in hand. With his soon-to-be ex-coworker holding the door open for safety precautions, Roe raised the container emptying the contents into the huge green receptacle. Just like that, he ducked back inside. Still feeling like she was being watched, Jakki shrugged it off as nothing but sheer paranoia brought on by the longwinded speech about the foolishness School Boy had done and how things were about to get hot.

Just as quietly as she'd crept up on the porch of the trap house she and her friends had hit the prior night, Jakki made her way to the metal Dumpster that stood at least a good foot taller than her. With both hands firmly gripping the sides, she lifted the weight of her body upward so she could look inside the smelly tomb where garbage came to die. Luckily the green plastic bag Roe had thrown in had an easily recognizable T-Mobile logo taped across it. Using the strength of one arm, Jakki snatched the bag out then ran back to her car. Throwing the bag in the rear of the trunk, she slammed it shut and smiled. Backing the car out the same way she'd driven in, the elated female was soon back at Burger King waiting for Roe, her temporary partner in crime.

Ripping the bag open, Jakki marveled how smoothly this electronic come up had gone down. *I swear this must be my week to shine!* Jakki was overjoyed with the bag's content. Counting at least fourteen Galaxy Note 4s, eight or so iPhone 6 Pluses, and countless Galaxy S5s, Roe, a certified and street official pill head of his word, had held up his end of the bargain even more so throwing in a few Android tablets and a gang of overpriced phone cases. Closing the trunk back down Jakki leaned over into her car's open window opening up her purse. She knew Roe probably could've stolen all this merchandise himself and tried flipping it out in the streets, but that type of slow moneymaking grind was not what most addicts, even nine-to-five having functional abusers, were used to. They wanted their cash or drugs as soon as possible and lucky for Jakki, they could never see the bigger picture. Choosing to bless Roe with a handful extra of pills she could easily sell around the way, Jakki was never known for being stingy. Yeah, she was hard as most guys she'd come in contact with, but never unfair. When Roe finally arrived, the two wasted no time settling up. Jakki, having business to tend to, drove off leaving Roe in the parking lot eagerly deciding which pill would get him where he needed to be the quickest.

Just like that Jakki was about to bring even more seemingly untraceable revenue to her beloved infamous family. Nothing at all like that reckless blood-tainted cousin of hers, she wanted to show her father loud money, like School Boy was determined on getting, wasn't always good money.

Chapter 7

Daybreak usually brings about a fresh start for most and Jakki was no different. Climbing out of bed with a bright outlook on her father's condition, something told her he would be better soon and back home where he belonged. No longer worried about who would take his place when he stepped down, the loyal daughter was now focused on him returning to stand at the head of the table. In the few days that he'd been incapacitated, it felt like the world was going crazy. She was spending every waking moment trying to bring her own flesh and blood down. At one point she and School Boy were closer than just first cousins; they were like brother and sister or best friends. Now, just like that, they were sworn bitter enemies.

Inhaling the smells of her mother's homemade biscuits, Jakki looked under her bed removing the bag of stolen phones. Ripping away at the plastic, one by one she laid them on the bed. Taking out her spiral notebook, she added an estimated actual value as well as street value directly under her calculations from the pills, cough syrup, and cash she'd gotten from a few nights back. After taking two new iPhone 6 Plus cell phones and a tablet for her mom, Jakki unselfishly placed the rest in a shopping bag to give to her uncle to add to the family pot.

Dressed in a robe, her empty stomach was starting to growl. Wanting to grab a few of her mom's biscuits before she took them down to her father, Jakki sped up her pace. Going toward the bathroom to brush her teeth and at least wash her face, she was surprisingly met in the hallway by School Boy. "What in the . . . ?"

"Yo, what's good, Jakki?" he nonchalantly asked looking high as a kite and exhausted all at the same time.

"What's good?" Jakki instantly repeated with rage. "Are you freaking for real? Are you kidding me? Negro, come in here." She snatched her cousin by the arm practically dragging him in her bedroom slamming the door shut. "Where you been hiding out at, dummy? You know me and Pops seen you all on the news? Geesh, all of Detroit seen you and that fool you run with!"

"Girl, chill, it ain't that serious." School Boy smirked still feeling the aftermath of the sometimes lethal combination of pills and lean. "Them fools ain't see our faces so we good!"

"You think so?"

"Yeah, I do. And why you hating so hard on what I do anyhow? You jealous of the lick I hit or what?"

"Me, of all people, jealous? School Boy, get your life and have several seats! Why in the world would I be hating or jealous about that stupid caught on *Candid Camera* mess you did?"

"Whatever, girl, me and my manz got a real come up from that store! When your pops and my other uncle do the count on that lick, you gonna be looking straight crazy!" School Boy tugged on his manhood like he was posted up on the street corner talking trash to one of his homeboys. "I'ma be the last man standing at the end of the day, flat the fuck out. And wait until you see what else I got planned in the next few days!"

"Something else planned? Oh hell naw!" Watching School Boy stumble, then fall back on her bed, Jakki insisted he sit up so they could clear up some things. "Look, cuz, I don't know how things got so foul between us, but this side eyeing ain't for me and you, not at all. You out here doing the most acting all buck wild and for what? It ain't what you do but how you do it. And besides, it ain't like my daddy about to really walk away from his position, at least no time soon."

"Yeah, okay, Jakki, you say that now, but for real, if you didn't feel that way, why you going so damn hard in the paint to show you really about that life?" School Boy was all in his emotions. "Running up in the pill spot on the east side! Yeah, cuz, I heard about it. You ain't the only one with they ear to the street."

Jakki tightened the belt on her robe and mockingly laughed. "Silly weak-made, Negro, I was born being about that life just like you. Matter of fact, let's keep it one hundred, I'm the realest nigga on your team any day of the week; not that simple-minded car-thieving bastard you run with or his stuttering, bun-biting sister you smashing!"

"Yeah, but—"

"Yeah, but my pretty ass," Jakki bossed up catching a hot fire hostile attitude. "Look, fool, I'm 'bout done trying to get what family loyalty truly is through to your thick skull. I gotta get dressed and go visit my father that you ain't once been to see since the day he collapsed."

"But—"

"But nothing," she cut him off yet again. "We got a family meeting at the restaurant later this afternoon. Can I tell everyone you coming or what?"

"For what? All they wanna do is talk that yang yang shit to a guy!"

"So ummm, is that a yes or a no? Because like I told you, I ain't got time. Matter of fact, do what you feel. I got thangs to do." On that note Jakki decided to skip the biscuits, take a shower, and hit the streets early. School Boy had worked her last nerve and tried to take her out her positive disposition. A steaming hot shower would surely get her back on track.

Left in his cousin's bedroom feeling a small bit of remorse, School Boy stood to his feet. Walking over to her dresser, the out for self young man took a hard look at himself in the mirror. "I don't know, my dude," he started talking to himself. "Can I trust her slick ass or not?" Reaching for some much needed lotion for his morning ashy face, he saw two brand new cell phones and a tablet. Knowing if this was last week this time, there'd be no doubt whatsoever in his mind that the extra iPhone 6 Plus had to be for him.

That's how he and his favorite cousin got down. They always hooked each other up.

Hearing the shower water running, School Boy took it upon himself to take the gift off the dresser he knew was rightfully his. Just to prove to Jakki he'd at least heard what she was saying, whether he agreed or not, the hardheaded thug dug deep in his left blue jean pocket pulling out one of several high-priced diamond rings he'd stolen in the highly publicized smash and grab robbery. Placing it down exactly where the phone was, he left out the front door without so much as a good-bye to cousin or his auntie. School Boy knew he could've sold the ring in the street for way more than the popular brand new in the box cell phone was worth, but blessing Jakki was more valuable. Maybe now she'd get off his back.

Arriving at the hospital, Jakki saw a few familiar cars parked in the valet section. Wanting to leave as soon as possible when the meeting was over, she opted to go into the garage and park herself. Having dropped off the bag of expensive cell phones to her uncle earlier, her overall attitude was positive. She knew when her family usually got together for one of their brainstorming conferences things could get out of hand. Accusations of favoritism would be hurled along with a public belittling from a parent if the child was acting out or worse than that strayed from the fold. Loyalty was first in the Crayton handbook and anything else including God Himself came in a distant second.

Jakki braced herself knowing today was definitely going to be one of those days. Why her dad would choose to hold such a surefire explosive get-together in the hospital family room was beyond her, but of course it was no way she'd question his judgment, not now. School Boy and his televised antics were sure to be at the top of the discussions, if not the only thing. And since his own father's death, School Boy and all he did, good or bad, was all on Ruben. After years of dishing out judgments on certain renegade branches of the family tree, it was now time for their fearless leader to finally stand accused of bad parenting.

When the few privileged rulemaking members of the Crayton Clan gathered inside the normally quiet room, talk of what Jakki's favorite cousin had done started immediately. Twirling the diamond ring on her finger School Boy left in exchange for one of the cell phones, Jakki couldn't help but believe there was still some hope for her wayward cousin and despite what her elders were saying about disowning him, family loyalty would still prevail. When her ailing dad, wheelchair bound, entered, a respectful hush fell across the room. Pushed by his wife toward the head of the table, Jakki hated to think she wanted to stand at that very spot so badly she almost caused her father to die. After hearing the family finances being spoken about from her uncle, Jakki at least felt like she'd made her father proud. Especially knowing he was about to take a sock in the gut for School Boy.

The minutes seemed to drag by. Each person took turns basically saying the same thing; Ruben either had to get the boy out the state to be ostracized from the rest of them or the virus had to be eliminated all together. They agreed bringing this much heat and possibly notoriety to the family name was not good for any of them. Before Jakki knew it, her father along with the others had nominated her to get School Boy to meet with them within twenty-four hours to either leave town indefinitely until things cooled down or turn himself in and take whatever it was like a man, facing all consequences that may come his way. He would be reassured his legal fees would be paid, but as far as anyone from the Crayton Clan publicly supporting him, that was a no-go. The decision would be left up to the troubled youth Ruben sadly hoped would one day stand at the head of the table. But whatever fate School Boy chose, it was up to Jakki to deliver him to the elders by any means she saw fit. Her uncle reminded her that no matter what amount of revenue she brought to the table, standing where her father stood took strength to do whatever had to be done if it endangered the family as a whole.

Chapter 8

Jakki didn't know if she could do what was asked of her, practically demanded. Her family, father included, wanted her to betray School Boy's trust to get him to sit down with them and figure out his options. She knew that was nothing more than a ploy, considering they'd already decided what would and had to take place. Not wanting to disappoint her dad or bring him any more shame, Jakki placed the call doing what she had to do. After three or four rings it was apparent her cousin wasn't going to answer and then confirmed hearing his profanity-filled music voicemail greeting.

Once again fumbling with her new diamond, Jakki wished she could turn back the hands of time. Pulling up in front of Carla's apartment building, Jakki hoped Paulette and Faye had already arrived. With a new hustle on tap to make money, she decided to put the situation with her cousin temporarily on the back burner and return to focusing on her own moneymaking ventures. There was no second-guessing she'd given up on the immediate idea of taking Ruben's place, but her getting cash was always going to factor into her daily life. Like her uncle reported at the meeting, bringing a prideful smile to her dad's face, percentage-wise, Jakki Crayton was turning in more revenue than most of the men in the family this week. The hard hustling Detroit-born diva knew every week couldn't be like this week, but today was like Christmas, Fourth of July, and her birthday all rolled into one. This week she was queen of the clan. The only downside to her celebrated reign was heartbreakingly she knew her own flesh and blood; School Boy would do anything to dethrone her.

Once inside the apartment, Jakki had each lady take a seat and pay careful attention of how things had to take place if they wanted to walk away on easy street. With three sets of eager eyes on her, she laid out the next illegal venture that would sponsor the down for anything females to continue going on shopping sprees, pay car notes and rent, and avoid shutoff notices. Being the boss to them that she was, Jakki promised the trio that this game they were about to run was sure to be epic. Just like the UPS driver tipped her off about the two old guys running the pill house, Jakki had yet another plug. This plug was not a knowing or willing participant to the crime, but so be it. There were always casualties in war and make no mistake about it, Jakki making money was a full-out battle. This time it was a guy she used to go to summer camp with back in the day when they were just kids. She'd bumped into him at Red Lobster and they exchanged numbers.

Lusting after her now full breasts and thick frame, Jakki would hook up with him from time to time mesmerizing him with her advanced sexual skills. Like most men, the white collar businessman thought with his small head instead of the one mounted in between his shoulders. Her ex–camp mate was not like Jakki one bit. He was a perfect square knowing absolutely nothing about hustling in the mean streets of Detroit. Having been snatched out the hood five or ten days after camp ended, he never knew struggle or what it meant to make ends meet. The wildest thing he'd ever done was allowing Jakki to seduce him in the executive bathroom of the corporate office where he worked.

Jakki, always on the prowl for a scam, had figured out his passwords to various accounts he was put in charge of. Peer pressured into hooking a few of his equally stick up in the ass friends of his with hers, they had agreed to meet late night at their office penthouse for some innocent fun in the Jacuzzi. Planning on drugging the men and taking not so flattering pictures to blackmail them with, along with transferring some of the accounts monies to Green Dot cards, Jakki knew this was gonna put her on easy street for months. After tonight's come up, she was going into semiretirement and let her father and uncle worry about the day-to-day bullshit.

Chapter 9

"Bae, what you think gonna happen to my big brother? You think they gonna let . . . let him go?" a worried Lena stuttered while looking out the front picture window.

"Girl, your guess is as good as mine." School Boy leaned back on the couch propping his feet up on the coffee table. "I don't know what that fool was thinking anyhow stealing a car just to joy ride around the hood in! He ain't need to pull that low-budget stunt and we sitting on all this cash."

Walking away from the window, Lena saw the plastic bag of stolen jewelry laid out next to School Boy's feet, the same jewelry he claimed they couldn't touch yet because it was too hot. "I told him he was gonna get . . . get caught. He was up in the middle of the . . . the intersection doing donuts!" She struggled to get the rest of her sentence out. "Like some little kid."

"Well I hope no matter what that fool stand tall and be a solider about his." He reached for the lighter. "I hope he boss up if need be, ya feel me?"

"What you mean, Bae?"

"Girl, you know what I mean. Stop acting so dingy. You seen us putting in that work all over the news."

"I know," Lena regretfully replied wishing her brother had never followed the man she loved.

"Well you know these non getting bread bums around here be on that snake tip. Whack hustle wannabe players don't want the next man to come up if they can't." He lit a Newport and shook his head. "Let's just hope ain't nobody rat us out. And if they did, let's hope your brother hold his head and his tongue."

Lena was infatuated with her older brother's friend and had been since she was about ten, but she loved her sibling and didn't want anyone, School Boy included, to start rumors about his snitching. "Bae, I love you, I swear I do. And you know I . . . I got your back, but don't be over here putting those misconceptions in the air about my family. My brother as solid as they come."

"Damnnnnnnn, look at you getting beastie around this raggedy piece of nothing house!" He loudly laughed.

Caught in her emotions, Lena headed back to the window wishing she'd see her menace to society brother stroll up the walkway like him being knocked was all a joke or a big misunderstanding on the cop's behalf. "Naw, it ain't that. But ain't you the one always around here talking that family first, blood in blood out, family loyalty stuff? Now look at you, pissed . . . pissed off not even talking to my homegirl Jakki. She always got your . . . your back and mine!"

"What?" He started feeling some sort of way, but kept his composure. "Slow your roll, girl, with that annoying stuttering. You getting out of order with all that speaking on mines. Stay in your damn place!"

"Dang, Bae, I'm just saying you might need to call her and at least go visit your uncle. He's like your daddy." Folding her arms Lena had tears starting to form. "I just wish my brother would come home or at least call."

School Boy, in deep thought, finished smoking his cigarette then leaned his head backward closing his eyes.

It was nearing ten and Jakki was getting ready to meet back up with her crew. After calling School Boy several more times, she'd completely given up on trying to encourage him to sit down with everyone and try to come to a middle ground. *Forget all of that! Let him keep doing him. I'm so over it,* she thought as she stopped to get gas and buy a pack of chewing gum. *Me and my girls is about getting that paper tonight and I straight like that don't need or want no distractions to my concentration courtesy of School Boy's self-centered attitude!*

Tossing the station attendant a twenty, the pump seemed to be moving extra slow allowing two different men to try to run slick game on Jakki. Amused, she laughed as she got back in her car. Glancing up in the rearview mirror, she checked her makeup.

Both guys coming at her sideways let her know she was indeed looking extra cute tonight. Starting the ignition, she was finally on her way to pick up Carla so they could meet up with Faye and Paulette.

Less than fifteen minutes from her destination, Jakki's cell rang. Turning down the radio, she reached over swooping her cell off the passenger seat. Without looking at the illuminated screen, she pushed talk assuming it was Carla.

"Hold tight. I'm almost there."

"Almost where?" School Boy blurted out.

"Hello?"

"Yeah!"

"Cuz, is this you?" Jakki asked pulling the phone back from her face so she could see the screen.

"Yeah, fool, it's me!"

"Well what number is this you calling from?"

"Girl, I'm calling you from my new iPhone 6 Plus this female blessed me with!"

"Oh yeah." Jakki giggled tired of being evil toward her blood.

"Yeah, my number one go-getter!"

"I got your go-getter, crazy, but where you been? I was blowing your line up all evening."

School Boy, for the first time in days seemed to be in a good mood and it showed in his voice. "I had it here at Lena's crib charging. I been rocking this new big boy all day."

"Dig that, well . . ."

"Well what, cuz? I know you ain't trying to rush a guy off the line. Where in the hell was you going anyhow? Who you thought I was?"

Jakki thought twice about telling him, but figured what was the difference. "I was about to go holler at Carla and blow one."

"Man, eighty-six Carla always coattail-riding ass! Come swing by Lena's and get lifted with your manz. I got that good fire over here!" School Boy demanded not willing to take no for answer. "I'm about to roll up a few blunts right now. So hang up, cuz, and pull up on a young, handsome moneymaker!"

With the scheme she'd perfectly plotted ready to jump, Jakki didn't want to be late, but at the same time didn't want to leave her family hanging, especially considering this was the first time he'd reached out ever since her father collapsed. *Damn this fool messing with my bread!* Busting a U-turn, Jakki called Carla telling her to let the girls know she'd be a little late. After that she texted ol' boy telling him one of the girls had babysitting issues but the party was definitely still on. *I'ma just smoke one blunt with his crazy ass, tell him what the family want him to do, and be out!*

"Okay now, cuz, I ain't gonna lie, this right here is some good weed." Jakki choked inhaling twice more before passing the blunt to Lena. "Whoever got this making a killing, I know."

Eyes bloodshot red and wired, School Boy cracked open a bottle of Rémy Martin 1738 and separated the three clear plastic cups he'd gotten from the corner store. "Yeah, girl, them trees is the deal. Me and Lena been getting high as three kites off an ounce for two days in a row."

"Yeah," Lena agreed after also choking. "I think this weed is what made my brother bug out and act a fool."

"Oh yeah?" Jakki grew confused wanting to know more.

"Yeah, sis, that's why he's in jail now." Lena's high started to deflate even thinking about her brother's present confinement issues.

"Jail?" Jakki, puzzled, raised her eyebrow at School Boy. "What she mean jail, cuz? What he in there for?"

School Boy wanted nothing more than to jump up and slap the spit out of Lena's mouth but put his anger on safety. "Naw, cuz, it ain't what you think." He reassured Jakki who was on pins and needles. "It ain't about that other thing, I guess."

"There the hell you go . . . go again with that. I told you he ain't nooooo snitch!" Lena, fist balled, jumped up like she was ready to do battle with a giant. "And don't think I don't notice that big, shiny diamond ring on her finger that was in that bag yesterday! I thought you said—"

"Yo, nosey trick, don't worry about what I said! And chill on all that stuttering before I stuff some of this big boy in your mouth." School Boy motioned down at his crotch. "Ain't nobody said that okay? I was just telling my little cousin when it comes to my manz, it's whatever."

"Y'all both chill," Jakki intervened thinking about the code of the streets. "As long as he keeps his mouth shut then everyone is good all the way around. Lena's brother always been a soldier."

Pouring the smooth-tasting liquor in the glasses, School Boy made a toast to family cruelly telling Lena she needed to sit this one out because she wasn't they blood. "Not you, Lena, you fall back!"

"Boy, stop that! This girl been rocking with you since she was in disposable diapers. Don't do her like that. She done helped us out more than a few times." Not wanting to tell School Boy she totally agreed with him and Lena was no more than an insignificant jump off who would do anything to fit in, she decided not to add fuel to the already scorching fire.

With everyone calmed down, the three of them continued to get white boy wasted. By midnight, Jakki had forgotten about her prior commitment to her friends and the plan that was gonna enable her and them to chill on the mindset of everyday monkey hustling. She knew they were counting on her and she hated to let them down, but at the end of the day School Boy was family and to her there was nothing greater than that bond friendship included. Ignoring the constant buzzing sounds of her cell, she was busy being twisted up in School Boy and her bonding over all the things his new phone could do. Out of nowhere, with Lena in the kitchen frying a bag of wing dings, Jakki dumbly decided to kill the mood by bringing up family business.

"Cuz, trust me when I tell your worrisome soul." He raised his slurring voice. "Don't nobody wanna hear that crap right about now."

"Dawg, I'm just saying," Jakki leaned in closely whispering in his ear. "You don't know what that stuttering jump off broad's grand theft auto brother behind them bars saying. You know guys just like females ain't loyal." She glanced over at the kitchen door making sure Lena's happy-go-lucky ass wasn't coming with their plates. "For all we know he in there telling them everything he can think of so he can come home."

"Cuz." School Boy shook his head laughing while rolling up yet another blunt. "You know they say jail builds character with some dudes!"

"Naw, fool, you know what they really and truly say is: first one in, first one out. He ain't blood." Jakki bargained trying to get her point across. "You need to talk to the family; well, at least my father. You don't wanna get mangled around in the system and don't have the full support of the Craytons do you?"

School Boy started to feel some sort of way, but decided to keep it to himself. Flicking the lighter, he blazed up. Finally no more words on the subject were passed as Lena, naïve to the game, returned to the living room with chicken, bread, and a big bottle of ranch dressing.

Chapter 10

It was getting late. Well after one in the morning. Jakki, School Boy, and Lena were definitely feeling the full-blown effects of their highs. Laughing at a DVD of a Kevin Hart comedy show, each seemed to outwardly forget their worries. However, School Boy wasn't really in the same place mentally as the females in the living room were. The more he drank and the more he smoked, he kept replaying in his mind what Jakki was urging him to do: throw himself at the mercy of Ruben. Yeah, he was ecstatic his little cousin wasn't tripping any longer and had come to hang out with him, but disappointingly to him, she'd brought the same bad vibe feelings she'd been displaying to him all week long since his uncle fell out in the street. Yeah, he was out doing his own thing, that most of if not all the family took as being pure renegade in nature; but so damn what? He felt as if he wasn't putting any of them in any real danger.

Unlike Lena's brother, School Boy felt he was bred for prison and if it came down to it he would do his time, no matter how long, standing on his head. Whatever was gonna happen was gonna happen and he wasn't one for living his life on his tiptoes, avoiding walking under ladders or trying not to break mirrors. School Boy was ruthless and rotten and had no off button and no home training since birth.

"Bae, you good?" Lena noticed her so-called man was zoned out seemingly in another world. "What you over there thinking about?"

"Yeah, cuz, what's good over there in that wild mind of yours?"

School Boy took his time in answering. Downing the last swig in the bottle, he finally spoke. "You know what, Jakki? I was thinking about what you said earlier."

"Earlier?" Lena cut in. "What she say? I missed it."

"Yo, fall back, girl," he insisted with an annoyed tone. "I'm talking to my family."

"Well excuse the hot piss outta me!" Lena sarcastically shouted while getting up heading toward the bathroom.

When the cousins were finally alone, School Boy felt more at ease to speak. "Look, I was sitting over here thinking about going to talk to Unc in the morning."

"Oh yeah?" Jakki was overly elated she'd gotten through to him to do the right thing. "That's good, cuz, for real!"

"Well, I can admit I've been out here messing up, but you know hearing you talk down on me seeing you father on the ground like that kinda had a nigga's brains fried. Ya feel me?"

"Yeah, I do. And seriously, I'm sorry I was saying them things. I was out of order. You pull your weight with the family just like I do."

"Thanks, cuz." School Boy grinned with a forever scheme floating in his head. "Well just for old times' sake before I go and holler at your pops and the rest of them fools in the morning, let's hit one more lick together."

"A lick? When and what you talking about?" Jakki frowned knowing that must've been the weed, pills, and liquor talking.

"Yeah, cuz; just something I've been plotting on since last month but never got around to."

"Last month?"

"Yeah, some real easy in and out work just for the hell of it."

"In and out?" Jakki thought about the money she'd missed out on from earlier and slowly began to consider his out of the blue proposition.

"You know me and you used to be on our Batman and Robin routine before last week." School Boy laid it on thick continuing to sell her on the idea. "And since I'm going to talk to Unc and probably be put out of commission for who knows how long, give a guy something to smile about."

"You beyond crazy," Jakki teased.

"It must be in my blood." School Boy stood up beating himself in the middle of his chest. "So you with me tonight or what, cuz?"

"Okay as soon as I smash this big, raggedy piece of metal into the back part of the building, you and

Lena grab the pillowcases, jump out your car, and rush in through the hole. I already cut the power lines running to the store so we should be good on time. Ain't no alarms going off."

"What's all in here, cuz? I mean what exactly should we be looking for and why you ain't coming in?" Jakki quizzed following the stolen pickup truck in her own vehicle.

"Girl, yo, stop with all the questions," School Boy quickly replied. "You almost worse than that crybaby Lena riding with you."

"I'm good, fool. I was just asking. You know I don't go around doing no spur-of-the-moment crap like this without checking it out first."

"Look, cuz, take my word for it. We good. I told you I cut the electric line and besides the owners live clear on the other side of town. Trust me, this gonna be in and out," School Boy swore as he revved the engine and braced for impact. "I'ma drive your car around the front and look out for any police."

Chapter 11

Using both of their smart phone flashlight apps Lena and Jakki grabbed everything in sight they thought was of value. Wasting no time with discussion of who would get what later on when they go home, the pillowcases were soon stuffed with dresses, shoes, designer purses, and leather jackets. Finding a flashlight behind the counter, Jakki was even more enthusiastic about the task at hand. Not hearing the ear-splitting, piercing sounds of any burglar alarms go off, the girls were at ease feeling like they were on an all expense paid shopping spree and not a petty B&E. Suddenly feeling the vibration of her cell Jakki removed it from her bra turning it around so she could read the incoming text message.

"Oh my freaking God! Not now of all times!" Panic quickly filled the room.

"Girl, Jakki, what's wrong?"

"I'll be damned, hell naw, not now! It was all good just a minute ago. This is mad crazy. That ill-bred snake School Boy got us all messed up with his hating ass! I know he did this."

"Jakki! Jakki! What? What's wrong? What is it? What he do? What, tell me!"

"This right here is some real bullshit! Why fucking me?" Jakki wondered out loud. Normally cold as ice, she was shook and it showed. Her mind traveled in a million different directions at once. She felt this obvious betrayal couldn't be happening. This couldn't be life, but it was. The so-called abruptly planned carefree night of thievery she and her cohorts intended on having had started to unravel. This was just supposed to be fun and not part of the contest. This whole thing was petty anyhow!

"Why we stopping? Wh . . . wh . . . why?"

"You wanna get us knocked or what? 'Cause a chick like me ain't trying to go back to jail! Your momma or grandma might bail ya slow, skinny ass out no matter what. But me, I'm hit; my pops still in the hospital. And my so-called loyal family, the bastard who dick you sucking, apparently he on some other type of cutthroat mentality this week!"

Practically dragging a lightweight Lena by the wrist, Jakki found a huge rack of clothing near the rear exit of the exclusive fashion boutique School Boy claimed he'd staked out for days. Receiving two text messages from her older cousin announcing the owners had pulled up in the parking lot and were getting out their cars, Jakki knew she and Lena didn't have time to escape the same way they'd come in: a hole in the side of the building School Boy crashed a stolen pickup truck through. If they did take a chance and tried it, Jakki wasn't brand new to the game and knew they ran the risk of being met with God knows what. At this point, they were trapped. It was bad enough they were taking such a gigantic risk by robbing who School Boy claimed was a retired pimp turned businessman, his bottom bitch's and partner's store, but now here they were, seconds away from possibly being caught red-handed.

Listening to whoever was clicking the light switches up and down, Jakki was relieved to know School Boy hadn't totally double-crossed her when he claimed to cut the electricity to the building, like his convenient misinformation about the guns. She had to believe it had to be nothing more than dumb luck that had brought the storeowners back in the middle of the night interrupting her criminal activities. After all what else could it have been? He had proven to be a snake earlier in the week, but claimed he was over all of that now and wanted to get past the drama.

Why did I even trust him? Ever since we was kids he been dirty. Jakki thought back remembering her and School Boy's sometimes turbulent childhood.

"Jakki, gimme some of your candy."

"Why would I do that? You could have come trick or treating like the rest of us." She spread her sweet treats across her canopy bed.

"Yeah, but I didn't!" School Boy barked mad at the world as usual. *"I told you that running around door to door begging people for candy ain't me! I let y'all fools do all that."*

Jakki tore open a snack-size Snickers with her teeth then took a bite. "Well what's the difference in you in my room begging me for my candy? You still a little beggar, boy," she teased sticking out her tongue to further mock him.

"Just gimme some candy and stop being so dang gone stingy before I really get mad!" Overpowering his little cousin, School Boy knocked her off the bed taking what he wanted from her colorful pile of sugar.

"Mom! Mom!" Jakki angrily screamed out in distress from her bedroom floor. "Help me! Help!"

In a matter of seconds Jakki's mother, School Boy's aunt by marriage, came flying through the doorway with a broom in hand and her younger daughter on her hip. "What's wrong, Jakki? What's going on in here?"

Not having any problem whatsoever in telling on her cousin, Jakki, with tears in her eyes, spilled the beans. "He shoved me on the floor, cursed me out, and then took some of my candy. I told him he couldn't have any and he took it anyway!"

Having been more than a few rounds with her nephew over the past week or so while her husband was away running the family-owned afterhours spot, the young mother warned School Boy for the last time to get his act together or he was going back home to his mother come the first thing in the morning.

"The morning?" The barely a teenager School Boy stood tall having a problem with authority, especially women, ever since his father had been murdered by his mistress a few years back. "Auntie, you don't have to wait until daybreak to send me to my momma. I can go home to my house right now!"

"School Boy, watch your tone raising your voice like that in my house!"

"Fuck your house, I mean my uncle's house, and you and this stingy-hearted candy-having little monster too!" Grabbing his small duffle bag, he stormed out the front door into the dark of the night getting no opposition from his aunt.

Not even bothering to see if the troublesome youth made it home, Jakki, her younger sister, and she went to sleep. By three in the morning Jakki was awakened by the strong smell of smoke. Opening her eyes wide, she was met by the wire screen in her window bent inward and bright orange and red flames that seemed to dance around the corner of her bedroom. Thankfully remembering what she was taught at school, the petrified young girl dropped to the ground and started to crawl toward the closed door. Momentarily looking back over her shoulder she saw her one white sheer curtain turn dark gray then disappear into nothing. Coughing, she then pulled her pajama top up to her face as a mask and reached up for the knob. Safely escaping out into the hallway, Jakki started yelling for her mother and little sister to wake up. Realizing the hot flames were chasing her, the young girl stood to her feet quickly helping her panicked mother grab what few belongings they could before fleeing out to the curb with her younger sibling in tow.

Hours later, when the suspicious fire was finally put out, Jakki and her mother were adamant in *blaming one person for their sudden almost deadly misfortune: School Boy. After hearing about the altercation earlier then finding the family dog underneath Jakki's bedroom window with a broken neck, Ruben's first thought was also his deceased brother's son. Enraged he practically kicked his sister-in-law's front door off the hinges trying to get to his nephew. Once inside, he found School Boy in his bed, lights out, fast asleep. With a sworn promise from both him and his terrified of her son mother that he'd been there all night, Ruben had no other recourse but to let it go. Since there was no real proof, as time went by School Boy was allowed to return and visit the freshly remodeled home, but that was only if he spent all his time with Ruben.*

Ruben's wife, although still infuriated and untrusting, put up with her husband's nephew out of devout loyalty to her husband. An innocent-minded Jakki, not wanting to believe her own flesh and blood really tried to burn her to death for not sharing her Halloween candy, slowly grew to forget about the near tragic incident all together and accepted him back into her heart.

Chapter 12

Snapping back to reality, Jakki nervously bit at the corner of her lip. She and Lena were terrified listening to the owner and his friends talk about what they were going to do if they caught them in their store. After trying like hell to be perfectly still, the enraged owners thought they heard something and were headed in their direction. Before Jakki knew it things went from bad to worse for her and School Boy's jump off.

Oh my God! Jakki held Lena even closer after seeing what she knew was a laser beam shine in the confines of the makeshift cave and on the girl's bare leg. In a matter of seconds both their fears were tragically confirmed. Jakki gouged her curved fingernails deeply into Lena's jaw line pressing down even harder over her mouth as three gunshots rang out inside the store. *Fuck! Fuck! Fuck!* was all she could think before, during, and after hearing the gunfire. Feeling Lena's skinny-boned body jerk and her head tilt back, Jakki knew the girl was hit.

Damn, now what? Shit! Where is the police when you need they dirty asses? Jakki, convinced she was also on her way to get called home, closed her eyes waiting for what was gonna ultimately happen after what came next. With School Boy continuing to blow up her cell, she knew her grimy intentions cousin was still close by if nothing else. *Family ain't about nothing. How that nigga gonna play me of all people? Something told me not to do this caper. How he ain't got me?* Of course she wondered why her first cousin hadn't burst through the door, guns blazing to save her from harm's way, especially after hearing gunshots, but now was not the time to figure that part out. Quickly coming to the realization she was on her own and her life was on the line, Jakki wasted no time getting her mind back right and focused.

The owner's girlfriend had no idea what'd she done. Lena would never be going home again to worry about her incarcerated brother. She'd never be around nagging School Boy for attention or cook some of her grand-mother's secret recipe extra-crunchy fried chicken. Jakki, on the other hand, had a chance to see tomorrow. Waiting Lena's killer and the two men out, thankfully they went out the rear door to get rid of the cat that also had taken a bullet.

Holding the shovel as far away as he possibly could, Maino carried the dying cat's body out the rear door. With a seething attitude, he slowly passed by the gaping hole the truck had made in the back brick wall of his business. Wanting nothing more than to have some sort of legitimate cover for the money he and his partner were making from all the pills and prescription cough syrup they were running out one of their trap houses, this was the last thing he needed or wanted to take place. Having taken a major loss the earlier part of the week, tossing a near dead stray into the Dumpster was like extra icing on the cake celebrating the world's worst week.

"I swear on everything I love and every broad I done pimped on in these Detroit streets, if I ever find the little punks who did this or run into them four sluts that violated, I'ma go to penitentiary for the rest of my days."

Scared of even seeing the bloodied fur dead body of the feline she'd mistakenly slaughtered, his woman eased behind him, eyes closed following the sound of her man's infuriated voice. "Baby, calm down and watch your blood pressure. I know it's sky high." She knew how Maino would get excited and get closed to stroking out and wanted to avoid that from happening. "Matter of fact did you even take you medicine this morning?"

"Hey, tramp! Shut up talking to me about that medicine now!" He turned around almost causing the suffering cat to slide off the end of the shovel and onto the ground. "I got a gigantic hole in my business and some young skeezers done stole all my product making me and my manz here the laughing stock of the neighborhood and you out in this alley talking about some medicine. I oughta beat your worn out in the womb self just for old times' sake; shooting a stray cat!" He shook his head before raising the shovel up in the Dumpster.

Quickly realizing the ex-pimp mentality in Maino had been revived and she ran the high risk of getting slapped to the concrete face first she stood down letting him vent.

Wanting to keep the peace, Maino's best friend and business partner removed a half-smoked joint out his pocket. "We all need this to calm our nerves."

Now all alone in the store, with the exception of Lena's recently deceased corpse, Jakki saw her opportunity at life. Acting as if they were giving away free cheese, butter, and honey to the first twenty people in line, Jakki took off running. Only a few yards from making a clean getaway, the frantic female stumbled to the floor tripping over the same pillowcase filled with stolen items she'd dropped earlier. Scrambling desperately to get back on her feet, Jakki heard one of the men yell he'd heard a noise back inside of the store. *Damn I'm about to get killed too! I know I shouldn't have broken into this spot without doing my damn homework! This is so messy.* At the same time she heard the sounds of footsteps rush through the back entrance she saw a set of high-beam headlights in the front of the building coming her way. *Lord, please let this be School Boy's backstabbing, double-crossing ass! Please!*

Chapter 13

With his head buried into his new cell, School Boy was feeling untouchable. Not only did he feel he was bigger than the game, he felt he was the game. Having plastered the same picture of the stolen jewelry that he'd braggingly sent to his cousin on Facebook and Instagram, he felt like the rules of the street and life in general didn't apply to him. Hearing the engine roaring sounds of a vehicle swerve up across the block and park in front of the boutique, a sinister smile of satisfaction graced his face. *Oh naw! Couldn't be! This night is going better than a nigga planned.*

Removing his baseball cap, School Boy felt his palms getting sweaty. With a huge thirst for vengeance, he casually texted Jakki that he believed the owners of the store was back and she and Lena probably needed to get in the wind. He'd promised them both that this burglary was going to be no more than a simple in and out caper and that part he truly meant. Seeing that the owners had surprisingly returned was not on his agenda for revenge for Jakki coming over earlier, smoking his weed, drinking his drink, and eating his jump off's fried chicken then blatantly stab him in the back by trying so hard to coax him into letting Ruben and the Crayton Clan elders sell him down the river, but so be it. Payback is always a motherfucker and karma is a bitch. Just like he'd told his beloved first cousin the other day in her bedroom, she wasn't the only person in the family walking around with their ear pressed to the streets. School Boy not only had heard about the infamous home invasion-style conquest Jakki and her forever devoted crew of female hood rats had so skillfully pulled off, the vindictive thug had gone the extra mile in investigating not only the amount of ill-gotten gain they'd come up on that night, but the complete rundown and pedigree of the two older victims who were now ridiculed in the street, marked for being straight suckers.

School Boy's original intention was to naïvely allow Jakki and Lena, who begged to tag along as usual, to go inside the upscale boutique, take everything they could get, and bring it home to "Big Daddy." His mindset was to take all the expensive priced items from the robbery along with the bag of stolen jewelry, including Lena's car-thieving brother's portion, and toss in on his uncle's hospital bed proving he was not just out running renegade in city, but on the come up for the overall good of the family. And just in case Jakki wanted to be a snake once more, he'd proudly announce her being a fool herself robbing the same very men she'd just robbed earlier in the week. School Boy knew Ruben didn't like taking unnecessary risk shining light on the family name and what Jakki was doing was just that.

Fighting with his longtime demons, when he noticed that all three of the people getting out the car were strapped, his conscience started to kick in. Having a small bit of remorse and sympathy for his blood, not like the time he allegedly tried to burn Jakki alive when they were small children, School Boy texted her once more this time informing her they had weapons drawn and were heading toward the door.

Damn, this is kinda messed up. I hate the grimy two-faced sneaky hood rat and all, but these old clowns 'bout to do her and my girl for real! I can't let this bloodbath go down. His thoughts and emotions were all over the place watching one of the men and a woman eagerly fumble with the keys at the entrance while the other man cautiously headed toward the rear of the building. *But on another tip.* He tossed his cell on the passenger seat of Jakki's car then removed his gun from his waistband setting it on his lap. *Hopefully they'll get their black asses out the store before ol' boy gets back there. But on the other hand, if cuz get knocked or even killed, I'ma be standing at the head of the table no competition, no questions asked.*

Holding tight for a few minutes, School Boy text Jakki once more wanting to see if she and Lena had safely gotten away, and if so, where he could pick them up at. Waiting on pins and needles the now on-edge troubled youth got the same response from Jakki as he did with the previous texts: none. Seeing the man reappear from the back of the building, School Boy didn't know what to think or what to do for that matter. Rubbing both hands back across his head, his heart seemed to be pounding out his chest.

Confused with what to do next, his palms continued to sweat knowing he had to make a move swiftly if he wanted to save the day for his cousin and jump off. Moments later his hand was forced. A thunderous few rounds of gunfire rang out causing him to instinctively take cover in the vehicle not knowing exactly where the close range sounding shots came from and who the mystery shooter possibly was. Starting the ignition, he came to the fast realization the shots fired were inside the confines of the boutique. The time had got for School Boy to shit or get off the pot so to speak when it came to his family loyalty to Jakki. Knowing it was now or never, he placed one hand on the steering wheel and the other on the gear shift. For the first time in a week, his decision was perfectly clear.

Jakki bolted out the front door of the boutique and passed a car, which had to be the owners, parked in the front. With the set of high-beam headlights somewhat blinding her sight, she trusted that it had to be School Boy in her ride signaling for her that he was there to save her from the enraged wrath of the owners who were hot on her trail. Knowing her cousin had to have heard the gunshots ring out as well, Jakki wondered why he hadn't just rushed inside and had a gun battle if need be to rescue her. After all, he was the one who sent her and Lena into what ended up being an ambush. Hearing one of the men yelling out to the other, her urgency to reach the car increased before she was forced to meet the same fate as Lena and the cat.

"Oh my God, oh my God," she repeated out of breath. The closer the panic-stricken diva got to the headlights, the quicker she realized it was not her vehicle heading in her direction. There was no School Boy, her favorite cousin to save the day, but instead a flat bed tow truck. *Where in the fuck is he at? Why he doing me like this?* As the driver changed gears making the engine seem to growl much louder, Jakki ducked behind a parked car a few stores down. Saying her prayers next to the missing hubcap wheel, the winded female hoped no one from inside the store saw which way she went. *Oh God, please help me, please. I swear if you get me out of this I'll do right.* Close to peeing on herself, she clenched her legs tightly and braced for the worst. Terrified of taking a possible bullet between the eyes, she raised up just enough to see over the hood of the blue Nissan. *Whoa!* A warm feeling of gratitude came over her believing her prayers were truly answered. One man was waving his arms telling the tow truck driver to pull behind the building while the other walked up to a police squad car that was just driving up. Seconds later the man followed by the cops went inside the still dark store.

After gathering her thoughts, Jakki then boldly hiked her blood-soaked skirt, took her panties off, and squatted on the otherwise deserted street. Using the thin layer cloth to wipe herself, she took off running for her life once more. Putting at least a good three-block distance between herself and the scene of the crime, she had to think quick knowing it was only a matter of time before the electricity to the boutique was restored and Lena's unresponsive body was discovered. Stopping at a random house using their water hose to rinse off her hands and some of her skirt and T-shirt still covered with the girl's blood, Jakki's anger grew. *Where in the hell is this grimy, demented idiot with my car? I swear to God he straight dead to me! That bastard set me and that stuttering Lena up just like it wasn't nothing!*

Reaching her hand into her bra to call School Boy, Jakki became more distraught realizing she'd lost her cell phone. With no money and no other options, she headed toward the hospital that was thankfully located only a half a mile away. She knew it was late and visiting hours were over, but if anyone could tell her what to do next, her father could.

Chapter 14

The seventh floor. School Boy read the numbers brightly painted on the door of each floor in the stairwell. Peeking out the small-sized center window, he continued to be just as careful as he'd been since sneaking passed the preoccupied emergency security guard. With the determination of three men, he cracked the door open as quietly as possible. Poking his head into the dimly lit hallway of the eighteen-story medical facility, School Boy started to grin with a crooked smile knowing he was seconds away from settling a long-standing debt. Caught in his warped emotions, he believed the next five coming minutes of his life was nothing other than destiny, a prophecy fulfilled. Hearing the beeping tones of multitudes of various machines and monitors to aid in saving and maintaining the hospital patients' lives, School Boy knew his task might not be as easy as he hoped, but stayed diligent just the same.

As he waited for the perfect opportunity to make his move, School Boy thought back on the evening he witnessed his father being brutally murdered at the hands of his jealous mistress. Tired of being second in his father's life, the spiteful woman vowed if she couldn't have him, no one could, including his wife and son. So with a sharp kitchen carving knife, the now also dead vixen slashed his father's throat while he and his younger cousin Jakki were forced to watch. Since that day Ruben stepped up to the plate, but nothing could take the place of a father's love. School Boy's mother was never right in the head again or him. Jakki on the other hand got therapy and seemed to readjust to a normal childhood. School Boy was who he was, a ticking time bomb who loved no one but himself, never getting attached to people afraid they'd leave him just as his dad did. Sadly, instead of embracing the loyal family he had left, he secretly hated their daily existence.

Making sure every nurse and night cleaning staff was out the general area, School Boy crept to room 702. Not once wondering if Jakki and Lena were dead or alive, he took a deep breath, mentally preparing himself to finally come face to face with his once beloved and respected uncle, Ruben Crayton. *He wanted to see me so bad, well now is his chance.*

Exhausted, looking disheveled, Jakki rushed through the hospital's front lobby. Relieved to make it to safety, the messy-haired female marched up to the information desk after finding out the elevators were locked down for the night. Taking notice no one was there, she desperately searched the room for anyone who could help her. Seeing a security guard in the far corner of the room buying himself a cup of coffee from one of the vending machines, Jakki ran up on him.

"Excuse me, excuse me," she excitedly spoke out.

"Yes, miss, how can I help you?" he replied wondering why a girl so pretty was looking so out of sorts with parts of her shirt and skirt obviously wet.

"I know it's late." She tried fixing her hair. "But I need to see my father."

"Your father?"

"Yes, Ruben Crayton."

"Was he brought through emergency?" the guard asked thinking this had to be the reason she'd come out the house looking the way she was.

"No, he's in room 702." Jakki rubbed at her temples trying to soothe a pounding migraine.

"I'm sorry, miss, but visiting hours are over and don't start back until ten." He pointed to the bright red digital clock on the wall. "You will need to come back then."

"Look, sir, it's an emergency! I have to speak to my father now!" Her voice echoed off the walls of the empty lobby.

"Okay please listen to me, miss, first things first. I'm gonna need you to please lower your voice." He towered over her trying to be diplomatic. "The hospital rules say ten and even if I wanted to break them I couldn't. These elevators are locked down being serviced until daybreak. That's their policy, not mine."

"Okay, but, I ain't crazy! I know that's not the only way up to the damn seventh floor where my father is at!" She raised her voice yet again not used to not getting her way. "This is so messed up!

"Look now, I've told you once. You have to calm down and lower your voice or leave the premises. I'm done telling you that."

"Okay, I'm sorry." She tried another approach attempting to reason with the man. "I know I must look a hot mess, but this is serious. This is very, very important! Please help me. I'm begging you."

The security guard felt for her, but certainly not enough to risk losing his job. "Hey, I can let you use the house phone and you can call his room and if he's possibly awake at this late hour and sees the flashing light, he'll pick up."

Feeling that may be her only option of speaking to her dad until morning, Jakki ran over to the beige wall phone snatching the receiver off the hook. Pushing in his room number she waited, praying her dad would pick up. Repeating the process several times, she returned to the guard almost in tears. "Look I don't have my purse with my money and ID. I messed around and lost my cell phone and the only thing I need to do is speak to my dad," she explained not knowing what to do or say next to convince him the urgency of her getting word to her father that she needed his help.

"I tell you what. I'll call the nurse's station and have her check in on Mr. Crayton and see if he's awake," he negotiated. "If so, I'll have her let him know you need to speak to him."

"Wow, okay. Thank you! Thank you!" As she stood there, tugging at her wet, filthy clothing hoping her father was indeed awake; she prayed the police wouldn't burst through the hospital doors looking to drag her back to the boutique in handcuffs.

After at least fifteen minutes and not receiving a response, the security guard placed another courtesy call. With the second desk nurse picking up, she carried the cordless phone with her to check on not only the patient, Mr. Crayton, but her missing in action colleague as well.

The hospital room his uncle had been occupying the past week was quiet. With the exception of the heart monitor making murmured beeping sounds every so often sending indicators to the nurses' station that all was well with the patient, you could hear a pin drop on the sanitized floor. Closing the door to shut out the intrusion of light from the hall-way, School Boy stepped all the way inside the private room. Standing in the shadow, perfectly still, the once loyal nephew watched his uncle's chest slowly move up and down. His forever hero was now reduced to no more than a helpless old man fighting to survive; however, School Boy seemed to have no mercy in his hardened heart.

Momentarily pausing to ensure no one was coming, he bent down removing the telephone cord from the wall. Leaning back up, with ill intentions he wanted to snatch the bedside phone off the nightstand and smash it across Ruben's head. Feeling confused as to why it had to be this way, his hands shook. Thoughts of why his uncle was trying to push him out of his rightful place in the family and disregard all the dirty work he'd selflessly put in over the years while his perfect princess Jakki was running around still playing with dolls, consumed his troubled mind.

Fuck my cousin and this fake old man too! With evil finally prevailing over good, School Boy grabbed an extra pillow from a chair in the corner of the soon-to-be chaotic hospital room. Standing over his sleeping uncle clutching both ends of the white fluffy pillow, the deranged young killer started speaking his final peace in a whispered but vengeful tone. Out of spite, he then hawked a huge glob of saliva directly into Ruben's face before raising the soft weapon of death over the ailing man's head. With no remorse, he lowered his arms.

"School Boy! What you doing!" Awakened by the feel of a warm slimy substance oozing down his jaw line, Ruben, once a strong street warrior in his prime, began using all his strength to stop what was taking place in the darkness of the supposedly quiet and safe hospital room. "Are you crazy?" He panted, out of breath and energy as his IV was ripped from his inner arm as well as the small clamps from the heart monitor. Fighting the good fight, the boy's uncle was about done.

Thankfully a small amount of light entered from the hallway when a nurse pushed the room door open. On her way to check to see if Mr. Crayton was awake by request of the security guard at the front lobby, she was shocked by the commotion and actions that were taking place. "Hey, hey, what's going on in here? What do you think you're doing?" Trying to intervene, she pulled at School Boy's shirt and was instantly met with an elbow to the face knocking her to the ground. Striking her head on the side of one of the many machines, she blacked out.

Knowing the interruption and noise was sure to bring others, School Boy, out his mind, bolted out the room and disappeared into the same stairwell he'd come from.

"The seventh floor nurses' station," the woman's voice answered.

"Yes, this is the front lobby security desk."

"Yes, how can I be of help?"

"Well I hate to bother you folks again, miss, but I spoke to someone about twenty minutes ago who was going to check on a patient in room 702 for me. His daughter is down here and says speaking to him is urgent."

"Oh okay I see. That must've been Nurse Simmons," she quickly replied in an agreeable manner. "She's not back yet but I can go check for you. Matter of fact if you can stay on the line I will take this cordless phone with me."

Within minutes of checking on the patient in room 702 as well as her coworker, chaos broke loose as the hospital went into mandatory lockdown.

Jakki, needless to say, was totally beside herself in the midst of the pandemonium. Being told limited information, the distraught female had to be physically detained by two security guards until the hospital, on high alert, could conduct a thorough search for the person who'd attacked one of their nurses and a patient rumored to be her father. With the actual Detroit Police Department now taking over the investigation, the reason Jakki was even down at the hospital at this late hour to speak to her dad had come into question. After a while she and her mother, who was immediately contacted by the hospital administrators, were taken to see their loved one.

Ruben, going in and out of consciousness, was tight-lipped claiming he had no idea whatsoever who'd attacked him. Sure he'd gotten a good look at his brother's son, even argued with him, but telling the law on kin was not in his character or part of his Crayton DNA. School Boy was blood and he'd be handled for his disrespectful, deadly intended transgressions the way family dealt with one another: privately.

With his visibly shaken wife trying to comfort her husband and Jakki now loyally posted at his bedside threatening a lawsuit for allowing him to almost be murdered on their supposedly secure hospital property, Ruben stood strong on his word; he knew nothing. No sooner than they were alone in the room, he had his daughter lean close. Whispering in Jakki's ear shockingly exactly who his assailant was, the physically and mentally exhausted man had tears in his weary eyes. She couldn't believe what she was hearing but at this point put nothing past that idiot who'd slept under their roof and eaten their food whenever he wanted since childhood. School Boy actually tried to bite the hand that fed him; however, now he was dead to them and could go hungry for all they cared.

Even more pissed about this act of betrayal than what that creep foul so-called family member had done to her and Lena's poor dead self, Jakki started to feel the same murderous rage in her heart as her out-of-control cousin. There were rules to the game and he'd recklessly broken them all. Not wanting to upset Ruben any further for the night, Jakki decided to put the information on hold that she too had been set up and victimized by his crazed nephew who her dad always thought should be next in line to stand at the head of the Crayton Clan table. Taking off the still damp T-shirt she was wearing, replacing it with two hospital gowns happily provided by the still upset staff, Jakki stared in the mirror vowing to make School Boy pay for his sins.

Chapter 15

The definitely proven to be stolen pickup was finally removed from its temporary resting place and loaded onto the huge flat bed tow truck. Left with uncertainty over what to do next, Maino finished speaking to the police officers who informed him there was not much they could do on the premises, especially since there was no electricity inside of the dwelling. Advised to take plenty of pictures and contact his insurance company to put in a claim, there was not much for them to do now but wait for the power to be restored. As he, his best friend, and his woman stood in the front of the building watching the tow truck drive away, they didn't notice Jakki's cell phone lying face down on the side of the curb near his driver's side car door.

Luckily, they didn't have to wait much longer as an emergency DTE van was dispatched to their location. Explaining what they believed to had taken place, Maino, still infuriated, led the technician to the rear of the building where the damage was done. After inspecting the cut wires, flashlight in hand, the man informed them he could have a portion of the boutique lights back on in a matter of minutes, but they'd have to request a full service work truck on the premises come daybreak to complete total restoration. In less than twenty minutes' time, the man had kept his word as half of the buildings lights flickered on.

Stunned to find the once perfect store in such disarray was almost more trauma than Maino could stomach for the week. At his wits' end and his blood pressure steadily climbing, he left his best friend and woman to start the sure to be tedious process of cleaning up and putting things back in order. Having not discovered the dead female body slumped underneath the clothes rack, in the still dark part of the building, Maino headed to his car to sit down and hopefully gather his thoughts. Stepping down off the curb, he saw a small bit of light blinking. Picking the cell phone up, he grinned realizing it must've belonged to one of the thieves who'd violated his property. Pushing talk on the only number in the call log, he waited for someone to pick up.

Jumping back into Jakki's car, School Boy pulled out the hospital parking as quickly as possible. Knowing he'd tried committing one of the most unforgettable acts ever, he knew his time running wild in the city since a kid had run its course. After driving a few miles he arrived back at Lena's house. Not sure if his cousin and Lena were dead, alive, or locked up behind bars he knew any of the three outcomes of the late-night robbery gone wrong would ultimately bring people over to the house. Rushing into the living room, he tipped the couch over grabbing the plastic bag containing not only his portion of stolen jewelry, but Lena's brother's as well. Almost knocking the bedroom door off its hinges, School Boy stuffed some of his clothes and a few other personal items into a duffle bag. Throwing the bag over his shoulder then grabbing the last few pieces of the chicken his jump off had fired earlier, he left back out the front door not even bothering to lock it.

Walking by Jakki's car, he tossed her car keys in the back seat landing them next to her and Lena's purses. Getting into his own vehicle, he drove off once more this time having no deliberate destination. He knew by now his name was mud with his family and probably ringing in the streets. Still in a murderous state of mind, his only regret was not being able to send his uncle on his way. Thinking about calling the hospital just to see what was what, he was startled by his phone ringing. Knowing Jakki was the only one person with the number to his new cell, he braced himself for what she had to say. "Oh I see you made it out alive huh, bitch!" he sinisterly remarked answering the line.

"Yo, who is this?" Maino barked out as his blood pres-sure jumped even higher.

"What?" School Boy was confused expecting to hear Jakki's smart yapping mouth trying to come at him sideways not some random man. "Naw, fool, who in the fuck is this?"

"Listen up, whoever you are. Your dumb friend dropped their cell phone after crashing a damn truck through the back of my store. Who cell phone is this? I'ma find out and when I do, I'ma kill 'em!" he firmly vowed thinking about the amount of damage that was done.

"Oh yeah, is that right?" School Boy, not new to the game, played it off not knowing if Jakki and Lena were in police custody and the cops were trying to trick him to incriminate himself. "Dude, I don't know who or what you talking about. You calling my phone this late on some bullshit."

Maino reminded School Boy in the manner he'd started the call. "If you don't know whose phone this is why did you ask did they get out alive? I ain't no fool, young blood!"

It'd been a long night and School Boy was fed up with the back and forth. Ready to put an end to the conversation and questions in general, he gave the man what he was looking for: answers. "I tell you what, old man, you've had a mad helluva bad luck week so I'm about to put you up on some game just on the humble."

All ears, Maino leaned back against his car as School Boy dry snitched on Jakki Crayton and her girlfriends for breaking into his pill house, then blamed tonight's robbery on her as well. Since he wasn't able to successfully murk his uncle, he decided to throw him under the bus as well. "Yeah, fool, my people's, the Crayton Clan, got it out for you in a bad way. The old man Ruben is the one who sicced his daughter on you in the first place. He the one you need to be talking about killing, player, not me."

"Say what now?" Maino puzzled out loud as he started to pace in front of the boutique. "Aww, man, why is they messing with me? Tell Ruben and his daughter they wrong as hell for this! This is foul!" He voice grew with every syllable. "We don't even run in the same circles; not now not ever! My house where I make my ends, now my goddamn store; for what? I ain't never had no beef with them Craytons; ever!"

"Well guess what, homeboy, the fuck you do now!" With those final words, School Boy was elated he'd planted the seed for a potential windfall of trouble. Powering off his cell, School Boy now had a destination and purpose. Maino had just let him know on the humble that Jakki and Lena must've escaped. So on that note, he made a U-turn. Heading toward Jakki's house in hopes of further settling some family business before he left town, once again School Boy had blood in his eyes.

Chapter 16

The sun was shining brightly through the car's wind-shield as Jakki's mother drove them home. Convinced her husband was stable health-wise and was promised extra security to ensure his safety she suggested to her daughter they both go home to get some much needed rest and to freshen up. Jakki, still dressed in a now dry, soiled skirt, no panties, and two faded hospital gowns, was quick to agree with her, feeling like a walking billboard for filth.

Having been preoccupied with her father's well-being and the heinous reality that School Boy had tried to end his life, Jakki gave little or no mind to the God-awful fact that Lena had indeed lost hers right in her arms. Sitting back in the passenger seat with her eyes shut, she wished she hadn't her lost cell phone to check the local news channel Web site updates about possibly a deceased female's body having been discovered in a botched burglary scene. Even though she and her cousin's jump off weren't that incredibly close, Jakki, unlike School Boy had a conscience for actions that harmed somewhat innocent people and bystanders who weren't totally in the game. They didn't ask for or welcome the fallout from street life; it just was forced on them. Sadly they'd have to start the sunny morning off by planning a funeral.

Wanting to at least contact Lena's people and tell them what exactly happened the night before when their loved one took her final breath, Jakki knew that wasn't an option.

Awakened out her emotional trance by her mother telling her to get out of the car Jakki felt a huge sense of relief seeing the front porch of her house. Raising her weary body upward, she climbed out the vehicle practically dragging herself inside the two-story dwelling. Walking by the kitchen door, she saw her mother, who should've been exhausted herself, had wasted no time putting water on for some coffee as if they just didn't have plenty down at the hospital.

"Hey, Mom, I'm going to take a long, hot shower. I feel like a dirtball or something."

"Okay, dear. I'm gonna fix us a light breakfast to go with this coffee."

Yeah, now that's what I'm talking about! Two soon-to-be dead Craytons for the low discounted price of one! School Boy had been parked a block over but could easily see his uncle's house in between the multiple scattered abandoned homes. With the same amount of inner rage he felt a few hours prior when trying to suffocate the man who raised him as a son, School Boy's blood started to boil when he saw not only Jakki but, who he perceived to always mistreat and be mean to him, his aunt as well. *Both them turncoat hoes gonna pay for trying to turn my family on me!* His warped mind kicked into overdrive as he stepped outside his car. Nonchalantly making his way through the debris-filled empty lots, the fire burning in his belly grew. *None of them loved me for real anyway. After I do them, maybe I'll go back by Lena's and kill that worrisome trick, too! I'm tired of everybody and they fake stuntin'.*

Having crept along the side of the house, School Boy solemnly stood outside of Jakki's bedroom reminiscing, wishing his childhood had been different. Knowing the neighbors wouldn't pay attention to him being in the back yard he'd grown up running around, playing tag, and having family barbeques in, he felt confident he'd not be interrupted. Peeping through the raised window's screen, he saw Jakki wasn't inside her private girlie domain. With ease, he used the same method he'd done years ago when he set her bedroom on fire after being scolded. Not only did he bend the corner of the wire back this time, School Boy snatched the entire thing out the frame tossing it on the direct spot he'd left the broken neck family puppy. Lifting himself up, he crawled his muscular frame through the window landing on the side of Jakki's bed.

Momentarily pausing he remained motionless. School Boy heard the sounds of the shower water and knew it was time to put his rotten plan into effect. Standing up, he walked over toward the door as quietly as possible avoiding the parts of the floor he knew always creaked. Poking his head out into the dim hallway, the deranged soon-to-be killer looked down seeing steam coming from underneath the crack of the bathroom door. He knew his cousin Jakki was famous for taking long showers and would nine out of ten be preoccupied for a while giving him time enough to solve one of his two problems. Having been raised in the household for years, School Boy inhaled taking a strong whiff of his aunt's fresh-brewed coffee and knew she was either in the kitchen cooking or planted in front of the television watching an episode of *The Price Is Right.*

Just as he hoped, his aunt had her back to him and was bending down putting some of her beloved homemade biscuits in the preheated oven. A coward, not wanting to see his aunt's face, he made little noise as his arm reached over to the kitchen countertop. Wrapping his fingers tightly around the handle of a knife, with ease he raised it upward out of the brown wooden block. School Boy's palms grew sweaty as they always did when he was about to do mischief. Reliving several events as a child when he felt his aunt had treated him wrong, his adrenalin kicked in and his mouth watered for the sweet taste of revenge. With the knife now up over his head seconds from smashing down into the center spine of the older woman's back he cruelly spoke out, "Auntie, you should've never treated me like a stranger, like I didn't belong! I'm a Crayton by blood; you just married into it!"

Getting chill bumps, feeling like someone other than herself was in the kitchen, Jakki's mother lifted up from the open hot oven door in just enough time to avoid certain death before hearing his salty words ring out. Instantaneously she could feel the intense fury imbedded deep in her nephew's soul as they locked eyes and he swung the knife once more this time slicing her arm. "Oh my God, School Boy! Why? Me and Ruben never did anything to you! Why? We took you in as our own!"

"Why?" He evilly repeated as she begged for her life to be spared. "More like why not? You never liked me. You took every chance you got to poison my uncle's love for me; you and Jakki!"

The devout churchgoing Catholic backed up into the refrigerator saying her prayers. Fearing this was the end and she'd soon meet the Almighty Creator, she braced herself to. Before the loving wife and mother could get the first Hail Mary completely out, School Boy's coldblooded expression of a hunter about to devour his prey was unexpectedly turned to that of a terrified victim. With his eyes now twice their normal size, his mouth fell open but no words of hate spewed from his quivering lips. With the balance of a man who'd drunk an entire fifth of Hennessy straight, he then staggered across the marble kitchen floor dropping the knife he was holding out his hands. Falling face first near the still open oven door and his terrified aunt's feet, the room grew eerily silent. Jakki, hair dripping wet, wrapped in a towel stood judgmentally over him having that same murderous rage embedded deep in her soul

School Boy just had in his. If there was any question as to if they were cut from the same cloth, they ended here, today, on this now bloodied kitchen floor.

In his short amount of time living, School Boy had done more than enough of his fair share of treachery and mayhem to shake hands with the devil in person. The always ill-intentioned thug earned that unvalued right years ago and Jakki had just made sure her cousin was well on his way to hellfire to get his just due. As she and her mother, nursing a small fresh wound, somberly watched their once beloved family member squirm, urinate on himself, then bleed out from the recently sharpened meat cleaver Jakki had just roughly lodged in the rear of his skull, she had a flash back to the day School Boy's father had been taken out the game of life almost in the same fashion: a female with a blade.

In less than a twelve-hour time span, School Boy, obviously snapped and becoming deranged, had tried to murder all three of his close family members without so much as a second thought. In each case it was only God that spared the trio, not any remorse on School Boy's behalf. Throughout a mixture of feelings ranging from sorrow, pity, and regret to anger and resentment, a huge sense of relief and satisfaction soon emerged and smiles graced both mother's and daughter's faces.

Chapter 17

Jakki had taken total charge of the wilded out situation that'd just unfolded. Having called her uncle to immediately come over to the house, she spoke to him in the living room first before leading him into the kitchen. Upon witnessing his wayward nephew sprawled on the floor, face first, in a pool of dark blood with his eyes wide open, he knew at least his brother's attempted murder the night before had been avenged by the very person who he and Ruben had fought not to stand at the head of the table: Jakki. Placing a call to a few of the other family members who handled this type of circumstance whenever it'd occurred, the older man consoled his brother's still in shock wife as his niece calmly made further needed plans to ties up any loose ends.

Of course Jakki was heartbroken that her once favorite cousin lay dead a few feet away and it was by her hand, but so be it. She knew he seemed relentless in his attempt to bring harm to her and her parents, so he had to go. Her only mission at this point was to make sure the family as a whole was good and would not have to suffer through any unwanted contact with the authorities.

After getting OnStar to locate her missing vehicle, Jakki got one of her trusted cousins to drive her to the address she recognized as Lena's house. Hopefully Lena's people or worse than that the police wouldn't be there investigating and she could drive off no questions asked. As she and her cousin bent the corner, they saw School Boy's car parked the next block over. Telling him to pull over, Jakki boldly walked up the window, which was cracked, reaching her arm inside to unlock the door. Grabbing a duffle bag off the rear seat, Jakki returned to the car using her government-issued Obama cell to call a crooked tow truck they always used to have the vehicle taken to a junk yard that required no paperwork and crushed for scrap immediately. Searching through her deceased cousin's bag, Jakki felt some of School Boy's recent sins were paid for after discovering the bag of stolen jewelry.

Fifteen minutes later, Jakki's prayers were answered as they turned on Lena's block. There were no people on her front porch crying, no neighbors being nosey acting like they gave a damn, no yellow tape, and thankfully no police. The only thing Jakki saw was her car parked in the front just as OnStar said it was. Wasting no time, she darted to her car, spare keys in hand. Jumping into the driver's seat she pulled off not even bothering to notice her and Lena's purses were in the same spot they'd left them in and School Boy, as a last goodwill gesture, had kindly left her car keys as well. Signaling out the window to her cousin that she was good, Jakki headed toward the hospital. Surrounded with a smug feeling of accomplishment, she wanted to be the one to break the news about his nephew's untimely demise and the circumstances surrounding his death.

Strolling through the lobby, this time dressed appropriately, Jakki pushed the elevator button. As the door open then closed, she thought she saw two of what seemed like familiar faces coming toward the other set of elevators seeing how they'd missed hers. Stepping off on the seventh floor, the proud daughter marched to her father's room and straight to his bedside where he seemed to be awaiting her arrival.

"Jakki, I wasn't expecting you back so soon, but I'm glad you're here." He reassuringly placed his wrinkled hand on top of hers after laying his cell phone down on top of the blanket. "We need to talk."

"Yeah, Dad, we do. I have something to tell you."

"Well sorry, baby doll, it will have to wait for now." He announced somewhat bursting her bubble, "Something important has been brought to me that needs both mine and your immediate attention."

"Is it about School Boy?" she confusingly asked hoping her uncle hadn't beaten her to the punch in delivering the tragic but much needed news. "Because that's who I wanna talk about!"

"Well yes, and no," Ruben quickly responded trying to adjust his pillow. "It's about the pills and cough syrup you put in the family pot earlier this week and whatever foolishness that supposedly happened last night."

"Last night?" Jakki was now even more bewildered about what her father was talking about not connecting the two crimes she'd committed together.

"Yeah, Jakki; last night before you got down here to the hospital to see me; some type of trouble you and that fool nephew of mine done got into."

"Push the button for the seventh floor," Maino instructed his partner as the door slid closed.

"I don't understand why after all this time we've been doing our thing Ruben Crayton would want to try to step on our toes. It don't make sense."

Maino felt the same way and was just as confused as his longtime friend. "Yeah, you right. None of it makes any sense. Them Craytons ain't never did business on our side of town and not once, even when I had my whores on the stroll, did they trick on his. Then all of a sudden, boom, here they come."

"Yeah, Maino, out of nowhere he puts his daughter and them foul skeezers on us." He stroked his manhood thinking about how the females had spitefully duct taped it and the enormous pain he felt taking it off. "I'm glad you found his number in her phone and reached out. We need to end this misunderstanding before it gets even more outta hand. They dipping in our pockets like it's their money not ours!"

Maino took a deep breath when the seventh floor light lit up. When he and his partner stepped off the elevator and into the busy hallway, he told him to just fall back and let him do all the talking. "Listen, the way the man was talking earlier, he seemed kinda lost about what was going down. It might've been all game and what that fool on the phone said was true, they is coming for our hustle." Maino grew more courage with each passing steps the duo took. "But whatever the case is, we got an ace in the hole; one that's gonna stop him and his family dead in their tracks."

Ruben had just started explaining to his daughter about the strange call he'd received on his cell, a call that was placed from her number. Only minutes into telling Jakki that School Boy had apparently spoken to the caller, who had her cell phone, and informed him Jakki Crayton under the instructions of the Crayton Clan had not only robbed one of his drug houses this week, but had crashed a stolen truck into the rear of his building causing thousands of dollars in damages, they were interrupted.

"Yes, excuse me." Maino came through the doorway as his partner stood outside. "Is this Ruben Crayton's room?"

"Yeah." Jakki looked over at the two men recognizing not only their faces from the pill robbery but shockingly their voices as well from last night's botched lick. "Oh wow!" she mumbled under breath. It'd been dark in the boutique when the owners came in and she was not able to make out their faces.

"Gentlemen, hello, please come in and close the door." Ruben used the hand controller to slightly raise his hospital bed. "You must be Maino correct? And if so, I believe we need some privacy."

Jakki, overly suspicious of the two visitors as well as protective of her father, moved to the other side of the room so she could watch. Having tasted the empowering feeling of sending a man on his way, the loyal daughter was prepared to do battle once more for the day if need been, twice if they pushed her hand. "What do y'all want with my father?"

"Naw." Maino had no problem bringing his issues straight to the table. "The question is what does your father and you want with us? We ain't never stepped out of line with you or yours. We let you do your thing and we do ours."

"Let?" Jakki started to feel some sort of way at the tone Maino was using and his choice of words. "What you mean let? You better pump your brakes, ol' man, nobody lets the Craytons do shit; we just do it!"

"Slow down, it's okay, Jakki. Let's hear them out," Ruben suggested still not feeling a 100 percent after School Boy's surprise attack on him in the middle of the night.

Maino and his partner heard Jakki's name and both looked at one another.

"So you're Jakki huh?" Maino squinted trying to imagine her with a bandana covering half of her face. "I guess you do look like the one who held a gun on me and my partner the other night and stole all our stuff and money."

"Gentlemen, what exactly can we do for you?" Ruben felt the tension growing but still tried to keep the peace. That's what he felt a good leader did if at all possible: maintained order. "Per our conversation you said it was vital you spoke to me face to face. Now as you see, I'm at somewhat of a disadvantage being under the weather and all, but I'm here to listen to your concerns over what harm you claim my child brought to you."

After beating around the bush, the reason for the call placed from Jakki's lost cell, and then the visit was revealed. Not only asking for the street value of their stolen pills and cough syrup to be returned, but also the total cost of repairing the gaping hole in his building, Maino had the nerve to ask Ruben for the possibility of blessing him and his partner with permission to open up another spot on their side of town. "I think that seems fair considering, don't you?"

Before Ruben could take the opportunity to respond to Maino's outlandish demands masquerading as simple requests, Jakki, fuming, stepped in. "Okay, listen up, Maino, or what the hell ever your name is. I don't know who you think you talking to or what piece of courage cookie you took a bite off of this morning, but as long as you alive, and that might not be that long, don't you ever speak to my damn father like that again. You not on his level to address him like that, so fall back!"

"Hold up, wait a minute." Seeing the young girl was up in arms, Maino tried to rephrase his statement but she wasn't done yet.

"Naw, you two pussy made Negros need to hold up. Y'all got the game and my family all the way twisted." Jakki tried keeping her voice down the best she could, but was losing the battle to do so. "How dare y'all stroll into my father's hospital room like some kinda official OGs in the streets talking that la la mess! Like y'all doing us some huge favor allowing us to make shit up to y'all. Fuck y'all! How about that?"

Ruben wanted to intervene and get Jakki to stand down, but she was on a roll representing the Crayton name and he was glad of it considering his weakened state.

Maino's partner had yet to mutter a single word, more than happy to fall back as he was asked in the hallway.

"Listen, do you really think it's okay that we take such a loss just like that? Do you think you dealing with men with no options, no pride or dignity?" Maino was indeed feeling intimidated by Jakki and the infamous Crayton Clan that stood behind her, but made up in his mind he'd die first before becoming some man's bitch. "Just like your father wouldn't just suck that up and move on, I'm not willing to either."

Having been focused on both visitors, Jakki finally looked over at her father. For the first time in a week he seemed to be getting his color back. Assuming it was him feeling like he was back in the game, even only having a bedside front-row seat, she grinned letting him know she had this. "Just for the principle of it, why don't you tell me what you plan on doing? Because point blank you not getting them pills or none of that cough syrup back!"

"So about that young lady." Maino finally played his ace in hopes of getting Ruben and Jakki to at least negotiate and return some of what was rightfully his.

"Young lady?" Ruben finally spoke wanting more details.

"Yeah, Mr. Crayton, the young lady your daughter left dead inside my store." Maino watched Jakki's facial expression change and knew she hadn't told her father the entire story of what had gone down the night before. Seizing the opportunity to bring the young girl down a few notches in her father's eyesight, if at all possible, he started explaining from start to finish.

When it was all said and done, Ruben was speechless; however, Jakki on the other hand was not. "Okay, guy, you had your say. And guess what, half if not all of what you say went down this week probably did. But that's part of the game. You and this other old man ain't new to any of this life. You know like I know when you spin the wheel sometimes you don't hit. Well this week your luck ran out." Jakki was not at all moved by him bringing up the fact that Lena's dead body was still slumped over underneath the clothing rack in his boutique and he was willing to not call the police and implicate the Craytons if they didn't meet his demands. "This week you got hit hard and instead of trying to keep it street you come in here, at my father's bedside like some little scorned female attempting to extort my family."

Maino, like his partner as well as Ruben, was now speechless after shooting his load.

"Well I got good news and bad news for you. The bad news is those pills and bottles of syrup me and my homegirls took from you is over. Not only are you not getting a dime in return, you need to get together a few more bottles just because and wait for my people to pick them up. That's the street life you chose to walk in." Jakki stood tall as she laid down the new law of the land where Maino and his partner were concerned. "Now the good news is the family is gonna step up and pay for the hole in the wall of the building. That's on us because your business is clean and we don't operate like that. Now as far as you even mentioning the police, that talk will get you killed on the spot. But since we about to be doing business together on a regular basis I'm gonna chalk that threat up as you temporarily losing your mind."

"Business?" Maino finally spoke as Ruben also curious as to what his daughter was going to say next looked on with pride of the true boss she'd become.

"Yes, business. You mentioned wanting to open an additional spot correct?"

"Well yes."

"Well don't worry, I'm gonna make that happen," Jakki promised staring a stunned face Maino dead in his eyes. "But for now I think it'd be in your best interest to go back to the boutique and wait for my people to show up and help you with that little problem."

"Yeah, but—"

"Listen, old man, you ain't the only one who done suffered through a bad week, so please just do like I asked before things get real hectic for you real quick."

"What?"

"You heard me and before y'all bounce, run me my damn phone!" Jakki held out her hand and twisted her lips.

Glancing over at Ruben, Maino could tell he was in a no-win situation as he gave the bossy female back her cell. Deciding to cut his losses he and his still silent partner conceded leaving to do as Jakki had requested as far as Lena's corpse went. Each hoped that after the head of the Crayton family was released from the hospital he'd be able to speak for himself and make things right in their eyes.

Chapter 18

Walking by two men that'd obviously left from Ruben's room, Jakki's uncle hurried his pace not knowing what had taken place. Only seconds away from possibly having to break the bad news about their out-of-control nephew's untimely but much needed demise, he turned into the open door of the room. Finding his niece sitting in a chair pushed all the way up near the bed's safety guard rail, he felt all was well. She'd not only proven herself to be a true hardcore hustler over the past week, but a delegator, negotiator, and strangely enough a cold and heartless assassin if need be who had no issue with taking out a weak link, even if that link was blood. If there was any doubt where her family loyalty was at, she'd stepped up to the plate and he respected her, now to the fullest.

"Hello, brother," Ruben, although feeling exhausted considering, happily greeted his family member.

"Hey, man, how you doing?" he replied with a raised eyebrow. Glancing at Jakki, he saw her wink then shake her head. Easily he took that to mean she'd yet to tell her father about School Boy.

"We good, Uncle. We just had a meeting with few new dudes we about to do business with. I'll fill you in on the details later." Jakki grinned hoping she'd made her father proud with the way she handled a potentially bad situation from exploding.

"Well, Jakki, I wanted you to know I took care of those things you needed me to take care of for you."

"What things?" Ruben inquired.

"Oh nothing much, Daddy, just some stuff that went on back in the neighborhood."

Ruben sat up reminding his daughter as well as his brother even though he was bedridden he was still very much in control and head of the family. "Look, don't hide anything from me. I might look weak here in this bed, but I'm not. My body may not be operating fully, but my mind is perfect."

"I'm glad you said that." Jakki got up shutting the room door. "Because I need to talk to you about something."

"What else have you been up to, Jakki? It's bad enough I had to meet with those assholes just now."

"Naw, it's not her, Ruben; it's that wild child School Boy again," his brother spoke up. "That's the one we was both wrong about."

"What about that disrespectful, disloyal animal? Has anyone in the family seen him?" Ruben's blood pressure started to rise. "I can't believe that fool and what he tried!"

Jakki lovingly stood on the side of her father's bed as her uncle stood at the foot. Realizing her old man was beyond salty with her cousin for the botched attempt he'd made on his life she still knew Ruben's blood could never, for whatever reasons, run cold for

School Boy. Throughout the years he'd done more than enough outrageous things to get him exiled from the family; of course, none were as crazy as the acts he'd tried to commit within the last twenty-four hours, but Ruben would intervene making excuses for his bad behavior. This time, however, School Boy's awful sins would and could not be pardoned by her father. This time her cousin had gone too far and it was up to her to break the tragic but much needed news to him.

"What, at my house?" Jakki used both hands to push down on her father's shoulders to stop him from getting out of the bed. "Are you telling me he was in my house and cut my damn wife? Where is she? I wanna talk to her right now, I mean it!"

"Dad, she's okay; if she wasn't you think I'd be here? I'd be with Mom!"

"Yeah, Ruben, don't worry, I swear she's good. Luckily it was only a small cut."

"Well I want y'all to find that ignorant nigga and bring him to me! He's gonna pay for what he tried to do!"

"Pop." Jakki paused looking dumbfounded.

"And what's the rest? It's something, I can tell by the way you two are looking at one another!" Reaching for the phone to call his wife, Jakki, ready to be a soldier in every sense of the word, stopped her father telling him he was correct there was more to the story.

***

Ruben knew eventually it had to be done. There was no stopping or changing the inevitable from jumping off. Having been the head of the Crayton Clan for so long, he was no fool and considering School Boy's unforgivable renegade actions—robbing people in the neighborhood, committing blatant high profile crimes, setting Jakki up to get knocked or worse than that killed, not to mention the callous attempts out of the blue he'd made on his and his wife's lives—it was only a matter of time. School Boy was and had been for a long time a ticking bomb on the verge of exploding. But nevertheless, even in the thick midst of thinking about all the heinous things he'd done since childhood, Ruben was outwardly in pain of his nephew's demise.

Seeing her father visibly shaken by the news that she knew he'd have mixed feelings about was almost more than she could stand. Walking away from his bedside, she stared out the seventh-floor window overlooking the hospital's parking lot. Always cold and in total control, Jakki was shook, refusing to look directly in his face for fear of breaking down not only over the fact she'd never see her troublemaking cousin again, but the gut-wrenching fact that she was the one who sent him on his way.

"Did anyone get in touch with his mother yet?" Ruben sorrowfully inquired of Jakki and her uncle.

"No, not yet. I didn't know how or if you wanted to handle it," his brother responded shrugging his shoulders. "I can go by the house and tell her if you want me to."

Quick to reply, Ruben reached for the glass of ice water that was sitting on his nightstand and took a sip through the straw. "Naw, do me a solid and go pick her up."

"And then?"

"And then bring her to see me. This is the type of thing I need to tell her face to face. I owe her that much."

As her uncle left out the room to do as he was asked, Jakki continued to stare out the window somewhat confused why even in death School Boy was still such an important factor in her father's life; after all, the lunatic did try to kill the entire family.

Chapter 19

"Yes, nurse, who do I talk to in order to get a special list for my father's visitors?"

"You mean like a restriction list?"

"Yes, after what happened last night, they promised us they'd put that in place." Annoyed, that Maino and his boy were allowed to just get on an elevator and casually stroll into her father's room was not okay with her. As she stood at the desk patiently waiting for a form to fill out stating who exactly was to be placed on the list, the elevators door slid open. She saw her stone-faced uncle return with School Boy's mother, obviously confused as to why Ruben had summoned her to his bedside. Jakki spoke to her aunt, seldom seen and mentally unstable at times, knowing in a matter of seconds her heart was going to be shattered in a million pieces.

Five short minutes later while adding the last name to the soon-to-be completed list, the elevator doors slid open once more. "Hey, Mom, what you doing here so soon? I thought you were gonna get some rest."

"I was, Jakki, but I know after your father found out about what that nutcase tried to do, he was gonna practically raise the dead until he saw me and knew I was okay."

Jakki laughed knowing after all the years her parents had been dating then married, no one in the world knew her pops like her mother did. "You right, he did keep asking how you were. Anyway, how is your arm?"

"It's good. It was nothing, just a little cut. It's gonna take more than something like that from that bastard School Boy to stop me!" she proudly announced. "And good riddance to his dead ass!"

Jakki moved over from the nurses' station and looked down the hallway at her father's doorway. "Shhh, Mom, chill a little before she hear you."

"She who?"

"Auntie Sheila is in there with Pops. He's telling her about School Boy and what happened."

"In where?" Jakki had never seen her light-skinned mother turn this red so quickly. "In your father's room?"

Practically running to keep up with her normally calm mother, Jakki was confused as to why she had gotten so heated.

"Ruben have you lost your complete mind in this damn hospital?" she shouted finding School Boy's mother sobbing in her husband's arms.

"Whoa, slow down." He pushed Sheila's tear-soaked face away from his chest. "You don't understand. I just told her about, well you know. School Boy."

Jakki's mother was not in the mood to have sympathy for her aunt's loss and let her feeling be known for all to hear. "Listen, Ruben, I done put up with this deception for years. I have stood by your side and put my feelings on the back burner and sucked it up," she raged as her voiced bounced off the serene colored walls. "But no more, it's finally over and I'm happy about it. I swallowed my pride and practically raised that no-good monster and what did he do in return but try to kill me, our daughter, and you!" The rant continued as Jakki's uncle tried unsuccessfully to get her to please be quiet. "Naw, I'm not gonna be quiet. I'm tired of all these secrets and skeletons piled up in the closets! Your brother and this half-crazy home wrecker messed around behind me and her husband's back and created that demented bloodline baby, so let them deal with the consequences!"

Jakki's mouth dropped opened. She couldn't talk let alone move. Not sure of what her mother had just blurted out she just stood there trying to process it all.

"Stop it!" Ruben demanded as his wife lunged at his alleged baby momma slapping her across the face.

"Naw, Ruben, let's be honest for once. Your brother would still be alive to this day if it wasn't for him coming home from prison doing time for the precious Crayton Clan and finding out you not only slept with his wife, but knocked the dirty tramp up as well! What kinda family loyalty is that huh? If he wouldn't been so messed up in the head behind finding out about y'all little affair, he'd never messed around with that other skank who ended up stabbing him!

See what all your secrets got you: a dead brother and son!"

Jakki couldn't believe her ears. What her mother said once, she just said twice. And if it was true, that would explain a lot: why her father always forgave her "cousin" no matter what and gave him special treatment; why her mother hated him so much; and lastly why her father was so adamant about wanting him to stand at the head of the table when he stepped down. "Son? Is this true?" After fighting to swallow the lump in her throat, she finally asked the million dollar question to everyone inside the room who seemed to have knowledge about this longtime scandal. "Is it true?"

The room grew silent. The only thing that could be heard was the sounds of Ruben's heart monitor and the tiny mournful whimpers from School Boy's shocked mother.

"Jakki." Ruben reached his hand out to his daughter, but she didn't move. "Look, what your mother said is true. School Boy is, I mean was, my son," he finally confessed. "But it never stopped or stood in the way of the love I had for you or your sister. I've always been proud of you both and for the past week you've made me even more proud stepping up to the plate holding the family down."

Jakki totally zoned out. It was like she was having a terrible nightmare, one she couldn't wake up from. "Your son?" she mumbled in a trance walking by his extended arm and out into the busy hallway.

For years she wanted, even fought for, her father's approval and to show him she could stand at the head of the table and now he'd just given her his blessing, but in her eyes it was too late for all that. *Son? School Boy was his son?* As she pressed the elevator button, Jakki stood there fighting with the fact she'd not only killed her cousin, but her brother as well. She wanted to scream. She wanted to cry. She felt like she even wanted to kill someone again. As the doors finally slid opened, in tears she stepped onto the crowded elevator not knowing where to go or what to do next. The only thing she knew for a fact was that family ain't shit!

Six Months Later

"Yeah, Carla, like I told you real bitches do real thangs!" Jakki walked out the door of the condo she and her homegirl shared ever since she'd moved out of her parents' house. "I swear if I didn't have to handle this business I'd be partying with y'all tonight."

Carla stood in the doorway shaking her head. "Yeah, all right, best friend, I hear you talking. You been saying that every since you started trying to go so hard."

"You know me, baby, that's what I do, go hard!" Jakki jumped in her new truck and headed to meet up with her uncle who was still doing what he'd been doing for years: keeping an accurate tally of the Craytons' assets. As she pulled up at their regular designated meeting spot, she got a call from one of the people she'd had making money for the family. "Yeah, hello."

"Hello, how's everything?"

"Everything is everything this way, Maino." Jakki turned off the truck's ignition and reclined her seat. "You got our half of that cheese or what?"

"Um we kinda short; you know this is the last week in the month."

"So what you saying? You think people who need to get high only get right the first three weeks and just magically wake up on the fourth and say oh well, forget getting blasted today? Hell naw, it don't work like that, homeboy, so we gonna expect a double up tomorrow."

Maino had been strong-armed into cutting Jakki and her infamous family into his and his partner's small-time hustle or cutting it out all together. Legendary in the treacherous acts they'd commit if they didn't get their way, he opted to just take the loss and make the best of it. He'd attempted several times to get in contact again with Ruben, but was met with opposition forcing him to finally give up and into Jakki's extortion with a smile tactics.

Ending her impromptu conversation with Maino, she placed another one to the florist. After getting over the initial shock of finding out School Boy was her brother, idiot or not, Jakki made sure he as well as his jump off Lena had fresh flowers once a month laid out on top of their unmarked graves that were located in the very rear left tree-covered unkempt corner of a cemetery run by a close longtime trusted friend to the family. Sure Lena's kin didn't deserve not knowing why their loved one supposedly ran off with School Boy and never once called home to check in, but that was part of street life that touched innocent people's world when their loved ones signed up for a bid in the game.

Finishing that task, Jakki finally went inside the building and into the small-sized conference room where her uncle along with the other family elders were waiting. Feeling a sense of bittersweet pride she stood at the head of the Crayton Clan table knowing she was not only groomed to but born to lead. Jakki listened to her uncle explain to the others that thanks to their new leadership in her, the family had obtained over twenty properties, both commercial and residential, and now had branched out having interest in several extremely lucrative projects that would have them and the next generation to come set for life.

When the short but productive meeting had concluded, Jakki was unexpectedly met in the hallway by her semi-estranged mother. Blaming both her parents equally for the decades of deception and lies, she was still not raised to be rude to her mother and was at least always cordial when forced to be in her presence.

"Hello, dear." She leaned over hugging her daughter. "I miss you so much."

"Hey, Mom, how are you?" Jakki's response was standoffish as she put little to no effort in returning her mother's hug.

"I'm doing okay, baby, I just miss you being at the house. It's so empty with everyone gone. At least your little sister is supposed to come home this weekend for a visit."

Jakki wanted to feel bad for her mother roaming around in the house by her lonesome, but knew that's what happen when your lies catch up to you. "Yeah, well you knew I was gonna move out someday and yeah, she texted me yesterday."

"Well that's really why I came by," she confessed, sensing Jakki's attitude was quickly going south. "I wanted to know when your sister gets home if all three of us can go visit your dad? I know it would mean so much to him if we were all there at his side." Jakki's mother was hopeful that her firstborn would be big enough and have enough compassion in her heart to let bygones be bygones and not only forgive her, but her ailing father as well.

"I'm gonna be busy that day," Jakki snidely remarked while pretending to be cleaning underneath her nails.

"Jakki." She knew her child and knew she could be stubborn when she wanted to and unfortunately this was one of those times. "Come on now, I didn't even tell you what day me and your sister planned on going."

Thinking back on how she was raised and all the school programs throughout the years her father missed out on while running the streets claiming he was doing this and that, she frowned. Or all the multitudes of times she wanted to just hang out with her dad, but instead he chose her cousin, now known to be her brother, treating her differently acting as if he was mad she wasn't born a boy. After her short trip back down memory lane, Jakki gave her mother an earful.

"Okay, Mom, if that's really who you are." Sarcasm filled the small outer hallway. "Please don't come in here trying to mess up my good mental mindset behind your cheating and lying husband. You chose to put up with him and his bastard seed and I ain't mad. That's on y'all. But me, I'm out for self! I'm not trying to direct be a part of his circus anymore; this cage animal done broke out and about to get it how I live out here. So if you think you're going to guilt me into visiting the old man in that sad, dreary nursing home you had to put him in a few months back after he had that stroke, trust, you're sadly mistaken. Maybe him being paralyzed is God's way of telling him that He ain't liked all the ugly he's done in the supposedly name of family."

Jakki's mother was mortified by the callous things her oldest child was saying about her husband, but deep down she couldn't blame her for being caught in her feelings. Holding back the scandalous truth about School Boy had been haunting her since his birth.

Now she was free of that secret but had lost her own daughter in the process. "Look, baby, I understand how you feel and you have every right to think like that. I get it, but since the day you walked out that hospital room, your father lost his will to live."

Jakki looked at her mother with disdain. "Come on now, him feeling like that ain't got shit to do with me. That's all about his beloved School Boy is gone. That's all that ever really and truly mattered to him. So guess what?"

"Jakki." Her mother's face grew even sadder know she was fighting a losing battle.

"I'm not gonna be able to visit your husband today, tomorrow, or even next week. See I gotta lot of business to take care of; Crayton Clan business." Jakki seethed knowing her words were cutting her mother to the bone. "My father will understand; after all, in his book loyalty to the family is above all else. Like he always used to say, when you stand at the head of the table heavy is the head that wears the crown. Well right about now, I'm rocking that bitch to the fullest and ain't got time for nothing else!"

THE END

Counterfeit Love

Prologue

Balil stood at the top of his basement stairs yelling down for his daughter, Sanaa, to hurry up.

In a rush, Sanaa turned the dial on the huge steel safe imbedded in the wall. She opened it, grabbed the large amounts of cash and jewelry inside, and began tossing the contents into the oversized Louis Vuitton bag she had on her side.

"Sanaa, you gotta get the hell outta here," Balil yelled again from the crown of the entrance. "They'll be here any minute."

Balil was referring to law enforcement and the many branches that were currently looking for his daughter. The State of Georgia wanted her on weapons charges, as well as an assault and battery case as well drug cultivation, and intimidating a witness; but the Feds had plans on trumping them with a warrant of their own for drug trafficking, counterfeit currency, and a possible RICO charge. If convicted by the Feds, these charges would surely put Sanaa away for the rest of her life.

"Call Joi and tell her that I'm ready," she yelled back up to him as she stuffed the last few stacks of money into her bag.

Sanaa was now officially on the run. She was going to need every dime she had if she was going to be successful in hiding out while the statute of limitations ran out on her current state and federal cases. The last two months the fools had added some additional charges that she had not been indicted on as of yet. She gave some girl a place to lay low and she got caught up with Ringworm; he pimped her ass out and the little bitch dropped her name. It felt like they were just making up shit to add to her charges to ensure she wouldn't see the light of day. Her lawyer had advised her to lay low for at least four or five years. The weapons charges would be dismissed by then and any witness on the assault and battery would be difficult to find and get to court to testify after so much time had lapsed. The federal case was going to be a lot more difficult so she was going to need the time to build her money back up for the long trail she knew was ahead. So for now Sanaa's destination was Philadelphia, her original place of birth, and where she had spent her early teenage years. She still had a lot of friends and family there, so her concern of being alone for the next five years wasn't that great. Well, that and the fact that her best friend, Joi, and her younger brother, Sleepy, would be accompanying her on the long trip back up North.

"Did you call her?" Sanaa asked, coming up the steps with the heavy bag over her shoulder.

"Yeah, she's three minutes out. She had to pick your brother up. You make sure you watch over her. Right now, she is only wanted for questioning, but you know how the police do. We can't afford to have her in custody at all," Balil told Sanaa.

She figured that was going to happen. Joi's photograph and license plate had been captured in connection with the shooting and possible murder of a former family friend. She would have to lay low until the investigation died down. Balil had learned from his source in the police department about the evidence implicating Joi, and decided it was best for her to accompany Sanaa and Sleepy back to Philly.

"So when am I going to hear from you?" Sanaa asked, looking into her father's eyes before walking over and peeking out of the front window.

"No contact for a while, baby girl. At least six months," Balil answered, walking up behind her.

Sanaa sat staring out of the window, thinking about the crazy run she had experienced in Atlanta. She had managed to turn the city upside down, and had the cocaine game sewn up on her part of town. Not only was she a major player in the drug world, she was also responsible for multiple shootings related to turf wars in and around her neighborhood.

Over the last couple of years, she had become a problem for the hood niggas as well as the local authorities who eventually had to call on the Feds for help. Once they stepped in, it took them less than eight months to build a strong enough case to indict her, as well as the people she ran with. She now had no choice but to go on the run or face going to jail. Sanaa had chosen option A. Being in the street would give her the chance to stack the cash she was going to need to find and retain the best defense lawyer for the federal charges.

"Here they go," Sanaa said, seeing Joi pull up to the house. "Daddy, I'm gonna miss you," she said, turning around and giving him a tight hug.

"I'm gonna miss you too, princess. Take care of your brother and be safe. Oh, and put some flowers on ya mom's grave for me." He smiled. "Now get outta here," Balil said, pushing her to the door.

As Sanaa walked down the steps, Balil hoped she wouldn't look back. It was hard watching his baby girl walk away, knowing this would be the last time he would see his family for a while. He and Joi temporarily locked eyes as the silent words "I love you" were mouthed with their lips.

Balil took a deep breath as he watched his family pull off; he instantly began to miss them. Less than fifteen minutes later, police cars, black-tinted SUVs, and the SWAT unit swarmed the block. They ransacked Balil's house looking for Sanaa. He silently said a thankful prayer to God, glad that she was gone.

Danielle jammed her hands into her jacket pockets as soon as she got out of the car. She was trying her best to keep warm from the constantly blowing midnight breeze. But on this evening, it would take more than cold weather to stop her from handling the business at hand. This kind of work always seemed to separate the boys from the men, or in this case, the little girls from the grown women.

"His car is still out there, but I don't think he's in the house," Royce, Danielle's partner in crime, said as he walked out of the Chinese restaurant to meet her.

Home invasions, breaking and entering, and robbery were at an all-time high in Philly. It had gotten so bad that even chicks were starting to get in on the action. Sky-rocketing cocaine and weed prices were the main causes of the problem, and those who were still somewhat relevant in the drug game became prey to the many wolves that roamed the dark streets, looking for that quick come up.

"So, let's just do this and get it over with," Danielle insisted, walking back to the car to grab her gun.

It was a simple B&E, but she knew one could never be too safe when it came down to taking another man's money, especially since the person she was taking from tonight was known in the hood for making people disappear. It was a risk that at this time Danielle was willing to take.

Royce felt the same way, knowing that the lick on this job could reach well into the six figures, not including the strong possibility of some drugs being in the home also.

"Fuck it, you ready?" Royce asked, looking into Danielle's eyes for any signs of fear or doubt.

She displayed no fear, and Royce just hoped that she would keep that same ice water running through her veins if shit ever turned sour.

They hopped in the car and pulled off down Third Street. Once they got to Norris Avenue, Danielle pulled over and parked. They both got out and walked the rest of the way down the dimly lit road until they reached Pethrobe Street.

The block was small, and so were the homes. Danielle wasted no time walking straight up to Rico's house and pulling out the set of keys she had manage to duplicate during the time she spent with him over the summer. Despite Rico's car parked right out front, she casually walked into the house as if she was still staying there.

Royce followed in right behind her, but stopped her at the door so that he could check to make sure no one had seen them enter the residence.

The house was clear, so Royce and Danielle went right to work. "In and out," he yelled before walking back into the living room where Danielle was waiting.

She already knew a few of the stash spots in the home, so she went straight to them. Royce stayed guard at the front door, just in case someone attempted to enter.

"Yo, come help me," Danielle yelled from upstairs. "Hurry up," she continued yelling.

"Keep it da fuck down," Royce whispered loudly as he joined her in the bedroom. "What da hell is you doin'?" he asked when he saw her standing on top of the dresser with half the ceiling tiles missing.

She pulled down two black trash bags and one small duffle bag from the ceiling. Royce immediately placed the bags on the floor and opened them to get a quick look at what was inside.

"Jackpot!" he said, seeing nothing but money in the trash bags and some guns in the duffle bag.

"I know he got another stash in the basement," Danielle said, jumping down off the dresser.

Royce lifted his head up from the duffle bag when he heard the loud bass from a car stereo outside. Danielle ran over to the window and slightly moved the blinds to the side. She almost pissed on herself when she saw Rico getting out of his man Style's car.

"Oh shit, that's him," she said, easing the blinds back. Styles got out of the car and headed into the house right behind Rico.

As soon as Rico turned the light on, Danielle greeted him with a chrome .45 automatic pointing right at his face. Styles attempted to reach for his pistol, but stopped when he felt a cold piece of steel pressed against the back of his head. Neither man had paid attention to Royce, who was behind the door when they entered the home.

"Danni?" Rico said, looking at Danielle with his face twisted in disbelief. "Bitch, you must have lost ya fuckin' mind," he snapped, looking like he wanted to walk over and choke the shit out of her. "You know who shit you fuckin' wit'?"

"Both of y'all muthafuckas sit down," Royce demanded, stripping them of their guns before they sat on the couch.

He walked over to Danielle, who kept her gun aimed at the men. Royce stood behind her, wrapped his arms around her waist, and rested his chin on her shoulder. The whole room was silent.

"Pull the trigger," he whispered in Danielle's ear.

Her heart almost jumped out of her chest. She had never shot anyone before. She hoped that Royce was bullshitting, but after he repeated himself, Danielle knew he was serious. She looked at Rico, who had a smirk on his face, as if he knew she wasn't built for the murder game.

"You sure you want me to kill 'em?" she asked, trying to stall. "Won't the neighbors hear it?"

Unlike Danielle, Royce had known from the moment Rico and his boy pulled up that he was going to have to lay them down permanently. It was inevitable, but Royce wanted to seize this moment to see if Danielle was ready to catch a body like the one she bragged about catching before. In their line of work, she needed to be prepared to murder something at the drop of a dime, and he needed to know she was able.

"Come on, babe, we'll both do it," Royce said as he raised one of the guns and pointed it at the two men.

Danielle was scared. This was more than what she had bargained for, but she was determined to see it through. Her palms grew sweaty and her heart began to race. At this point, she knew it was either kill or be killed, because there was no way Rico was going to let her live after this.

Out of nowhere, Rico lunged forward in a stupid attempt to grab one of the guns. Danielle just closed her eyes and squeezed the trigger. The bullet hit Rico in his face, knocking him backward onto the couch. She opened her eyes and couldn't believe what she'd just done.

Royce quickly fired three shots into Styles, who seemed to be frozen in the chair. He released Danielle from his embrace.

She stood motionless, staring at the bullet hole in Rico's head and the blood that leaked out of it. She had actually never witnessed someone being shot and her stomach begin to knot up as she could feel the bile moving up her throat. Danielle took a deep breath and swallowed it back down, not wanting to look weak. She tried to look away, but watching the life leave Rico's body was mesmerizing. It took Royce throwing the duffle bag over her shoulder to get her to snap out her trance. Once she did, they both exited the home, but not before Danielle took one last look at Rico's body as she passed it.

Chapter 1

Krystol sat on the bed, breastfeeding Raven and watching with a scowl as Royce walked back and forth from the bathroom to the bedroom, getting dressed for the day. The attitude displayed on her face said it all, and Royce knew that it wasn't going to be easy getting out of the house in the next twenty minutes, as he needed to in order to be on time for his meeting. Royce took his time, making sure he looked perfect. Krystol knew without any doubt that he was doing all of this for another woman.

As with her and many other women Royce had a routine. He would work out to make sure his muscles were swollen; he only wore Gucci cologne when he was going out to prowl, or going to pleasure. He sprayed the cologne in the air, and then sprayed it on his shorts while they lay on the bed. He slipped them on and checked himself out in the mirror. This was his mating routine, giving the flies honey to buzz around. The Gucci cologne applied to the wrist and crotch section of his shorts confirmed her thoughts.

"You doin' all that just to go to work?" Krystol sarcastically asked, popping her breast out of Raven's mouth and placing the fully fed baby on the bed. "Damn, you can at least put some shade on what you're doin'," she continued as she walked to the bathroom.

Royce just smiled, looking into the mirror as he continued brushing his hair. Moving to Atlanta a couple years ago hadn't worked out the way that he thought it would, so he had moved his family back to his hometown of Philadelphia about ten months ago. He was on a mission to set him and his family straight forever, after a chance meeting with a financial advisor who had informed him that with a goal of $1 million cash, he could ensure that they would never have to worry about money again. It was as simple as placing that same million into an escrow account that would gain 20 percent interest annually, which would mean a $200,000 yearly payout for Royce. Two hundred grand a year consistently sounded great to him, considering all the lows and highs of the dope and stickup game. Royce was growing tired, and he knew that either death or prison was eventually going to catch up to him.

"Yo, it's not what you think," he said, grabbing Krystol's arm as she came storming out of the bathroom.

At that moment, she couldn't stand the sight of him, and she definitely couldn't stand to sit there and hear him lie to her face again. Instead, she just looked at him with disgust, rolled her eyes, and walked off, snatching her arm from his hand.

Krystol was starting to regret the move from Atlanta, which was where she was originally from. If it weren't for the fact that Raven was only seven weeks old, she would have truly considered moving back home. It seemed that ever since Royce had gotten back to Philly, he stayed in the streets. Although he always used the excuse of working, he was always complaining about money. He had put her on a strict budget, and he kept telling her that she was going to have to get used to living on a fixed income once he retired from the streets. Krystol had dated a few hustlers in her life, and she knew that most of the time this was just pipe dreams that all of them had about leaving the life.

"B, on the real, stop acting like dat," Royce said, walking over to the bed. "You tellin' me that you don't trust me?" he said, picking up the baby.

"So, where you going, and who you meeting?" she snapped back.

"I'm goin' to . . ." he began, but stopped. Royce was stuck. He was about to tell Krystol he was going to help his sister out at her club, but he could tell by the way she asked the question that she already knew he wasn't going there today. He didn't know what to say or whether he should tell her the truth of who he was meeting.

He stared back at his two girls while Krystol waited to hear his excuse. Royce looked directly into her eyes, and at that moment, he knew that the truth would be to hard to explain to Krystol; so instead, he did what any man who really loved his woman would do. He prepared himself to lie: something he really hated to do, because he knew Krystol could always tell when he wasn't telling the truth. But before the words could leave his mouth, she bailed him out.

"Just like I thought," Krystol said, grabbing the remote control off the nightstand and turning the TV on. "Nigga, just put my daughter down and go where you're goin'."

Royce glanced up at the clock on the wall. It was getting late, and he really didn't have time to get into it with her right now. He chose to take the out and not even respond to her last comment. Instead, he just looked down at his baby girl as she lay cradled in his arms. Raven suppressed any anger that was building up.

"Look, we'll talk when I get back," Royce said, laying Raven down on the bed next to Krystol.

"Yeah, maybe I will find me somebody, and call it work," she said in a smart manner. Krystol knew she had a way with her words that could make a nigga mad instantly.

"Fuck is dat supposed to mean?" Royce said, stopping at the bedroom door.

"Nigga, you know," she uttered in a sarcastic tone.

"Know what, B? Say what you say!"

Krystol just looked off into the TV, as if she didn't hear him, hoping it would make Royce mad. In some odd crazy way, she wanted to argue and fight with him, knowing it would mean that he would have to stay home.

Royce kept his cool and didn't entertain the last comment. Instead, he just chuckled, told her that he loved her, and left.

***

Sanaa sat at the bar talking to Joi, who was drying the glasses that had just come out of the dishwasher. The two ladies were exhausted from the long weekend at the club. Club All In was Sanaa's baby, and Joi was the aunt. The three-level club consisted of the large bar and grill area on the first floor, and an even larger dancing area on the second level. Poker tables and slot machines where housed in the basement area. This was where the majority of the money was made, and normally where all the headaches and drama were as well.

The club was coming up on its one-year anniversary, and for the two women, it would mark their fifth year of being best friends. The great connection they had with each other proved that their bond was just as strong as blood sisters, even though there was a fourteen-year age difference between them, Joi being the elder. The two women enjoyed each other's company, and it was a good thing, because they had spent every day of the last year together.

At times like this, Sanaa could guess what was going on with her friend before Joi could even say anything. "What's wrong?" Sanaa asked, seeing the sad look on her best friend's face that Joi was so desperately trying to hide. "I know you miss him, and I do too, but we can't go back yet. It's still too hot, and if he comes this way, they will follow him."

"Damn, but don't you feel trapped sometimes? Don't you?" Joi asked, pointing at the bottle of Jack Daniels so that Sanaa could pour her a drink.

Joi sure as hell was feeling trapped, and had been feeling that way ever since they moved back to Philly. Joi was used to a different type of lifestyle in Atlanta, where she had moved over ten years ago: a life where she could get up and go whenever she wanted. It was a life where she surrounded herself with dope boys and niggas who took money. That was until she had a chance meeting with the only man she had ever really loved in her life.

Balil was an old Philly hustler that Joi had started messing with when she was only nineteen. Although he was old enough to be her father, and had children nearly her age, Balil was still a very attractive man, who kept himself feeling young by not dating anyone in his age bracket. His and Joi's relationship lasted a few years, but as she began to age, Balil desired for something younger, just like he had done with the girl before Joi. But that was years ago, and water under the bridge, as far as Joi was concerned.

She had run back into him at a club in Atlanta. Balil had moved his gambling empire down South, for a chance at semiretirement, and Joi had hoped that included his womanizing and cheating behavior. Everything was going so well for the two of them, and the icing on the cake was his daughter, Sanaa, who she found to be a kindred spirit and had developed a relationship with.

Things in the ATL eventually began to come apart, and she and Sanaa had to go on the run. Philly looked like their best bet at remaining free. Although being stuck behind the bar at Club All In wasn't her idea of real freedom, she knew that after the shit that went down in the A, she had to make some changes in her life. But this was a little much.

Before Sanaa could respond to Joi's questioning, the sound of the bells ringing on top of the front door caught both of their attention. It was mid-afternoon, so pedestrians were allowed to drink at the bar, but when four men walked through the door dressed in suits, Sanaa knew it wasn't her regulars coming in for a drink. Instinctively, she eased her hand toward her waist where her gun was holstered, while watching the hand of everyone who entered the establishment.

Joi also inched over and got closer to her pistol, which was sitting under the bar.

I hope this ain't the Feds, Sanaa thought, hesitant to pull her weapon on federal agents.

But as the men got closer, she recognized a familiar face she hadn't seen in a while. Boo, with his classic smirk that showed the one deep dimple in his left cheek, walked through the door. He was the last person she had expected to see; he was a bully, and she thought for sure someone had planted a bullet in his brain by now. Seeing Boo generally meant that you needed to be strapped up, or have enough people with you to handle beating his stupid ass down. The long scar on his neck was a reminder of how people felt about him. The cut was only millimeters from his jugular. He was hated and feared by many niggas in the hood. She and Boo were not on the level of doing more than passing each other.

"I see nothing's changed," Boo said, walking up to Sanaa and taking a seat on a stool next to her.

"Yeah, they say the more things change, the more they remain the same. What can I do for you?" Sanaa asked, curious about this unexpected meeting.

"You got somewhere we can talk in private, or is this open for everybody's ears to hear?" he asked, looking over at Joi, who had her eyes on everything that was going on.

"Nah, we good right here. Whatever you got to say, you can say it in front of her, unless you don't trust your people," Sanaa interjected, picking up the bottle of Jack Daniels and pouring herself another shot.

Boo stared at her for a minute. Sanaa was a true wolf in sheep's clothing. Her face reflected her young mother and older father's timeless genes. She wore her naturally curly hair in an afro Mohawk. Her eyes were like black coal and had a piercing effect, as if she was able to look right into a person's mind and thoughts. Boo temporarily closed his eyes and gave his head a slight shake, as if he was clearing it from his physical attraction to Sanaa. He knew he had to stay on point, because although beautiful, she was dangerous.

"Well, first of all, I do believe a thank-you would be nice, considering I gave you a grace period to get your little business up and running. Now I know you didn't think that you was going to eat in my hood and not show me any love," Boo said, grabbing the bottle of Jack Daniels from the bar and pouring himself a shot.

Sanaa really didn't care for Boo. She knew he was a grimy nigga who would sell his own momma if he thought he could get rich from it. Plus, he was known for putting his hands on females, a fact that she knew first hand after Boo smacked up one of her girlfriends who used to date him. The smacking turned into an everyday beat down for her friend, and Sanaa was the one there taking her to the hospital damn near every other day.

She looked at him like he was crazy. He had many people in the hood shook, but Sanaa wasn't one of them. She had put in some respectable work herself over the years, which had earned her a lot of street credit from both men and women. It was only recently that she had turned it down a little, considering the authorities were sitting back waiting for her to mess up.

Boo motioned for one of his boys to come over to the bar. In his hand was a small black trash bag, and without Boo telling him to do so, he dumped the contents onto the bar right in front of Sanaa.

She looked down at the stacks of twenties and fifties in a curious manner. Not sure what to say, she just looked up at him.

"I'm trying to get rid of this counterfeit money and you going to help," Boo said, throwing back his shot glass.

"Oh, I am, am I? And how you figure I'm doing that?" Sanaa said, picking up a stack of twenties and peeling off one of the bills. She closely examined the bills, hoping that none of the gamblers had passed any to her recently. "How in the hell can you tell it's fake? Shit looks real as fuck to me," she said, raising the bill up to the light, unable to find its flaws.

"I can tell because I made it," Boo said, reaching over the bar and grabbing one of the sodas that was about to be put in the refrigerator.

"Nigga, when you start making funny money?" she asked in shock. Sanaa had played around with some phony money back in Atlanta for a while, so she wasn't a stranger to the counterfeit game. She had changed over large amounts of it during her many drug transactions, and she was never caught. This money looked a lot like the high grade she had back in the A. The ink was on point, and the paper. She had a hard time being certain that it was counterfeit, due to her limited handling of the funny money back in Atlanta. Her boy Manny was the expert in regard to how to print it, and how to spot it.

"Yeah, I get busy a li'l. I know you got a nice li'l hook up in here, plus you and ya crazy-ass brothers be making moves. I figure you wouldn't mind doin' some business wit' me," Boo explained, throwing back the shot of Jack Daniels.

As he and Sanaa talked, Joi listened carefully, and the more she listened, the closer she inched toward her gun. His demeanor was somewhat aggressive, and Joi didn't take too kindly to it. Boo was trying to muscle in with a soft press. Whatever the case was, Joi didn't care because she was armed, clutching the Ruger P80 under the bar.

Sanaa was well aware that he had no problem turning her club upside down, but at the same time she also knew that Boo would try to be diplomatic about the situation first, before it got to that level. He just went on and continued explaining to Sanaa how the money was made, and how it was able to go undetected.

"You see you got to get your paper from them sand niggas, the plates and ink from them Africans. They know how to make your shit legit."

She still wasn't quite convinced about the funny money because she still couldn't see the flaws in the bills. She turned to Boo, her hand still on the butt of her gun, and pushed the twenty back to him. Boo sighed, and grabbed the club soda from the counter. He allowed a few drops to fall on the face of the twenty, after a few moments, the ink turned red, and began to run. Sanaa picked up the twenty, and placed it in the glass of water. Within minutes the water was red, and the paper only had the impressions of the symbols of the money.

"So now what?" Sanaa asked Boo as she picked up the dripping ink-stained money.

"Well, that's up to you. I got loads of this shit and I can give it to you for cheap," he replied, pouring himself another shot of Jack.

Sanaa looked over at Joi, who was still looking down at the money. She too couldn't believe how real the money looked. Sanaa's mind began to turn. Although she was doing okay with the bar and gambling spot, a come up like this could be life changing, and it didn't come along often. However, at the same time, she didn't trust Boo as far as she could see him, nor did she like his attitude most of the time. But this was business, and not personal, so she was keeping an open mind.

"So, what the prices for this shit look like?" Joi said, easing her hand off the butt of her gun.

Sanaa saw Joi's question as a statement, letting her know that she was interested as well.

Atlanta

Doughboy pulled over, jumped out of his car, and ran into the corner store. It was pouring down raining outside, and it took a minute to get through the crowd of people taking refuge in the entrance of the store. Once at the counter, he ordered his three Dutches, a pack of Newports, and a bottle of Pepsi. He quickly paid for the items, and then made a break back to his car through the rain.

"What da fuck?" he mumbled to himself, looking over and seeing a car blocking him in.

A tap on the passenger side window caught his attention, instantly causing him to reach under his seat and grab his gun. He rolled the window down just far enough to see the pretty face of a woman looking right at him. The rain beaded off her face, and the sounds of cars honking in the background indicated that she was probably the driver of the vehicle.

"Can you help me push my car out of the street?" the young woman asked in the most innocent voice Doughboy had ever heard. "I'll pay you if I got to," she suggested.

"No problem," he said, tucking his gun back under his seat.

As soon as he unlocked his door to get out of the car, the driver side door swung open. By the time Doughboy looked up, the chrome .380 was pointed directly in his face. The passenger side door opened, and into the car jumped the same pretty face that had been asking for his help. This time, she had a gun in her hand, and it too was pointed at Doughboy.

Once the female passenger had him at gunpoint, the driver side door closed, then the back driver side door opened. Another female jumped in the back and sat right behind Doughboy. It was total silence in the sedan, except for the sound of the raindrops falling on the outside of the car, sounding like steel drums being hit with each drop on the metal of the sedan. He looked into the rearview mirror at the assailant in the back seat, trying to figure out who was stupid enough to hold him at gunpoint in his own hood. Since it was two bitches, he had thoughts of reaching under his seat for his gun. He thought twice about that once he felt the barrel of the .380 pressed against the back of his neck through the headrest.

"What y'all bitches want?" Doughboy asked with an attitude, mad as hell that he had fallen for this bullshit setup.

"Where's ya boss, Doughboy?" the woman in the back seat asked, pressing the gun farther against the back of his neck.

"What da fuck is you talkin' about, and how da fuck do you know my name?" he asked, trying his best to remain gangsta.

What seemed like a long time ago for Doughboy only felt like yesterday to Ariana. She could vividly remember looking up at the ceiling in her hospital room, wondering if she was going to survive her wounds. "Sanaa," Ariana snapped back. "Where da fuck is Sanaa and her no-good-ass friend, Joi?" she asked, moving her face over so that Doughboy could finally see who he was talking to.

When he locked eyes with the female through the rearview mirror, his eyes shot open wide like he had seen a ghost. He couldn't believe that Ariana was sitting in his back seat. He knew her well, considering her relationship with Sleepy. He also knew that she was about her business when it came down to the gunplay. All that tough shit went flying out the window, and now he realized that this was a life or death situation, and he had better comply.

"I thought you was dead," Doughboy said as he glanced at a few people running past his car.

"I did too. Now, where is she?" Ariana yelled through her clenched teeth.

Her patience was running low, and her girlfriend, Olivia, could see it. She reached over and jammed her gun into his crotch, causing Doughboy to tense up.

"Yo, Sanaa just up and rolled out. She didn't tell me where she was going. She just said she had to get out of Atlanta. The police was on to her, and her name was coming up heavy on some federal indictments," Doughboy reported.

Something was telling Ariana that Doughboy wasn't telling her the truth about what he knew. He was hiding something and she could tell. She glanced over at Olivia, who then cocked the hammer back on the gun. She was just about to pull the trigger when Doughboy decided to talk. The last thing he wanted to do was lose his dick by way of a bullet. He'd rather take one to the head first.

"Man, look, the last time I heard, she moved up North. I don't know where, but I think it might be Philly. She said she had family up there," Doughboy explained.

"Was Joi wit' her?" Ariana asked, jabbing the back of his head with her gun.

That was one question Doughboy really didn't know the answer to, mainly because he didn't know Joi. He wasn't aware of the whole situation that had gone on between her and Sanaa, and the last and only thing that he could remember about her was that she had disappeared at the same time Sanaa did. To him, it was like one day Sanaa was there, and the next day, everybody was gone.

Ariana wanted both of their heads, and she wasn't going to stop until she had them. Thoughts of the last meeting she had with Joi haunted her. It was that day that changed Ariana's life forever. Just thinking about it made her furious, and it was unfortunate that Doughboy was on the other end of her gun as the horrible thoughts ran through her mind.

Ariana didn't even realize that she'd pulled the trigger until she heard the loud sound of the bullet discharging from the gun's chamber, and saw the blood from Doughboy's neck splatter onto the front windshield. The bullet tore through his esophagus, causing blood to rush down his throat and into his lungs within seconds.

The initial shock of the gunshot subsided immediately, and instead of waiting for another bullet to hit his head, Doughboy reached for the door handle in an attempt to exit the car. He managed to get the door open, but that was about it. Olivia raised her gun to the back of his head and squeezed the trigger twice, putting two holes in his skull the size of a quarter.

His body fell into a puddle on the sidewalk as the rain continued to fall from the sky. The people who were in the store scattered like roaches, no longer caring about the nasty weather. They were trying to avoid two things that could get them killed: flying bullets and being a witness to a murder.

Ariana and Olivia hopped out of Doughboy's car, pulled their hoods over their heads, then jumped into the car that had blocked Doughboy in. They were on some gangsta shit, and Ariana was at the head.

Chapter 2

Royce pulled into the parking lot of Daisy's Diner just in time. He took a few seconds to check himself out in the rearview mirror before making the phone call that prompted a beautiful white, five feet five inch, 135-pound blond-haired, blue-eyed French bombshell to exit the diner. She wore a knee-length floral sundress, a pair of Bernardo leather sandals, and Gucci oversized square-frame sunglasses. Her curly blond hair was wrapped in a bun, and for a moment, it seemed the sun had dipped behind a cloud just to give her some time to shine.

Respectfully, Royce got out of the car, walked around to the passenger side of the vehicle, and opened the door for her as she made her way to the awaiting chariot. She clutched a large Diane Von Furstenberg tote as she climbed into the car, making herself comfortable for the long ride to the other side of town. Royce's dick got hard just thinking about what was about to go down. It was a long time coming, and despite the fact that he'd been lying to Krystol about going to work every day, looking over at Danielle made him look past his deceit.

"So where are you taking me today?" Royce asked, focusing on the road ahead of him. "You know I'm supposed to be working with my sister today," he joked, thinking about Krystol.

"Not far at all," Danielle responded with a devious grin on her face. "You know you can't keep lying to that girl. Eventually, you're gonna have to tell her," she encouraged him.

"Yeah, well I'll do that when the time is right. I don't think now is a good time," Royce shot back.

"It will never be a good time, especially doing the kind of things we do." She giggled.

"How about we change the topic?" Royce suggested, trying to avoid the guilt.

Danielle wasn't about to let up on him. She wanted to be sure that Royce was going to be in it for the long haul. She was investing a lot of time into Royce, along with her trust that he wouldn't disappoint her. She liked Royce, and could see potential in him, but if he couldn't be truthful with his girlfriend about what was going on, there was no way Danielle could move forward in their relationship. She knew he had a goal of reaching millionaire status, and she had a plan to get both of them there. But she also knew that he couldn't have any distractions, and an unhappy home was one that could derail them both.

"So, where are we going?" he asked again, still not sure of the destination.

"It's our first time doing something on this level, so I want it to be special. You just make sure that when we get there, you put it down like you're supposed to," she responded in a seductive manner.

Before he knew it, they were pulling into the Four Seasons hotel parking lot. Danielle jumped out, followed by Royce, and the couple walked hand in hand toward the entrance. Royce threw on a pair of Raf Simons aviator sunglasses, trying to be as incognito as possible in case he ran into someone he knew.

Once at the front desk, the clerk already had the room key waiting and passed it off to Danielle without saying a word. Royce wrapped his arms around her waist and walked behind her, in sync with every step she took toward the elevator.

The hotel had thirty floors, but Danielle and Royce were only going to the fourteenth: room 1417, east wing, to be exact. Royce stopped Danielle in the middle of the hallway, pressing her back against the wall. He had to admit to himself that she was indeed a ray of sunshine. He leaned in to hug her, resting his chin on her shoulder, and at the same time, looking up at the single security camera. His heart was racing uncontrollably, and had been ever since they pulled into the parking lot, due to the fact that Danielle had briefed him on what was about to go down.

"You ready?" she asked, wrapping her arms around Royce's neck, and at the same time glancing up at the camera.

As soon as the little red light on the side of the camera switched off, Danielle pushed Royce back, reached under her sundress, grabbed a ten-shot 9 mm, and screwed the silencer on to it quickly. Royce did the same, reaching around and grabbing a seventeen-shot Glock from his back waistline. He screwed his silencer on as they both made their way down the hallway to room 1417. Danielle placed her tote bag on the side of the door, wanting all her limbs free to react to whatever was inside the room.

She passed Royce the keycard to open the door, and with one swipe of it, the door was unlocked. There was no time to waste, so as soon as the green light flicked on, Royce was through the door firing at the first body he saw, which was an armed man standing by the window off to the left.

Danielle was right behind him, letting several shots fly into the two men sitting at a table putting money through the money machines. She didn't hesitate to hit both men from the neck up.

So focused on her targets, Danielle didn't see one of the men racing across the room in an attempt to tackle her, but before he could reach her, Royce shot him in his chest. His body fell right in at Danielle's feet.

Royce quickly moved across the hotel room, checking every door, until he was satisfied that there were no more physical threats. Off the break, Royce noticed the large amount of cocaine sitting on the bed, packaged in brick form.

Danielle walked out into the hallway and retrieved her tote bag. She pulled out another trash bag from it and threw it to Royce. "We're only taking the money," Danielle instructed, walking over to the table where the cash was.

"Are you sure?" Royce asked, nodding at the cocaine on the bed.

"Yeah, that coke belongs to somebody else. We are only here for the money," she said, bagging up the cash from the table.

Royce didn't even think twice about it. He walked over to the table and helped Danielle bag the currency. This was Danielle's lick, and Royce was just along for the ride. It was a good lick, too. Five hundred grand was the total take, but Royce only saw two hundred grand of that. The lick didn't come for free, so Danielle had to pay $100,000 and the dope, which left her with two hundred grand herself. She had to pay off a few different people who helped put it together. That was just the nature of the business she was in, and for a female, she did it damn well.

They both walked out of the hotel heavier than what they were when they first walked in. A simple wink of the eye told the hotel clerk that he could go and collect his cocaine. That's where his cut, along with the head of security's cut, came from. Today was the day everybody got paid.

Sleepy walked into the club with a Louis Vuitton leather bag containing twenty-five grand, which was being used to purchase some of Boo's funny money. One hundred grand of fake money for twenty-five grand in real money was hard to pass up, especially seeing how good the money looked. Although Sleepy wasn't completely sold on this funny money idea, he was going to ride with his sister. Besides, he needed something to take his mind off his constant obsessing about Ariana. Everyone seemed to think that she had just taken off, but he knew better. Their love was real, and she wouldn't just bounce on him. As soon as he was able, he was going back to Atlanta to find his woman.

Sanaa had thought it over, and being one who was always down for a fast come up, she decided not to pass this by. She made a mental note to call up her other brother, Royce, and get him on board. Although none of the siblings shared the same mother, Balil had made sure they came up as tight as any brothers and sisters raised under the same roof. Whenever it was time for some real shit to go down, Sanaa made sure she had family around. Her two brothers were known killers, and that helped when doing business on the streets.

"Ya money," Sanaa said, walking over to the table and placing the bag right next to Boo's plate of Buffalo wings.

Boo didn't skip a beat while eating his food. He just looked at the bag and smiled as he continued to chew the mouthful of chicken. Ranch and bleu cheese dressing were all over his hands and face. It got to the point where he had to release his top button.

"Sit down. I wanna talk to you about something," Boo requested, pointing at the chair across from him with a chicken bone.

"No, I'll stand," Sanaa shot back. "And I really don't think we have anything else to talk about."

"Look, I apologized about ya girlfriend a long time ago. Now sit down, I have something I wanna talk to you about," Boo insisted in a more serious tone.

It was quiet for a moment, but Sanaa eventually pulled out the chair and took a seat, only willing to hear what he had to say so that he could hurry up and leave.

Boo nodded for his boys to back away from the table so that he could talk to her in private. It was obvious that Sleepy wasn't invited to the conversation, and from the look on his face, he felt some type of way.

"It's cool," Sanaa told Sleepy, nodding for him to back away from the table.

Boo grabbed the Louis Vuitton bag and emptied the money out on the table. He took his orange soda and poured it over a few of the bills. He wanted to make sure he wasn't getting any fake money in return.

Sanaa scooted up in her chair and took a good look at him. She could tell that Boo had something on his mind, and because she had history with him, she knew it was some type of scheme boiling in his head. "What do you want, Boo?" Sanaa asked, wanting him to get straight to the point.

"I don't know about y'all, but I'm hungry. I'm tryin'a eat," he said, looking over his shoulder at Sleepy, who kept his eyes on him.

"Again, get to the point, Boo," she said, cutting him off.

"I wanna move five million in counterfeit money through ya club. I got everything from one dollar bills to one-hundred dollar bills," he said, hoping to get her attention.

Sanaa's attention was in his grasp. She looked at him like he had lost his mind. Moving $5 million of funny money through her spot was out of the question, and that was something Sanaa didn't have to think about. "What makes you think I'ma move five million dollars of ya funny money in my place?" Sanaa shot back.

"Listen, Sanaa, you and I both know that I didn't come here to ask you. I'm pretty much telling you you're gonna move dis money through ya spot," he replied, giving her a stern look. "Look, I respect you and your brothers, and even your pops, but if I have to kill each one of you, it's no problem for me. I have a whole crew; you got maybe five or six people. How you figure you going to win?"

If it wasn't before, shit had just got real at the table. For a second, Sanaa couldn't believe what was coming out of Boo's mouth. This wasn't a proposition, nor an offer. This was a demand, and the price Sanaa and her family would have to pay if she didn't go along with the scheme would be heavy. Sanaa wasn't stupid; she knew right now wasn't the time to be taking on a nigga like Boo. But by no means was she about to let him know that. Shit, she too was a gunner in her own right.

"I can make that to be ya last meal," Sanaa threatened out of anger.

Boo's confidence and arrogance was through the roof. He just looked at her and laughed, picking up another Buffalo wing and sticking it in his mouth. Fear was nowhere in his eyes.

"One thing I know about you, you're not stupid," Boo said, pulling the chicken bone out of his mouth. "If you wanna start a gun fight right here and now, then that's fine wit' me. We can all die up in dis muthafucka. My guys got a green light to put a bullet in ya head the moment things get out of hand," Boo informed, cleaning his hands off with the face towel.

Sanaa looked back at Boo's boys, two of whom were looking directly at her. By the time she turned back around to face Boo, one of his hands had found its way under the table, and the look in his eyes said that he had armed himself. Sanaa just chuckled, trying her best to keep her cool.

"So what if I say no?" she asked, leaning back in her chair. "You gonna set it off right here and now?" She smiled. "One thing I know about you, Boo, is that you don't wanna die, especially by my hands."

Boo blew her off, as if what she said was an insult. Her comments rubbed him the wrong way, but in a way, he could see that she was serious about her work. He really didn't want no problems with Sanaa. All he wanted to do was get some money, and convincing her that the come up was beneficial for both of them was his main objective.

"Look, Sanaa, if you say no, then you just say no. But I know that you're not stupid enough to turn down this kind of offer. Most banks don't even know the difference in the money I print out, and to be honest wit' you, I can print out as much of it as I want. One million was all that I brought wit' me. I can change the American currency if given enough time," he bragged. "Look, I just want you to think about it," Boo said, standing up. "You know where to find me when you ready." He tucked the large-caliber gun he had clutched under the table back into his waist.

Sanaa just sat there as Boo walked past her and made his way out the door with his boys. From the look on her face, Sleepy could tell that she was in deep thought when she walked back over to him. Boo had given her more than enough to think about. It was like he had anticipated and visualized the endless possibilities of all that Sanaa could do with the counterfeit money.

"So what's all that about?" Sleepy asked, taking a seat at the table.

Her mind was racing so fast, it took a moment for her to even realize Sleepy was there. "We need to have a meeting," Sanaa said as she got up from the table and headed straight for the bar.

Chapter 3

Royce walked into the house only to feel a totally different vibe in the atmosphere. The living room looked a mess, with clothes tossed about on the floor and the couch. He could hear Krystol's voice upstairs sounding like she was talking on the phone, which she was when Royce finally made it to his bedroom. Raven was lying in her crib while Krystol continued to separate the clothes she was pulling out of the closet.

"What's up?" Royce said, holding a curious but very serious look on his face.

His presence startled her a little, since she hadn't even heard him come into the house, let alone creep up to the bedroom. It was a good thing that he was there, because she had a lot to get off her chest, and he was the reason why. She quickly got off the phone with her sister, tossing the cordless phone onto the bed. She walked over, grabbed Royce by the arm, and pulled him into the bathroom in order to get away from the baby.

"I'm moving back to Atlanta," Krystol said, closing the bathroom door.

"What the fuck? Is that supposed to be a joke?" he replied, looking at her like she was crazy.

"Naw, Ro, you a fuckin' joke. Whatever bitch got ya ass open like that, tell her she can keep you. I'm done wit' dis bullshit," she snapped.

"Are you serious? I told you I wasn't fuckin' around on you. You need to stop trippin'."

"You a fuckin' liar. And you been lying to me for over a month now, Royce. I talked to Sanaa, and she told me she ain't seen you in nearly a month, but every day you leave out of this house in the morning, claiming you going to work at her spot!" Krystol yelled, poking Royce in his forehead.

Royce sat there with a grin on his face, somewhat amused by Krystol's investigation. He also was smiling because he couldn't figure out how he could have been so sloppy with not calling Sanaa and letting her know he was using her as his excuse with Krystol. Truth was, his mind was so on his money and the future for his family that he wasn't thinking about the bullshit. He sat there confused on if now would be a good time to tell her about Danielle, and what he'd been up to. Royce lived by the code of the streets, and a real gangster never discussed what he had going on with his wife. That way, if anything ever went down, the police couldn't indict Krystol because she was unaware of what he was doing.

It was an ugly situation, because here he was, trying to protect her and his family, and if he didn't tell her, he could risk her leaving him. If she thought that he was cheating on her, she would still leave him. Krystol had made that clear before she moved to Philly, and she swore on her mother's soul that she was going to stand by that if it occurred.

"Yeah, just what I thought," Krystol said, covering his face with her hand.

He grabbed her hand and threw it down, giving her a stern look. "I told you I wasn't fuckin' wit' nobody," he snapped back. "We got bills to pay, and I'm out there doing what I gots to do."

"And what is that, Royce? Because I don't see the money from you doing what you got to do. If you doing all this, where's the money at?" Krystol asked with an angry but disappointed facial expression.

"Look, B, you just gots to trust me on this; just know it's the best thing for us, babe. For our family," he answered, looking her in the eyes.

"How can I trust you, and you won't trust me enough to tell me what you got going on? I want to believe you, but, Royce, I smell her perfume on your clothes every time you come back in. I seen the lipstick smudge on your shirt. Tell me you not seeing another bitch!'"

"No, I'm not fucking anybody," he answered.

She sat there and looked at him for a moment, trying to look into his eyes to see if he was lying to her. Something in her heart told her that he was telling the truth, but it was also something inside of her that told her that Royce was doing something he didn't have any business doing.

"You're a fuckin' liar," she calmly said, and then tried to walk out of the bathroom.

When she reached for the knob, Royce pressed his back against the door, closing it shut. He could see the stress in her face, and that was something he hated to see in the woman he loved. He grabbed her by the waist and tried to pull her closer to him.

She resisted for a moment, but ultimately gave in.

"I told you I wasn't fucking with nobody, and I give you my word on that." Royce spoke gently. "You just gotta trust me, B," he assured her, gazing into her eyes.

Krystol and Raven were his world. They were the core reason why he woke up every morning and did what he did.

"Man, fuck Boo," Sleepy said angrily, looking across the table at Sanaa. "He got us fucked up."

"Calm down, li'l bro. It ain't that serious," Sanaa said, pouring a shot from the whiskey bottle sitting in the middle of the table. "You know, it's really not a bad idea. It ain't like we can't relocate," she said, pushing the bottle over to Joi.

"So how is we suppose to move that kind of money without getting caught?" Joi asked, wondering what Sanaa had in store.

"I got a poker table, bar, and food and drink. It's not really the question of if we can move it, it's just how fast we can move it," Sanaa said, passing both Sleepy and Joi one of the twenty-dollar bills Boo had left behind. "As long as we keep it away from soda and shit like dat, we should be all right."

Everything seemed to have been going good until Boo showed up with another one of his money schemes. It was only after careful thought about what Boo said that Sanaa decided to take him up on his offer. With the problems she had back in Atlanta, it was best that Sanaa stack as much money as she could, in case she had to run, or, in a worst-case scenario, had to prepare a legal team. The little bit of money she was making in the club right now wasn't enough to do either. She kind of felt like her back was against the wall. It was at times like this that Sanaa wanted out of the game altogether.

"What are you thinking about?" Joi asked, seeing that Sanaa had gone off into a daze for a moment.

Her mind was racing a million miles per second. She was gifted in making good decisions at the drop of a dime, and nine times out of ten, her choices and ability to weigh the pros and cons was on point. This was one of the reasons that Joi yielded to Sanaa, even though she was older.

"I think it's time we start thinking about our future," Sanaa began. "We can't keep living like this and expect for us to keep ducking prison or the grave. We've seen it happen all too many times to think that it won't happen to us. Do you really think we can do this forever?" she asked, looking around the bar.

Everything Sanaa was saying caught Joi and Sleepy by surprise. It was like she came out of left field with it, and as crazy as it may have sounded coming out of her mouth, her words held a lot of weight. She had

Sleepy thinking about what he wanted out of life. He knew that he someday wanted to have a family like his brother, Royce. He thought that he would have it with Ariana, and some parts of him still believed that he would.

He looked over at Joi, and she seemed to be deep in thought. He had really tried to like her, but something in him just did not trust her. They were cool at one time, but in the back of his mind he had suspicions that she was involved with Ariana's disappearance. They had never gotten along, and he didn't think it was a coincidence that Joi had to get out of town at the same time that Ariana seemed to have vanished. *Yeah, I'm going to watch this bitch,* Sleepy decided as he returned his attention to his sister.

"Look, I say we just move as much money as we can, then try to start over. I think that we can at least stack a million apiece before we make the spot hot. That should be more than enough to start fresh," Sanaa suggested, throwing back the shot of whiskey.

It was obvious by the tone in Sanaa's voice that she was tired. There comes a time in every criminal's life when they just want to fall back and get out of the game. But at the same time, most criminals who feel this way also feel like they got one last run in them. One last chance to make enough money to put them where they want to be. Sanaa was no different, and neither were Joi and Sleepy.

"So dis is it?" Sleepy asked, reaching over and grabbing the whiskey bottle. "And you're sure about dis, right?"

"Yeah, I'm sure about it," Sanaa said.

"What about you?" he asked Joi, pouring the whiskey into his glass.

Looking into Sanaa's eyes, Joi spoke. "I'm wit' you on dis one, baby girl," she affirmed.

Chapter 4

Danielle walked around to the back of the house where Kemo was sitting at the table by the pool. She took a seat in the empty chair and tossed her keys and clutch onto the table. She could tell by the look on his face that he was mad about something, so like always, she waited for him to initiate the conversation. She knew her place, being Kemo's girlfriend for the past couple of years.

"I got hit again," Kemo said, looking off into the swimming pool. "They got me for a nice chunk, too."

With a shocked look, Danielle played the role as if she was surprised at what Kemo had just told her. It was really no surprise to her, considering the fact that she was the one behind his missing drugs and money. She had been robbing Kemo for the past six months in order to support her own wants and needs.

"You should think about hiring some new guys who can handle the responsibility," Danielle suggested.

"Yeah, well you should think about finding a new drug dealer for a boyfriend. You robbing me more with ya shoe fetish than the niggas out on the streets," he shot back with an attitude, taking his anger out on Danielle as usual.

That was one of the main problems in the relationship now, and had been for about a year. He knew that Danielle was high maintenance when he met her, but as of late, he was starting to regret taking her on. What he didn't know was that by bringing her into the world of crime, she would pick up a few tools along the way that would teach her how to survive. She learned how to take money, and once she did that, she started making Kemo pay.

"Don't make me out to be the bad guy," Danielle said, turning her chair around to face him. "You knew who I was when you met me, and that's part of the reason why you fell in love with me. But I fell in love with you not because of your money, but because of the kind of person you are."

"Bullshit." Kemo laughed, knowing how money hungry she was, or at least how money hungry she used to be.

"Think about it, babe. When was the last time you gave me a large amount of money? I haven't even asked you for money lately, because I know you've been having some financial issues. But look at me, still sitting here right by ya side, without a pedicure, a manicure, and my eyebrows look like I belong in a werewolf movie," she joked.

Kemo just smiled, realizing that Danielle was speaking the truth, and it was him who was placing blame in the wrong place. He was so open for this white woman, he didn't even see the one-two punch coming his way. Danielle only became more submissive because she had something bigger planned for Kemo. Something that was going to take him being totally comfortable with a certain aspect of his business around her. The moment he was in his most vulnerable state, Danielle would execute her plan. For now, it was all about Kemo, and Danielle knew exactly what Kemo needed: a good shot of pussy.

Sanaa looked out the window, watching Royce pull into the parking lot of the Waffle House. It was crowded, as always, but this was one of the few spots they liked to meet up for lunch. He walked in with a smile on his face, knowing that this last-minute scheduled lunch was about more than eating. He knew his big sister all too well.

"What you smiling at?" Sanaa asked, smiling back at her baby brother.

"You crazy, sis. What's goin' on?" he asked as he took a seat at the table.

"I'm trying to figure out why you been telling Krystol you with me, without letting me know," Sanaa teased.

"It's not what you think. I just been having a lot of shit on my plate. Trying to take care of Krystol and the baby is a headache by itself," he complained. "But you know, it is what it is. So, what you call me down here for?" Royce asked, wanting to get to the core of the meeting.

"What, I can't just have lunch wit' my baby bro without wanting something?" she joked.

"No," Royce shot back, waving for the waitress to come and take his order.

"I need you at the club for real. I got something big goin' on, and I need to be surrounded by my family on this one," Sanaa said, lowering her voice as the waitress took Royce's order.

"Come on, sis," he semi whined as he dismissed the waitress. "Now ain't the right time, yo. I got B all up my ass, and I got something I'm working on."

"I got a hundred fifty grand for you if you ride wit' me on this one," she said, cutting Royce off and grabbing his full attention. "No bullshit, I'm dead serious."

One eyebrow shot to the sky as Royce put on the most curious face. A hundred and fifty grand added to his last score would put him nearly halfway to his goal.

For the next hour, Sanaa broke down everything, including her plans on exiting the game. At first, Royce was a little hesitant on moving the funny money, but since Sanaa and Sleepy were both down, he was all in.

"I'll do it under one condition," Royce requested.

"And what's that?" Sanaa shot back.

"You gotta make sure you keep me covered with B until I get the rest of my shit covered, and no, it don't have nothing to do with no other bitch," he added.

"A'ight, you know I got you, li'l bro. By the time Krystol look up, y'all will be unpacking y'all shit into a new home," Sanaa promised.

Chapter 5

Atlanta

Ariana pulled up and double parked on the corner of Rosehill Street where Toughy sat, smack in the middle of his crew of five. Ariana and Olivia both jumped out of the car with large caliber automatic weapons in their hands and headed straight for the crowd.

One of Toughy's boys took off running, thinking the two women were the narcs. Toughy knew it wasn't the cops, but by the time he could tell his worker, he had already bent the corner. When he turned back around, Ariana was only a few yards away from him, while Olivia played the background, keeping everyone else in eyesight.

"What up, Tough?" Ariana said, holding her gun down by her side with her finger on the trigger.

"Damn, shorty, I haven't seen you around here for a minute," he said, trying to appear as if the gun she was displaying didn't bother him. "You comin' through here kind of heavy." He laughed, looking down at her hand.

"Where is ya boss?" Ariana said in a disrespectful tone, unaware of the movement that was going on around her.

"Boss? Bitch, I am the boss," Toughy shot back, feeling disrespected by her comments. He was well aware of who she was asking for, but Toughy had moved up in the game since Sanaa took her show on the road. He was also far from having any bitch in his blood, so he wasn't about to bite his tongue, not even with Ariana having him on the jump.

"Cut the tough guy role and tell me where Sanaa is before I blow ya fuckin' head off," Ariana threatened.

Toughy eyeballed her for a second before turning around to crack a joke with his boys. "Yo, this chick think she got a dick down there," he joked.

Everybody chuckled at his comment, but as he turned back around to answer Ariana, he whipped out a .40-cal from his waist. Ariana didn't see it at first, but Olivia did. She raised her gun and pointed it at Toughy. Ariana did the same.

Toughy also raised his gun and pointed it at Ariana. It was silent for a moment, until one of Toughy's boys cocked a bullet into the chamber of a large assault rifle. The sound of it alone caught Olivia's attention. She looked over to the far right of her at a man holding something with a banana clip. Silence took over again, and everyone looked around at everyone else.

"If you bitches tryin' to work, den bust off," Toughy taunted. "Other than that, get da fuck back in ya car before I tear ya ass up."

"I just want Sanaa and Joi," Ariana said, not backing down from the possible gunplay.

"Yeah, well if you find da bitch, you let me know, 'cause I'm lookin' for her too," Toughy shot back.

Sanaa left a bad taste in his mouth after leaving without giving him a dime. After all the work he'd put in for her, he felt like he deserved some type of compensation, and she had provided none. Not only did Sanaa leave him without any money or a connect, she also left behind some old beef with a couple of go hard niggas. It was only natural that Toughy had ill feelings toward her.

"Now get da fuck out of here before I force ya hand," Toughy said, gripping his gun tighter.

Ariana took a good look around, calculating the odds that were stacked against her. At the same time, she wasn't a big fan of Toughy's mouth. He was talking to her like she wasn't ready to pull the trigger. It wasn't an ounce of bitch in her blood either, and in fact, she was more inclined to set it off just because.

She took one more look around before squeezing off the first shot. The bullet hit Toughy in his shooting arm, but not before he got off a shot too. The bullet grazed her cheek as she backpedaled to the car, firing several more bullets in Toughy's direction. Everyone around him, including Toughy, scattered like roaches.

Olivia fired a couple shots in the direction of the man with the Mac 90, but it was of no use. The sound of the assault rifle alone was enough to make Olivia and Ariana hit the deck, taking cover behind parked cars. The multiple shots didn't give either of the women a chance to return fire. They scurried back to the car, letting off a couple shots in the gunman's direction, or at least where they thought he might have been. Olivia ran around to the driver's side, damn near diving in the seat and slamming the car into drive.

If it weren't for Ariana crawling into the passenger side, she would have left her.

As they pulled off, bullets ripped through the back window. The girls got as low as they could, sideswiping a couple of cars on their way off the block. They barely escaped with their lives, and Ariana still didn't get the information she was looking for. The only thing left was the gun smoke lingering in the night air.

Chapter 6

Sanaa sat in her office staring at $1 million in counterfeit money. She really couldn't believe how real the money looked. She began separating the bills and running them through the money machine to make sure it was all there. The first million was more like a test run in Boo's eyes. He wanted to make sure she could move the money before he dropped five million at her doorstep.

"So this is what a million dollars in funny money looks like," Sleepy said, walking into the office. "Dis shit look real as hell." He walked over and grabbed a stack of twenties off the desk.

"Yeah, dis shit is crazy. I was sitting here thinking about the fastest way we can move the money, and I came up wit' a few ideas."

"You're gonna need more than a few ideas. Dis a lot of paper," Sleepy replied, tossing the money back on the desk.

Sleepy was starting to think that maybe Sanaa had bitten off more than she could chew. The only good thing about the cash, aside from it looking so real, was the fact that the bills consisted of ones, fives, tens, and twenty dollar bills. Sanaa requested that specifically, because fifty and one-hundred dollar bills would be harder to get rid of.

"I want you to take some money and go buy all the supplies we need for the kitchen and the bar," Sanaa directed. "Instead of going to the big name companies, hit up the local supermarkets and liquor stores. Even hit up the boosters and the food stamp chicks. We have to stay off the radar with this money."

Sleepy caught on quick, realizing that local stores would be less likely to check the bills, as opposed to big name vendors who scanned every dollar before passing it on to the bank. It would also be easier for the large vendors to track where their money came from, because they had a set line of customers.

"What about the poker money?" Sleepy asked, amazed at how his sister's brain functioned at times like this.

"Don't worry about poker. Just help Joi out with the bar and kitchen. And I need you to go and make some flyers for tomorrow and Saturday. We got to get this place poppin' for the weekend," Sanaa instructed as she continued to stuff money in the money machine.

Sleepy didn't hesitate for a moment. He grabbed a stack of twenties off the desk and headed out the door. He still didn't know exactly what Sanaa had in store, but it really didn't matter because he trusted that whatever she came up with would be official.

***

Royce patted lightly on Raven's back while she laid on his stomach. He was hoping to put her to sleep so that he could attend to some other business, mainly Krystol. He had purchased her some lingerie and had a bottle of champagne chilling on ice. With everything that had been going on as of late, they barely had time to themselves. Tonight, it was on, just as long as the baby was asleep.

Royce looked down at Raven, who was fast asleep. Just when he was about to move her into the other room, his cell phone went off. It had never sounded so loud. He tried to lean over and grab it off the nightstand, but he just couldn't reach it to quiet the sound.

Krystol, who was coming out of the bathroom, quickly grabbed the phone, looking at Royce with a devious grin before answering it.

"Hello," she answered, taking a seat on the bed right next to Royce.

The sound of a woman's voice asking to speak to Royce damn near sent Krystol up the wall. Danielle's sweet, soft, and sexy voice only added fuel to the fire. Instead of snapping out and drawing a scene, Krystol just politely passed him the phone.

"Yo, what's good?" Royce answered as he continued to rub Raven's back.

"I hope I'm not disturbing you," Danielle said. "I was calling to let you know that it went down tonight. If you want this easy money, we got to get at it right now," she advised.

"What's the take on it?" Royce asked, watching Krystol jump up off the bed and head back to the bathroom.

"I don't know the exact number, but I can assure you that you won't leave with less than a hundred grand."

A hundred grand was a nice piece of money to add to whatever he was going to make from Sanaa with her lick. It was an opportunity that he didn't want to pass up. Baby Raven's eyes were now wide open from being awakened by the phone. The only thing left to do was chase some money. But then again, there still was a chance that Royce could salvage what was left of the night.

"Yo, let me get back to you," Royce said, looking at Krystol standing in front of the mirror changing out of the naughty tennis player outfit.

He laid Raven down on the bed, got up, and walked over to Krystol. She had already taken the top off, and was working on taking off the jewelry and hair ties. The night was pretty much ruined, and Krystol's flame had been put out.

"You mad at me now?" he asked as he walked up behind her and wrapped his hands around her waist.

She reached back without turning around, and pushed Royce off of her. It was obvious she had an attitude, but Royce didn't care. He actually thought it was kind of cute seeing Krystol a little upset.

He walked right back up to her and tried to wrap his hands back around her, but again, she pushed him away. This time, a little more aggressively.

"Ask ya girlfriend for some pussy tonight," she said, stepping out of her heels. "You must think I'm a fuckin' fool."

"That's not my girlfriend." He chuckled. "And I know you're not a fool," he said, and approached her again.

When he tried to grab her waist again, Krystol snapped, turning around and landing a punch to the side of his eye. The punches kept coming, and before long, it turned into an all-out fight, at least from Krystol's standpoint.

Royce would never hit her, nor were Krystol's punches hurting him. He simply just grabbed her arms as she continued to swing. The wrestling match ended quickly as Royce overpowered Krystol, turning her around and pinning her against the dresser with her face pressed against the mirror.

"I swear on Raven's life that I'm not fucking her, nor will I ever fuck her. She's not my girlfriend, and if I'm lying to you, God can take our daughter's life right now," Royce argued.

When Royce swore to God on Raven's life, Krystol knew instantly that he was telling the truth. Royce would never swear so hard on Raven's life unless he was telling the truth. But even though she might have felt that he wasn't lying, she was still mad, mainly because her face was smashed against the mirror and she could have sworn that in the midst of the fight, Royce had tagged her. She tried to get up, but Royce wasn't sure if she was done swinging, so he held her there.

"Do you believe me?" he asked, seeing that she was still struggling. "Do you believe me?" he yelled again.

"Yeah, now get da fuck off of me," Krystol yelled back, still trying to get out of his grip. "I believe you, I believe you," she pleaded.

Reluctantly, he let her go, and she finally got up and turned to face him. It looked like she was about to cry. Royce leaned in and grabbed the back of her head, pulling her into his chest.

"Babe, you got to trust me. I will never cheat on you," he said with sincerity.

Krystol just sniffled and tried to pull away from him. She believed him, but she was still mad, and, for some odd reason, all the wrestling and fighting had turned her on. She went back into fighting mode, throwing several punches Royce's way. This time it was different. They were playful punches, and Royce playfully defended his face. They both laughed and wrestled.

Royce spun her around and pinned her against the dresser again. Her face pressed against the mirror for the second time. She started to fight back, until she felt Royce kicking her legs apart like a cop when they're about to search somebody.

"Stop fuckin' playin' wit' me," Royce said, hiking up Krystol's miniskirt.

Bent over on the dresser, Krystol resisted a little, feeling the tip of Royce's dick breach the walls of her pussy. He stuffed the whole of his dick inside of her, keeping her crammed up against the mirror. The whole dresser rocked back and forth with every stroke. The mirror damn near fell off its hinges. Although it was a bit awkward being in that position, Krystol loved every bit of the back shot. She felt powerless with him behind her, pounding away like a madman.

The sex felt so good that for those moments all the problems of the outside world didn't exist. It was so good neither of them paid attention to baby Raven lying on the bed innocently playing with her pacifier.

Chapter 7

The line to get into Club All In damn near wrapped around the corner. The capacity of the club was to its max, and even still, cars were pulling up, and more people continued to flock. A crowd this big only meant two things: free food and cheap drinks. Those things were enough to get almost any black person in the building.

Not only was it packed inside, the women outnumbered the men three to one, which meant the amount of drinks being purchased would go through the roof. Joi had even managed to turn the whole third floor into a strip joint. She had several strippers walking around giving lap dances for dollars, along with dancing on the tables in a private booth like it was a stage.

The music was loud, and the dance floor was packed with just about everybody dancing. Not a stool was empty at the bar, and at times Joi couldn't keep up with the orders. Beautiful women were all around, and handsome men coming up with their best pickup lines were there to entertain them.

To see the club doing it this big in such a short period of time was amazing to Sleepy, who stood off to the side and took in the whole atmosphere. All the money they had spent on advertising was really working out, and they had spent a lot, but it didn't matter because it was all fake.

"You need some help?" Sanaa screamed over the loud music to Joi, who was running around crazy behind the bar.

This was the hardest Joi had worked for some money and Sanaa knew it. Joi was like a wild lioness, and Sanaa was trying her best to domesticate her and give her a different life from the murderous one she was used to living. For the love of their friendship, Joi was willing to try anything once.

"No, I'm fine. Go back downstairs. We're fine up here," she screamed back over the music.

Downstairs, the poker tables were pretty much packed as well. Sanaa allowed her wealthiest clients to bring somebody with them as a tagalong, provided they were gambling. That turned out better than what she had expected. Every table was full to the max, and for the first time there was actually a waiting list to get a spot at the tables. Even Boo was impressed with the way things looked.

Everything was moving, but at the same time every-thing had a purpose. Real money was being generated throughout the whole club. For instance, Sleepy took a couple grand of funny money and purchased pounds of Buffalo wings, French fries, boneless chicken breasts, hot dogs, hamburgers, and all the accessories to go with them, all of which was bought from the local supermarket. The method behind it was to draw people into the club with free food. He then purchased alcohol, which was sold for a cheaper price at the bar. The average drink cost two dollars, and the top shelf drinks cost three dollars, filled to the top of the cup. When patrons paid for drinks, Joi would take the real money and put it in a separate register. If somebody needed to get change back, she would give them the counterfeit money. Sometimes, the counterfeit money was recycled back into the bar, but they had marked every counterfeit bill, so Joi was on point with distributing the funny money and withholding the real stuff.

The strippers on the second floor served a purpose also. Sleepy was on deck, exchanging large bills for singles, so dudes could make it rain. Every time someone wanted change for a fifty or a twenty, Sleepy would give them counterfeit one dollar bills, and in some cases, five dollar bills. Joi even got a kickback from the strippers for allowing them to dance on the third floor.

The poker tables were the jackpot of the whole operation. Sanaa ran them with an iron fist, monitoring every dollar that passed through the hands of the dealers. Each time someone cashed in, they got chips. The real money was secured in the slot boxes near the tables. During the course of the game, if that person wanted to cash out, he would go to the window and get the counterfeit money for the chips. The funny money would be pushed back out on the floor if any of it was mixed in with the real money. It was also good for business for the occasional hot hand to win big at the tables. It fueled others to drop more cash, in an attempt to do what all gamblers wanted to do, and that's break the house.

The sex was so explosive it put Krystol and Royce to sleep. The lick that Danielle had for Royce was back on, despite the missed opportunity he had the night before. Royce crept out of the bed, leaving Krystol and the baby asleep, or at least that's what he thought he was doing.

Krystol woke up the minute she felt Royce's body leave the bed. She knew that eventually he was going to leave the house, having been there all day with her and Raven. She was just waiting for him to make his move, which he was now doing.

He even had the nerve to be sneaky about it, taking his clothes and getting dressed downstairs so he wouldn't make any noise that would wake her up. He was a little heavier than just his clothes. He also had his vest, a Glock, and an extra clip to go with his outfit.

As he was getting dressed downstairs, Krystol was getting dressed upstairs. She had promised herself that the next time Royce left the house she was going to follow him. She wanted to know what in the hell he was doing when he left their home.

Chapter 8

Atlanta

Shannon pulled up in front of his house with his infant son in the back seat. He was trying to hurry up, drop his son off, and head back out the door for some playtime. He was moving so fast unstrapping the baby from the car seat, he didn't even notice the pretty-faced young lady who was sitting on his porch. It wasn't until he got on the steps that he noticed her. At first, he thought it was one of his baby mother's friends, but the gun in Olivia's hand quickly made him realize that she was a foe. He clutched his son tighter as he climbed the steps, not knowing where this confrontation was about to go.

"I know you?" Shannon asked with a slight attitude about the gun being out around his baby.

"Naw, she don't know you, but I do," Ariana said, walking up the stairs behind Shannon.

She too had her gun out, and it was instinct that made Shannon reach for the .38 snub in the baby bag draped over his shoulder. Had he not thought twice about it, the result would have been fatal for him and possibly his son.

"You was one of Sanaa's security guards," Ariana began. "You was one of the smart ones. Always making good decisions at the right time," Ariana added, trying to get him to think about the situation he was in, and how important it was for him to comply.

"What you want, shorty?" Shannon shot back, wanting her to get to the point.

"Where is Sanaa?" Ariana asked, walking up so close to him that she was only a couple feet away from the baby.

Shannon smiled, remembering who Ariana was. He had remembered her from Sleepy, but didn't understand why she was asking for Sanaa in this manner. "She moved out to Pittsburgh." Shannon wasn't about to tell this chick nothing about Sanaa. Her aggression told him she wasn't bringing anything good to Sanaa. Shannon lied, thinking that would be the end of it. Shannon took a step toward his door. Ariana laughed. He had given her that information too quickly; she knew that he was way too loyal to just give old girl up that easy.

"Now, before you consider sticking to this lie, you might wanna think about ya li'l man. You might wanna think about who's more important between the two. I'm guessing by the looks of things, you love ya li'l man a lot. Don't be—"

"All right, I hear you," Shannon said, cutting her off.

He knew what Ariana was getting at, and he also knew from Sleepy that she was no stranger to putting in work. His son meant more to him than Sanaa on any given day, and since Sanaa had up and left without so much as a good-bye, Shannon didn't see a reason to be loyal to her.

"She moved to Philly," he confessed out of frustration before trying to walk off.

"What part of Philly?" Ariana asked, stepping in front of the doorway he was headed for.

"I'm from Atlanta. Do it look like I know anything about parts of Philadelphia?" He shot back with irritation in his voice. "Now that's all I know. I'm tryin' to get my son in the crib now, if you don't mind."

Ariana stepped to the side, and so did Olivia.

By the time Shannon got his key in the door and turned around, they were gone. There was no need for them to stick around after eliciting that information. Ariana had a strong feeling that Shannon was telling the truth; he was the second person to direct her to Philly. If he was lying, it wouldn't be anything for her to travel back to Atlanta and kill him. For now, she was on the next thing smokin' to Philly, but not before making one more stop.

Royce swerved in and out of lanes on the highway before getting off on exit 13A. Krystol stayed at a distance, but she was right behind him, following his every move. She kept looking back at baby Raven, who had already fallen asleep from the ride. She regretted bringing the baby out, but she was determined to find out what Royce was up to.

After a few more turns, and a little more weaving through some light traffic, Royce pulled into the parking lot of a small strip mall. He pulled the car beside the only other vehicle that was there. Krystol didn't pull into the parking lot, knowing it would look too obvious. Instead, she parked across the street where she couldn't be seen. Although she was a little far away, she could still make out what Royce was doing.

"What is your daddy up to?" Krystol asked baby Raven as she stared into the parking lot.

In a matter of moments, the driver of the other car had exited the sports car. Krystol had most of her face glued to the window, and she damn near choked on her own spit when she spotted the blond-haired white woman walk over to Royce's car and get into the passenger seat. Royce backed up and pulled right out of the lot.

"Oh, dis nigga like white bitches," Krystol mumbled to herself as she frantically tried to get the car started. "A white bitch," she kept mumbling to herself the whole time she tried to catch up to Royce's car.

It was a short drive to the motel Krystol had followed them to, and she got there just in time to see the two of them open the door and go into one of the rooms. It was one thing for a black man to cheat on his girl, but it was a totally different thing when a black man cheated on his girlfriend with a white woman. It was a pride and ego trip, which caused many insecurities in a woman's ability to please her man. Krystol couldn't help but to think about what this woman was doing for him that she wasn't doing for him at home.

I'm pretty, I suck good dick, my pussy stay wet, we've done every position you could name, and I even let him put it in my ass. We have rough sex, soft sex; we make love on the regular. I dress up, we have role play, and I even swallow every now and again. Those thoughts raced through Krystol's head as she sat outside the motel, debating on whether she should get an extra key from the clerk and bust in the room. She looked back at Raven, who was now awake, and backed the car into a parking space in the parking lot of the motel.

Danielle stood by the bed, wrapping her hair in a bun while Royce started to peel off his clothes. She did the same, first pulling her T-shirt over her head, then unzipping the tight-fitted jeans she was wearing. It was hard for Royce to concentrate on doing what he was doing as he snuck a few peeks at Danielle's body. Her stomach was flat with a pierced belly button, her breasts were perfectly round, and a glimpse of her hard nipples peeked through her designer bra that matched the panties, which hugged her hips. She looked like something out of Victoria's Secret catalog. If any man would ever cheat on his lady, it had to be with someone of her caliber. Even Royce couldn't stop his dick from getting hard, which was a bit of an embarrassment when Danielle noticed the bulge in his jeans.

"Now, you got to be on point with this one," she said, snapping her fingers to get Royce's attention. "It's gonna be fast, and whatever you do, don't shoot at the second car. That's where the money is," Danielle explained.

"Well, what if the second car starts shooting at us?" Royce asked, watching as Danielle slipped into some overalls along with the bulletproof vest.

"Just let me take care of the second car. You just make sure nobody is left breathing in the first car."

After hearing the plan from Danielle a couple of times, Royce got dressed too, slipping into the black overalls provided by Danielle. She too snuck in a few peeks at Royce's eight pack before he put his vest back on. There was a little bit of sexual tension between the two, but they had never crossed the line. Both understood that the relationship was based on business, and that needed to be respected. Also, Royce wasn't willing to lose Krystol or his family.

After everything was all said and done, Danielle and Royce headed out the door of the motel ready for work call.

"Yo, slow up a li'l bit. I got too much money in this car for you to be getting pulled over," Kemo yelled at his driver as he looked off into the road. "And call them niggas up there and tell them to slow the fuck down too," he continued, pointing to his boys who were in a separate car in front of him.

Kemo wasn't the boss of Philly, but he was one of the top niggas who supplied the streets with heroin. He had a little crew, mainly consisting of five people, but those five people had crews of their own. He was considered the boss, but even bosses took losses, and for the past few months that's all that had been happening with him. He was on a vicious downward slope, and the $400K in his car was the last chance he had to get back to where he needed to be. That was just enough for him to buy five bricks of heroin, which would be a hell of a start in his mission back to being on top.

The dark suburban streets provided the perfect cover for a dope deal to go down in the middle of nowhere, but before Kemo got to the drop spot, he made sure everybody was on point. They pulled up to a red light, just a few blocks away from the site.

The flashing lights seemed to come from out of nowhere. The unmarked car pulled right up behind him, and if there were something more than money in the car, he would have told his driver to pull off.

"Just be easy," Kemo told the driver as he looked at the car through the rearview mirror.

The driver quickly flashed his headlights to the car in front of him so the crew could see what was going on. When the light turned green, they drove up a little and pulled over while Kemo's car sat there.

Danielle took one good look around the dark street before pulling the hockey mask over her face and exiting the Crown Victoria. She had a Mossberg pump in her right hand down by her side as she quickly approached Kemo's car. The flashing lights made it hard for Kemo to see anything, and by the time he did, it was too late. The gunman was already at the driver side door.

When the driver looked up at the window, all he could see was the flash, and the sound of what seemed like a grenade going off. He didn't even feel the buckshot hit his face when it crashed through the window. The small pellets tore chunks of flesh from his face and the other pellet or two hit Kemo in his neck as well.

In a split second, Kemo was looking down the barrel of the shotgun.

The commotion caught the attention of the boys in the front car, but before they could react, a second masked gunman jumped on the hood of their vehicle and released multiple shots into the driver and the passenger. The two men never even had a chance to draw their weapons and shoot back, as the bullets crashed through the windshield and into their bodies.

Danielle walked around the front of the car with Kemo at gunpoint the whole time, but when she got around to the passenger side, she glanced over to see Royce jumping down off the hood of the other car. That was her only mistake. By the time she focused her attention back on Kemo, he had a gun in his hand and was squeezing the trigger.

The first bullet hit her smack in the middle of her chest, causing her to fall backward. The impact from the bullet made Danielle squeeze the trigger of the pump, firing it off, but not hitting anything.

Seeing her hit the ground, Royce opened fire as he ran across the intersection toward Kemo. Kemo jumped out of the car, still squeezing his trigger, mainly at the gunmen on the ground in front of him. He hit Danielle again in her gut while he ran past her. Royce was on his heels, but he stopped chasing him when Kemo ran into the wooded area. Instead, he ran back over to Danielle, who was slowly trying to get up on her feet. Neither of the bullets had pierced her vest, but she was still shook up a bit.

"Hold this," she told Royce, passing him the shotgun before going into Kemo's car.

A few buttons pushed here and a couple latches lifted there, and the whole back seat came out. Inside were several stacks of money in a duffle bag. She wasted no time taking it out, then headed back to their car. They both jumped in and peeled off into the night.

All Kemo could do was look from the woods as his money drove away.

Chapter 9

The last few heads staggered out of the club as it closed for the night. Everyone looked tired as hell from the long night, especially Joi, who was damn near asleep behind the bar.

"Come in," Sanaa yelled, hearing someone knocking on her office door.

When Sleepy walked in, there was money everywhere. Sanaa sat behind her desk running bills through the money machine. In her hands was a small calculator and she was tapping away at the numbers. Sanaa too looked tired, with her hair somewhat sweated out.

"So how did we do?" he asked taking a seat on the edge of the desk.

"We did good, but not as good as I thought we would," she responded without even picking her head up.

The casino did the best with the counterfeit money, hauling in a little more than $100,000 in real money, and that was after all the payouts. The bar and grill, along with the strippers, raked in about $21,000, and that included the fee of admission.

"So why the long look on ya face?" Sleepy asked.

"I mean, the numbers look good, but we're taking a hit in the long run. We made a $121K in real cash, but it's only $800K left in counterfeit," she explained. "It costs us almost half the profit just to flip the money over, and it's coming from the payouts in the casino, and the register at the bar," she said as she continued to punch in numbers.

"So what now?" Sleepy asked, knowing Sanaa had a plan.

"I got to call Boo. If we're going down the middle with everything, he's going to have to take a hit on his profit too."

One thing Sanaa was good with was math, and in order for it to add up right, some changes needed to be made, especially since she was taking the biggest risk. It was a sure thing that moving $5 million in funny money was going to be more of a challenge than what she'd initially thought.

"We got to find a way to move this money a little bit faster," Sanaa mused, leaning back in her chair.

"So what do you have in mind?"

Sanaa just sat back in her chair with a zoned-out look on her face. Sleepy knew what that meant, so he just sat there and let her thought process go. It took her a few minutes, but when it came to her, it was like a light bulb clicking on in her head.

"I think I got a couple ways to move it," she said, snapping out of her trance. "I'm gonna need you to make some more flyers and get ready to call the radio about a new ad."

***

The whole drive home, Krystol regretted not getting the key from the hotel management and busting up in the room on Royce. All she could think about was the words that so easily came out of Royce's mouth. *"You gotta trust me."* All that trust shit went out the door, and as she lay in the bed crying her eyes out, the sounds of Royce walking through the front door caught her attention.

She quickly cleaned her face off so he wouldn't know that she had been crying. She really didn't know what she was going to do to him or if she'd even say a word about it. All she knew was that her heart was hurting, and tonight was more than likely the beginning of the end.

The first thing Royce did when he came into the bed-room was head straight for the shower, something typical of him after coming in from being outside. To Krystol, it was the typical behavior of a man who had to wash the smell of a woman off of him before he got into bed. Her head was so messed up it skipped her mind that this was a regular routine from him. Everything he did at this point was enhanced to something bigger than what it was.

The shower was quick, and before she knew it, Royce was climbing into bed naked, sliding up right behind Krystol under the silk sheets. He thought she was asleep, but she was wide awake, fighting the urge to turn around and let him have it. Instead, she just lay there in tears as he wrapped his arms around her, not knowing what she now knew.

***

Danielle sat in the dark living room, waiting for Kemo to come home. She had been there for more than thirty minutes. When the cab pulled up to the house, she ran up the stairs and headed straight for the bedroom. She hopped right in the bed and sat there in her Juicy Couture pajamas as if she'd been home all night. The sound of the door slamming and furniture being kicked around told the tale of him being hot under the collar.

When he finally made his way to the bedroom, Danielle jumped out of the bed and tended to him as he fell through the door. He had his driver's blood all over him, and a little blood of his own ran down his neck.

"Baby, what happened?" Danielle screamed, putting on her best award-winning act.

He could barely talk through his alcohol-slurred voice. It was obvious that he had made his way to a bar before he got there, and clearly, he had more than his body could handle. He finally got to his feet with Danielle's help, and it wasn't long before the vomit came up. He was sick, but not the typical type, rather the mental. Nothing could compare to him seeing the last of his money driving away.

"Mafuckas got me, babe. Dem mafuckas got me," he managed to get out while leaning over the bathtub. "I'm broke, I'm broke," he cried out between spurts of vomit.

Danielle just sat on the edge of the tub, patting his back and rubbing her fingers on his bald head. She found it hard to hold back the urge to laugh at how pitiful he sounded. It was a vicious game she was playing, but in her eyes, she had him right where she wanted him.

Chapter 10

Everything around her had stopped moving, or was moving at a slower pace. Joi lifted her head up from the bar; the bags under her eyes, her pale skin, and chapped lips made her appear to be one of the walking dead. As she turned her head she saw the glimmer of Ariana's chrome revolver flicker in the light. Joi grabbed her gun from behind the bar. Ariana stood only a few feet from her smiling.

"What the fuck?" Joi said, staring wide-eyed at Ariana. Joi began firing at Ariana, who never attempted to dodge any of the bullets that were coming her way. Joi blinked her eyes as she tried to see what the hell was coming out of her gun because the bullets appeared to disintegrate before reaching Ariana. Ariana smiled at Joi when she heard the clicking of the gun, signaling that her clip was empty. Joi turned and jumped over the bar; she began to run as Ariana chased her. Bullets shattered bottles of alcohol as Ariana continued firing at Joi. Joi screamed as a bullet ripped into her back causing her legs to stop running, and her body to fall to the ground. She felt a sting in the center of her back, that took her to the ground.

"Bitch," Ariana growled as she walked up to Joi, and kicked her in the stomach with such that it

knocked Joi on her back. Joi looked up at the barrel of the gun, as the hammer clicked.

"Joi! Joi! Wake up!" Sanaa yelled, shaking Joi's shoulder.

Right at the moment Ariana pulled the trigger Joi woke up out of her nightmare. She was out of breath, and had the fear of God in her eyes when she grabbed Sanaa.

Sanaa wrapped her arms around her, but not before almost falling off the bed. "It was a dream, Joi," Sanaa whispered in her ear as she tried to comfort her.

Joi wasn't convinced right away, still feeling the bullet wound to her back where Ariana shot her while she was asleep. It took a few minutes, but eventually Joi reached over and grabbed the bottle of spring water off the nightstand.

"Dis shit felt so real. She was about to kill me," Joi said, holding back the urge to cry.

This wasn't the first time Joi had a dream like this. Ever since she left Atlanta, she'd been having similar dreams to this one. Visions of the day she shot Ariana raced through her mind, and although she knew in her heart that Ariana was dead, it still haunted her.

"She's gone, Joi. You don't have to worry about Ariana anymore," Sanaa spoke.

"Yeah, I know, Si, but damn," Joy replied in frustration. "Did you talk to your dad? Is he still coming up here?" she asked.

"I talked to him, and he said he'll be up this way in a couple of days. He also told me that the cops are still looking for you, and the Feds stopped by his house again, looking for me and Sleepy."

"Damn, the Feds are fucking relentless," Joi said.

Ariana wasn't the only trouble they had back in Atlanta. Sanaa and Sleepy had sold more drugs than a little bit, and right around the time that Joi and Ariana were going through their situation Sanaa was selling large amounts of cocaine to a federal informant. Sleepy was doing the same, but instead of selling the informant cocaine, Sleepy was selling him heroin. Luckily, by the time the Feds kicked in their doors, Sanaa and Sleepy were on their way back to Philly. At the request of their dad, they had brought the now wanted Joi along with them.

After Joi and Balil had hooked back up, knowing how he was around women, especially young ones, Joi stayed on point whenever new girls came around. Although she was aware of Sleepy and Ariana's new relationship, she had also found out that Balil and Ariana had shared a romance as well. Balil tried to convince her that it was a one-time sexual thing, and now that Ariana and Sleepy were in love, it was nothing to worry about. But Joi couldn't stand having Ariana around, and it didn't help that she had a smart mouth and a temper to go along with it.

One night, after words had been exchanged the two ladies had begun fighting. While Sanaa was attempting to break it up, Joi got to her gun and managed to get three shots off, with two hitting Ariana in the stomach. No one knew that she was pregnant, and unable to call the medics without attracting law enforcement to their spot, they decided to try to drive her. Ariana kept going in and out of consciousness. When it seemed like she was no longer breathing, the girls decided it would be best to just drop her body off in the parking lot of the hospital. Both Sanaa and Joi still believed that she was dead.

In the midst of all of the confusion, they had completely forgotten about the emergency room cameras, which had snapped a picture of the car coming and going. Although the photo was somewhat blurred, it had a full frontal view of Joi. Sanaa happened to have her back turned, while trying to attend to Ariana, who was laid out in the back seat. The photo alone was not what brought detectives to Joi initially. The parking garage camera had caught the license plate of the vehicle they were driving. The automobile was registered to Joi, and it was only going to be a matter of time before things would be put together. But, with all the murders in the ATL, it wouldn't take long for Ariana's case to be tossed into a cold case file cabinet. The truth was she was a black woman, and like their male counterparts, there was never too much attention dedicated to their cases. Balil had people connected to the local law enforcement office to keep him aware of the progress of the case, which was why he had decided to send Joi to Philly.

The relationship between Joi and Ariana had affected the whole family and crew, forcing people to take sides. Although Balil had told his son that Ariana had always been flighty, and whenever relationships got too close she would bail, Sleepy just couldn't believe she would up and leave him without saying anything.

"Come on, let's go get ya mind off of her." Sanaa smiled, patting Joi on her lap.

"Where we goin'?" she asked, not really up for doing too much of anything.

Sanaa had a huge smile on her face. "Let's go spend some of this money," she said, jumping up and heading out the room.

Boo walked over and looked into his security monitors at some movement that was going on outside his house. He was especially on point around this time, due to the fact that he was printing out money. He really didn't want anybody knowing when he was doing it, not even his right-hand man. The money plates were the most important part of his process, and he was willing to guard them with his life.

"Ay, Mi Mi," Boo yelled into the intercom that went from the basement, straight up to the bedroom.

"Yeah, Papi," she responded, walking over to the small black box hanging by the door.

"Tell dem niggas to come back in a couple of hours," he said, looking at Tee Tee, Wax and Sticks walking up to the house.

Once Mi Mi dismissed the guys, she went right back into her bedroom and closed the door. She knew that when Boo was in the basement, he didn't want to be bothered by anyone, not even her.

"A'ight, let's get dis money," Boo mumbled to himself as he walked over and hit the "on" switch to the printing machine.

Today, Boo was only printing out twenty-dollar bills. It wasn't an actual printing machine like the ones the Franklin Mint used, but it was a mini replica that was capable of printing out one size bills at a time. Although small, the machine was loud, so to drown it out, Boo bumped Meek Mill through his stereo system.

To that day, nobody knew how Boo got the plates to make the money, and more than likely that secret was going to die with him. What he did have was a constant reminder for himself of what he had to go through in order to get them. As he did every time before he printed money, Boo lifted up his shirt and rubbed the large stab wound on the left side of his chest. The incident that almost took his life was well worth it to him, and as the first sheet of money rolled out of the printer, Boo looked at it and smiled.

"Come on, babe," he said, pulling the sheet of twenties from the printing machine.

Sanaa had called everyone to the club, and everyone showed up except Royce. He was always busy in his own little world. Sleepy and Joi must have thought it was happy hour, because they were behind the bar sipping on Patrón.

"A'ight, listen, y'all. We gotta see what dis money do," Sanaa said, pulling out one hundred grand and placing it on the bar. "Before we really start moving dis shit, I think it's only right that we treat ourselves to some shopping," Sanaa said, tossing stacks of money to Joi, Sleepy, Yellow, and E-Money.

Everyone nodded happily in agreement. Ironically, no one in the room was afraid to spend the funny money. It looked, felt, and even smelled like real money, so for them, it wasn't going to be a problem.

"I don't know about y'all, but I'm about to tear King of Prussia Mall down," Joi said, counting her money.

Sanaa's phone vibrated in her back pocket. Only two people had the number to that line, and the screen did not show a name or face on it. It only displayed the name Joe Jackson. Sanaa laughed before answering.

Joi could tell from the bright look on her face that the person on the other end of the phone had to be Balil.

"Hi, Daddy," Sanaa answered, walking away from everyone. "Is everything all right?" she asked.

"What, I can't call and check up on my princess?" Balil smiled, taking a puff on his cigar.

"Come on, Dad, I thought we agreed that you wouldn't call until the heat cooled down, unless it was an emergency."

"Well, the Feds haven't been around for a few weeks, and they stopped sitting on your and ya brotha's house," Balil informed her. "Your pops knows how to cover his tracks. I hoped you would find the name funny and answer. As soon as I finish talking to you the phone will be destroyed and it can't be traced. It is cloned off some teenager or some shit is what Peanut told me. Anyway. Wassup wit' Joi?"

"You know she's standing right here staring down my throat," Sanaa joked and looked over at Joi.

Sanaa walked over and gave Joi the phone, knowing she wanted to talk to him. She missed the hell out of Balil, and the distance plus the lack of communication was killing her. At times, she regretted doing what she did to Ariana.

"Hi, handsome," Joi said, turning away and walking to the other side of the bar.

"How are you holding up?" Balil asked, standing up and walking out to the back patio.

Hearing his voice for the first time in months felt so good tears began to fill her eyes. She wanted to go back home bad. So much so, she didn't care what was waiting on her when she got there, just as long as Balil was there. "I miss you," Joi whined.

"Hold on, babe," Balil told her, distracted by the two females who had entered his backyard.

Balil couldn't believe that he was standing there looking at Ariana, who had a large chrome automatic weapon in her hand. Olivia was strapped too, but she stood at the bottom of the balcony steps while Ariana joined Balil.

"Let me call you back," Balil said, hanging up the phone before Ariana inquired about who he was talking to. "Long time no see," he said, placing his phone on the patio table before taking a seat.

"You good people, Balil, and you know I got love for you. I really don't wanna hurt you, but if you don't tell me where Joi is, it's going to get ugly," Ariana said flat out.

"Damn, you don't wanna catch up on old times?" Balil joked, trying to play it cool.

Ariana smiled at his humor. One thing she could always count on was Balil being Balil. She had to be honest with herself. Shooting Balil wasn't going to be easy; it was almost like shooting her own dad. Although she had slept with him, their relationship to her was never about sex. Balil offered the father figure and adult guidance she never had growing up. He taught her about life, and how to survive. It was Balil who helped her get her first car and apartment. And even when they were no longer sexually active and she began liking Sleepy, he never once came between her and his son's relationship. In fact, it was the opposite. He told Sleepy what a good woman she was, and that he should not make the same mistake he had by letting her go.

Maybe it was the last statement that made Balil's new woman, Joi, so hateful toward Ariana. Whatever it was, Ariana didn't have time to try to figure it out now. The lines had been drawn, and either Balil was with her or against her. There was not going to be any playing the fence.

She asked him again, "Where is Joi?"

"Ariana, you know I can't tell you that. I don't know what happened between you and Joi, but I'm really not tryin' to get involved," Balil said.

Ariana turned her head for a moment. She became frustrated hearing him talk like he wasn't trying to choose sides. "You know, I looked up to you," Ariana snapped. "Dis bitch tried to kill me, and that's the best you can say is that you don't wanna get involved in it?"

"She's my wife," Balil snapped back, raising his voice in anger.

"And ya wife killed ya grandbaby," Ariana yelled, lifting up her shirt to show Balil the bullet wound in her gut. "Fuck ya wife, Balil," she said, getting up from the table. "And you know what? Fuck you too."

Ariana raised the gun and fired two shots into Balil's gut, knocking him backward out of the chair. She walked over and was about to put another bullet in his head, but she just couldn't. Looking into his eyes, she could see Sleepy, and almost immediately, she regretted pulling the trigger.

She turned and began to run.

Olivia followed, and both women disappeared just as quickly as they had arrived.

Chapter 11

Sanaa had a beautiful home in the suburbs of Philly. She lived in the Balla Kenwood area, in a house with four bedrooms and four and a half bathrooms. It had a large chef's kitchen, a deck with a swimming pool in the back, and it sat on three acres of land. She got it for a good price, $250,000 to be exact, and purchased it under her dad's name, Marvin Anderson.

She sat out on the back deck trying to get some peace of mind before it was time to get back to the club. It was going to be another busy night, and a little relaxation was needed. Joi must have been thinking the same thing, because she found her way out to the deck as well, not bothered at all by Sanaa's presence. Even though Sanaa had convinced Joi to stay with her, it wasn't often they got a chance to sit down and talk, and Sanaa wasn't about to pass up the chance to unload some of what she had on her mind.

"I love you, sis. I'm glad you're here wit' me right now," Sanaa started. "I swear, I hope I don't go to jail. If they catch me, they're gonna put me under that motherfucker," she said, taking a sip of her lemonade.

Joi smiled, and Sanaa couldn't help but to notice it. "What are you smiling at?" she asked with a curious look on her face.

"No matter how many times I hear you say it, I can never get tired of hearing you call me sis," Joi confessed, smiling from ear to ear at the thought of it. "And what are you talking about jail for? Do you really think I'm living in this house with you so that I can watch you go to jail? That's the last thing you should be thinking about. Shit, it wouldn't be a prison bus safe in America, as long as they got you in custody," Joi joked.

It may have been said in a joking manner, and they both actually did laugh, but every word that came out of Joi's mouth was the truth. Sanaa felt it, although she didn't say anything. Joi was crazy for real.

"Oh, I meant to ask you earlier, do you think you could open up tonight? I gotta go holla at the hotel manager in a couple hours about that thing," Sanaa said.

"What thing?" Joi shot back with a curious grin. "And you know ya brotha don't like me like that," she added.

"The hotel party, and wait, what makes you think Sleepy doesn't like you?"

"I think he knows I had something to do with Ariana. You know dat boy fell in love wit' dat girl. You're probably the only reason why he hasn't put a bullet in my head yet," she joked but was dead serious.

Joi was right. Sleepy had all kinds of animosity toward her, and the only reason he dealt with her was because of Sanaa and his father, and the fact that he wasn't 100 percent sure about her involvement in Ariana's disappearance. He would need to be sure before going against his family. Sanaa didn't see it, but Joi did, so for that reason she stayed on point when she was around him.

"But look, I'll open for you. You just got to call him and let him know what's going on," Joi said.

That was the last of the conversation between the two. For the next couple of hours, they just sat back on the deck and enjoyed each other's company. As usual, Sanaa's brain was moving at a fast rate, thinking about the hotel party she had planned, and how she was going to start moving the rest of the counterfeit money. It was a great idea, but Boo didn't think she was going to be able to pull it off. He didn't know Sanaa very well. When she was focused on a job, she saw it through, and more than likely, the job was going to get done, especially with that kind of money involved.

Chapter 12

I knew a young woman would be the death of me, Balil thought as he lay bleeding on the ground. He couldn't believe that Ariana had actually shot him. Immediately, his survival instinct kicked in, and he knew that his only hope of survival was immediate medical attention. He lifted his head slightly and looked around. To his dismay, he didn't see his phone anywhere on the ground.

Each breath was painful as he laid his head back and used his right hand to apply pressure to his stomach wound. In his peripheral vision, he noticed his cell phone sticking out over the side of the patio table. Now, all he needed to do was get to it. The over-turned chair that he had fallen out of lay between him and the table. With his left hand, he pushed the chair out of the way, and then slowly dragged himself over to the table.

The three feet he had traveled to the table felt like 3,000 miles in his weakened state. For a moment, he could only lie still as he tried to catch his breath. His body seemed to weigh a ton, and he was beyond exhausted. The cell phone was so close; all he had to do was reach up and grab it. Just reach up. But he couldn't; his arm refused to move. Short of breath, Balil felt the fight leaving him. He had never been afraid to die; he just wasn't ready yet.

"If I perish, I perish," Balil whispered as his eyes slowly closed.

Instantly, Sanaa's image emerged in his mind-scape and his eyes flew open. He had to warn her about Ariana. Dying would have to wait; his baby girl was in danger. He took a deep breath, and with all his might, he willed his body to follow his mind. A loud grunt escaped as he moved his right arm from his wound, and bent it at his side to steady himself. As he raised his left arm, he leaned on his bent right arm for support, until finally his phone was in his hands.

Balil dialed 911, and immediately an operator answered.

"I've . . . been . . . shot. Please hurry," Balil whispered as he lost consciousness.

Royce returned to his house after putting the $200,000 he'd made the night before in his stash. He rarely kept that kind of money in his home. When he walked through the door, he knew something was wrong. He dropped the lunch he had brought back for Krystol, reached into his back pocket, and pulled out his gun. The total silence in the house made him walk cautiously from the living room, up the stairs. Clothes were all over the place, including on the stairs. Royce had only been gone a little over two hours, and the house was definitely not in this condition when he'd left.

He crept up the stairs and headed straight for his bedroom, but when he got there, the room was empty. Even more clothes were strewn around, and every dresser drawer looked like it had been emptied out. Even Raven's small dresser was completely empty.

"Krystol," Royce yelled out, breaking the silence in the home.

There was no answer. Royce walked through the whole house, clearing every room, as if he was a part of the SWAT unit. Nothing and no one was there. He flipped out his cell phone to call Krystol, but when the phone started ringing on the other end, he could hear Krystol's phone ringing in the bedroom. He walked in to see it lying on the entertainment system, next to an envelope with the word READ on the front.

Royce feared picking the envelope up, thinking it might've been some type of ransom note, but when he finally did get the nerve to see what was inside, he realized that it was something worse than a ransom note. For a moment, he wished it would have been a ransom note instead of what his eyes were seeing. He walked over to the bed, took a seat, and placed his gun on the bed next to him. The picture in front of the letter was of him, Krystol, and baby Raven.

Dear Ro,
I sat up in bed writing this letter all night as I watched you lie asleep right next to me, and I caught myself on a couple of occasions

pressing your gun up against your head, willing and ready to blow ya fuckin' brains all over the pillow. This is how mad and hurt I am right now, but even still, I would never be able to bring myself to hurt you. I guess you're probably wondering why I would feel this way. Better yet, you probably already know. I followed you last night when you left out, and I watched you meet up with a woman. A white woman at that. I followed you to the motel where I watched you go into room 308 with that bitch. I sat there feeling stupid, before I just decided to leave. The thing is, Royce, I already had a feeling that you was cheating on me. I just didn't want to believe it. You kept telling me to trust you and I did, not because you are a great liar, but because I wanted to believe you. This hurt so bad, because I loved you so much. You was my first, and the only man I wanted to spend the rest of my life with. I guess the love that you had for me didn't equal out to be the same. Damn, Ro, you truly broke my heart. It saddens me to even write this letter. I never cried this much in my life. I hope that she makes you happy and that she could be to you everything that I couldn't be. If she could take you away from me, then she deserves to have you. Please just let me go and find someone who can love me and only me. I will contact you when I get on my feet and get

established, so that you can remain in Raven's
life if you choose to do so. Take good care of
yourself, Royce.
    Love always,
    Krystol

Royce's eyes were glued to the paper, and for the
next ten minutes, he just kept reading the letter
over and over again. He couldn't believe Krystol had
gone this far, and had he known it was going to come
to this, he would have taken his chances with just
telling her the truth about what he was doing. He
was sick, and the more he read the letter, the sicker
he became. Krystol meant everything to him, and
to know that she was out there somewhere with his
daughter made him feel weak. He couldn't protect
them or watch over them without knowing where
they were, and that ate at him. Could his chase for
money really have cost him the love of his life?

He flopped back on the bed in frustration, and
then he quickly hopped up, figuring that she couldn't
have gotten that far. He was going to check every
train station, bus station, and even check the airport.
He walked over to the closet to check the petty cash
box and see what kind of money she had to work
with. It was empty, which meant she had anywhere
from $1,500 to $2,500 to work with. Thinking about
it, Royce knew that it was enough cash for her to get
where she wanted to go. And if she needed more, it
wouldn't be anything for her to hit the bank and have
access to an additional six grand.

He raced down the stairs and shot to the garage to see if she had taken her car, but it was still in there. He then raced to his own vehicle, jumped in, and pulled off to a destination he hadn't figured out yet. All he knew was that he didn't want to lose Krystol like this. He wanted the chance to tell her the truth. Being unfaithful was the last thing he wanted her to think about, nor did he want that to be the reason why they broke up. Especially since he had never cheated on her.

"Come on, B, where you at?" he mumbled to himself, looking up and down every street he went through.

The hotel manager stared at Sanaa like she was crazy, not knowing how serious she was about what she was offering. The Loews Hotel was one of the largest hotels by the airport, and probably one of the most expensive.

"You know what you're asking me to do is illegal. If I don't report that kind of money to the IRS, I could get in trouble," the manager told Sanaa, reaching into his lower desk drawer and pulling out a bottle of Scotch.

"Look, Mr. Bosworth, I'm not here to talk to you about what's legal and what's not. You got the power to say yes or no. I personally just want to throw a party at ya hotel, and I'm sure you can find a way around the IRS if you wanted," Sanaa shot back in her most professional tone.

She was right. Bosworth had ways of making things happen with the books, especially when it came down to putting a few extra dollars in his pocket. This wasn't the first time he'd entertained a hotel party.

"I'm willing to give you ten grand in cash if you can make it happen for me," Sanaa threw out there, getting every bit of his attention.

He sat there for a second, throwing back the shot of Scotch he had poured in his cup. Ten grand sounded like a beautiful number to him, and it wasn't long before he rolled his chair over to the file cabinets. He rolled back over to the table with a large black book, slammed it onto the desk, and flipped through the pages.

"I'm not even sure if we have that many rooms available in the hotel," Bosworth said, looking into the reservations log.

At that point, Sanaa knew she had him. If there was one thing in this world that spoke louder than words, it was money. It really did make the world go 'round, even if it was fake.

"Don't worry, babe, you're gonna do fine," Danielle encouraged Kemo as they sat in the car outside of Club All In. "Here, I've been saving this for a little while, and I want you to have it," she said, reaching into her pocketbook and pulling out fifty stacks. She placed the money in his hand.

Kemo knew better than to ask about how she got the money. His ignorance about some parts of her lifestyle was his peace of mind. Still, as any good street dude would be, he was curious, and he had been doing a little bit of research into how she grew her loot. A couple of times when she thought he was sleep or off in another room, he had overheard bits of conversations. He looked at the money she handed him, and placed the envelope in his pocket.

At the bottom of the barrel, Kemo had to go back to doing the only thing he knew best, which was counting cards in the lovely game of blackjack. It was something he tried to leave in his past after getting into the drug game, considering he'd been banned from entering any casino in Atlanta City or in Las Vegas. A card counter lived a very different kind of life, and even though the money was good, it was a lot of work and long nights. It had the risk of prison time, and depending on the casino, it could cost a life, and that was something Kemo had nearly experienced a few times in his short career. Like anything—counting cards, street hustle, or producing a product niggas wanted to buy—it all came down to the numbers. You had to weigh your options, and your risk factors.

"Remember, babe, this is only a warm-up to get you back in the rhythm of things, before we go out to Atlantic City," she coached. The larger casinos didn't always watch things as they should. Kemo knew he could get by some of the security; he could grease their palms a little to look the other way.

Danielle almost seemed to be talking to a child she was dropping off at school on his first day. This was where she wanted him, knowing the potential he had, and how easy it was for him to be a millionaire almost overnight. Those were the good old days she was used to having when she first met him, and all she wanted to do was get back to those times.

Counting cards and moving weight were two of Kemo's talents. Both could give the government his life or, worse, the streets could take it. Either way, he needed and wanted money. He couldn't adjust to being a basic nigga. Living from paycheck to paycheck for damn pennies. Kemo was a dude who always had that ace in the hole, even when he appeared to be against the wall, and down to his last. He wasn't as good at drug dealing as he was at counting cards, and the money didn't even equal up. It was crazy, because Danielle's whole plan for robbing Kemo was to get him to dig up a couple million he had put away when he stopped counting cards. She was simply going to take the money and go on about her way, but after she found out that he was completely broke and had dug that money up a long time ago, she had to improvise and persuade him to do what he did.

Kemo walked to the back of the club where the door to the poker tables was. This was his first time there, only having heard about it from a couple of his boys. He wasn't even sure if they were going to let him in, but in the event he had any problems getting in, his man Troy had told him to use his name. That's exactly what he had to do, because Joi didn't see his name on the list, and wasn't going to let him in.

"Coffee, soda, juice, or tobacco," the waitress announced, walking past the tables.

It was bigger and better than Kemo thought, a place he felt he should have already been coming to. It really looked like the floor of a casino, boss pit included. He found his way over to the blackjack table, where only a couple people sat. It had been so long since he counted cards, but it seemed like it all came back to him at once. He looked over and saw the sign that said NO LIMIT, which brought a smile to his face.

"Coffee, soda, juice, tobacco," the waitress announced again walking past the blackjack table.

"Let me get a shot of Hennessy straight," Kemo ordered. "And let me get some chips," he said to the dealer, placing $12,000 on the table.

Kemo didn't play the first couple of hands because the deck was almost finished, so he just waited it out so that he could get a fresh start on the cards. He was only there for a few minutes, and had already planned to break the house. He took in the security posted up around the floor, and he noticed the two cash-out booths on the side by the slot machines. He took inventory of everything, including how many people were in the building. Those were just some of the things a card counter had to look out for in the event that a speedy exit was needed, something Kemo was also good at.

***

Sanaa pulled up to the club, and it seemed to be even more packed than it was the night before, which only meant that the money was moving according to plan. She decided to take the back way to get inside. As she walked to the back door, Sleepy sitting in the alleyway in the dark startled her. Off instinct, she pulled her gun and held it in front of her until she recognized who it was.

"Boy, you scared da shit out of me," Sanaa said, tucking her gun in its holster on her hip. "Why you ain't inside, and what happened to you last night?"

"Let's deal with one thing at a time," Sleepy replied, grabbing Sanaa's arm and pulling her farther back into the alleyway.

"What's going on?" she asked, as he led her almost to the end of the alley.

When they got to the end of the alley, Sleepy went behind the large green Dumpster and grabbed a man who was still somewhat knocked out. Sanaa didn't know what the hell was going on. She didn't recognize the man at all.

After a few smacks across his face, the man woke up in a panic. He looked directly at Sanaa, who he knew to be the owner of the club.

"What da fuck is goin' on?" the man yelled, sitting up on his elbows.

"You want to tell her what you told me inside?" Sleepy asked the man.

"Young'un, all I said was that I want my money back, because this shit y'all paid me with is fake!"

"Fake, what makes you think that?" Sanaa asked, wanting to see what the man knew.

"Yeah, it's fake, and just know that I know," the man continued.

Sanaa wasn't sure if the man was an old school hustler who recognized counterfeit bills, or if he was just a simple man making a guess. Either way, her main concern was who else he might have told this to. If something like this got out, it would surely blow the spot, and possibly put Sanaa in prison faster than she'd thought. Even worse, the streets might take justice into their own hands, and end up killing her and the whole crew. Philly was known for a nice body count every year, and she wasn't trying to add herself to it.

"Who else knows?" Sanaa asked the man. "And how did you find out?"

"I was at the bar, and the bartender spilled some seltzer water on the tip I left her. The ink started to fade away, but the bartender took the money before I could say anything. Come on, man, I didn't tell anybody, and I promise I won't say nothing," the man pled, seeing that maybe he had put himself in a bad situation by complaining.

He might have been telling the truth, but Sanaa couldn't afford to take the chance of this little secret getting out. She drew her weapon from her hip, aimed it at the man's head, then pulled the trigger. The hollow-point bullet entered his skull and exploded in his brain before exiting the side of his head.

Sleepy was taken by surprise. He looked down the other end of the alley to make sure that nobody saw or heard the shot. Everyone at the other end of the alley toward the club was so worried about the car show going on in front of the club, and the loud music, they didn't even hear the shot. At the other end of the alley was a bunch of car traffic, and nobody even paid attention to what was going on in the alley, so the coast was clear.

Sanaa took her gun, wiped it down with her shirt, and then tossed it on the ground right next to the body. She walked away as if nothing ever happened.

Sleepy followed her and was about to ask her if that was a good move, murdering a man so close to the club. But before he could get a word out, Sanaa's phone rang.

"So what happened to you last night?" Sanaa asked Royce, not even saying hello.

"I was busy taking care of something," he responded. "But fuck that right now; did Krystol say anything to you today?" he asked, hoping Sanaa would know where she was.

"No, why, where is she?"

"That's the problem, I don't know. She left this morning and I don't know where she went."

"Hold up," Sanaa said, stopping in the middle of the alley. "You mean to tell me you don't know where she's at?" she asked in a concerned manner.

"No, I have no idea." Royce had driven around all day trying to find her. He checked bus stations, train stations, and he damn near boarded the only flight to Atlanta, which he eventually found out that she wasn't on.

"So where is my niece?" Sanaa asked.

He just shook his head, because he couldn't answer that question either. That's what made him so sick. He worried most about Raven, and if he had her safe with him, it would have eased his heart.

"Look, sis, I don't have any of them answers right now, but if she comes by, just hit me and let me know, okay?"

"No question, brah, and you call me and let me know when you find them."

Sanaa and Sleepy finally made it into the casino, and the first thing she noticed was the large amount of people there tonight. She also couldn't help but to notice the crowd of people gathered around the blackjack table, and the loud cheers coming from the players. Kemo was making the best of his skills, and the people around him were enjoying it. He was a little rusty coming out of the gate and losing the twenty grand Danielle gave him in the car, but he rallied back with his last three grand, and he was now on a winning streak.

"What's goin' on?" Sanaa asked as she walked to the pit where Joi was standing.

"He cashed in about twenty-three grand, lost twenty, and now he just got his money back," Joi reported. "He's been on a streak for the past twenty minutes."

"What about everybody else?" Sanaa asked, look-ing around at the other tables.

"The house is winning," she answered with a smile on her face.

"Good, I'll take it from here. Oh, and I need you to get upstairs and relieve Pam from the bar. She's fuckin' up," Sanaa yelled over the cheers coming from the blackjack table.

As the night cooled down and the last few people left the casino, Sanaa crunched the numbers again, and this time she had done a lot better than before. The club was starting to attract a lot of attention, just the way she wanted. It was a successful night, despite the fact that Kemo had left with seventy grand. It was nothing compared to the $143,000 that Club All In had made for the night. As usual, the casino made the bulk of the money. She had even done better with exchanging the money, and she still had around six hundred grand left.

From this point on, it only looked like things were going to get better; that is, if she could prevent people like the dead man sitting in the alleyway waiting to be found from finding out about the funny money.

Chapter 13

Detective Thomas squatted down over the dead body in the alley, pointing with his ink pen at the entry hole in the victim's skull. The forensics unit was on the scene as well, taking pictures and collecting evidence from the victim's body and the surrounding area. The most obvious piece of evidence that caught the detective's attention was a neon green band around the victim's right wrist. It had the words SINGLE ADMISSION written around it.

"What you think this is?" Thomas asked his partner, pointing to the band.

"I don't know. It looks like something you get when you go to a club or something," he answered.

Detective Thomas stood and looked up and down the alley. He started walking down the alley toward the opposite end, looking up at the buildings as he passed them. He walked all the way around to the front of the building, and the more he walked, the more neon-colored wristbands he saw on the ground. It was like a line of clues that eventually led him right to the front door of Club All In.

"Who's the manager?" he asked Yellow, who was behind the bar cleaning glasses.

"Who's asking?" he shot back.

Thomas moved his suit jacket to the side, flashing his badge and gun. As he was doing that, Sanaa came out of her office with some financial papers in her hand. The detective caught her by surprise, and for a minute, she thought that it was the Feds finally coming to get her.

Yellow, not knowing about Sanaa's legal problems back in Atlanta, pointed right at her.

Sanaa was about two seconds away from taking off like she was in the one hundred yard dash. The only reason that she didn't was because the detective looked at her like he didn't know who the hell she was. If it was the Feds, she'd already be on the ground with her hands behind her back.

"Can I help you?" Sanaa asked boldly, making her way over to the detective.

"Yes, I'm investigating a homicide that took place last night in the alleyway behind your building."

Again, Sanaa was ready to break. It didn't help any that she had a compact .45 automatic sticking out of her back waist. That alone was probable cause for him to dig a little deeper.

"We believe he was at your club before he got shot. He had on one of your admission bracelets," the detective continued.

"Oh, God," Sanaa said, placing her hand over her mouth in shock in her best shocked expression. "Who was he?"

The detective went on to explain as much as he could about the victim, but he wanted Sanaa to come out back to see if she knew the guy. Reluctantly, she agreed, but she was more concerned about what she was going to say when the detective saw the gun in her back. As Sanaa followed the detective out the door, Yellow came from behind the bar and acted like he was going to follow them out, but he didn't. Instead, he simply walked up behind Sanaa, grabbed the gun from off her back, and tucked it away in his back pocket.

Sanaa felt it and was relieved as she headed around to the alley with the detective.

Ariana's flight landed in Philly at just after two o'clock in the afternoon. She and Olivia hated flying, but they had made the sacrifice for the greater good of the mission.

"'Hotel party. Best Bikini. Best Dancer. Win Grand Prize,'" Olivia read from a flyer she had picked up off the floor. They were all over the airport. "Look, they even said it's going to be some local rappers there, too," she said, showing Ariana the flyer. "You think we can have some fun while we're in Philly?" Olivia asked.

Ariana smiled, knowing how much of a party freak she used to be. The weather was so beautiful, even Ariana fought the urge to party a little. But of course, business always came before pleasure. She didn't plan to draw out the confrontation between her and Joi anyway. On sight, no matter who was around or what Joi was doing, Ariana was going to kill her, and that was going to be the end of it. If Sanaa was there, she was getting hit too. The only problem Ariana had at this point was getting guns and ammo for her and Olivia, that along with finding out where Joi was.

"So, are you ready for Atlantic City?" Danielle asked Kemo as he walked into the room, drinking a bottle of spring water.

"No, not yet. The club is having a party at the Loews Hotel. They got a nice chunk of money, and I know I can take the house," he told Danielle. "I can't take 70K out to Atlantic City and expect to do what I do. Getting caught ain't what I plan on doing. They would put me away for the rest of my life, or get my ass beat down. I'm damn Billy the Kid in most of these places. They might shoot to kill, instead of sending my ass up the river! My face would be posted in every casino if I get caught."

Kemo had learned from the mistakes he made in Las Vegas and in other casinos. This time, he had to be a lot smarter if he was going to walk away from one of the United States' largest casino strips with millions of dollars. Right now, hitting Sanaa for a few hundred grand was a good start.

"I need more money before we go out there. We should be good by next week."

Danielle put up no argument with what Kemo was saying. She knew that when it came down to cards,

Kemo knew what was best. All it took on her part was being a little patient, something she'd been for over a year now.

Kemo walked over to the bed where Danielle was lying, grabbed her by the ankles, and pulled her to the edge of the bed. He stood over top of her with nothing but a pair of sweatpants on, showing off his ripped body and dark chocolate skin tone. Whether she liked it or not, it turned her on to see him focused the way he was on making money.

As he reached in to try to take off the tank top she was wearing, Danielle quickly remembered the two bruises on her chest and stomach from when Kemo had shot her. She had tried to nurse them, but her white skin made it virtually impossible. Kemo was far from stupid, and if he saw those bruises, it would take him no time to grab the gun off the nightstand and put a bullet in her head. Danielle knew it, and she had to think fast on her feet.

She smacked his hands down, sat up on the edge of the bed, and snatched his sweatpants down to his ankles. She looked up at him, taking his half-hardened dick into her mouth. With one hand rubbing his chest and the other hand on his waist, Danielle pushed his dick as far down her throat as she possibly could. Kemo just threw his head back and closed his eyes, enjoying the warm, wet, soft mouth of Danielle. She took his hand and placed it on the back of her head, encouraging him to guide her head to the rhythm of his choice.

"Shittt," he grunted, grabbing a handful of her hair and pushing his dick farther down her throat.

His hand went from grabbing her head, to sliding down the center of her back. Before Danielle could react, he had pulled the tank top over her head. She backed up just enough for him to remove the tank top. At this point, Danielle looked over at the gun on the nightstand. If anybody was going to get to it first, it was going to be her.

Think, think, think, she thought, looking up at Kemo.

In one swift move, Danielle rolled over on her stomach, arched her ass up in the air, and looked back at Kemo. There was hesitation, but not because Kemo had seen the bruises; rather he took a moment to admire the scene. She knew how to use her body when it counted, and without further ado, Kemo stepped up, placed his hand on the top of her ass cheeks, and guided his thick, long dick into her soft, warm jelly jar. She inhaled through her teeth, taking it all in, looking back at her ass clapping against his pelvis. He started pounding away, watching through the mirror in front of him as Danielle's titties bounced around low to the bed. Danielle had to hurry up and get it over with, despite how good it was feeling.

She reached back, grabbed her ass and spread her cheeks apart so that Kemo could go deeper inside of her. "Deeper, deeper," Danielle yelled out. "Harder, K. Fuck me harder," she screamed, throwing her ass back at him.

Kemo could feel himself about to cum. He kept stroking, harder and deeper. Danielle's pussy was so wet he could hear his dick splashing around in her. He grabbed her waist with both of his hands and sped up his strokes. Danielle knew that he was about to cum. She could feel it. She could also feel herself at the tip of a climax.

"I'm cumming," she yelled, slamming her ass against him.

Kemo was at his point too, and released his thick, warm cum inside of her. He kept stroking until every bit of it was out of him and inside her. The cum from Danielle's pussy formed a creamy-colored paste around the base of his dick.

Danielle fell to her stomach, using the opportunity to conceal the two bruises. This gave her all the reasons she needed to lie there until the opportunity presented itself for her to put her clothes back on. It happened sooner than she thought, because Kemo headed straight to the bathroom and turned on the shower.

Sanaa walked back into the club where Royce and Yellow were waiting. Yellow did his best to bring Royce up to speed about what was going on, as if Royce didn't know already. She didn't say a word, but headed straight to her office. Royce followed, waving for Yellow to stay put.

Royce could see a bit of irritation in Sanaa's face as she plopped down in her chair. The detective had a million and one questions for Sanaa, even after she was unable to identify the body. It appeared that the man was in the club at some point, which prompted Thomas to ask questions about the club's security and surveillance. He was adamant about finding out what happened, but as much as he tried to dig, Sanaa dismissed everything that suggested the club could be the reason for his death. For a minute, it felt like he was starting to interrogate Sanaa. That's when she cut the interview short, leaving him with one of her business cards as a form of contact.

"You know you can't go around killing everybody who finds out about the money," Royce joked, but in a serious way.

"Yeah, I know," she replied, rubbing her temples. "That's why I got to hurry up and move this money before dis shit gets out."

"No, you need to reconsider that deal you did wit' Boo and just stop while you're ahead," Royce sincerely suggested, plopping down in the chair in front of the desk.

Sanaa had already considered that, and had set up a meeting with Boo for after the hotel party. She felt she had maybe bitten off more than she could chew for the first time in her life. She just didn't want to cut Boo off and be on bad terms. It's crazy, because if Sanaa wanted to, she could have moved every last counterfeit bill, given time. Either way, something was going to have to give, because at this rate, she was going to end up going to jail anyway and maybe for something far worse than what she was doing.

Ariana and Olivia checked into the Loews Hotel having gotten the idea from the flyers in the airport. The flyers were everywhere and not just the airport. Ariana figured she would let Olivia let her hair down a little, since they didn't have their guns yet. A little networking tonight would change the firearm situation. Philly was known for guns. Ariana knew that, because most of the guns floating around in New York came from down South. Getting the guns was just a matter of who you knew in the city, and with pretty faces like hers and Olivia's it wasn't going to be hard for them to find some young thugs to accommodate them with what they need.

Chapter 14

Some of Philly's most beautiful women poured into the Loews Hotel, some as guests and others just there for the party. The music from the DJ mixing on the turntables greeted everyone the moment they walked into the lobby. For those men and women who had keys, they were able to go straight to their room without having to check in at the desk.

The setup was crazy. Sanaa had rented out one hundred rooms, occupying the entire fourteenth, fifteenth, and sixteenth floors of the hotel. The east wing was connected to the indoor Olympic swimming pool, which Sanaa pretty much owned for the next two days. The access to the ballroom was a plus, too, where people had a place to dance during the evening hours.

Sleepy was in charge of selling the rooms, at which he did an excellent job, having sold eighty-five rooms out of the hundred in less than three days. Most of the hustlers jumped on the rooms immediately, anticipating fuckin' at the end of the night. The females who purchased the rooms were mainly strippers, who knew that the majority of their hustle would be taking place that evening after the parties were over.

Joi was the star of the show when she made her debut into the pool area. When she took off the extra-large T-shirt, all heads turned, and there were a lot of beautiful women there. She had a Charlie polka dot and stripe print bikini, and a pair of black Bernardo leather sandals. On her face was a pair of large, blue square frames. To be the age of forty-one, she gave every female in the building who looked like something a run for their money. No fat, no stretch marks, and definitely no signs of aging. Joi had to be in the top three out of about 250 women at the party.

Sanaa looked tough too, rockin' a one piece, open-stomach Louis Vuitton bathing suit, some sandals, and a pair of large-frame Gucci shades. She too was getting a lot of attention, especially from one of the lifeguards.

The party was doing everything Sanaa had expected it to do. The pool area was jumping. People were vibing to the party music, niggas on the bleachers were kicking their best game to the lovely ladies, and a group of people had even turned a small section of the deck into a dance floor. It was bananas, and there wasn't a displeased look on anyone's face.

"You might have outdone yourself this time, baby girl," Joi yelled to Sanaa over the music.

"I know. We should have been done this," she responded, playfully dodging some water from a nigga doing a cannonball right in front of them.

Not only did the party have a financial purpose; it also served as relaxation. It gave Joi and Sanaa the opportunity to let their hair down and have some fun for a change. It was just the thing they needed in their lives.

"Are you going to need my help upstairs?" Joi asked Sanaa, knowing that it wouldn't be that much longer before Sanaa made her way up to the rooms for another portion of the party.

Even through all the fun she was having, Sanaa was still in business mode, having set up shop in the hotel for some executive gambling. She had taken five of the largest suites and converted them into gambling rooms. Although she couldn't bring some of the portable replicas of the poker tabletop game she had in the club, she managed to make do with the blackjack and slot machines. She had even made a ticket for the basketball finals, with odds taking Miami over Oklahoma in less than seven games. Yeah, Sanaa was having a little fun, but her mind was still on the money and the money was always on her mind.

Ariana looked out her window at all the cars pulling up to the hotel, and she could see crowds of people walking around and into the building. She was up so high on the twenty-second floor that she really couldn't see the faces of the people at all, plus she was on the west wing of the building, away from the action.

Just as she was looking out the window, Olivia came bursting into the room, excited and half dressed. Ariana looked at her with a silly grin, remembering what she had left out in, and amused at the fact that she was now returning wearing a bikini and some Daisy Dukes. She even had a bottle of Ace in her hand, chilled as if she had just pulled it out of a bucket of ice.

"Since you ain't goin' to the party, I'm bringing the party to you," Olivia joked, popping the top of the bottle.

"Girl, I ain't got no time to party right now. I'm about to meet up wit' the dude, Nick, to get the guns," Ariana replied, turning back to finish looking out of the window.

She had gone straight to the hood last night after getting settled in and she met a dude who knew another dude who sold guns. Because she was a female, Ariana set the meeting up to take place in a public place in the middle of the day. She was staying on the safe side, being in a foreign land. Cute face and all, Ariana was taking a chance that could turn out to be detrimental for her health, fuckin' around in the streets of Philly.

Ariana just stood by the window, rubbing her finger inside the bullet wound in her stomach. It was the same bullet that took her baby's life, and she took comfort in touching the only memory she had left of her unborn child. It was a pain she had to live with for the rest of her life, and at times, when she drifted off into space, Olivia could tell that she was thinking about it.

"Don't worry, baby girl. You'll get ya chance," Olivia said, walking over to stand next to Ariana by the window. "You just make sure that when you do, you go hard as a muthafucka. And know for sure that I'ma be right wit' you until we bury everything moving, or get buried ourselves," she assured.

Despite only knowing each other for a few months, they had become best friends. Olivia was actually the one who found Ariana's body lying in the parking lot of the hospital. She was only a nurse's assistant at the time, but she was able to get a weak pulse after performing CPR on Ariana for about three minutes. From that day forth, they were inseparable, and Olivia chose the street life under the guardianship of Ariana. For her, she was willing to go the distance.

"Now, I'ma be down by the pool area if you need me," Danielle told Kemo, who was standing outside the door of the blackjack room.

Her position was clear, and that was that. If Kemo was to get into trouble with the cards, she would come get him up out of the there, even if it was by force. She was also the decoy he needed in the event he hit for a large amount of money and it was time to go. At the same time, if Kemo miscounted the cards, and was starting to lose the money, she would come get him off the table so that he could restart. She had her purpose for being around, and the things she did were needed.

Kemo walked into the room, and from the beginning, he liked what he saw. A couple of local ballers he was familiar with sat around at tables smoking cigars and sipping on hard liquor. Walking farther in, he could see that the room was adjacent to another room that held another blackjack table.

"Coffee, soda, juice, cigarettes," the waitress announced, walking past with a bikini on, holding a tray.

Kemo just took in the scene for a moment before finding his way over to the table. It was like some mob-style shit goin' on, and Kemo fit in perfectly, slamming fifty grand on the table and asking for chips.

Off the break, Carla, the dealer, recognized the counterfeit bills and immediately looked over at Will, the pit boss. He was even stuck for a second, wondering what he should do. Carla looked at the money on the table; without touching it she immediately recognized the flaw in the seal around the president's face. She only recognized it having seen one or two nights ago, and having been educated by her boy, Dolpha. Dolpha was an engraver and he had sold some moneymaking plates a few years back to some of his boys. They had later complained about the flaw in the plate to him; they damn near beat the shit out of him. He was spared because he was a master at what he did, and they knew it.

Kemo looked up at both of them, trying to figure out why his money was still on the table. Sanaa walking through the door was like a savior. She was immediately summoned to the table.

"Is it a problem?" Kemo asked, looking up at Sanaa.

Sanaa looked down at the money then back up at Kemo. She had recognized his face from the night before, figuring he was just trying to pick up where he left off. Without further wait, she let him play, and grabbed counterfeit money off the table. She gave Will the directions to recycle the money into the payouts, and not to mix it with the real money. Just like that, Kemo was back on.

Ariana and Olivia left their room, en route to meet up with Nick for the guns. It was Olivia's idea to take the east wing elevator to get out of the building, so that Ariana could pass through the pool party and see how much fun everyone was having. She really just wanted to cheer her up a little.

They bent the corner of the hallway to get to the east wing, and the unthinkable happened. It was as if someone took a sledgehammer and knocked Ariana's chest into her back, and for a split second, she felt like she was about to pass out. She never thought in a million years she would run into Sleepy again after hearing that he had moved out to Cali. But there he was, standing in front of the elevator looking dead at her.

After doing a double take, Sleepy couldn't believe his eyes, and wondered if his mind was playing tricks on him. He just stood there staring at her as Ariana slowly walked up and stopped a few feet away from him. Olivia didn't know what was going on, having never met or seen Sleepy before. In fact, she'd never seen any of the people Ariana told her about, and up to this point, she only knew them by name.

It was a confusing and awkward moment for Ariana and Sleepy, and neither of them knew what to say. Sleepy had never stopped thinking about Ariana, and had held on to the love he had for her. Ariana had nothing but murder on her mind. Until now, she'd really never thought too much about Sleepy, but more so about the seed he had put inside of her. Right now, she was just stuck, and so was Sleepy.

They stood there in silence staring at each other. Olivia knew that something was up from the looks on both of their faces.

"A, you cool?" Olivia asked, clutching the Ace of Spade bottle, ready to crack Sleepy upside his head.

"Yeah, she good," Sleepy answered for her. "She just got a lot on her mind right now," he said, inching closer to Ariana.

It was like all of her anger, all of her confusion, all of her stress, and all of her problems had subsided the instant she heard his voice and confirmed who she was standing in front of. All the memories she had hidden inside came rushing back to her at once. Tears filled her eyes, and unconsciously, she reached for what comforted her the most: the bullet wound on her stomach.

"And who da hell is you?" Olivia said, stepping up to get between them.

Sleepy didn't even pay her or her question any mind. He simply reached out for Ariana's hand. "You got a room around there?" he nodded toward the west wing.

Ariana shook her head yes, still not able to form words in her mouth.

"You wanna go back to your room so we can talk?" he asked Ariana, still with his hand out, waiting for her to take it.

It took her a moment, but her hand eventually reached back out for his. She slowly walked up to him and melted in his arms as he wrapped them around her. Her tears flowed from her face, onto his chest. It was at that moment, without his name ever being said, that Olivia knew exactly who he was. In the several months of knowing Ariana, Ariana only told Olivia one time the story of the first and only man she ever fell in love with, and by the looks of things, this had to be him.

Just being with him again was so overwhelming. Ariana's knees got weak, but before she could fall to the ground, Sleepy scooped her up in his arms while Olivia led the way back to the room.

"Yo, why you always staring at me?" Royce joked with Joi, who was standing poolside.

"Because you look just like ya dad," she replied with a smile.

"Yeah, well I'm a little more handsome," he joked before the next best thing to Joi walked into the pool area.

She wasn't the only snow bunny there, but she was by far the best looking. When Danielle dropped the towel from around her waist, the same heads that turned for Joi turned for her and she became the center of attention. Royce had to admit to himself that she was the baddest white chick he'd ever met in his life.

The bikini she had on showed off all her curves, along with the little ass that she had. Her long, curly blond hair was pulled back into ponytail, and the light pink Prada frames complemented her fresh manicure and pedicure. Her olive skin glistened in the sun; he noticed that some areas on her back were a darker shade than the rest of her body. Nothing that took away from her sexiness, it appeared she may have fallen or something, and bruised her skin slightly. She dove into the pool like an Olympic swimmer, not bothered at all about getting her hair wet.

Royce didn't even excuse himself from Joi; he took off his sneakers and dove right into the water. Joi just smiled, watching him swim underwater across the pool.

He swam all the way up to Danielle, who was still in the water leaning against the wall.

"Oh, you can swim, too?" Danielle said as Royce came up from under the water. "A man who can hold his breath that long has a quality all women can use," she joked in a playful but seductive tone.

"Stop being nasty," he responded playfully. "So what brings you out?" he asked, knowing she wasn't there just for the party. He knew Danielle well enough know that she was there for one reason, and that was to work. There was somebody here she was sitting on, and Royce was curious to know who it was.

"I told you I was working on something big," Danielle began. "If you're around when it falls through, I'ma make you a millionaire."

"Yeah, I been hearing that a lot lately," he shot back.

"Yeah, well I'm not everybody else who told you that. You of all people should know that I'm about my business, and ten times out of ten, if I say I'ma do something, it's gonna get done," she said with a look of sincerity.

Royce had to agree. Every time she said she was going to do something, she came through. Plus, he knew firsthand how vicious she was with a pistol. He couldn't take anything away from her.

"So, I guess I'll let you get back to work then," Royce said, playfully splashing a little bit of water into her face.

She laughed and splashed him back. "I guess you should do that then." She smiled.

"I'm in room 2009 if you need me. Oh, and you look good in a bikini," he complimented her as he climbed out of the pool.

He left Danielle there blushing, and had it not been for the fact that Kemo was in the building, she would have tried to kick it with him longer.

A knock at the door caught Sanaa's attention as she looked on at the poker game that was heating up. She watched as Yellow looked through the peephole then looked back over at her with a dissatisfied look on his face. It prompted Sanaa to walk over to the door. She looked into the peephole, and to her surprise, Boo was standing there looking back at her.

Sanaa threw her head back in frustration, not really sure how Boo knew about the poker room. No one who wasn't invited was supposed to be there. Luckily, for Boo, Sanaa had a few things she wanted to talk to him about anyway, mainly concerning money.

"Damn, what, a nigga money ain't good up in here?" Boo said when Sanaa opened the door.

Sanaa cut her eyes at him about his comment; he was the master of funny money. She stood to the side and allowed him to enter. He stared Yellow down when Yellow reached out to pat him down.

"Easy, Boo. It's too much money up in here for niggas to have guns on them. If you strapped, you'll get it back when you leave," Sanaa told him in a calm and civilized manner.

He respected it, reaching in and grabbing the .40-cal off his hip and passing it to Sanaa. Yellow wasn't done yet. Boo still had a Louis Vuitton shoulder pack with him that needed to be checked.

"What's in the bag?" Yellow asked, not yet moving from Boo's path.

"Damn, nigga. It's money," Boo said, trying to walk past.

Yellow stood there and still didn't budge. Boo looked over at Sanaa, who only shrugged, standing by Yellow's position. She wanted to make sure everyone in the room was safe.

Reluctantly, Boo opened the bag, but only showed Sanaa the contents. He had every right to want to protect what was inside, and once Sanaa saw the money plates in the bag sitting on top of a pile of money, Boo was no longer hassled.

"Come with me," Sanaa said, leading him into the bedroom. "Yellow, give us a little privacy," she said, closing the bedroom door behind them.

Yellow did just that, but stood close to the door just in case something foul popped off.

"Don't tell me you're tryin' to sell those," Sanaa said with a curious look on her face.

"Don't be silly, Sanaa. I'm not that stupid," Boo answered, walking over to the bedroom window.

Boo was actually in the process of transporting the plates and the printing machine to another location. He had concluded that having the machine and the plates in the same place where he rested his head wasn't a good idea.

"Well, look, while I got you here, I wanna discuss business," Sanaa said, walking over to the closet. "I wanna buy some more money. I don't know how much you got on you, but I'll take all of it off ya hands for the right price," Sanaa said, placing the shoebox she had taken out of the closet onto the bed.

It was only a few days since she'd bought $1 million in counterfeit money, and now she was ready to buy more. At that moment, Boo knew that Sanaa was ready for the $5 million in funny money he was ready to drop in her lap. The only thing was Sanaa wasn't trying to be fronted anything. Whatever she got from Boo she wanted to buy on her own, and with her negotiating skills, Sanaa was going to get as much as she could for as little as possible.

Balil had several surgeries before doctors could stabilize his condition. The bullets had done so much damage to his insides, that it was only an act of God that he managed to survive. His cell phone sitting on the patio table was the only thing that saved him.

As he finally opened his eyes in the recovery room, all he could see was a blurry image of a nurse standing by his bed checking his vitals. He so desperately wanted to contact Sanaa and Joi to let them know that Ariana was more than likely on her way to Philly.

"Nurse, Nurse, I need a phone," Balil whispered through his dry throat.

"The detectives are in the process of contacting your family. Right now, you really need to get some rest," the nurse told him.

"Please, please," Balil pled, holding his hand up and pointing to the phone.

The nurse, feeling sorry for him, looked around before grabbing the receiver to the phone on the stand next to the bed and reaching it out to him. Balil began spitting out Sanaa's cell phone number while the nurse pushed the buttons. After the phone started ringing, the nurse left the room so that she wouldn't get into any trouble for helping Balil get on the phone in the recovery room.

Sanaa was letting Boo out of the hotel room when her phone went off in her back pocket. She didn't recognize the number, but knew from the area code that the call was coming from Atlanta. She felt that more than likely it was her father, as he was the only one in Georgia who had her cell phone number.

"Yes," Sanaa answered, walking back toward the bedroom. "Hello," she shouted, irritated that nobody was saying anything on the other end.

She was just about to hang up when she heard a faint voice whispering. It was hard for her to make out what was being said, but she could hear the beeping sound of the heart monitor in the background. She took a seat on the bed and listened more carefully to the whispers.

"Coming . . . for . . . you," Balil whispered, going in and out of consciousness.

He was so tired from all the pain medication and the anesthesia that was wearing off from his surgery he could barely keep his eyes open. Feeling his body getting weaker, he tried to speak again, but instead, the phone just fell out of his hand and landed on the side of the bed.

"Well, come get me," Sanaa snapped, unaware of who she was talking to. She hung up and tossed the phone onto the bed next to the money she had just purchased from Boo.

"You good?" Yellow asked Sanaa, knocking on the door to get her attention.

"Yeah, I'm good. Come in." She waved, telling him to close the door behind him. "It's a hundred grand there," she said, pointing to the money. "Circulate it into the poker game. I can't mark it, so you and Lisa gotta be on point," Sanaa said, getting up from the bed and walking over to the window. "Remember old Ben has a flaw in his halo," Sanaa said speaking of the kink in the circle surrounding Franklin's face of the funny money.

Yellow understood and nodded as he walked over to the money. Sanaa just stood by the window looking out at the crowds of people flocking into the hotel. She was on a mission, and determined to make the best out of the situation that had fallen into her lap.

Chapter 15

It was ten o'clock in the morning and Sleepy was still wide awake. He hadn't been able to get one bit of sleep after Ariana confirmed everything that happened between her and Joi. He still hadn't made up his mind about what he was going to do to Joi; he had a lot to consider in the event that he decided to kill her. His only problem was having to explain to Sanaa and his father why he did it. He knew in his heart that Sanaa just wasn't going to accept him killing her best friend for a female. Balil wasn't going to be any happier. All these thoughts and more raced through Sleepy's head all night.

Ariana let out a small yawn, opening her eyes to see her body wrapped up in Sleepy's arms. He looked down at her with a smile, removing the loose strands of hair from her face so that he could lean in and kiss her on the graze she got from the shootout with Toughy.

"You know I'ma kill Toughy when I catch him," Sleepy said with a serious look on his face.

Ariana chuckled, burying her head into his chest and tapping him on the side. Not that she needed one, but it felt good to have a knight in shining armor who was willing to kill for her. That was one of the many reasons why she was so in love with him.

She always felt protected. In their moments alone Ariana felt like she could take off her armor, and be a woman. She could be soft, and feminine. Instead of being a soldier, she was the protected queen. Sleeping was a foreign affair to Ariana, but with him around, he was like her Tylenol PM. She was able to relax, and know that nothing would get past him, and nothing could hurt her.

"You know I gotta go take care of that," Ariana said, sitting up in the bed.

As bad as she wanted to lie up with Sleepy, she knew that there was still work to be done. Now knowing that Joi was in the building, she wanted to make the best out of the opportunity. Sleepy could see it in her eyes that her mind was made up, and had been for some time. How could he blame her? Joi took her baby's life and left her for dead. What woman wouldn't want revenge?

Sleepy had to think this one through. Ariana, if given the opportunity, would go in blazing her gun at Joi and wouldn't care who stood in her way. She would sacrifice the lives of others just to kill one, and he couldn't afford for Sanaa to be anywhere around her when bullets started flying.

"I can't sit here and let you kill my sister," he said, giving Ariana a stern look.

"I don't wanna kill ya sista. I just want Joi."

"Yeah, but if my sista is there, she's gonna shoot at you. In fact, she's gonna end up killing you as soon as you start gunning for Joi," Sleepy advised.

"So what da fuck am I supposed to do?" Ariana screamed, frustrated with Sleepy's comments. She really didn't care who was around Joi when it was time to work. Sanaa was just going to have to do what she had to do, if not get killed herself. "She killed my baby. She killed your baby, Sleepy," she cried out.

"All right, all right," he said, grabbing her and pulling her into his arms for comfort. He was feeling her pain. "Listen, let me get my li'l brotha and my sista out of the way. I'ma text you and let you know it's a green light," he calmly spoke, wiping the tears from her cheek.

"And what's gonna happen to us after this?" she asked with a concerned look on her face.

"Don't worry about that. We gonna be all right. I just want you to be careful," he shot back, walking over to the nightstand and grabbing his gun. "You got ten shots in here," he said, raising the gun. "When you go to my room to get ya girlfriend, it's another clip under the mattress."

Sleepy hated for it to go down like this. He didn't care much for Joi from the day he met her, and now knowing she had killed his seed made his heart even colder toward her. If it weren't for Sanaa, he would have done it himself, and he was still considering doing so as he watched Ariana grab the gun. She checked to make sure a bullet was in the chamber before tucking it away in her back waist.

***

Royce woke up to the sensation of his dick being smothered in something warm and wet. Before he got the chance to open his eyes, he could hear the spit along with his dick, slashing around in her mouth. When he finally cracked open his eyes, he could see long, blond, curly hair draped over the bobbing head. The head felt so good he decided not to stop her, even after pulling some of her hair back and seeing Danielle looking up at him seductively. It looked like she was making love to his dick, slowly licking up and down the shaft before taking him deep within her throat.

"How you get in here?" he asked, exhaling from pleasure.

She took his dick out of her mouth to answer him. "The front desk gave me a key," she said right before kissing the head of his dick then licking down the shaft.

She kissed his balls while slowly jerking his dick. The spit from her mouth was a lubricant. As she jerked, pre-cum began to leak. She didn't hesitate to take him right back into her mouth. She could feel his dick pulsating in her throat. It was an indicator she was well aware of, and she only added more spit in her mouth as she increased the speed of her head motion. Royce grabbed the back of her head with both hands as he felt himself cumming. The cum squirted into her mouth, and she swallowed every ounce of it until nothing was left.

Sitting up on her knees, she unstrapped her bikini top. Her breasts fell out of the top, arousing Royce and keeping his dick brick hard. She then stood up and unstrapped the bikini bottom, but the moment she tossed it to the side, her cell phone rang. She tried to ignore it, but knowing it was Kemo, she couldn't.

Royce was stuck in a trance, looking up at the light, faded landing strip of hair running to her clitoris.

She straddled him as she reached over and grabbed her bag. The phone was screaming when she pulled it out, as she took a second to get herself together before answering it.

Royce could feel the tip of his dick rubbing up against her entry point. His heart was pounding. He wanted to sample the good stuff, but when he went to grab her waist to push her down onto his dick, she jumped up and began putting her bikini back on, the whole time still talking to whoever it was on the other end of the phone.

"I gotta go. I'll call you later," she said as she headed out the door.

Royce didn't even have a chance to ask her about was going on. He just sat there in the bed, looking at the clear fluid from Danielle's pussy on the tip of his dick.

Sanaa sat in her suite stuffing the last stack of money into the money machine. The numbers were looking good from the night before, despite Kemo shutting down the blackjack table. She made fifty grand off the hotel rooms alone, and then pulled in twenty-five grand from the bottles of champagne she sold, plus ten grand from the regular bar she set up in the ballroom. The only people who were able to get into the pool area and the ballroom were those who had room keys. Everybody else had to pay a backdoor access fee of fifty dollars, except for women, who got in free. Backdoor access pulled in fifteen grand easy. The casino, like always, was the money train. It pulled in two hundred and seventy grand before 4:00 a.m. Three hundred and seventy grand was the take, and tonight they expected to do better numbers, due to the local rap artist who would be making a guest appearance.

An unexpected knock at the door quickly caught her attention. She reached for the large chrome .50-caliber Desert Eagle on the table and proceeded to the door. Only three people knew she was in this room, and if it wasn't any of them, it was going to be a problem. She waited for the second knock, which was a secret one they all knew. The series of taps confirmed that it was safe to open the door. When she did, Sleepy was standing there with a smile on his face.

"Where's Royce?" he asked, entering the room.

Danielle walked through the door of the hotel room, and the first thing she saw was several stacks of money sitting on the bed. It was more than what she'd expected him to come up with. Kemo walked out of the bathroom with a towel wrapped around him. He had just gotten out of the shower.

"Where was you at?" he asked with an attitude, having been back in the room since five o'clock.

"I was out getting an outfit for today," she lied, unaware that Kemo had been there waiting for her. "I see you did good last night," she said walking over and grabbing a stack of twenties off the bed.

"Yeah, I hit 'em for about three hundred racks," he bragged, popping the top on the bottle of Ace he had sitting in a bucket of ice.

He started to snap on Danielle for being out so late, but he took into consideration that she was a party freak. He didn't really need her for anything anyway. As he made his way over to the bed, he caught a glimpse of the two bruises peeking out from under her bikini. The concealer she had applied earlier to the bruises was wearing off. Earlier the bruises appeared yellow and pink due to the concealer, but now the dark blood on some of the bruises were rising to the surface again. Her swimming had caused the blood to flow faster, and also caused the bruised blood to rise.

"What happened to you?" he asked, nodding at the bruises.

Her heart dropped to her stomach. She had forgotten about them when she changed into the two-piece bikini in Royce's room. It was too late for her to try to cover them up, so she did what she did best: lie.

"I got into a little altercation in the ballroom," she said, reaching for the bottle in Kemo's hand.

He looked at the bruises a little closer, and when he walked over to Danielle, she got nervous and dropped the bottle of champagne onto the bed. She quickly picked it back up, mainly to knock Kemo upside the head with it if she needed to. He walked up and stood behind her, wrapping his arms around her waist.

"Nervous?" he asked, reaching for the bottle.

"What da fuck!" Danielle slightly yelled, looking down at the bed.

Kemo was about to flip on her until he too looked down at the money on the bed. The ink was starting to smudge some of the bills the champagne had fallen on. Danielle reached down and grabbed some of the money, lifting it up to her face. They both stood there in shock, watching the ink rub off on Danielle's finger.

Kemo grabbed another stack of the money and poured some Ace on it. The ink started running off in seconds. He poured the rest of the champagne onto the rest of the money, getting the same results. Silence took over the room and both of them just froze, looking down at the money. There wasn't a word in this world that could describe the rage boiling inside of Kemo as he looked down at all his hard work fading away.

***

The afternoon came fast, and it wasn't long before the scorching heat had crowds of people flocking to the pool area of the hotel. The DJ had already started blasting the music, so the party was officially on and poppin'. It was a repeat of yesterday, but even better. Girlfriends called their girlfriends, and dudes called their dudes, which meant that the place was packed.

Joi sat next to the lifeguard station checking her schedule for the day, making sure everything was going to run smoothly. She couldn't afford any fuckups, with all the money at stake. It was the last day of the hotel party, and possibly the ending of the first million dollars in counterfeit money they had changed over.

"I need twenty bottles of Moët and forty bottles of Ace on ice like yesterday," she directed one of her workers. "Is all your staff here?" Joi looked up and asked the lifeguard who was sitting on his deck chair.

"Yeah, we're good," he replied at the same moment he was blowing his whistle at a nigga trying to get in the pool with a bottle of champagne.

Joi was so engrossed in her preparation she didn't even notice Ariana entering the pool area. It wasn't like Ariana blended in with the rest of the women, having on a pair of jean capris, a white T-shirt, and a pair of Air Max sneakers. She had on no disguise, no glasses, no nothing, just Ariana in the flesh.

At first glance, Ariana couldn't spot Joi through all the women that were there, but then it happened: Joi poked her head out from behind the lifeguard's chair.

Ariana's heart pounded at the sight of her. She pulled the 9 mm from her back pocket and covered it with a towel as she made her way around the swimming pool toward Joi. Water splashed everywhere from people diving in the pool, but Ariana kept her eyes on Joi like a lion watching his prey. Twenty yards away, and Joi still didn't have a clue of what was about to happen.

Although Joi wasn't paying attention, the lifeguard next to her happened to glance over and see Ariana walking up from the side of the pool. He could tell by the look she had in her eyes that Ariana was up to something. Once the towel dropped and the gun was exposed, he knew for a fact that it was about to get ugly.

The sound of his bare feet hitting the ground grabbed Joi's attention. She turned back around to see what in the hell he was running from, and froze like she had seen a ghost.

She had trouble registering the fact that she was looking at Ariana coming toward her, and was raising a gun up to aim and shoot.

The first shot woke Joi up, bringing her out of her daze. The bullet hit one of the legs of the lifeguard's deck chair, right in front of Joi's face. The crowd of people barely heard the gun go off over the loud music, but when Ariana began letting off multiple shots from the 9 mm, everyone caught on to what was happening.

Hearing the bullets hit the legs of the chair and knowing she could hide behind it no longer, Joi dove into the water, Prada bag still on her shoulder. She swam underwater straight into the crowd of people who were screaming and trying to get out of the pool. Ariana kept firing, trying her best to hit Joi while she was underwater. Bullets whizzed right past Joi's body in the water, just inches from hitting her.

A woman getting out of the pool took one of Ariana's bullets to the back. Another woman was hit in the chest right next to Joi, when she came up for air. Ariana dropped the empty clip, reached in her pocket, and grabbed another one.

While she was slapping it into her gun, Joi unzipped her Prada bag under water, reached in, and grabbed the .45 ACP. She hoped that the gun would still work, as she turned down the safety latch. She brought the gun from under the water, aimed, and squeezed the trigger. The pin hit the back of the bullet and ejected a hot lead ball in Ariana's direction going a million miles per second. The bullet knocked a chunk out of the vinyl tile right above Ariana's head. The .45 roared, sending several more bullets Ariana's way.

Ariana wildly returned fire as she ran down the side of the deck toward the exit. Another one of her wild bullets hit a woman on the side of her head. Joi tried desperately to hit Ariana, knocking holes in the wall right behind every stride Ariana took toward the door.

It was pandemonium as people scattered out of the pool. Joi had to move the lifeless body floating in front of her to the side, so she could get out of the water. She climbed up on the deck, far from being done with Ariana. As everybody poured out into the lobby, so did Joi, looking for any signs of Ariana. She had spotted her trying to get on the elevator and wasted no time barking the .45 at her.

The crowd in the lobby dropped to the floor when they heard the shots.

Ariana returned fire, taking off for the staircase.

"Put the gun down," an armed off-duty police officer yelled, pointing a gun at Joi from across the lobby.

She spun around and fired several shots at him until her gun cocked to an empty chamber. She took off running through the hotel lobby for the exit door, and if it weren't for the fact that one of her bullets hit the off-duty cop in the hand, he would have taken off after her.

While sitting in the room contemplating what to do, Kemo could hear footsteps racing past his door. He grabbed his gun from the bed and cautiously proceeded to the door. He cracked it open, only to see more people running past. Danielle jumped out of the chair to join him at the door.

"Yo, what's goin' on?" Kemo asked one of the females who was running by.

"They downstairs shooting," she screamed as she continued to flee to her room down the hall.

Kemo looked up and down the hall and could see that people were getting their shit and leaving. "Get ya shit," he told Danielle, pushing her back into the room.

She scrambled around the room grabbing her things while Kemo bagged up the funny money. He walked over to the window, which had a view of the pool, and he could see a body floating in the water surrounded by blood. It looked like another body was lying on the deck, face down. He knew that it was definitely time to exit stage left, which he and Danielle quickly did.

Sanaa had walked over and grabbed a bottle of water from the cooler when she noticed the loud music in the pool area had stopped. She walked over to the window and peeked out of it. She closed her eyes and reopened them, to make sure she had really seen what she thought she'd seen. The female's body was still face down in the water and a crowd of people was gathered around the second body on the deck. She couldn't believe what she was looking at. Listening a little closer, she could hear sirens approaching the hotel.

"Come look at this," she told Sleepy, who was putting the last bit of money into the duffle bag.

"Oh shit," he said looking down at the pool. "It's time for us to go," he said as he grabbed Sanaa by the arm.

There wasn't a stutter in her step as she threw her things in a bag and headed out the door in a flash. Sleepy was right with her, toting the large bag of cash. As she walked down the hallway toward the elevator, she made a phone call to the pit boss to shut down the whole casino.

When Sanaa got onto the elevator, she hit G for the ground floor, but when it got to the seventeenth floor, the elevator stopped. The doors opened, and standing there waiting to get on was Ariana. Sanaa looked up and met her eyes. Sleepy was shocked as hell to see her standing there himself. Sanaa looked at her, then looked down at the gun in Ariana's hand.

Flashbacks of Ariana shooting up her car raced through her mind. She reached, but struggled to get the large .50-caliber out of her bag, and as she wrapped her hand around the grip of it, the elevator doors started to close. Ariana looked like she was about to shoot Sanaa, but a swift, stern look from Sleepy made her change her mind.

That didn't stop Sanaa from getting the gun out and firing several shots through the door as it closed shut. The large bullets ripped through the door, almost hitting Ariana, who got out of the way in the nick of time. The elevator filled with gunsmoke as it continued to go down. Sanaa tried to stop the elevator at the next floor, but Sleepy stopped her.

"Yo, we ain't got time for dat," he said, putting the bag of money around his shoulders. "We got to get da fuck out of here."

The elevator stopped at the lobby, but when the doors opened, they could see police coming through the front doors of the hotel. Sleepy quickly pushed the B button for the basement, stopping some of the screaming guests from trying to get on. Sanaa jumped on the phone without saying a word to Sleepy. She was trying to contact Joi, and then she thought about the two bodies in the pool. Joi not answering the phone only made things worse.

"I gotta go back up there," Sanaa said, pushing the G button, then passing Sleepy her gun.

"What you mean?" he shot back when the doors opened to the basement.

"Look, it's my party. It's either I deal with this now, or let them come to the club and start snooping around," she said, thinking about the cops. "Plus, I still gotta find Joi and get Royce from out of his room."

Sleepy couldn't argue with her. He didn't have the time to, because his window of opportunity for getting out of the building safely with the money was fading away.

"Call my phone as soon as you get a chance," he said stepping off the elevator.

Royce got off the elevator on the lobby floor where everything was still crazy. Police were everywhere, and people were still pushing their way out of the side doors. He just stood by the elevator and looked around at all the chaos. The sound of the elevator next to him reaching the floor caught his attention. When he looked over to see who was getting off, it was Sanaa.

"Damn, sis, what da fuck is going on?" Royce asked.

Sanaa couldn't even think straight enough to answer him as she headed for the swimming pool. All she could think about was if it was her girlfriend lying face down in the water. Ariana was the main source behind all this, so it was very possible that Joi could be dead. She couldn't believe that Ariana was still alive, and neither could Royce, once Sanaa told him.

"Thank God," Sanaa mumbled to herself after seeing that neither of the bodies was Joi.

What she did notice was the Prada bag floating in the water. It looked just like Joi's, but before Sanaa had the chance to fish it out of the water, the police were forcing her away from the crime scene.

Royce was still shocked that Ariana was alive, but what was even more shocking was to see Danielle leaving out of the side door with Kemo. He'd remembered Kemo's face very clearly from the robbery, and more specifically from the two bullets he put in Danielle's chest. He stood there and watched them leave out the door, but before they exited, she looked back and locked eyes with Royce. The crowd behind her pushed her out of the door before Royce could say anything.

Chapter 16

Sanaa, Joi, Royce, and Sleepy all sat in Sanaa's office trying to get some understanding about what was going on. The one thing they all could agree on was the unexpected guest crashing the party. Joi still couldn't believe that she was alive, when she had sat and watched Ariana take what she thought was her last breath. Joi couldn't even look Sleepy in his eyes, thinking that he might have known about the baby. Sleepy, on the other hand, just played it cool, opting not to even get involved in the conversation they were having about Ariana. Sanaa insisted on his word though.

"So you think you can talk to her, li'l bro, to see if we can bring this to a peaceful resolution?" Sanaa asked Sleepy, knowing that he felt some type of way about the whole situation.

"If you was her, would you wanna talk?" He looked hard at Joi when he spoke. "Left for dead by you, and then shot at by you today, you two do the math," Sleepy said, pointing at Sanaa and Joi.

"I swear, I thought she was tryin' to kill ya dad," Joi began. "You know what; I don't have to explain nothin' to nobody. I did what I did, and whenever I see Ariana I'ma blow her fuckin' head off," Joi snapped back, tired of walking on eggshells around Sleepy.

"Look, everybody just calm down," Sanaa yelled, slamming her hand on the table. "Now, Ariana is just gonna have to deal with the consequences of her actions if she so chooses to pursue Joi. And let's not forget that everybody in this room is family, and we cannot allow for an outsider to come in and break this family apart, I don't care who it is," she said to everyone, but directed her last statement to Sleepy.

Before Sanaa could get another word out, her office phone started to ring. She picked it up and slammed it right back down without answering it. Sleepy understood what she was saying, but didn't feel her last comment, so he just turned around and left the room. Nobody in the room understood his personal feelings or why he had the connection he had with Ariana. She wasn't just carrying any old baby, it was his baby, and the more he thought about it the more he wanted to kill Joi himself.

"I'ma go talk to him," Royce said, leaving out of the office behind him.

The office phone rang again. This time Sanaa pushed the speakerphone button and answered. "All In," she said, speaking into the phone.

"Yo, I been sitting here thinking about you all day," a voice spoke out.

It sounded like some perverted shit, so Sanaa was about to hang up the phone until the man continued.

"You know, you got a real nice setup moving this counterfeit money," Kemo said, looking at one of the fading bills. "You gotta be raking in a nice penny," he continued.

"Who is this?" Sanaa asked, looking at the phone in confusion.

"You gonna find out in a minute, because you're gonna give me my muthafuckin' money," Kemo threatened sternly.

Joi and Sanaa just looked at each other and shrugged. They didn't know who was on the other end of the line. "Well, how much do I owe you, sir? Maybe I can get you squared away today," Sanaa said.

"You owe me three hundred grand and I want mine in an hour," Kemo answered.

When he said the number, Sanaa knew exactly who he was. She remembered Kemo from the hotel. He was the only person who hit that night, for that kind of money anyway. One thing was for sure, Sanaa wasn't about to give up three hundred grand in real money, no matter who it was.

"Well, do you got somewhere for us to meet, or could you just come here?" Sanaa suggested.

"Yeah, stay by the phone. I'll call you back," Kemo said then hung up.

Sanaa took in a deep breath and sat back in her chair. This wasn't the type of exposure she was looking for. She knew what needed to be done the moment Kemo hung up the phone. Then the thoughts about what Royce said picked at her brain. *"You can't go around killing everybody who finds out ya little secret,"* she remembered him saying. Sanaa felt that she didn't have a choice, and Kemo wasn't the type who was going to keep the counterfeit secret all to himself. This was the type of move in the game that could keep his name in the streets with respect and envy from haters. He liked to flex, and his flexing could destroy everything. Although his moves were smart, and efficient, his mouth and ego were a detriment to his success at times.

The office phone rang again, breaking the silence in the room. Sanaa put him back on speaker. "Yeah, go ahead," she answered.

"I'll be there in an hour," Kemo said then hung the phone up again.

Sanaa looked up at the clock then back at Joi. She had one hour to come up with a plan to get rid of him without drawing any attention to the club. Joi was already ten steps ahead of Sanaa. This was what Joi did, and she was great at it.

"I'll take care of it," she said, getting up.

Sanaa didn't have any doubt whatsoever in her friend's ability, so she didn't even ask any questions nor make any suggestions. It was all on Joi.

Detective Thomas sat at his desk going over all the evidence that was recovered from the double homicide at the Loews Hotel. His plate was full for the next couple of months, because not only was he the lead investigator in the hotel shooting, he was also the lead on the alleyway murder that took place near Sanaa's club.

"Come take a look at this," Thomas told his partner as he locked in on the computer screen. "You're not gonna believe this."

Thomas pointed to the screen once Detective Boyd walked over. From all the statements they took from the guests at the hotel, several of them stuck out. Each one of them claimed that the owner of Club All In was who had hosted the party.

"It seems like every time this chick throws a party, somebody ends up dead," Detective Boyd said, looking at the screen. "Who is the owner of the club?" he asked.

"The building is owned by the same woman I got this from," Thomas said, passing him the card Sanaa gave him when he interviewed her about the alleyway murder.

"Sanaa Douglas," Boyd said looking at the card. Sanaa Douglas was the fake name she used in Philly. She wasn't ready to divulge her real name, given her lifestyle. "I think we should have a little talk with Ms. Douglas," Detective Boyd suggested, passing the card back to Thomas.

They both grabbed their things and were headed out of the office until Thomas's desk phone started to ring. He answered it, but quickly had to pull the receiver away from his ear because of all the yelling coming from the other end. Detective Boyd looked on while Thomas took down some information before hanging up the phone.

"We gotta make a quick stop before we see Ms. Douglas," Detective Thomas said with an excited look on his face. "I think things just got a little more interesting." He smiled, leading the way out of the office.

Ariana stood by the window and watched as Sleepy pulled into the Days Inn motel parking lot. It was always a sense of relief when he came around, even during the not-so-good times. Ariana had already watched the news and found out that Joi was still alive. She was hoping that one of the two bodies was Joi, but the news anchor announced the victims' identities and neither was her target.

She opened the door and stood to the side, putting her head down from the shame she felt for missing her target and killing two innocent people. Sleepy, on the other hand, didn't care two shits about those women and was only concerned about Ariana's well-being. He showed that with his actions.

"Are you all right?" he asked Ariana, lifting her chin up with his index finger.

She nodded her head yes, closed the door, and walked over to the bed. Sleepy couldn't help but to notice the variety of handguns sitting on the bed with extra ammo to go with it. She even had a vest and a silencer. Right after the shooting at the hotel, Ariana made it to the meeting with the gun dealer that she'd rescheduled. They had everything she needed and then some.

"That's a lot of guns." He laughed and walked over to the bed.

"Yeah, I had to get rid of yours, and now that Joi knows I'm still alive, I expect for it to be a war." Ariana wasn't stupid. She knew exactly the kind of chick she was dealing with, and knew that it was going to take a lot to accomplish what she needed to get done.

"Oh, I got you this," she said, grabbing a P.40-cal from the bed, cocking it back and passing it to him.

Sleepy grabbed the gun and smiled. He wasn't smiling at the gift, but rather at Ariana, who looked so beautiful to him. The connection between them was electrifying. She looked up at him and couldn't resist being submissive. He grabbed the back of her neck and pulled her in, pressing his lips against hers ever so gently. Ariana melted like warm butter in his arms. His kisses were mesmerizing, and they put Ariana in a trance. This had been the first time they'd kissed in almost a year, aside from the time he kissed her graze wound back at the hotel. She needed this bad and wanted nothing more than to feel Sleepy inside of her. The aggressive pursuit of Sleepy's tongue made it clear where this was going. Before Sleepy knew it, he had been pushed back onto the bed and Ariana was climbing on top of him while pulling off her tank top.

Good thing Olivia had decided to get a separate room.

***

Detective Thomas and Detective Boyd sat in the executive office of the Loews Hotel in awe at what they were hearing from the regional manager of the Loews chain. He was explaining that a large deposit to Bank of America was rejected after the money was discovered to be high-grade counterfeit. They had confiscated the bills, turned them in to the FBI, and fined the Loews chain.

The detectives couldn't believe it, but what was more shocking was that the hotel manager, Mr. Bosworth, still had some of the counterfeit money. In fact, he had most of the $10,000 Sanaa had given him for letting her throw the party. When Detective Thomas heard that, he demanded to see the money.

When Bosworth pulled the money out and set it on the desk in front of the detectives, Thomas took some of the bills and examined them. So did Detective Boyd.

"So you said the owner of Club All In is who paid you with this?" Detective Thomas asked.

"Yes, that is correct," he answered.

Detective Thomas looked over at his partner and passed him the money. Sanaa's name was coming up way too often for her to be clean. Then it hit him. He remembered that the guy who was found murdered in the alleyway had money in his pocket, which was why they had ruled out robbery as the motive. Thomas got on the phone with the evidence room and had them pull the money and check it for counterfeit. It didn't take long for them to call him back and confirm.

Detective Thomas got out of the chair. It was definitely time for them to have a talk with Sanaa. They had to be careful though. A drunken hotel manager who was trying to keep his job could never be credible enough alone to place the counterfeit money in Sanaa's hand. They needed something more concrete.

"Oh, and what happened to the surveillance footage I asked you for?" Detective Thomas asked.

The regional manager just looked over at Mr. Bosworth. "I turned off the video feed of the whole east wing and the swimming pool area, elevators included," Bosworth said, putting his head down. Thomas just looked at him and shook his head in disgust before leaving the office.

Kemo and Danielle parked right in front of the club, along with two more of his boys in a separate car right behind them. Danielle stayed in the vehicle, while Kemo and one of the two men in the second car headed for the front door. Sanaa stood at the entrance, unlocking it and allowing the two men in. Before she locked the door back up, she quickly scanned the outside to see who else was with them. Sanaa was well aware that there was no way he would agree to meet on her turf unless he had adequate backup.

The bar area was empty, but Yellow and Joi were definitely in the building. Kemo was on point though, and so was his boy, who was strapped. All Kemo wanted to do was come and pick up his money with no further incident. Violence wasn't his first choice, but if he had to, he would surely end with it.

Sanaa walked around to the back of the bar and grabbed a bottle of vodka from off the top shelf. "So how do I know you're not gonna tell anybody else about the money?" Sanaa asked as she reached under the counter and grabbed three shot glasses.

"I'm cool with the drink," he told Sanaa before she could pour the shot. "And if you want some insurance that I'ma keep ya little secret between us, you need to be trying to add an extra hundred grand to what you already owe me," Kemo demanded.

Sanaa took his demands and his refusal of the drink as an insult, but kept her cool. She poured the vodka in all three shot glasses anyway, filling them to the rim.

Kemo and his boy just stood there waiting for a reply to his demands, but it never came. Instead, a red dot appearing on his partner's head caught Kemo's attention. He followed the trail of the beam all the way to the second-floor deck where his eyes landed on Yellow, who was holding a 30-30 rifle like he was a professional hunter. Kemo's boy also followed a beam that was on Kemo's chest across the dance floor. He went to reach for his gun, but the sound of a hammer being cocked back made him think twice about it. They both looked back over at Sanaa, who was holding a large .44 Magnum with both hands, aiming it right at them.

"You must not know who I am," Kemo said arrogantly. "You think we here by ourselves to pick up three hundred grand?"

"Naw, I know you're not here alone," Sanaa said walking from around the bar as she kept them at gunpoint. "You did exactly what I thought you would do," she continued, walking over to Kemo and patting him down.

She took the gun he had on his waist, then turned around and stripped the weapon off of his partner. Joi came from behind the jukebox, keeping the men at gunpoint, while Yellow made his way down the stairs, also keeping the beam on the men. Kemo was hot under the collar about this, but not to the point where he was about to try something stupid.

"They got two cars out front," Sanaa informed them, pulling the zip ties from her back pocket.

"You know you're gonna have to kill me," Kemo threatened.

Yellow walked up from behind him and hit Kemo on the back of his head with the butt of the rifle. Kemo dropped to his knee as he bit down on his bottom lip in pain. Kemo's boy didn't give Yellow the chance to hit him. He opted to take a knee on his own. He still got kicked to the ground, along with Kemo, before Joi tied their hands behind their backs.

"I plan on doing just that," Sanaa said, pulling out her cell phone.

Seeing that this wasn't turning out in his favor, Kemo made a last chance attempt to get Danielle's attention. He started to yell at the top of his lungs, but only got about two seconds of yelling before Yellow kicked him dead in the mouth. One of his front teeth shot straight down his throat.

"911," the operator said into the other end of Sanaa's phone.

"Yes, hi. I'm calling because there are two strange looking cars outside of my establishment," Sanaa told the operator. "It was just a murder in the alleyway behind me a few days ago and I'm just a little concerned," she finished, and then gave the operator the description of the two cars Kemo came in.

Joi and Yellow lifted the two men to their feet and forced them down the steps, through the casino, and out the back door. Before they knew it, Kemo and his sidekick were being tossed through the slide door of a stolen minivan parked in the alley. Yellow had switched his rifle to a handgun and jumped into the back of the van with the men. Joi looked up and down the alley to make sure she wasn't seen by anyone, before she got into the driver side and pulled off.

Sanaa stood at the front door of the club, watching and waiting for the police to pull up, and they did, in a matter of minutes. Two police cars pulled up right behind the car that was parked behind Danielle. As they got out of the police cruisers and approached the lone driver, Danielle took that opportunity to pull off from the scene. She couldn't afford for the police to start snooping around in her car, knowing that the three hundred grand in counterfeit money was sitting in the back seat, along with two handguns under the driver and passenger seats.

As Sanaa looked on as the cops harassed Kemo's boy, she was startled by two detectives popping up at the door. Detective Thomas flashed his badge through the window and identified himself for the record. Sanaa hesitated for a second, not knowing if Yellow and Joi had left yet. She stalled them, putting up a finger, as if she had to go and get the keys for the door. She ran back to her office and looked out the window to make sure the van wasn't still in the alley.

Danielle figured she'd just go around the block and allow the cops to leave on their own, but when she bent the corner, she watched as the officer put the handcuffs on Kemo's boy. Another cop was holding a gun in the air by the butt, which they got out of the car. Danielle didn't even think about slowing down as she passed by. When she passed by the club, she looked over at the front door to see if Kemo was trying to get out, but she noticed the two well-dressed men standing at the front doors of the club. Once she saw that one of them had a badge on his waist, her mind was fully made up. Kemo was on his own.

Sanaa ran back to the front door, keys in her hand. She opened the door and allowed the two detectives inside. "Can I get you guys something to drink?" she offered, trying to show some hospitality.

"Ms. Douglas, we need to have a talk," Detective Thomas said with a serious face, ignoring Sanaa's offer. "You just threw a party at the Loews Hotel the other day, is that correct?"

Sanaa could tell by the way he was asked his question that he already knew the answer to it. That's how it was most of the time with detectives, and Sanaa was well versed in dealing with cops like this, coming from the fast city of Philly.

"Yeah, I had a party there, and it's tragic what happened to those women," Sanaa sympathized. "I'm still thinking about whether I should file a law suit against the hotel for not allowing me to have armed security there," she explained, trying to put the blame on the hotel for what happened.

"Well, why didn't you stick around to give a statement?" Detective Boyd cut in.

"Well, Detectives, when bullets get to flying, my life becomes number one priority. I got the hell out of the building, like everyone else."

"So did you see anything or know something that can help us in the investigation?" Detective Thomas asked.

"No, just like I said, once I heard it was a shooting in the pool area, I exited just like everybody else."

"Ms. Douglas, you paid for this party in cash, right?" Thomas asked, digging into his back pocket.

"Yeah, why?" Sanaa shot back with a curious look on her face. "I run a club. I always use cash."

"Does this look familiar?" Thomas asked, holding up one of the ink-faded bills.

"Should it?" Sanaa asked with one eyebrow up.

"Yeah, hotel management said that you paid for the rooms with this money. The whole balance, including a little pocket money for Mr. Bosworth," Thomas said.

Sanaa could see where this interview was going, having noticed the change in the detectives' demeanor and line of questioning. This was easily turning into an interrogation, but she kept her cool. She knew that if you just let the police ask questions, eventually they would start to divulge the real reason why they were there. Sanaa wanted to see just how much they knew, and what evidence they had thus far, so she played along.

"Did you ever catch the person who killed that man in the alleyway?" she asked, taking a seat on the barstool.

"As a matter of fact, I found—"

Detective Boyd tapped Thomas before he could say another word. He could see that the detective was about to give up too much information about the case to a possible suspect. Detective Thomas quickly got a hold of himself, seeing that Sanaa was starting to get under his collar. The last thing he wanted to do was blow either one of the cases.

"Do you own a gun, Ms. Douglas?" Thomas said with a bit of aggression behind his question.

"Do I need a lawyer?" Sanaa asked. She was beginning to get irritated with all the questions.

"Do you?" Detective Boyd asked.

Sanaa looked at both of the detectives. This interview was over in her eyes, and there was only one way to get them out of her sight that she was aware of.

"I'm not answering any more questions without my lawyer present," Sanaa requested with a slick grin on her face. "Now, if you're not gonna arrest me for anything, I'm going to have to ask you to leave," she said getting up from the stool and walking to the door.

Detective Thomas wished he had something to arrest her for, because it looked like Sanaa was taunting them a little bit with her slick choice of words. But the detectives knew that this line of questioning was now over. She had requested a lawyer, and once a suspect requested an attorney during an interview or an interrogation, all questioning had to stop.

As the detectives were about to leave, Detective Boyd looked down at the floor in frustration. When he did, he noticed a small blood stain in the wood floor. He looked at Thomas, who looked down to what had his partner's attention and noticed the same thing. It was the blood from Kemo's mouth when Yellow kicked his tooth out. Sanaa noticed what they were looking at and tried to rush them. Even if it was blood, that alone wasn't enough for them to claim probable cause and get a warrant. They needed more, so they decided to give Sanaa the first round, but both felt that it wouldn't be long before they would have enough to get a warrant.

Yellow had his eyes glued to the rearview mirror at a cop car that had just pulled in behind the van.

Kemo and his boy were sitting up in the rear seat with their hands still tied behind their backs. Yellow was in the seat right behind them with his gun pressed against the back of their chair. His heart was racing, and every case scenario ran through his head of how this was going to end if the red and blue lights began flashing.

"Just be easy," Yellow told Joi as he peeked out of the back window.

Kemo looked in the rearview mirror himself and saw the patrol car behind them. He nudged his boy with his leg, making him aware of what was going on. He too looked into the mirror and saw the cop car. This was the only chance Kemo had to get out of this situation alive, and he knew it. He'd be damned if he wasn't going to take advantage of the situation. His boy, Bread, felt the same way.

"Don't do nothing stupid," Yellow threatened the two.

A red light brought the van to a stop, trapped behind a couple of cars. *It's now or never,* Kemo thought as he noticed the cop car had its turn signal on. He swung his legs around, pressed his back against Bread, and kicked the side window. It didn't break the first time, so he kept kicking. Yellow yelled at him, and even punched him in his jaw, but that didn't stop Kemo. He kicked until his feet went clear through the window. The shattered glass blasted out of the frame and onto the car next to them.

All the commotion got the attention of the police officer, who immediately turned on his lights. When the officer got out of the car, he drew his weapon and cautiously advanced toward the minivan.

Trapped, Joi stepped on the gas, crashing into the car in front of her. She kept pressing on the accelerator, trying to move the vehicles out of her way.

"Turn the fuckin' car off," the officer yelled. "Turn the fuckin' car off," he screamed again.

In an instant, the side door of the van opened and out jumped Yellow. He hit the ground running.

Kemo managed to squeeze out of his restraints. He reached up and wrapped his arm around Joi's neck, right before she popped opened her door and was about to take off. She tried to reach for the gun under her lap, but it fell to the floor. Kemo had a tight grip around her neck and was squeezing so hard she thought she was about to pass out.

"Get ya hands in the air," the officer continued to yell, walking up to the driver side of the car.

Seeing that the cop was itching to pull the trigger, Kemo let go of Joi and threw his hands up. Joi put her hands on the steering wheel, trying to catch her breath.

Two other cop cars pulled up within minutes to assist the first officer. "Gun," one of the officers yelled when he opened the slide door and saw a gun sitting right by Kemo's feet.

During the struggle, Joi had kicked the gun from her feet, all the way under her chair to the back where

Kemo was. He hadn't even noticed what she'd done, being so engaged with trying to break her neck. That one move had put her in a better position. In order to find out whose gun it was, everyone was going to have to go down to the police station. And that's just what happened, all except Yellow, who was out of sight and halfway back to the club.

Ariana woke up from a quick nap to feel something rubbing against the bullet wound on her stomach. She reached for it and grabbed a hold of Sleepy's hand.

"It's okay, it's me," Sleepy said in a low, calm voice, into her ears as he lay behind her.

This was something personal for Ariana, and for a moment, she felt violated. Until now, she had been the only one who rubbed the wound or even touched it for that matter. But it was something in Sleepy's tone that told her that she was safe. She kind of felt like he had just as much right to touch it as she did; he too shared the loss of their baby. She put her hand on top of his and guided Sleepy's finger to the rhythm she used to rub it.

"I think about her every day," Ariana confessed, leaning back against his body. "She would have been a couple of months right now," she said, almost bringing herself to tears.

"And what makes you think it was going to be a girl?" Sleepy joked. "She could have been a he." He chuckled, play biting her neck, trying to make Ariana laugh.

"Yeah, you right." She smiled. "As long as we had a healthy baby, I would have been cool, you know."

"Well, maybe after everything is all said and done, we can try again," Sleepy suggested.

It got quiet in the room. Ariana wasn't even sure if she could have kids after all the damage the bullet did to the inside of her stomach. It wasn't just that, but it was also a mental thing. Ariana had trouble dealing with not knowing whether she was in fact ready to have another baby. She felt like she couldn't even protect the first one, so how was she going to be there for another one? Then there was her lifestyle. She knew beyond a shadow of doubt that along with being a mother came responsibilities. The kind of responsibilities that would force her to put down her guns and become civilized, something she wasn't sure she was ready to do.

"Listen, Ariana, I love you," he said, turning her over to face him. "And I know things look kind of crazy right now, but you gotta believe me when I tell you that everything is goin' to be all right. I swear on my life that I'm going to protect you and be here for you until I take my last breath," he said with sincerity in his eyes.

"I love you too, Sleepy, but what's gonna happen after I kill Joi? What's gonna happen then?" she asked.

Ariana couldn't help but to think about their future. There were a lot of things Sleepy wasn't taking into consideration or he just refused to acknowledge. It was a fact that one of two things was going to happen, and that was either Ariana was going to kill Joi or Joi was going to kill Ariana. Either way, somebody had to die, and if it was Joi, Sanaa was never going to rest until she got revenge. And that was just one part. What would happen if Sleepy somehow found out that she had murdered his father? Ariana was now having regrets for shooting Balil; she wasn't ready to lose Sleepy again.

"From now on, I don't want you to worry about Joi. I'ma take care of that myself," he told Ariana. "After that, we're gone. We can start a life somewhere out of the country for all I care," he said with all seriousness.

Ariana could tell that he was serious and it brought her a sense of security. She felt calm and relaxed and loved the idea of running off with him. That was exactly what she needed to build her confidence to one day start a family. If there was anybody she could spend the rest of her life with, it was Sleepy. She just had to make sure he was going to go through with killing Joi, because if he didn't, she sure as hell would.

Chapter 17

Kemo and Bread sat in the holding cell waiting to be booked. Kemo was facing gun charges and Bread was being charged with joy-riding in a stolen vehicle. Joi was in a separate cell, waiting to be charged with the stolen car and the gun that could have easily been hers also. But at this point, the officers were just trying to sort things out.

No help was coming from any of the accused, because nobody was doing any talking. Kemo was an OG and he wasn't doing any telling, even if he was kidnapped and almost murdered. Bread just rode with Kemo on whatever he was doing, despite the fact that he was the only one in the car with restraints on. The detectives who interrogated everyone had a feeling of what was going on, but they couldn't get a confession. It was frustrating for the detectives, because they had no idea what to charge everybody with that would stick in a court of law.

The floor officer pulled Kemo out of the cell so that he could be fingerprinted and photographed. The fingerprinting station was right by the female holding tank where Joi sat looking through the thick Plexiglas. Kemo looked over and gave Joi a sinister smile that said, "I'ma kill you!"

Joi gave him the same grin in return, but hers said, "I almost already killed you!"

The female officer tapping on Joi's window brought her out of her stare. She pulled Joi out to be processed and fingerprinted, unaware that Kemo had just tried to strangle her. It really didn't matter though, Kemo definitely wasn't going to do anything to her while they were in the police station anyway. At this point, all he wanted to do was see the judge so that he could get bail and get out before Joi.

"Mr. Turner, could you step over here?" The officer motioned Kemo to the photo area.

Another officer led Joi over to the fingerprinting station, and when she looked down, she noticed that the previous officer had left Kemo's personal information on the table. She hurried up and tried to read as much as she could, but was cut short when the officer remembered his paperwork and came back to get it. Joi only got as far as knowing his first and last name, and his date of birth. His birthday was what stood out, which made him forty-six years old. He didn't look more than thirty-five. He was in excellent shape, and that was probably because he had done almost half of his life in prison, eating healthy and exercising regularly.

"Brandon Turner," Joi mumbled to herself, making sure she didn't forget his name.

She looked over and saw Kemo taking off his shirt so that the officer could take pictures of his tattoos. He looked like an action figure the way his body was ripped. She could see every bit of the ten years he had done in a state penitentiary around weights.

Above all things, Joi did get a good look at a couple of his tattoos before he put his shirt back on. He had a picture of the Liberty Bell in the center of his stomach with the numbers 215 over top of it. He had another tattoo with the name ANGEL written across his chest. All this was documented into Joi's memory, because these were the very things she was going to use in order to find and kill Kemo the day she got out of the police station.

Yellow called Sanaa ahead of time to tell her to meet him at the back door of the casino. She called Royce, sensing that something had gone wrong, and she was unable to get a hold of Sleepy. When Yellow finally walked up, Sanaa looked at how tired and dusty he was. He walked right into the casino, stepped behind the bar, and grabbed a bottle of Christian Brothers off the shelf. Sanaa and Royce just took a seat at the bar and waited for him to get his thoughts together.

"Ya girl is locked up," he said after taking a swig out of the bottle.

"What?" Sanaa yelled in shock. "What da fuck happened?" she asked, grabbing the bottle out of his hand.

"A cop pulled up behind us and ya boy made a move," he told her.

Sanaa put her head down into her hands and shook her head. She instantly felt responsible, and it weighed heavily on her. It felt like everything was starting to go south, and the end result wasn't looking good for anybody. Sanaa jumped out of the stool and headed straight for her office. Royce and Yellow followed, Yellow explaining everything that happened before he jumped out of the car and ran.

"So now what?" Royce asked Sanaa.

"So now I'ma go bail her out," she said, opening her safe against the wall and taking a few stacks of money out.

"You don't know what she's locked up for."

"It doesn't matter what she's booked on, if she get a bail, I'ma be standing right there wit' the money," she said, grabbing her pocketbook and leaving the office.

As they were walking out of the club, Royce's phone began to ring. He looked down at it and completely stopped moving, seeing that it was Krystol calling. His heart raced, knowing that she had to be at home in order to call from her cell phone.

Sanaa stopped at the door and looked back. She smiled at the excitement on his face when he answered.

"Yeah, what's up," Royce answered, slowly walking back over to the bar and taking a seat on the stool.

"Hey. I just wanted you to know that I brought Raven by. I know you wanna see her, and I think that me and you should talk," she told Royce in a low, soft, and sweet voice.

Just hearing her voice meant a lot to him. He had been worried sick about Krystol and the baby, especially not having the slightest idea where they had gone.

"Yeah, I'll be there in about an hour," he told her, hanging up the phone and heading to the door.

Sanaa looked at him, wanting to know if she and the baby were all right. She knew how important family was, and would never stand in Royce's way when it came down to his.

"You go get ya family. I'll be fine," she told Royce, giving him a hug. "What can go wrong at the police station?" She laughed. "I'll stop by when I'm on my way home."

Royce took off running to his car. He wanted to see Krystol and his baby girl so bad, and if Krystol thought they were going to be leaving again, he had another thing planned for her.

Detective Thomas needed to make a connection between Sanaa, the money, and the murders. He stared at the screen of his computer, waiting for the results of his local and federal search of Sanaa, and her employees. He knew she had something to do with the funny money, but they had been smart enough to keep the cash circulating with the legit cash. They also let it flow with the patrons; that way, he couldn't say definitively it was connected to them or the business. He needed more, a witness or something else to give him the break he needed for that damn warrant.

When the computer stopped, Thomas damn near broke his neck sitting up in his chair. He read the contents of the federal case involving one Sanaa Anderson, and although the last name didn't match, this woman had also owned a night club where a murder had occurred. The case was from out of Atlanta, and although it was a long shot, he decided to pick up the phone and call the case agent who was over the investigation, Special Agent Razor. He answered almost immediately. Thomas began breaking down everything to him about what was going on in Philly.

"Hey, Dave," Detective Thomas yelled out, calling Detective Boyd. "Come here for a sec, buddy," he said picking up his phone. "Take a look at this," he told Boyd, pointing at the screen.

"Well, do you have a picture of her?" Detective Thomas asked Special Agent Razor, who was on the phone explaining the case.

"The case pictures that I took were lost in evidence. They really weren't that good anyway," Razor explained.

"Well from the way you've described her, I think we might be dealing with the same girl," Detective Thomas said.

This wasn't the first time Agent Razor had gotten one of these phone calls. Most of the time they just ran him into a dead end, having him start back over from scratch. He'd never gotten any word that she had traveled up North, and as far as he knew, she was still in Atlanta.

"This is what you do. Take a few pictures of the woman you believe is Sanaa, and send them to me. I'd know her if I seen her. That would possibly save me a flight to Philly," Agent Razor suggested.

This song seemed all too familiar to Thomas. Everything that he'd done thus far in the investigation hadn't come easy, especially trying to get a warrant from the judge. It was frustrating for Detective Thomas, but if the Feds wanted to see some pictures of Sanaa, then that wasn't going to be a problem at all.

He looked at Detective Boyd after hanging up the phone with Agent Razor. Boyd could see it in his eyes and knew they were in for a long night.

"You up for a photo shoot?" Detective Thomas asked his partner.

"Yeah, sure, rookie." Boyd chuckled, leading the way out of the office.

Chapter 18

Sanaa stood outside the police station waiting for Joi after paying the $5,000 bail that was set in her case. She was mindful to watch where the cameras were positioned; although she was confident that she was cool, she didn't want to take any unnecessary chances that some overzealous detective might have seen her picture on the Feds' wanted list. She needed to get Joi, and get the hell out. This was the first time Joi had been arrested for anything, and due to the bizarre circumstances and the lack of cooperation, the judge really didn't know what else to do but give a lowball bail. The only charge that was likely to stick anyway would be the stolen vehicle charge.

Sanaa had a lot of time to sit outside in front of the building and think about her next move. The sound of a familiar voice snapped her out of her daze. The bass in it sent chills down her spine, and if she wasn't standing in front of a police station, she knew that this would have probably been the last voice she heard.

"Was it worth it?" Kemo said, standing next to Sanaa by the bench.

She jumped up, scared out of her mind, but also ready to react. Sanaa backed up, reached into her Louis Vuitton bag, and grabbed her .380. It didn't matter where she went; she always had a gun on her.

Kemo looked at her and just chuckled, unfazed by Sanaa reaching. He knew she was too smart to make a scene out in front of the station where there were cameras everywhere.

"You should have just left it alone and got rid of it, just like I had to," Sanaa said, keeping her hand on the gun in her bag.

"Yeah, well, that's three hundred grand, and if you don't know who I am by now, I'ma be the first one to tell you that I'm not the right one to be fuckin' wit'," he said as he looked back and forth for his ride to pull up.

"Let's make a deal," Sanaa began. "I'll give you—"

"Bitch, you got me fucked up," Kemo snapped, cutting her off. "You think I wanna deal right now?" he said, lowering his voice as the police officers passed by, going into the station. "You tried to kill me, ho. It ain't no fuckin' deals. I'll see you in traffic," he ended, walking out to the pavement where his ride had pulled up.

Sanaa clutched the gun a little tighter and walked out to the pavement behind him. She took the safety off and took a good look around to see in anybody was watching her.

Danielle looked from the driver's side as Sanaa was getting closer with her hand still in her bag. The concern in Danielle's eyes convinced Kemo to turn around and see what she was looking at. When he did, Sanaa stood about ten feet away from him with an intense look in her eyes.

"Bitch, pull the trigger," Kemo dared, standing there like he was made of steel. "'Cause this is the last chance you eva gonna have to kill me," he taunted.

They both stood there for a moment staring at each other in silence. Sanaa was so zoned out she didn't even notice the few police officers behind her going into the station. She was seriously considering getting it done and over with right there, but a very important thought entered her head at the right time. She really wasn't ready to go to jail. She just nodded her head with a nasty grin on her face, and then backed up slowly.

"I thought so," Kemo teased, opening up the passenger side door and getting into the car.

Just then, Bread walked out of the station, giving Sanaa the ugly face as he passed by her and jumped into the back seat of the car. He made a gun gesture with his hand and pointed it at Sanaa through the window before Danielle pulled off.

"How long have you been out here?" Joi asked as she walked out the front doors of the police station.

Sanaa almost didn't hear Joi. She was focused on Kemo's car pulling into the street. She wanted to see which way they went, so that she could go the opposite. It wasn't because she was scared; she just knew she wasn't really prepared for a gun battle to erupt on the streets. A .380 wouldn't have gotten her far in a war and she knew it. She had to be smart, and being smart meant that she didn't have time to make stupid emotional mistakes.

It took Joi and Sanaa almost two hours to get home, a ride that would've normally taken no more than thirty minutes from where the police station was located. The extra hour and ten minutes came from Joi taking a number of routes in order to shake anybody who may had been following them, specifically Kemo and his crew.

"So what now?" Bread asked Kemo, who was sitting at the head of the fifteen-foot-long table in one of Kemo's trap houses. "We gotta kill dis bitch tonight," he suggested, pacing back and forth with a gun in his hand.

Kemo felt his pain, but he also had other plans on how and when he was going to kill Sanaa and her people. It wasn't something that had to happen right away, and for somebody like Kemo, who was much more experienced in the game, he knew that he would be the number one suspect on the police list, since he was just caught by the police with his arms around Joi's neck.

"We gotta wait a couple days," Kemo said, twirling two Baoding balls in his hand. "She just tried to kill us and failed, so you know she's gonna be on point right now. We not gon' make this shit no harder than what it has to be," he calmly said.

"Well what about the money?" Danielle added, hoping nobody had forgotten about that. It was her only reason for still being around, and if he wasn't going after it, there was no need for her to stay.

"Aaahhh, I see somebody is thinking." Kemo applauded, giving Danielle a wink of the eye. "Now how can I get my money if she's dead?" he asked hypothetically.

That was something Bread hadn't thought about, and that was because Bread didn't have the same financial problems Kemo had. Bread was the type who didn't even care about money that much. His only talent was pulling a trigger, and truth be told, he wasn't really good at that.

"So how do you plan on getting your money?" Bread asked with a doubtful look on his face.

Kemo was starting to take Bread's words and actions a little personal. It seemed like he was losing respect for Kemo, but Kemo was one who knew how to regain power and control.

"What, you forgot who da fuck you was talking to?" Kemo snapped back, rising from his chair with anger written all over his face. "You need to calm da fuck down."

"Dat bitch was about to kill me. How else am I supposed to feel?" he yelled with his eyes filling up with tears. "She was going to kill you too, and all y'all are worried about is some damn money," he snapped, slamming the barrel of the gun onto the table.

Although Bread's message was raw and a bit disrespectful, Kemo could understand how he felt. He too thought about the ride in the van with his hands tied behind his back, waiting to be taken somewhere and murdered. He understood all of that, but at the same time, he could see an opportunity to gain financially, and he could have done that either with or without Bread. Setting aside his pride, he decided to have Bread riding out with him on this one.

"Look, we wait a day or two, take da bitch for everything she got then put a bullet in the front of her head," Kemo demanded, giving Bread a stern look. "I need you on this one," he confessed, getting Bread's attention.

Kemo never needed anybody for anything, and to hear this come from out of his mouth made the difference in Bread's eyes. He placed the gun down on the table, pulled out the chair and took a seat. Kemo eventually took a seat too and they all just sat there in silence for a moment.

"All right, and tell me what you got planned," Bread said in a low and submissive voice.

"It's gonna go like dis . . ."

Joi and Sanaa were on their way to the club to meet with Boo to discuss some business. The expressway wasn't that crowded, so it wasn't hard spotting the patrol car creeping up a half mile back. Joi discreetly put her seat belt on and advised Sanaa to do the same. The speed limit was sixty-five miles per hour and Joi had slowed her down to sixty-eight miles per hour from doing seventy-five miles per hour. All the precautions were being taken, because guns and a large amount of money were in the car. Not to mention the fact that she and Sanaa both had bulletproof vests on.

"So you think Boo is going to go for it?" Joi asked, trying to make conversation while keeping her eyes on the rearview.

"I don't see why not. Two million in real cash for ten million in counterfeit money is a good deal."

"A good deal for what? We barely moved a million in a week, and now you're talking about ten million. What's goin' on, Sanaa?" Joi asked.

Sanaa just sat there looking out of the window at cars passing by. "We'll talk about it later on," Sanaa said, wanting to wait until Sleepy and Royce were around.

Before Joi could even attempt to get Sanaa to talk, the patrol car had pulled up within a couple cars back. It switched lanes a few times and ended up right behind Joi. She took in a deep breath then exhaled. Sanaa was also attentive to what was going on, looking at the cruiser through her mirror. When the police lights started flashing, both of their hearts dropped.

"What you wanna do?" Joi asked as she continued to watch the blue lights.

Whatever Sanaa wanted to happen would have been done by Joi. If she wanted to go on a high-speed chase, it would have gone down. Stop and have a shootout, it would have gone down. That's how much love she had for her friend and sister.

"Pull over," Sanaa instructed, taking her chances with the possibility of Joi just getting a ticket.

Joi did as she was told, pulling over to the shoulder of the highway. The cop sat behind them for a moment before exiting his vehicle. He walked up slowly to the driver side door.

Joi automatically reached for the sun visor to grab her registration and her license. She rolled her window down to pass it to the cop before he could ask for it, but was surprised by his command.

"Step out of the car, ma'am," the officer demanded in a relaxed tone.

Joi looked at Sanaa then reached for the compact .45 automatic inside the center console.

Sanaa stopped her hand before she got it open. She nodded for her to just get out of the car, which she did.

"What's goin' on, Officer?" Joi asked, looking up and down the highway for a good direction to run.

"You know, the last time I saw you, you had a pair of arms wrapped around ya neck," the officer said.

Joi looked at him closely and then remembered that it was the cop who arrested her and Kemo. He looked different and younger, and a lot cuter than before.

"Yeah, you look different," Joi shot back.

"Yeah, all cops look different when we're putting handcuffs on you," he joked, managing to get a chuckle out of Joi. "So do you normally let ya boy-friend choke you out and don't press charges on him? You know those kind of relationships could get out of hand," he said with some concern.

"That's not my boyfriend, and don't you think you're asking me the wrong questions?" Joi said with a flirtatious smile.

"You'd rather me ask you about the bulletproof vest you got on or the possibility of you having a gun in the car wit' you?" he replied, letting her know that he really wasn't trying to be a dick.

"So what do you want, Officer Waters?" she said, looking at the name on his shirt.

"Honestly?"

"Yeah, honestly," Joi said.

Waters didn't know how to explain it. He'd never felt this attracted to a woman before, let alone one that he had arrested. But there was something about Joi that grabbed his attention and he didn't know why.

"When I saw that guy with his arm around ya neck, I thought, 'he must be crazy.' I don't think someone as beautiful as you should be subjected to something like that."

This was the first time anybody had complimented Joi in this way in a long time. She was so used to having a stern, warlike expression that most men didn't approach her. It made her blush as if she was a teenager again.

Waters knew that he was getting beyond himself going this far with Joi, but sometimes the heart makes people do some strange things.

"So what, I'm supposed to ride off wit' you into the sunset, like this some type of fairy tale?" Joi asked, looking off down the highway.

"No." He laughed. "I just want to take you out one time. After that, if you don't ever want to see me again, that would be the end of it."

"I don't know about dat," she answered, not too sure about going out with a cop.

"Well listen, if you change ya mind, call me," Waters said, taking out a pen and writing his number down.

Joi took it then got back into her car. She wasn't sure if she would ever use it, but just in case, she stuck the phone number into her pocket. She just might have some use for it in the future. Anything could happen, and having a cop on standby could come in handy.

Raven drooled into Royce's mouth as he lay on the bed, lifting her up and down into the air. He was so happy to have his family back that he hadn't even said much to Krystol about her disappearing act. He knew that once he opened that situation, he and Krystol would be pulling an all-nighter. They both had a lot they needed to get off their chests.

Royce glanced over at Krystol through the corner
of his eye. She was just as beautiful as the day
he met her. Although she had put on a few pounds
since then, she was still just as sexy to him. He laid
Raven down as he began to feel his dick harden at the
thought of the love of his life. Well, that and the fact
that the only sex he had gotten since she left was the
head Danielle had blessed him with nearly a week
ago.

A sudden knock at the door caught both Krystol's
and Royce's attention. Not moving off the bed, Royce
nodded for Krystol to answer it. When she did, she
couldn't believe who was standing in front of her
face. It was Danielle, looking as beautiful as ever.
Krystol held the door, and stared at Danielle; she
thought she was looking at a ghost. Something inside
her told her that if she wasn't a ghost, she should be,
and the nerve of her to knock on her door after all
this time caused Krystol to see red. She focused on
her breathing; she was gripping the door so hard
that her hand began to cramp. She thought about the
gun she had in the foyer closet, she thought about
slamming the door, her mind was racing, and she
couldn't focus.

Danielle smiled at Krystol. She studied her for
a moment, and then slowly stepped back allowing
Danielle entry into her home. Her keys lay on the
table with Mace on the keychain, and she quickly
grabbed them. Something about Danielle made the
hairs on her arms stand up. She cursed to herself
as she looked at the door of the closet. The gun was

locked away, this bitch was stepping into her home, and she was going to make sure that if one of them had to leave in something flashing she would be the one leaving out feet first.

"You must be Krystol," Danielle said, walking into the living room.

She didn't even notice Krystol walking behind her with a can of mace in her hand. She had already planned in her head that she was going to Mace Danielle, and then beat the dog shit out of her. Royce coming down the steps broke her out of her concentration, but Danielle turned around and caught her trying to ease the spray back into her pocket. Krystol carried Mace and a switch blade with her when she went jogging. They were small, compact, and easier to carry than a gun. If she were ever to get in a confrontation and someone took them away from her to use against her, she had a better chance of surviving the attack, versus a gun ending everything. She was cautious, and a good judge of people. This bitch standing in her house right now was bringing some trouble.

Danielle looked at Royce as if to say, "You better get dis bitch before I shoot her."

Royce tried to give Krystol the baby to cool her down, but she declined, wanting her hands to be completely free to use them. Royce just held Raven, hoping that the situation wouldn't get out of control.

"I see you two have met," Royce said, bouncing Raven in his arms.

"Met? We ain't meet," Krystol said with an attitude.

"Well, Krystol, this is Danielle. Danielle, this is Krystol, the mother of my daughter as of right now," he said with his own little attitude. "Now, Krystol," he emphasized, "I was supposed to go out and meet Danielle somewhere, but instead, I told her to come here. I think it's time."

"Wait, just let me say something," Danielle interrupted, turning to face Krystol. "Your daughter's father is a good man, and I can't say that about many men. Not one time did he ever make any advances at me nor did he ever respond to the many times I flirted with him before he told me about you. I honestly thought that he might have been gay or something because not too many men can turn me down." She smiled, tooting her own horn just a little. "The bottom line is that Royce never cheated on you with me, and now that I know him a little better, I don't think he will ever cheat on you with anybody. He really does love you, and that's all I got to say about that. Now, I'll let him explain the business aspect of our relationship," she said, turning it over to Royce.

Krystol felt insulted by the way that Danielle was speaking to her. If this was to make her feel more secure in regard to Royce's commitment to her, it was doing the opposite. This bitch held herself in high regard, and basically was telling her that Royce had turned her down for a basic chick like her?

She looked at Danielle's smooth complexion, and hourglass shape. She was fashionable, and exuded confidence, enough confidence for Royce to have some type of admiration for her. Royce having any type of emotion for another female made Krystol's blood boil. She kept a poker face as Royce asked her to take a seat.

For the next twenty minutes, Royce broke down the whole takedown relationship he and Danielle had. He told her about the robberies, the setup, and he even made Danielle lift her shirt up to show her the light bruises she sustained from Kemo shooting her the night Krystol followed them. He would have shown her all the money he'd been saving, but Danielle was there. He knew just how hungry she was for money and how she didn't have no picks. He wouldn't dare put himself in harm's way like that, messing around with a chick who he knew would kill for a dollar.

After listening to everything, Krystol had become convinced that Royce was being faithful the whole time but still had lied about how he was getting money. It was a bittersweet moment. It was definitely something they had to talk about, outside the presence of company. For now, she was willing to set that aside for the greater good of saving their relationship.

Royce was happy to be building a life for his family, but there was something nagging him. He had tried to let the past go, and move forward just being grateful having the chance to love and be with them, but the voice of doubt was speaking louder as the days passed. The voice told Royce he would not be able to relax and rest until Krystol told him where in the hell she had been with his daughter. Everything needed to be on the table, and right now he knew he was missing an entrée.

Chapter 19

"I called everybody here today for a reason," Sanaa said, walking into her office where Sleepy, Royce, and Joi were waiting.

She had a few very important things to talk about with everyone and establish the direction she was heading in for the future. She sat at the desk looking around at her family, hoping that she was making the right decision. The love for them was incomparable to any love she had for anything or anyone, and that, along with their safety and well-being, had brought her to this point.

"Look, this weekend is going to be our last weekend with the club," she began. "I think that it's time we cut our losses, make some money, and get the hell up out dis city," she said leaning back in the chair. "I made a deal with Boo. He's gonna give me ten million in counterfeit money for two and a half million in real money."

"How in the hell are we supposed to move that kind of money in two days?" Sleepy asked, knowing that it was impossible.

A short moment of silence took over the room. Everyone was waiting for an answer. Sanaa took in a deep breath then exhaled. This might have been the hardest thing she ever had to do in her life.

"We're not gonna move the money in the club. It's more like a parting gift from me to you," she told them.

"Fuck is that supposed to mean?" Royce shot back, not at all enthused by what she said.

"What I'm saying is that I'm done with this life. It's time I grew up. Hell it's time we all grew up. Look at you, Royce. You got a woman who loves you unconditionally. You got a baby girl who needs you. You really got to start thinking about your family," she told Royce. "Sleepy, you got to start thinking about your future as well," she said turning to him. "You're better than this, and you got the potential to do whatever you want. And, Joi, well you're already grown. I just want you to stay around for a while. I really do need you in my life."

Sanaa's words put a lot of things in perspective for everybody in the room and nobody was in disagreement. The only sad part about the whole thing was that Sanaa made the decision that everyone should take their money and go their separate ways. That part of the plan didn't sit well with anyone.

"This shit right here ain't a good look. We should keep it tight and stay together," Sleepy said pacing back and forward. It was to no avail; Sanaa had already made up her mind.

"So what about the beef we got?" Joi asked, thinking about Kemo, Bread, and, most importantly, Ariana.

"Simple. Find them and kill them all," Sanaa ordered, leaving nothing else up for discussion.

Sleepy was going with everything until that point when Sanaa ordered the hit on Ariana. That was one order he wasn't going to stand on. Joi was going to die first, and that too wasn't up for discussion with him. He just had to do it at the right time and right place so that it couldn't fall back on him or Ariana. That would be the only way he and Ariana had a chance of being together without Sanaa killing her.

Detectives Thomas and Boyd sat across the street from Sanaa's club on the roof of a pet store, waiting with a camera. They'd been there for a while now, but had only gotten some bad pictures of Sanaa when she and Joi entered the club. They knew they could get better pictures of them coming out of the club and decided to wait. Detective Thomas was beginning to get frustrated; he started to go down there and just ask her for a picture. Just when he was about to get down off the roof, Sanaa and Joi stepped out of the club. Thomas snapped picture after picture, but he still couldn't get a good shot with the large Carrera shades Sanaa had on, covering most of her face.

"I can't get a good damn shot," Thomas said, rolling back over on the roof. "The sun is about to start going down, and I know we won't be able to get a picture tonight," he added.

"Don't worry, if we don't get it today, we'll get it done tomorrow," Detective Boyd encouraged him.

Thomas was impatient. He didn't want to wait until tomorrow to get the picture to Agent Razor. He got off the roof and headed around to the front of the building. Boyd was in his ear the whole way, telling him he might blow the case if he tried it and failed. Detective Boyd, the more experienced of the two, had seen cases where suspects disappeared after finding out the law was investigating them. They would just vanish into thin air, and the detectives couldn't figure out where they went wrong. That's the path Thomas was now heading down.

As they bent the corner of the front of the building, Sanaa and Joi were nowhere to be found. No one was standing in front of the club, and the car Sanaa and Joi pulled up in was gone. Detective Thomas and Detective Boyd just stared at each other before turning around and heading back to their car.

Chapter 20

People poured into the club by the dozen, and it seemed like everyone that was at the hotel party had shown back up, despite the shootings. As usual, the food was free, the drinks were cheap, and the strippers on the second floor were working hard for their money. The club was jam packed within an hour, and there were so many people that a small party popped off outside the club, as people waited to get in. This was by far the biggest party Sanaa had ever thrown at the club.

Downstairs in the casino, Sanaa stood in the pit station watching as large amounts of money exchanged hands. The casino was just as packed as upstairs, leaving only standing room for those waiting to gamble. Tonight, Sanaa ran the largest poker tournament ever. It consisted of eight tables, twelve players, and a $25,000 sit-in fee. Winner takes all. The tournament drew a large crowd, but so did the blackjack tables. Sanaa set the decks of cards to where the table dealt more winning hands.

Joi, instead of working the club area, had decided to take up security, knowing there was a strong possibility that anything could go down tonight. There was drama coming from all directions. She kept somebody armed at just about every station in the building, even by the bathrooms. Before the party even started, everyone was briefed to be on lookout for Ariana. Joi had kept pictures of Ariana for sentimental reasons, but had used them to show her staff what she looked like. With no pictures of Kemo, she had to just rely on herself, and that's why she stayed close to the door, watching everybody who came in and out of the club.

"So, this is where you work at," a voice yelled out over the music at Joi from behind.

When she turned to see who it was, she was kind of shocked, but also impressed to see how Officer Waters looked outside of his uniform. He looked like the average dope boy in the hood who was getting money. He had on a pair on Missoni Chuck Taylors, seersucker shorts, and a Polo pocket T-shirt. His Braves fitted hat complemented his outfit, along with the diamond chain that matched his iced-out watch.

"I'm starting to think that you're a stalker," Joi joked, keeping her eyes on the people coming through the door.

They shared a quick laugh. Waters, on the other hand, couldn't get enough of how sexy Joi looked in the tight hip-hugger jeans she was rocking along with a gray tank top that showed off her A-size breasts and flat stomach.

"Why didn't you call?" he yelled, tapping her on the waist.

She turned back around to face him. *Damn, he looks good.* She pulled her cell phone from out of her back pocket and went straight to her call list. "I've been busy, but as soon as I get free, I'll call you," she said as she held the phone up so that he could see his name and number locked into her phone.

He said nothing else and just backed off of her and headed toward the bar. It only took that small conversation for Joi to be unaware of Detective Boyd walking right past her. Detective Thomas was right behind him, and the two were now headed for the bar. Detective Thomas was determined to get Sanaa's picture to the FBI in Philadelphia. Something in the club was going to give him what he needed and he knew it.

He walked up to the bar and ordered a dry martini with seltzer water on the side, passing the bartender a one hundred dollar bill. In moments, the drink and his change was returned to him when Thomas walked off and headed for the bathroom. He couldn't help but notice a man standing guard in front of a red door toward the back of the club. It struck his curiosity because none of the club goers were even trying to go inside the door.

"Did you see that?" Detective Boyd asked Thomas, closing and locking the bathroom door behind them once they got inside.

"Yeah, I wonder what's back there," Thomas replied, pulling the bills out that he got from the bartender.

He held it over the sink and poured the seltzer water over it. The ink immediately ran off the bills

and into the sink. He quickly bagged it as evidence,
then gave Boyd another one hundred dollar bill so
that he could repeat the process just to be sure it
wasn't a onetime thing. Leaving out of the bathroom,
both detectives could see that the man was still
standing guard at the door. For kicks, Thomas walked
over to the door and tried to enter it. He was denied,
and damn near assaulted in the process. Detective
Thomas walked away with more information than
he had before. That guy was standing in front of the
door for a reason. He was protecting something, and
nine times out of ten in situations like this, it was
something illegal.

"Let's just get our evidence and get the hell out of
here," Detective Boyd said.

Bread sat outside in a stolen car waiting on his cue.
His cell phone going off got his attention as he sat
across the street from club.

"Let's get it," Kemo said, giving Bread the green
light.

Bread drove the car into the alleyway and smack
into the back door, pinning it shut so no one would
be able to exit from it. The casino was so loud, Sanaa,
nor anyone else, even heard the lightweight crash.
As the detectives were heading out the front door,
Danielle, her friend, Destiny, and three other guys
were entering the club. Destiny being the last one in
walked up behind Joi, pulled the .40-cal from her
waist and jammed it into her back.

"Do what I say or I'll blow ya fuckin' back into ya stomach," she threatened, grabbing the gun Joi had in her back waist.

Danielle and her three goons all fanned out into the club, pulling their firearms but keeping them down by their sides.

"Lock the door and don't let nobody else in," she ordered Joi. "And tell ya doorman to go help out at the bar."

Joi, feeling the barrel of the gun jammed in her back, did exactly as she was told. Destiny was so cool, calm, and collected, nobody even noticed what she was doing.

"Y'all know you won't be leaving the club alive," Joi shouted over the music, looking at Destiny through the mirror in front of her.

"Yeah, well we'll see about that," Destiny told her, doing a little two-step number behind Joi to make it look like she was just dancing.

Gee, one of Kemo's men, went up to the second floor where he took a seat right next to Yellow in a booth. He stuck the gun to his side, and gave him strict instructions not to move. He disarmed Yellow before Yellow could even think about making a move.

Danielle went straight to the back of the club were E-Money was holding up the door. He let the Jimmy Choo heels, Bridge shorts, and a white crop top fool him, not to mention that she was a bad-ass white girl. She brought the Highpoint 9 mm from the back of her thigh and slammed it into his gut.

"You move, you die," she told E-Money, stripping him of his weapon. "Open the door," she demanded, pressing the gun a little deeper into his stomach.

He turned around and opened the door before being forced down the steps by the back of his collar. Master and Boogie, the other two men, followed right behind Danielle, closing and locking the door behind them. The loud volume in the casino covered the sound of the gunmen coming down the staircase. Master and Boogie spread out across the floor while Danielle decided to wake everybody up.

Danielle fired three shots into the ceiling, causing everybody to get low to the ground. Sanaa drew her weapon, cupping it with both hands and aiming it right at Danielle, who was using E-Money as a shield. Mel, Sanaa's other guard, also drew his weapon and aimed it in Master's direction. Mel wasn't even aware of Boogie walking up behind him until he felt the barrel of a gun pressing against the back of his skull.

"You shoot me, I shoot him," Mel said, holding Master at gunpoint.

A crowd of people ran for the back door but couldn't get it open. The only other way out was through the front door of the club, which nobody dared try to use with Danielle blocking their way.

"This is what you call a robbery," Danielle announced to everybody with a smile on her face.

"Like hell it is," Sanaa said, gripping her gun a little tighter.

There was silence in the once loud casino, and for a moment, everyone who had a gun held stares with each other. What broke the silence and possibly shattered Sanaa's ability to hold the robbers back was the sound of a safety being taken off a gun, and that same gun being pressed against the back of Sanaa's head.

"Don't make me do this, Sanaa," a woman's voice spoke from behind. "Just put the gun down, please," the woman pled.

It was a voice Sanaa was familiar with, but couldn't believe it was her. As Sanaa slowly lowered her weapon, she was struck in the back of her head with the butt of the gun. Sanaa's gun dropped and she hit the floor, only to look up at Kia, her very own cashier. Kia was in charge of cashing out money, but Kia was also Master's little sister and Kemo's goddaughter. She was the one who gave up all the intel on the operations of the club and casino.

Mel followed suit and decided to lower his weapon, seeing that he was outnumbered. After all the threats were secured, Master went to work. He walked over to Sanaa, snatched the single key from around her neck, and started popping open the cash boxes on the dealers' side of all the tables. He emptied out every box, and then went for the cashier's booth that Kia had left open for him. He took everything out of the booth and put it in a separate bag away from the real money.

"Damn, Kia, I treated you good," Sanaa said looking up at her. "Dis how you gonna do me?"

"I'm sorry," Kia whispered in response.

Sanaa was in her feelings, but she had to get some control of herself so that she could make the best out of an opportunity that hit her when she looked up at the Glock strapped to the bottom of the pit boss's table. She couldn't reach for it without spooking Kia to the point where she'd pull the trigger. Sanaa couldn't afford that, because Kia's gun was pointed directly in her face.

"Can you at least get the gun out of my face, Kia?" Sanaa begged. "You're scared and you might shoot me by accident."

Kia agreed. She was scared as hell. She moved the gun slightly to the side, but enough where it wasn't in Sanaa's face. The Glock under the table was about five feet away, reaching distance for Sanaa if she moved fast.

Master was already done clearing out the casino when Bread got the phone call for him to move the car away from the door so they could exit the building. Bread placed the car in drive and allowed it to creep up just enough to clear the door. He jumped out of the vehicle and waited. Once Boogie opened the door from the inside, Bread ran in while Danielle, Master, and Boogie were coming out. His only mission was to kill Sanaa, and as he desperately looked around the casino, Kia called out to him as she slowly backed off Sanaa.

"She's over here," Kia yelled, while backing up and walking away toward the back door.

Sanaa could see Bread from the ground, making his way over to her with a gun in his hand. She leaned up and reached for the Glock under the table, rolling over and taking cover behind a wooden podium. She jumped up and started firing in Bread's direction. He dropped to the floor and returned fire as he crawled backward toward the door. Sanaa just kept firing, hitting the tables right next to Bread's head.

Kia was at the door when one of Sanaa's bullets knocked a patch out the side of her head. She dropped to the ground right in the doorway.

Bread fired again, forcing Sanaa to take cover behind a wall. That was enough time for him to get to his feet and run out the back door, stepping over Kia's body.

Upstairs, Destiny and Gee were making their exit out of the club as well. Gee came down from the second floor and left out first.

"Well, baby girl, this is where we depart. It was a pleasure," Destiny told Joi before leaving out of the front door.

Joi scrambled through the club and went into Sanaa's office where Sleepy was counting the money from the bar and strippers. He had no idea what had gone on in the last ten minutes.

"I think they just hit the casino," she said, opening the closet door and grabbing two guns before running back out of the office.

Sleepy grabbed a gun too and followed Joi. They both raced through the club and down the steps of the casino. When they got down there, everybody was still in shock. Some were trying to push the back door open, but couldn't because Bread had slammed the car back up against it and left it there before leaving the scene.

"You good, you good," Sleepy and Joi yelled, running up to Sanaa who was looking at Kia's body.

The crowd of people saw that it was safe to leave out the other way, and they did, like a herd of buffalo. The large amount of people poured out onto the dance floor and ran out the club in panic. The people on the top two floors were unaware of everything that had just happened. Between the loud music, the naked girls, and the large amount of alcohol being consumed, no one was paying much attention to their surroundings. But now seeing people running to the exits, the rest of the crowd just followed suit.

"We got to get out of here," Sleepy said, grabbing Sanaa's arm and leading her upstairs.

Joi followed, bringing up the rear. As they walked through the club Joi looked over and could see Officer Waters sitting at the bar watching her and two other armed men escorting Sanaa out of the building. Waters sipped the whisky; he did nothing to help stop the panic. He was feeling a light buzz, and was in no rush to perform his civic duty to restore order. They seemed to be finding the exits without issue. He looked at Joi, who shook her head for him to stay where he was; she didn't want to involve him any further in the issues at hand. He turned his eye to the crowd, and watched as people continued to hurry out of the exit. Within minutes the panic dissipated; he took a swing of his drink, and headed for one of the exits. He got up from his stool in an effort to lend his help, but Joi shook her head no, not wanting to involve him. He just waited for everybody else in the club to leave before he got up and left himself.

Detective Thomas and Detective Boyd were at the police station waiting to hear from the judge when they got the call that shots were fired at Club All In, and at least one was dead. It blew both of their minds because they had just left there. They didn't even stick around for the judge as they bolted out the door and raced to the scene. When they pulled up, there were mainly red and blue lights flashing and just a handful of partygoers off to the side.

"Where's the body?" Detective Thomas asked the uniformed cop at the front door of the club.

He pointed to the door in the back of the club that led to the casino. The detectives knew there was something going on behind that door, but they had no idea what they were in store for as they entered the casino. They both could smell the gun smoke in the air as they looked around in awe. Blackjack tables, craps tables, slot machines, poker tables. It really looked like a mini casino. Chips were all over the place, and some bets were still on the table. Thomas made sure that the forensic unit took pictures of everything.

"The bullet never left her head," Detective Boyd said as Thomas walked over to the body. "It looks like she was trying to get out of the door," Boyd said, pointing with his pen.

It was obvious that Sanaa was nowhere to be found, and that was a good thing, because Detective Thomas now had more than enough to arrest her. With all the evidence he had, he didn't need the warrant anymore to search her establishment. Hell if it came down to it, he would say he thought someone was in danger. He could simply say he heard a struggle; whatever he needed to say he had to make this move, and make it now. Detective Thomas pulled out his cell phone and pushed a couple of buttons. There was one person he wanted to call to see if any of this sounded familiar to him, and when Agent Razor answered his cell phone, halfway asleep, Thomas knew exactly what was going to wake him up.

"Agent Razor," he answered.

"Hello, Agent Razor. I hate to be calling you this time of night, but I needed to know something about the woman you were looking for," Thomas spoke.

"Yeah, go ahead," Razor responded.

"What would you know about illegal gambling and a full-scale casino?" Thomas asked, looking around at the few poker tables.

Agent Razor sat up in his bed, all too familiar with those details. His heart was racing, and before he knew it, he was getting dressed while Thomas stayed on the other end, explaining in detail what he was looking at. The more he talked, the more Agent Razor felt that this was his girl. They talked all the way up to the point when Agent Razor decided he was going to catch the next available flight to Philly.

Chapter 21

Sanaa crossed Parkside and headed into Fairmount Park, where everyone was supposed to meet. In her trunk, she had $10 million worth of funny money and about five hundred grand in real money. She also had plenty of guns and ammunition with her in case a full-blown war popped off.

"Sanaa! Sanaa!" Joi said, snapping her out of her trance as she drove down Parkway. "Are you even looking at the road?" she inquired in a sarcastic tone.

"Yeah, girl, I was just thinking," Sanaa shot back.

"About what? I see you got some shit on ya mind, so spit it out. And why are we in Fairmount Park?"

Joi didn't know about the money Sanaa had gotten from Boo early that morning, nor was she aware that today was going to be the parting day for Sanaa. Joi could feel something wasn't right, but she couldn't put her finger on what it was that was making her stomach tighten. Sanaa could be somewhat tight-lipped at times, and hard to read.

"You should go back home to my dad. He really misses you," Sanaa said as she looked in her rearview mirror.

"Girl, as much as I love and miss Balil, it's no way I'm leaving your side, especially now."

"Joi, right now shit is just crazy. Don't you think we need to let everything die down?"

Before Joi could respond, Sanaa pulled over on the side of the road where Sleepy was sitting on the trunk of his car waiting for her. It was a little secluded area, and just as she put her car in park, Royce pulled in right behind her.

Royce was mad as hell that he wasn't at the club to help protect his sister. All he saw was red and all he wanted to do was kill something. It didn't matter who was responsible for the attempt on Sanaa's life, Royce wanted them dead by the end of the day.

"Yo, I ain't got no rap. Who da fuck was it?" Royce spazzed out the moment he exited his car.

"Man, where da fuck was you at?" Sleepy snapped at Royce, a little mad that he wasn't around when they needed him.

They were about to start arguing but Sanaa stopped them. Now wasn't the time for the family to be falling apart.

"Look, we not here to place the blame on anybody. Right now, everybody needs to listen to me, 'cause this might be the last time any of you may see me for a while," Sanaa said, walking to the back of her car and opening the trunk.

"Fuck is you talking about, Sanaa?" Sleepy asked with his face twisted up as he followed her to the back of the vehicle.

Sanaa reached in and grabbed a duffle bag. She tossed it to Sleepy, and then reached back in and

grabbed another, then another, tossing them to
Joi and Royce. Everyone unzipped the bags at the
same time to see the money inside. Royce wasn't
impressed.

"What's this?" he asked, about ready to throw the
bag back at her.

"It's that parting money we talked back at the club.
I came, I did my thing, and now I'm gone. I'm already
wanted by the Feds in Atlanta, and now, more than
likely after last night, I'm probably wanted in Philly."

"So what are we supposed to do?" Joi asked with
an attitude, not really feeling the parting comment.

"It's two and a half million in funny money in each
bag, plus an extra hundred grand in real money. You
guys can go wherever you want. My suggestion is that
you get out of this city before it either kills you or put
you in prison for the rest of your life," Sanaa spoke.

"So you telling me that's it. Fuck the family, we just
take the money and go our separate ways?" Royce
said, pissed about the whole idea.

Sanaa knew what he was getting at, and as bad
as she didn't want to do it, the time and opportunity
for her to put this life behind her was now. No more
drugs, no more violence, and no more looking over
her shoulder wondering if the next bullet was meant
for her. It was bad enough that the Feds and the local
authorities were on her trail. The best thing for her to
do was lay low for a while, or at least until the statute
of limitations ran out.

"It ain't like we not goin' to stay in touch," Sanaa tried to justify. "We will always be family. You makin' it sound worse then what it is," she said, looking over at Royce.

Royce just shook his head and tossed the duffle bag full of money at Sanaa's feet. Sanaa tried to say something to him, but he walked off with a full-fledged attitude then jumped into his car and sped away. Sanaa, Sleepy, and Joi stood there in silence for a moment. Each of them not knowing if they should say something, or what to say. The time had come for all of this to end. Sanaa grabbed the bag, she looked at Sleepy and Joi. Everything had always been on ten for them, and now as the three of them departed, the silence was louder than any of the drama they had been through. Not seeing each other would be the sacrifice they needed to have a chance at surviving.

"Okay, we got the warrant for her arrest," Detective Boyd said, coming out of the judge's chambers.

After the incident at Club All In the night before, there was enough evidence and probable cause to arrest Sanaa. Among other things, illegal gambling and murder were at the top of the charges against her. Somebody had to answer for the female's body found in the club, and since nobody stuck around after the shooting to tell what happened, Sanaa was going to bear the weight of it for right now. She had been seen with a firearm, and it was known that there was bad blood between them according to witnesses. The judge had granted the warrant mainly based on the way it was presented to him, and it had not been an easy task. At the last minute Judge Harrison nodded and signed it, reminding them he was still not happy with how flimsy their evidence and the case appeared to him.

"Before we execute the warrant, we gotta go pick up Agent Razor at Philly International," Boyd said as they left the courtroom.

Razor was very adamant about catching up to Sanaa and bringing her back to Atlanta to face drug trafficking charges; he really wasn't that concerned about the illegal gambling aspect. With the Feds, Sanaa was facing a minimum of ten years for her role in a drug conspiracy. Agent Razor was hoping Sanaa would save herself and help him bring down her connect, who was one of Atlanta's biggest drug kingpins.

"Do we still have somebody at the club?" Thomas asked, hoping Sanaa would show up.

"Yeah, we got plainclothes officers on surveillance," Detective Boyd answered.

"All right then. Let's open up the blinds on this chick," Thomas said, getting into his Crown Victoria.

Kemo walked into his bedroom and took a seat in the chair that sat next to the bed. He pulled out his lighter and lit a cigar. Danielle was still asleep in the bed resting peacefully as Kemo looked down at her. He couldn't put his nose on it, but there was something wrong with her that she wasn't sharing. He knew her well enough to know when she was up to something, and the longer he sat there staring at her asleep, the more he thought. His senses were in overdrive, he had been getting shivers down his spine for a couple of days now. She had begun taking her phone calls away from him now, something she had not done as frequently before. He searched the bed for the phone; for the last few nights she had been sleeping with it under her pillow. He slowly slid his hand under the pillow, being careful not to wake her, but he didn't feel anything. He had called her a couple times when she was out, and she cut their conversations short, like she didn't want who she was with to hear them.

"What you got goin' on?" Kemo mumbled to himself, taking a toke of the cigar.

When Danielle rolled over to where the front of her body was facing him, he got a glimpse of the two bruises. Suspicious of her actions over the past few days, Kemo got up. He walked over and grabbed her Birkin bag from the nightstand. He moved quietly, making sure not to wake her, and walked into the bathroom. He looked back at her one last time before he closed the bathroom door.

"I'ma kill you if you cheating on me," Kemo said, opening the bag and dumping everything out on the floor. "Tell me something."

The first thing that he grabbed was her cell phone. As he looked through the outgoing and incoming calls, nothing seemed out of whack, mainly because his number was the most frequently used in her call log. He wasn't done there, because he went straight to her text log. The first few were to Kemo, but after that, things got a little interesting.

> He's about to leave. We gotta go now.
> I'm on my way. Wear ya vest.

Kemo looked at the phone sideways, not believing what he was reading. There were a few other texts of Danielle giving her location and letting Royce know that she was home safe. The most disturbing text was Danielle texting to Royce, He still don't know!

Kemo was mad as hell. He stormed back into the room and threw Danielle's phone at her. It hit her on the side of her head, waking her right up. When she opened her eyes, Kemo stood over her with anger in his eyes and a gun in his hand.

"What da fuck is all this about?" he snapped, pointing at the phone with the gun he pulled from his waist.

"What are you talking about, baby?" Danielle said, going through her phone. Danielle said looking at the phone; she looked at him standing there with his gun in his hand. "Kemo?" She looked at the screen; she saw the text between her and Royce. Her heart stopped and her stomach tightened as she realized it was from the night they had robbed Kemo. She cursed; she was sure that she had deleted all of the texts between her and Royce. She looked at Kemo; the vein on the side of his neck was visible, and her blood ran cold when she realized he was holding his gun.

Danielle was slipping, and it didn't stop there, because the tank top she had on was droopy, so much so that the bruise on her chest was showing. Her tank top fell forward exposing the bruises on her chest; she looked at the phone, the bruises, and back at the gun that was now pointed at her face. Had he put it together? Shit, she needed to stay calm, and figure out if he had pieced things together or if he was being a jealous lover.

"Baby, this is nothing," Danielle pled, sitting up the bed. "This all stemmed from last night," she lied.

Kemo glanced down and saw the bruise on her chest then looked back up at the fear that was pouring out of her eyes. He reached over, grabbed her tank top, and ripped it clean down the middle. The other bruise on her stomach was just as dark as the one on her chest, and that's when Kemo's brain really started to go into overdrive.

Visions of him shooting the masked gunman when he got robbed raced through his mind. He remembered shooting him once in the chest and another time in his stomach as he ran past him. The bruises on Danielle were identical to where Kemo had had shot him.

"It was you this whole time?" Kemo asked, twisting his face up at her; his brain felt like it was trying to jump out of his head. He ran his hand over his face trying to stop his mind from spinning. Shit his fucking instincts had been thrown off because he allowed some pussy to get into his heart, and head. The hurt he felt quickly left when he thought back to the text. *He still doesn't know.* What a fucking joke he must have been to her and this dude!

Danielle sat there frozen, feeling that her time on this earth was just about up. "Please baby, I'm sorry," she pled, hoping he would forgive her, and for a moment, she thought that he would when he lowered his gun. The hurt in his eyes stared straight into her soul, his expression softened, and he turned around to leave the room. Danielle was afraid to move, but exhaled slowly.

Kemo stopped. He turned around, as if he was about to leave the room, but spun back around and cracked Danielle on the side of her face with the gun. The blow knocked her clean out, and when Kemo leaned over to whisper something in her ear, he could hear a light snore coming from her nose.

"This is only the beginning of your nightmare," Kemo whispered in her ear before turning around and walking out of the room.

The drive back home was silent for the most part. Joi was still trying to grasp everything that was happening right now. Ariana was hot on her tail, and was going to stop at nothing until she got her revenge. And now, it seemed like the only real family she had was breaking up. At this point, she really didn't know what she wanted to do or where she wanted to go. Sanaa, on the other hand, didn't have that problem.

"Look, I just gotta run to the house and grab a few things. After that, I'ma pick up the rental car for you and then I'm out," Sanaa said, looking out into the highway.

"Damn, you ain't wasting no time. I thought we would at least be able to chill for a minute, and process all this shit," Joi shot back with an obvious attitude.

Sanaa knew how she felt, but right now wasn't the time for sentimental stuff. She could feel the heat around the corner, and the last thing she wanted to do was get caught slipping. She had the Feds in Atlanta on her heels, the local police in Philly closing in on her, Kemo wanting her dead, and Ariana was on her own warpath. The situation was ugly, and Sanaa knew that it was time to blow town and move on to the next.

"Oh shit. Check it out," Sanaa said turning down Fifty-eighth and Pine Street.

They were a little in the distance, but Sanaa could see clearly that the cops had the street the club was on blocked off completely. Philadelphia detectives were all over the place, pointing and talking on their cell phones. Sanaa knew for sure that if she went anywhere near that club, she was going straight to jail. Sanaa bit her bottom lip as she recognized the signs of a bust that was about to happen. Too many cars, and people walking around trying to appear casual. Their posture gave them away, as well as the way their eyes were scanning the street. One in particular, a blonde, was anxious. He wore a T-shirt, and tattered jeans, but his face was smooth and clean. As cars drove by he stared at them too long trying to see who was in them.

Sanaa had been watching shit like this her whole life; she knew what a setup from the Feds and local pigs smelled and felt like. The number of cars and their position was also a giveaway to the setup. She thought back to being in North Carolina with an ex of hers. Normally the street he had his trap houses on were busy, but the traffic had increased, and Duley had pointed out how clear some of the crackheads' eyes were who walked past them. That day they had been driving her car. His boy Tae drove past them and into the driveway of one of the houses. Once he pulled into the garage, agents swarmed from everywhere. Duley laughed, and told her to always be careful when you on the run or when you get that damn feeling in the back of your neck.

"See, this is exactly what I'm talking about," Sanaa said to Joi as she turned up Spruce Street, away from the crime scene.

It was one thing for Joi to hear Sanaa say how hot it was, but to see it with her own eyes was even more shocking.

"Fuck it. I'm not going back to the house. The cops might be there, too. So what I'ma do is take you to Avis, get you a rental car, then I'm gone," Sanaa said, speeding away, trying to get as far away from the club as possible.

"Dis bitch think she got all the sense," Royce mumbled to himself, pulling over and grabbing his phone.

He was a little late with it, but eventually, Royce realized that Danielle sent him on that dummy mission the other night to get him out of the way for when she and her people ran up in the club. He really never got a chance to confront her about leaving the hotel party with Kemo that day; so many other things were going on at the time, it had slipped his mind.

"Answer the phone," he said, looking out at the heavy traffic passing by his car.

Danielle wasn't going to answer anytime soon, and Royce came to that conclusion after she didn't answer for the third time. Royce hurried up and dialed another number, knowing that the person on the other end of this phone was going to answer. He wasn't feeling any of what Sanaa was talking about as far as leaving Philly. He'd left Philly once before to move to Atlanta with their dad, but since he'd been back in the city, he remembered how much he loved the streets of Philly. He wasn't trying to go anywhere, and if he had to go through Danielle to get to Kemo and kill him so that he could live comfortably in the city, then that's what it was going to be.

Although he'd been gone for a while, Royce still had a few niggas who went hard. All it took was this one phone call and it was on. Adding a million dollars in funny money to get the job done, Kemo would have more problems on his hands than what he could handle. Always the one to be prepared, he had skimmed some of the funny money here and there. He had enough stacked, and at the moment, he may have another source to get him more.

"Can I pay for this in cash?" Sanaa asked the clerk at the front desk of Avis.

"You can pay with cash, but we still need a credit card before you can drive one of our cars off the lot. After you return, we'll be happy to take cash," the woman advised.

Sanaa reached into her bag and pulled out her American Express card. She really wanted to limit her chances of being tracked down by the law, but the sooner her and Joi got out of the city, the better off they would be, or at least that's what Sanaa was hoping.

"When you get to Atlanta, you tell my dad that I love him and I miss him," Sanaa said, walking Joi out to the garage where the Dodge Charger was waiting. "I'll contact you guys in a couple of weeks with my new numbers."

Joi stopped at the driver side door, turned, and faced Sanaa. She wiped a tear that was falling from her eye then reached out for a hug. They both hated this part. Saying good-bye never was easy, especially for people as close as Joi and Sanaa.

"Girl, drive safe," Sanaa said, giving Joi a kiss on the check.

Before Joi could say anything, the sound of tires screeching caught both of their attention. Two all-black SUVs sped into the garage area, heading straight at Sanaa and Joi. Instinctively, Sanaa reached into her bag and wrapped her hand around the .45 automatic she carried. Joi did the same thing, only she gripped a 9 mm.

Both cars came to a screeching halt right in front of the girls. Men jumped out from both cars with guns drawn. "Get ya fuckin' hands in the air!" the men yelled as they cautiously approached.

Sanaa was hesitant to pull her weapon, thinking that it might have been the police. Joi was simply scared shitless from all the guns that were pointed at her. It wasn't until Sanaa noticed Bread in the midst of the men that she realized they weren't the cops. By then, it was a little too late.

Joi took her chances and fired off two shots through her Gucci bag. One bullet struck one of the gunmen in his chest while the other hit the hood of the car. Sanaa whipped out her gun, and squeezed the trigger. The gun didn't fire because the safety was on.

Joi was about to let off several more shots, but Bread responded with a single shot that hit Joi in her face.

Sanaa looked over and watched as Joi's body fell to the ground. "Joi!" she yelled, running over and dropping down to her knees next to her friend.

Joi's whole face was covered in blood. Sanaa was furious at this point. She didn't care if she died in a gun battle, and it took all but a split second for her to pop the safety off her gun. She clutched it tightly, picked her head up, spun around, and saw nothing but the butt of a shotgun rushing toward her face. It hit her right in her nose between the eyes, knocking her out before she could get a shot off.

"Let's go!" Bread shouted, walking back to the truck.

Two of the men walked over, threw a pillowcase over Sanaa's head, and carried her unconscious body back to the car.

Joi was left there to die, while the two cars sped out of the garage with Sanaa, as was ordered by Kemo. He had come to the conclusion that he wouldn't reap any benefit by only killing her. He had something more sinister on his mind, and if Sanaa didn't regret playing around with his money by now, she would, once she was taken back to him. Which could possibly be her final destination.

Chapter 22

Danielle woke up with the side of her face feeling like it had been caved in. She got out of the bed, walked over to the mirror to see that the whole right side of her face was black and blue and she could also taste dry blood in her mouth from the cut lining her inner cheek. She wanted Kemo's head on a silver platter for this shit.

Looking around the room for something she could bust him upside the head with when he came back into the room. Her eyes locked onto a metal bowling pin trophy sitting on the dresser. It had some weight on it, too, and with one right swing of it, Kemo was sure to go out like a light bulb. Clutching it tightly in her hand, she crept up to the bedroom door to get an idea of where in the house he was.

She cracked the door open slightly. Danielle could hear what sounding like Kemo talking to a couple of his boys downstairs. Now knowing that he wasn't alone, her immediate plans on splitting his wig open were put on hold. Instead, she closed the door walked back and sat on the bed, contemplating what else she could do. It was impossible for her to leave out of the house without being seen by someone. And at the same time, sitting there waiting to be dealt with by Kemo didn't sound like a good option either.

"Where's my phone, where's my phone," Danielle whispered, looking around the room. "Come on," she mumbled, as she rambled through her purse that was lying on the floor.

For a minute she thought that Kemo had taken it but he didn't. She found it and thought about calling the cops, but it was a little premature. Kemo bluffed many of times when it came to hitting her so Danielle wanted to see how it played out. Also she knew that Kemo could be soft when it came to attractive women. He would try to go hard, but always ended up apologizing. If she stayed patient and played like she was forced to do it, maybe just maybe he would believe her.

Royce pulled into Sanaa's driveway hoping he could catch her before she left the city. He had to voice his opinion to her about them splitting up, and wanted for Sanaa to reconsider the notion. As soon as he got out of his car his phone started blaring off. He quickly answered it once he saw Danielle's number pop up on the screen. Not wanting her to hear the anger in his voice, Royce answered the phone as calmly as he could. He could barely hear her as she started whispering into the phone.

"I need you to come get me. I don't know what he's gonna do," she whispered while looking at a car pull up outside of her window.

"What are you talking about?" Royce asked.

"He knows about us. He knows everything. I don't know what—" Danielle stopped midsentence and almost dropped the phone when Sanaa was being pulled out of the back seat by Bread. Her face was bloody and her clothes were stretched out like she had been roughed up pretty good.

"Danielle, you gon have to hold up. I'm looking for my sister right now."

"She's here," Danielle said cutting him off.

"I'm not in the mood for jokes."

"I'm not joking. I swear they just pulled up with her."

Royce stood there on the porch and looked around. Only one of Sanaa's cars was in the driveway. He wasted no time kicking in her front door then ran through the house like a madman, screaming and yelling her name, all while keeping Danielle on the phone.

"Where da fuck is you at," he snapped into the receiver.

Danielle knew that he was good and pissed, just the way she needed him to be. She thought that if it was anybody who could come in and save her, it would be Royce. Sanaa being held captive at the same location was more than enough incentive to get him to move out just a little bit harder. She knew for his family he was about to go nuts.

"Search warrant!" Detective Butler yelled before kicking in Sleepy's door. "Get on the ground. Get on the ground." Sleepy's address was listed on the business licenses and Butler was hoping that it would be this easy to find Sanaa.

Sleepy was upstairs but he heard the commands loud and clear. Ariana rolled out of the bed and grabbed her gun from off of the nightstand, cocking it back slightly to make sure it was a bullet in the chamber. The police rushed the stairs with tactical gear on and in their hands were fully automatic submachine guns. It looked like something out of a movie. He took the gun from Ariana and threw it under the bed before they got to his bedroom. His quick thinking saved both his and her life because if they had seen the gun or if Ariana would have started firing, the police would have killed them both.

"What da fuck is y'all doin' in my house?" Sleepy screamed from the ground while being place in handcuffs.

Ariana was also placed in handcuff but was taken out of the room immediately. Detective Butler walked through the crowd of officers, reached down and pulled Sleepy up onto his feet.

"Where's ya sista, Sleepy?" Butler asked, sitting him down on the bed. "You can't hear now. I asked you, where is ya sister?" he asked again after Sleepy didn't answer him the first time.

Sleepy chuckled, shaking his head at Butler's stupidity. "Do you honestly think I would tell you where my sister is so you can put her in jail? You got me all fucked up, cop."

Butler's eyes became bloodshot red. Sanaa wasn't nowhere to be found and one of the few people who knew where she was at was sitting right in front of his face unwilling to cooperate. It was as if he hit a dead end.

"You know, when it's all said and done, I'ma put you, ya brother, and Sanaa in jail for a very long time. One thing I know for sure is that she can't hide forever," Butler said then motioned with a head nod for the officers to take Sleepy into custody. As far as he was concerned, Sleepy was an accessory to all of the crimes Sanaa committed. Even if the charges didn't stick, he was going to jail this evening. He and Ariana.

Sanaa took blow after blow from Kemo, all the while with her hands bound together behind her back. He was treating her like a man, punching her in the face and kicking her in the stomach while she was on the ground. Even Kemo's boys couldn't stand to watch as he continued to punish her small frame.

"Whoooo, dis shit is like a workout," Kemo joked flopping down onto the couch. "I give it to you, bitch. You damn sure can take a punch." He laughed wiping the sweat from his face.

Sanaa spat large amounts of blood from her mouth and even managed to crack a smile at Kemo. She wanted him to know that there was nothing he could do to faze her.

"Oh you think dis shit is a game huh? We gon' see if you feel the same way a couple of hours from now," Kemo threatened.

Sanaa hog spit blood on his boots before laughing at him. Kemo laughed; he had to give it to her, she was one helluva chick. Not only was she bad, but the broad had heart.

Danielle had been watching the last few minutes and couldn't take it any longer. "That's enough, Kemo," she yelled from the top of the steps.

Since she was now on Kemo's bad side, her words meant nothing nor held any weight. "Bitch, shut up. Yo' ass is next," Kemo yelled back upstairs.

Danielle ran back into the room and closed the door behind her, thinking that maybe she had mistakenly thought that Kemo didn't have the heart to stay angry at her or any beautiful women.

Kemo grabbed a handful of Sanaa's hair and dragged her body over to the plastic tarp he had laid out. He reached his hand out to Bread for his gun and once Bread gave it to him he jammed the barrel of it into Sanaa's mouth. "Playtime is over," he leaned in and told Sanaa.

He took the safety off then wrapped his finger around the trigger. Sanaa closed her eyes and braced for impact.

Just when it seemed like Kemo was going to squeeze the trigger, he pulled the gun out of her mouth. "I'm not gonna kill you." Kemo laughed, tapping Sanaa's forehead with the gun. "I need my money. After you gimme my bread, then I'll kill you."

Sanaa wasn't going to tell Kemo where the money was at and she had good reasons not to. First of all, he had killed Joi, which was the worst of all. The second was because she knew that he was going to kill her either way, so if he was going to do it there wouldn't be any financial gain in it for him.

Kemo handed Bread the gun back and was about to continue beating Sanaa's face in until she gave him what he wanted, but then his cell phone started to vibrated on the glass coffee table.

Detective Butler walked back to the holding cells where Sleepy was, lying down on the bench. He looked super relaxed, using the cheese sandwich they gave him as a pillow. Keeping him in jail on some bullshit charges wasn't going to get Butler any closer to Sanaa. He'd looked all over the city, had all of his informants' ears to the street and still he had nothing. It was as if she'd disappeared in the middle of the night.

"You can't just hold me here without charging me with anything."

"Yeah, I know, that's why I'm letting you go," Butler responded. "I think you might wanna change ya mind about accepting my help. Joi was gunned down in an Avis garage earlier today. Your sister was the last person to be seen with her and witnesses only heard shots and then saw two SUVs speeding away once the firing stopped. So it looks like we are not the only people looking for your sister and it seems whoever else doesn't mind killing to get at her. So you may be safer here than out on them streets."

Not recognizing the number that popped up on his screen, Kemo answered the phone with an attitude. "What?" he yelled while walking from the coffee table over to the window.

When Kemo moved the curtain to the side he was in shock to see Royce standing in front of his car at the end of the driveway. To make matters worse, he noticed that Royce had brought what looked to be some of Philly's most dangerous men with him. Kemo counted six gunmen placed strategically around his home.

"Check dis out, homeboy, you got my sista in there wit' you. Let her go and you can have this," Royce said, kicking one of the two duffle bags at his feet.

Kemo snapped his fingers and motioned for Bread to come over by the window. "Aw, man, you got da game fucked up, young'un. Ya sista in too deep," Kemo spoke, looking over his shoulder at Sanaa lying on the ground.

"Dis shit ain't up for negotiation. Come out here, get ya bread, then let my sista go. It's either that or I'ma wake ya neighbors," Royce threatened, nodding for his boys to cock their weapons. The heavy artillery the men had ready to let loose got Kemo's attention quickly.

"Oh shit dis nigga ain't playin'," Kemo said holding the phone down by his side so Royce couldn't hear him. "What you think, my nigga?" he asked Bread.

Aside from Kemo and Bread, there were two other men inside of the house with them. They had guns in the home but not as big as the ones Royce's crew was brazing. Kemo had two options. He could take the money and release Sanaa or he could take his chances in a shootout. The choice for Bread was obvious.

"Yo, I'm not bitchin' up, K, but I think we should just let da bitch go and take the money," Bread advised. "But if you wanna take the other route, you know I'm with you either way."

"Nah, nah. We gon' play it smart," Kemo said placing the phone back up to his ear. "How much do you got in the bags, nigga?" he asked.

"It's two million, half funny money, half real."

Kemo's mind started to race thinking about what he could do with the real money. He had already made plans to split the fake money among Bread and the rest of the crew.

"How I know you not pulling some funny shit?" he questioned Royce.

"Look, nigga, you think I'm going to play with my family's life over some paper I can get again?" Royce responded. Kemo could tell from the sincerity in his voice that Royce wasn't bullshitting. But just in case he decided to send Bread out there to make sure.

Slowly opening the front door Bread stepped out on the porch to meet Royce and view the contents of the large duffle bags. Satisfied that Royce did indeed have the cash he promised, Bread stepped back in the house and gave Kemo the nod signaling all was good.

Kemo walked over to Sanaa. "Well it looks like you live to see another day," Kemo said as he untied her wrists. He dragged her by her arms over to the door then pushed her out onto the porch. Bread stepped out onto the porch as well holding the AR 223 in both hands.

Royce quickly grabbed the duffle bags. Neeno and Hasan were right by his side while everybody else kept a watchful eye out. He dropped both bags onto the porch then immediately attended to Sanaa. Seeing her battered face and bloody clothes had him furious. Sanaa was still alive but was injured to the point where she couldn't really walk. Royce carefully swooped her up into his arms and headed for his car, whispering some words of comfort to his sister as he got her to safety.

"Do you want your other bitch?" Kemo yelled as he pushed Danielle out the door. "I was just going to kill her anyway, but shit since I'm up a million, I'm feeling generous and why waste such a pretty face?" he joked.

Danielle took off running toward Royce's car. He hadn't planned on saving Danielle, but she could be useful in recouping the money he had just lost.

Danielle jumped in the passenger side while Royce gently placed Sanaa in the back seat. The rest of his crew got into the minivan that was parked behind Royce's car. He looked back at Sanaa as he was pulling out onto the main street. She was beaten up pretty badly, but he knew that the blood that ran through her veins was strong. They shared the strength of their father's DNA so he knew that she would be okay in the long run.

He reached in his pocket and pressed the contact labeled wifey. Krystol answered in a soft tone, having just laid Raven down for her afternoon nap.

"Hey, baby, what's going on?" she whispered.

"Yo, Krys, I need you to pack a small bag for you and the baby, and be ready to go. I should be there in about thirty minutes." Royce spoke with distress in his voice. Krystol recognize the stress in his voice and could tell something was wrong. But she didn't question him knowing that now wasn't the time. They had been in situations like this before and she understood that time was generally of the essence.

Royce hung up and quickly scrolled down to Sleepy's name. He had tried him a few times on his way to Kemo's house and didn't get an answer. The phone rang five times before going to voicemail again. Royce hated to leave town before speaking with his brother but he knew Sleepy was a big boy and could handle himself. His main concern at the moment was taking care of Sanaa.

Thirty minutes later he pulled up to the house. Krystol was peeking out the window and immediately went and grabbed baby Raven. As she was heading out the door Royce was coming inside.

"Where're the bags at?" he asked.

Krystol pointed to the side of the couch nearest the door. He went and scooped them up in one swift motion. Heading out the door he turned, making sure that the door was locked and the alarm had been set. He wasn't sure when they would be back, but he knew they surely would. Philly was their home and it would take more than a street hustler and the Feds to keep them away. Royce knew that the minute Sanaa was healthy enough they would be returning. But for now it was time that the family regrouped and gave the City of Brotherly Love some distance.

Sleepy and Ariana waited for the deputy to buzz them out the intake center door of the police station. Detective Butler had decided to release them, knowing that he wasn't going to get any info from either.

"So, you think he's gonna contact his sister," Detective Butler asked watching both as they exited the building.

Special Agent Razor stood next to Butler. "One thing I know about this family is that no matter what, and how much they go through, they will never be able to separate. The bond that they have is too strong and their ability to adapt in any environment makes our jobs even harder. We might not never see them again," Razor said.

"So now what?" Detective Butler asked, wondering what the next move was going to be.

Razor knew from experience that the chance of catching Sanaa right now was slim to none. He wasn't even about to waste any more time or manpower chasing after her. More than likely she was hundreds of miles away, on her way to God knows where.

"Now, I go back to Atlanta and you, my friend, try to get some rest. They'll open up shop in another city eventually, and when they do we'll get our chance again," Razor said before walking off.

About the Author

Blake Karrington is more than an author. He's a story-teller who places his readers in action-filled moments. It's in these creative spaces that readers are allowed to get to know his complex characters as if they're really alive.

Most of Blake's titles are centered in the South, in urban settings, that are often overlooked by the mainstream. But through Blake's eyes, readers quickly learn that places like Charlotte, NC can be as gritty as they come. It's in these streets of this oft overlooked world where Blake portrays murderers and thieves alike as believable characters. Without judgment, he weaves humanizing back stories that serve up compelling reasons for why a drug dealer might choose a life of crime.

Readers of his work speak of the roller coaster ride of emotions that ensues from feeling anger at empathetic characters who always seem to do the wrong thing at the right time, to keep the story moving forward.

In terms of setting, Blake's stories introduce his readers to spaces they may or may not be used to: streetscapes with unkempt, cracked sidewalks where poverty prevails, times are depressed and people are broke and desperate. In Blake storytelling space, morality is so curved that rooting for bad guys to get away with murder can some-times seem like the right thing for the reader to do, even when it's not.

Readers who connect with Blake find him to be relatable. Likening him to a bad boy gone good, they see a storyteller who writes as if he's lived in the worlds he generously shares, readily conveying his message that humanity is everywhere, especially in the unlikely, mean streets of cities like Charlotte.

Contact

Facebook: Blake Karrington
Instagram: BlakeKarrington
Twitter: @theblakekarrington
E-mail: Blake@karringtonmediagroup.com

Sack Chasing Star

by

T.C. Littles

Chapter 1

"Hey, girl, you hear me honking this mother-fucking horn. Get your thirsty ass over here," an untrained Rello yelled out the driver's seat of a canary yellow Dodge Challenger at LaStar. Floss faking in his uncle's custom whip, he checked the young girl's ghetto swag out with deceitful intentions. *Damn, those thick chocolate thighs looking tasty and delicious. I know it won't take much to impress her to get up in between them.*

"I'm coming damn," Star snapped at him, slamming the black rat tail comb she was doing hair with down onto the porch. "My bad, Tanisha, give me a second to see what's the word with him and I'll be right back."

"Don't be all day, girl. I'm trying to get my hair braided up so I can pull me a few ballers too." Tanisha pointed out the undone sections of her hair.

"Yeah, whatever. I got you so quit being a hater." Nonchalantly waving Tanisha off, Star strutted with a ghetto booty switch toward what she assumed was Rello's car. Tanisha's words went in one ear and out the other as she focused in on the most recent dude on her roster.

How dare he show up embarrassing me in front of the whole neighborhood? The first thing he's about to do is explain why he played me last night. He's about to get straight clowned. Lying to herself, everything in Star's immature mind made her think she was about to work Rello more than he was already working her.

"What's up? Why am I just hearing from you? Did you have amnesia last night that we were supposed to hook up?" Leaning into the passenger window, Star gave Rello a taste of her raw urban attitude.

"Don't start running your mouth recklessly, ma. Just get in." He threw the car into drive.

"Boy, stop it. You had your chance last night and no one plays a star," she said sarcastically, and shifted her pudgy weight while rolling her cheap makeup-packed eyes.

"Look, it was business in the streets with my name on it. I couldn't be stashed somewhere hugged up with you missing my money," he lied through his teeth.

Tapping his fingers onto the steering wheel, Rello knew Star's money-wandering eyes had zoned in on the bling and shine of his ticking Rolex.

"Wow, that's a nice-ass watch. I see you out here doing it big." Star fed into Rello's hallucination of having a flashy boss calling card. Little did she know, he'd spent a long hard hour scanning the gas stations' $39.99 cubic zirconia bezel imitation Rolexes for the perfect Presidential-style knockoff.

"That's what I'm trying to tell you, girl. It's nothing but boss things like this all day." Rello's words were as bogus as his watch was; but Star was naïve enough to believe it all.

"Did that business bring you closer to getting me those sneakers I asked you for last week? It's about time I get out here flossing too." Star was thirsty in the worst way, checking for any dude in Detroit willing to upgrade her low-level status.

"You'll never know if you keep running your mouth. So quit wasting time and get in the car." Rello smirked, patting his half-empty pockets insinuating her wishes were deep in them. "You got me fucked up if you think I'm about to keep sitting here playing fifty questions. I'm a busy man, Star."

"I'm not getting in for nothing, Rello." Star pouted her lips.

"If I ask again then I'm pulling off on your dusty, begging ass." Having a lot of nerve to call someone out, he jerked the gearshift into drive basically giving Star an ultimatum with zero time to decide.

Star was a true product of her society: a struggling teen trying to make it in the gritty streets of east Detroit. Whenever there was money on the table, Star was on cleanup duty. She didn't care how men treated her or talked down about her hood-like ways. Having a tarnished reputation wasn't a worry or concern for her. The game was called sack chasing and by nature, Star was knee deep in winning.

"I'll be right back, Tanisha," she called out to her friend while climbing into the car. "You better be giving me some money for those sneakers, Rello."

She slammed the car door. Star was playing the role of ghetto girl for him to see but was smiling inside. She saw the envy in Tanisha's eyes and loved it.

"Chill your hype ass out," he silenced her, turning the radio up on blast.

Star thought about giving him a quick comeback but decided against it after looking him up and down. Being trained by the grittiest ho in the game, she knew not to ruin a good thing before benefiting. *Oh yeah, bitch, keep calm; this just might be the one. At least get ya money up.* Getting comfortable in the buttery soft leather bucket seat, Star was impressed with everything about Rello. Her mind was dizzy thinking she'd landed her a true player in the game. Unbeknownst to her, not only the car but his entire wardrobe was his uncle's.

The neighborhood was flooded with cliques listening to music, drinking, gambling, and enjoying the daytime hours before ricocheting bullets were bound to fly. Every small-time gang, wannabe dough boy, and young hustler with no reference was posted up on the block getting money or plotting to take someone else's.

Rello loved to stunt and have people turning heads at his arrival. Having studied his uncle's swag many times from the same passenger seat Star was sitting in, he imitated his style, rubbing his neatly trimmed charcoal black goatee with one hand while gripping the steering wheel with the other. Every few seconds he'd glance over at Star feeling his cockiness rise.

Yeah, I've got her ass right where I want her. I'm glad I swerved up on her two weeks ago at the bus stop. She's eating me and this car up.

Star reveled in the limelight riding shotgun in the flashy whip. Coming up, she'd only seen nice cars speeding up and down the block or doing donuts at the infamous neighborhood car races. This wasn't something she was accustomed to on a daily, normally approached by local supermarket bag boys or book bag–carrying schoolboys who couldn't do nothing for her hungry pockets. Star was hoping Rello turned out to be more beneficial to her than the typical bums who gave her overly developed body attention.

Each street they rode down through the east side of Detroit turning heads and bending corners, Rello thought about how he could get young Star to give into his manly needs without him paying out the duffel bag in the back seat. Knowing the few crumbled-up five dollar bills in his pocket weren't nearly enough for the sneakers he'd promised her, he played the role like a boss refusing to admit his shortcomings. *Damn my uncle needs to put me on so I can stop being on this fronting shit.*

His time was running short. Not only had the gas light just come on, but his uncle Banko was texting asking about his whereabouts. Pulling into the parking lot of a half-abandoned apartment building, he turned the ignition off then pulled out the tightly packed joint of Kush.

"Why are we here? What's this all about?" Star asked, sucking her teeth.

"Chill out, baby. Hit this." He passed her the joint after taking the two long puffs. "I'm trying to see what you're working with." Licking his lips hoping she'd read into his innuendo, he wanted this hood legend licker badly. Light skin with braids, baby face, and hazel-brown eyes, Rello chose to use his pretty boy looks to his advantage.

What attracted Star, however, was the smell of money underneath her nose every time he came around.

"Oh it's like that? So what you talking?" Star wasn't a stranger to earning her keep or making her change. In today's world, it is what it is and you better get it how you can.

"Just a little lip action, baby." Rello rubbed on his growing cock, shifting so it could pop out, fully standing at her attention. "You got me?" he asked, realizing the young girl was all in.

"You should've been said that, Rello. It would've saved me from thinking you weren't like the others." She sunk back into the seat realizing this was just another day in her scummy lifestyle filled with the same bullshit. "Show me the money. You know how this goes." Star had been down this path before and the least Rello could do was prove he was worth her spit.

"Damn, it's like that? I've gotta pay my girl for some head? You tripping." A played-out Rello tried blocking Star from getting her deserved cash.

"Then that's even more reason why you should be giving me the cash: 'cause I'm your girl." A fast-thinking Star wasn't getting sidetracked. "So let me see the dollars, nigga." Star was persistent. If he set her up swell, no doubt in her mind she'd be checking for the role of wifey. She wanted to see how much Rello was really working with in addition to what he was willing to offer.

Damn, I can't show this chick how low balling I really am. I'm just gonna run Banko a lie about why the count is coming up short. Feeling backed into a wall, Rello hesitantly reached into the back seat unzipping the duffel bag of rubber-banded cash.

Star's eyes lit up like a kid in a toy store at the uncountable amount of loot. Energy surged through her body making her jump to grab Rello's exposed member. Sliding her smooth palm up and down his shaft, she was eager to lick her way to the jackpot. Not knowing he was just a small-time errand boy, Star was geared up for the greatest slob job in history.

Seeing the thirst in her eyes, recognizing it many times across the faces of his uncle's plethora of glamorous women, Rello tightly held the banded stack of twenty-dollar bills totaling $500 and slid them across her jaw line. "Make it good, ma, and I've got you."

Not wasting another moment of time, she obliged, swooping her hair to the back and bent over into his lap. Once he felt her big wet lips across the tip of his dick, Rello settled into the bucket seat himself, knowing the blue pill he'd swallowed right before picking her up would have Star bobbing down to his balls for a while.

Star effortlessly gulped his dick down. Not because she was a pro at slob knobbing but because Rello wasn't king long dong ding-a-ling. Not caring about his shortcomings or the fact he could barely touch her throat, Star made him jerk with each pull and tongue tickle on his balls. Rello was falling in love with her young mouth, knowing the ringing rumors of the hood were true. She was in fact a hood licking legend.

Lost in the moment, Rello gripped the back of her head relentlessly forcing Star down until the tip of her nose tickled his public hair. She fought back gagging at the disgusting mildew with the thoughts of dollar signs. Fifteen minutes of spit gushing dick sucking, Rello finally let a long, thick stream of semen release into her throat. Star had tasted better and sucked bigger; but had gotten paid way less.

"I ain't never been with no nigga who went that long." Star juiced Rello's head up wiping the excess nut from around her mouth. *If he can swipe the insides of my mouth for what seemed like an eternity, ain't no telling what damage he can do to this aching vagina.* Sucking dick always made her horny.

"I'm that real deal nigga out here, baby. You fucking with the right one." He watched her eyes scan down to his still rock-hard, throbbing penis. Quickly pulling his too big, hand-me-down Levis jeans back together and zipped, he hoped she hadn't peeped the true sign of an ecstasy popper.

"Show me then." Star put her hand out begging for the *dinero* she'd swallowed a mouthful for. "And you can take me to the mall to cop those joints, too," she said, batting her fake eyelashes in an effort to win him over. By no means did she want to hop on the bus after riding shotgun with him. *Chicks would drop dead of envy no doubt if I hopped out this fly car with bags in hand.*

"I can't even fucks with you like that right now, ma. My manz been blowing me up since I swooped up on you at your house." He checked his phone's missed calls and messages from Banko. "We've gotta link up on this business tip but I had to squeeze in some time to cake with your fine ass." It was true that Banko was blowing him up but other than that he was keeping Star spent on stories. Lucky for him she was easily blinded and persuaded.

"Oh okay, that's what's up, big fella. I see you're out here making big things happen." She pointed toward the back seat, never taking her hand out from its begging position. "You can run my money and I'll be up out your hair. Besides, ol' girl is on my porch with a half head of braids. I can get my shoes after I get done with that."

Rello knew he couldn't back down on his word to Star. She'd seen the pickup money, ridden shotgun in the custom ride, and heard him boast about getting bread in the streets. If he reneged on his promise, she'd without a doubt clown him throughout the hood ruining his already suspicious reputation. Handing her the stack of twenty-dollar bills, he regretted even promising her more than the few Abe Lincolns to his name. Once again his high hopes of being a paid hustler had overstepped his reality of only being a leech and a liar.

"Thanks, boo." Star pocketed it fast seeing the regret in his eyes. Before he could contest the amount he'd given her, she moved in for the kill by throwing sex his way. "So, are you trying to work me out tonight or what?"

"Fa'sho, ma. I'm all in that tonight. Let me feel that right quick." He leaned over, placing his hand between Star's thick thighs. Seldom getting close to a fat camel toe willing to cream for him, if Banko weren't going crazy about him getting home with his cash and car, he'd finish Star off in the back seat bent over. "I'ma beat this pussy up."

Rubbing his hands across the fat imprint they both wanted him to have, Star grinded back. Money made her cum and he'd handed her enough to squirt as far as her little mind was concerned. "Don't be on no bullshit like last night." She twisted her ghetto princess lips.

"I got you. Please believe I'm planning to tap that fatty out." Starting the car up, feeling it putter and slightly hesitate, he hurriedly backed the borrowed whip over broken glass and trash carelessly pulling into traffic. Running out of gas then being embarrassed or called out wasn't an option. Had he not been cruising, doing more than just the planned pickup and return home, he wouldn't be in the predicament to be exposed for the broke bum he actually was. But once again his desperation for flash had fucked him.

Ignoring traffic and pedestrians, Rello broke every traffic law as he sped and coasted up the side streets to drop Star off. There were no good-byes, thankfully for him, as she hopped out the gas-guzzling car. Honking as he flew up the street, she didn't even turn to wave being that she was too busy gleefully flashing the stack of cash to her girl.

"Sissy, I'm hungry." Savannah, Star's littler sister, poked her small head out the front door.

"Then go knock on your momma's bedroom door and tell her," Star snapped, knowing their mother probably put Savannah up to asking anyway. *I won't be spending this cash on her brats today.* Knowing the food stamp card had just been loaded, she knew Bonnie could stock the fridge with fresh groceries so she shooed Savannah into the house.

Savannah balled her face up like she wanted to cry then disappeared back into the house. At only eight, she didn't understand why or what it meant to go back and forth between her mother and sister. The only thing she did adapt to was getting yelled at. Joining their baby sister Samantha on the couch, they both sipped from a big cup of water and waited for someone to feed their grumbling stomachs.

Rello, now far removed and unconcerned about Star, replaced the gas nozzle from putting one of his last five dollars into the Challenger then picked up his government-issued Obama phone dialing Banko back. Without clearly coming up with a well thought-out lie, he tried spinning him with a diversion to keep clear from his uncle's warpath.

"Where you been at, li'l nigga?" Banko shouted into his Android phone. With sweat dripping from his nose, he'd been pacing the living room floor seething to attack since confirming with his main runner Rello picked the cash up. His nephew hadn't been answering his calls, making him worry he'd been flicked by the cops and folded under pressure.

"I'm on way, Unc. I had to jump stupid on your house boys for coming up short on your package," he lied, as every cent was accurate and had been accounted for.

Banko went from worry to rage, being straightforwardly lied to by the young nigga he kept so close to his fortune. "Oh straight up, killa? I'm on any nigga out here fucking my dough up." He drove his point in with hostility and emotion. He hated being lied to, especially by one in his bloodline. Banko took respect, loyalty, and love for his family seriously. Therefore, he'd been allowing Rello many privileges that other cats associated to him weren't privy to. Rello, however, was starting to take what wasn't being handed out. *Yeah, my good acts of faith for his mother are starting to run out.*

"You've gotta let me in on it, Unc. I could be cranking and keeping them jokers in line." Rello started his traditional begging spree.

Rubbing his thick black goatee, Banko felt his blood pressure rising. He hated entertaining the young pipe dreams of his sister's son; and as of late they'd been coming up more often. There was no way he could trust him on no real power moves when he was coming up missing on nickel and dime runs. He hung with true blood killers and hustlers, Rello didn't have the same gangster DNA that ran through Banko. "Ay, li'l nigga, just pull back up in my ride. I'm trying to secure my paper." Banko felt his blood pressure rising.

"Okay, I get it. You ain't gotta go all street on me, fam. I'm on the way."

As the flashy car sputtered with little gas up 94 West toward his home front, Rello thought of ways to impress Banko so he could continue flossing for Star. He imagined her warm mouth and big lips wrapping around his still stiff manhood. Pulling his semi-hard member out and jacking it a few times, Rello couldn't wait to get home to satisfy his nut. The performance she'd given him had his mind spent. *Yeah, that girl is a star for real. Her moms named her right. I've gotta find a way to dip off into that tonight.*

Chapter 2

"Give me some money to buy your greedy sisters some food," Star's mom Bonnie yapped, barging into her daughter's cramped bedroom to beg as usual. Not caring about the flimsy door being closed, which was a clear indication that Star wanted privacy, Bonnie stayed focused on herself and the petty plot she was about to run down on her oldest girl. "I'll pay you back when the caseworker turns my cash assistance back on," she lied through her teeth.

Star was tired of her mother's normal routine so she didn't reply with remorse. "Ain't nobody tell you to keep bare backing for babies. Besides, what happened to the food stamps on your bridge card? The government paying enough for ya kids to eat so I don't have to step in, don't you think?"

Bonnie was itching to smack the stale dick smell out of Star's mouth for talking recklessly. However, knowing she needed to feed Savannah and Samantha, she swallowed her pride but not without a tight jaw. "Ain't nothing wrong with helping your mother out."

When Star sensed her mother backing down, she went in for the jugular. "Damn, Ma, but for real, every month you fuck up the stamps, the cash, and even the free boxes of food they send up in here from the neighborhood church. You need to find a way to do better; and unfortunately that don't mean running me dry." Star showed no signs of backing down. With the platform to speak, she wanted to break Bonnie down or at least shake her off her back. *Them kids ain't mine and I ain't about to be playing Mommy either. Shit, where's my birth control at anyway?*

"Oh so 'cause you're grown now you can question and curse at me? Don't forget who brought who into this world." She stared down on her now nineteen-year-old daughter. Bonnie looked at Star and saw an exact replica of what she used to be. "I'll lay your ass up and out." Interlocking her fingers, cracking her knuckles, Bonnie let it be known she wasn't to be taken lightly. Once representing a cold, fierce, "out to get it" bitch, Bonnie was a beast in her heyday.

"Dang, Ma, why it gotta be like that?" Once ignoring her mother, Star now stood at attention and dared to turn her back. She'd seen Bonnie tag another pill popper in the middle of the street once before, not to mention the countless *WrestleMania* pay-per-views that went down between her and old dude; so Star knew Bonnie would fight tooth and nail to prove a point.

"Because I ain't ask for your smart mouth comments, that's why. What I asked for was a few of those dollars you tricked for earlier. Your sisters saw you leaving with some boy so cough it up, LaStar."

"Don't come up in here for my Lucky Charms, Ma. Them kids will be all right; and if not, that ain't on me. I'm telling you the same thing I told Savannah earlier." Star ignored her mother's quest to hand over her motherly responsibilities. "You are their momma. And for the record, you only trick for you so I only trick for me. Please close my door on the way out." She might've sprouted from Bonnie's tree, but Star had little respect for her mother, a once diva wasted on a nigga with no money, ambition, or potential. Now she insulted her whenever the opportunity presented itself.

"I don't know how you got to be so stingy and evil. You're such a little bitch." Her mom stared coldly at her first born. Star was a miniature version of the beauty queen she once was with a devilish personality to match. Bonnie knew exactly where the menacing attitude came from, being the one responsible for training Star up in the first place.

"Please, you're killing my vibe with all that, Ma. If I give you a twenty or two, you'll run in there and give it to his dusty ass before I blink." She casually pointed toward the front room where her stepfather lazily sat with his hands deep in his pants. Star's passionate hate for Jerome wasn't a secret. She adamantly spit venom each time his name came up.

"Shh! Keep your mouth down," Bonnie hissed, clasping her own mouth while simultaneously shaking and begging for her daughter to do the exact same. Having gotten her ass handed to her on several occasions on account of her kids, Bonnie tried to spare her babies and keep them out of Jerome's way. Star locked eyes with her mother in pity, pissed that she'd once again chosen a man over their relationship and the bond she should've been building with Savannah or Samantha.

"I'll take your children to McDonald's for a value meal, Ma, but I ain't putting no cash in your hand for their father to pimp you out of." Star couldn't hold the stare down as she watched mother's eyes brighten.

Bonnie was elated and could barely wait to tell her trifling boyfriend he could sell the remainder of her food stamps. Only fulfilling a few snacks for their late-night munchies, the kids she'd birthed high as a kite weren't accommodated when it came to nutrition once again.

"Thanks, baby, you're the best sister those two girls could have."

Star watched her mother anxiously run out the room, not to get her half sisters ready for the walk or free meal, but to present leverage for her sisters' dirt ball dad to stay. *I'll never let a nigga have me that dumb and tripping. She got me up here feeding these damn kids she made a priority to have for that sludge rock of a man; and he ain't raised a finger but to ram in her saggy coochie. It can't get more pathetic than that.* Turning her nose up at the thought of her stepfather and the dysfunctional family they were all supposed to be, Star couldn't wait to get enough money to move on her own. And despite her not wanting the responsibilities of being a parent, she knew leaving her siblings wasn't an option. LaStar was the only hope Samantha and Savannah had.

After putting a chair underneath her doorknob to stop Bonnie if she tried barging in again, Star resumed rummaging throughout her drawers trying to find the perfect outfit to mask the rolls hanging over her jeans so she could meet back up with Tanisha on the porch. Unfortunately, starving herself to death couldn't remove the lodged double cheeseburger meals she'd strictly dieted on for months. *I swear I need to start an exercise program ASAP.*

Instead of dwelling over what to wear, she picked up the phone to dial Rello's cell with high hopes he'd answer. She instantly felt déjà vu from last night when the generic voicemail greeting answered her call instead of his raspy voice. Huffing and puffing, she slammed her phone down onto the bed in aggravation. *This nigga bullshitting. I'm trying to get laid and paid while doing so.* Star felt he could be the money train out the run-down house she called home. It had been nothing but a migraine headache for her watching Bonnie live in a pity party by housing a no-good worthless nigga and ultimately ruining her innocent life.

"Come on, you two brats, let's go," Star yelled out to her sisters, moving the chair from underneath the door so they could go.

Bonnie watched her three daughters walk out of her shabby house and into the world where she secretly wished they'd stay. All they represented to her was lingering responsibility. Only spreading her legs to keep their daddies, she never had the nurturing gene women turned on after entering motherhood. The same gritty chick she was before giving birth, was the same gritty chick she was after being a mom for over nineteen years.

"Here, nigga, it's only ninety dollars left. See if you can sell them dollar for dollar. They cut my case down to a hundred dollars for me not letting her sneaky ass in last week for the annual visit," Bonnie lied, having sold the other $150 for her own gain. Handing her latest two kids' father the state-issued orange Michigan welfare card, she stood with no shame, not knowing how her daughters would eat come morning or for the rest of the month. With bare cabinets and a refrigerator of spoiled uncooked food, Bonnie was an example of the type of neglectful parent child welfare services made surprise visit days for. Her offspring didn't stand a chance.

Jerome stood looking sloppy in his worn navy blue pajama pants and stained gray T-shirt with his hand held out for the card. "Shit, woman, you've got to be joking. Even if I was successful in hustling some old bitty grandma out of her cash, we can only cop enough nose candy and liquor to wash it down with for a few days, if that. What are we supposed to do until then?" Jerome was never a strong companion or provider to Bonnie. Since after the first night of her bringing him home, he'd only been capable of mooching off the government assistance she received along with guzzling twelve packs daily of Milwaukee's Best beer whenever he could. Not only did he abuse drugs, but he abused women as well.

"Shit, I was thinking you could figure that part out. It ain't nothing else I can do since I'm bleeding and all." Bonnie was elated inside that she didn't have to sell her high miles pussy once again to get them through another month. While most women hated for their monthly cycles to come, Bonnie cherished the days because Jerome wasn't roughing her up to work.

Taking a seat on the duct taped leather couch, her stomach growled from having not eaten either. She was hopeful that Star would get her babies meals to go so she could take one for herself and make them split the other. The money she'd gotten from selling her stamps secretly was used to get high and pay back a few debts to the streets. Jerome might not have cared that young bosses who slung dope was on their heads, but she did.

"Well I ain't got nothing. So who you calling for some head?" Jerome stood over Bonnie boldly daring her to refuse the warm mouth he'd come in several times a week. With prison chiseled muscles and an itching fist, he patiently waited on her response. Ready to light her face on fire if she gave the wrong one, it would be his regular daily workout, one he looked forward to anyway.

"Why can't you just sell the stamps first and we'll talk about that later." Bonnie still tested his thirst to control and degrade her. Taking a sip of the beer they were sharing, Jerome smacked it out of her hand onto the floor, spilling their last, ultimately pissing himself off in the process. "Oh shit, why you do that for? Now what?" Jumping up to wipe up what she desperately wanted to lick up, Jerome used his foot to kick and keep her down, placing his bare foot across her neck. Frantic and panicking, Bonnie struggled to breathe with his weight on top of her tiny, frail neck.

"See how your neck really ain't shit to me unless you've got it bobbing and weaving for this family?" Jerome's words were viciously spat. He enjoyed watching her whimper and begging for him to stop.

Even though she knew her weakness gassed his ego, a blackout was coming and she didn't want her girls to walk in on her limp body. Last time he knocked her out cold from a beat down, she was out for hours and probably left to die.

"Now get up and get your shit together. I'm about to go sell these stamps. Your mission is to bring this family home enough to sustain us through the month." When Jerome mentioned family, his greedy bum ass really meant just him. Having no shame for her, just wanting the money her deep throat had a reputation for making, Jerome was callous and heartless.

Bonnie grabbed her neck in agony when Jerome lifted his stale-smelling feet. She gagged for air, thankful he'd left the room. Disgusted with her choice of men and poor decisions in life period, she grabbed her now turned off Sprint phone searching through the contacts for a dude who'd enjoy some head. Having burned through them many times before, she doubted they'd pay more than a few bucks for the normalcy. Now checking for the females she once called friends, Bonnie would be down for anything: girl on girl, or even threesomes to meet Jerome's quota. She had to be down for whatever to keep her partner around.

"Look, Momma! Star got us some toys and let us pick what kind of Happy Meals we wanted." Savannah, her middle daughter, burst through the door with a huge grin flashing her toy in front of her mother's face. Bonnie was the only mother she knew so had no option but to love.

"Yeah, yeah, yeah, that's nice." Bonnie pushed the meaningless toy from her face, opening the bag to snag a few fries. "Where's your sister?" Throwing them down her dry throat, finally having the taste of food made her hungrier.

"Her out front eating with Star." Not knowing her mom couldn't care less about her baby child, only being six herself, Savannah stood nibbling on a half-eaten nugget.

"Did you eat some fries on the way home?" Bonnie questioned Savannah with evil intent in her pill-popping prostitute eyes.

"Yes." Struggling with the plastic wrapper of the Happy Meal toy, like all children her age, was her main focus and goal.

"Oh, well then after you eat that nugget, you've had enough." Snatching the bag of food along with the toy, Bonnie tore the My Little Pony open, giving it back, and shooed her daughter to her bedroom. Rushing into the kitchen shoving more than a mouthful of nuggets into her starving mouth, Bonnie didn't regret swiping the food from the child she was responsible to feed. Nor was she concerned with the nightly belly aches Savannah and Samantha suffered from only eating junk food and outdated food from pantries. Gobbling the remainder of the McDonald's, leaving not one burnt fry tip or nugget crust, she tossed the bag into the trash.

"So you about to be on the ho stroll?" Jerome appeared from the bedroom, now in gym shoes ready to go.

"I'm trying to get something lined up. When you get back to watch the girls I can have more freedom to make a move." She hoped for more time.

"Oh, you can send they asses to bed right goddamn now. I ain't for all that loud playing and running through the house nonsense you allow anyhow. Fuck that, good night," he shouted through the almost bare house to his daughters. Savannah and Samantha unfortunately got to see their deadbeat dad do absolutely nothing but abuse them.

"Okay, I'll take care of it." Bonnie bowed to his request but wished she didn't have to. Already being a horrible, "give less than a fuck" mother, the one thing she did allow her little ones to do was play, laugh, and enjoy being children. It was only six and they'd taken a nap so she was sure they were still wired to go for hours. But to bed for the day they'd go. "Get in this house, Samantha, time to go night-night."

Chapter 3

Banko's reputation was unblemished and his name carried heavy weight in the streets. He'd singlehand-edly shut the pill game in Detroit down running a few illegal pharmacy spots throughout the city. Never having generic brands, he thrived off heads looking to pop the absolute best in large amounts. Having made it out of the Sojourner Truth Homes, pushing his own soldiers up and through the townhouses now, he'd arrived but was now carrying the dead weight of Rello heavy on his shoulders.

Grabbing an ice-cold Budweiser from the stainless steel fridge, he unzipped the duffel bag of cash Rello left on the counter before jetting up the back stair-case. He already knew his knuckleheaded nephew was guilty of ripping off a few bills, but for what was the question he wanted an answer to.

Banko hated having his sister's son in his home, but felt it was his job as a man since she was a single mom with issues. Patrice had chosen a loser as a baby daddy who was more addicted to drugs than handling his responsibilities. When he became more of a liability to Patrice and her son than an asset, Banko ran him away with death threats promised to be carried out if he returned. He didn't want his sister coupled with a woman-beating junkie. Patrice raised Rello the best she could singlehandedly until his testosterone took over, then passed her one and only child to her brother to be groomed into a man. Granted he'd taken Rello in without a qualm; but his faith was diminishing daily that his knuckleheaded nephew could follow in his footsteps within the game. Yet and still, Banko tried drilling his street knowledge and hood cred down to his only male bloodline left.

"Hey yo, Rello, get down here so we can chop it up for a few, nephew," Banko yelled upstairs, taking a seat at his breakfast bar. Eyeing the rubber-banded stacks, Banko had been in the game long enough to know his cash had been tampered with. Separating them into three neat stacks—his payout, re-up, and savings portions—he shorted Rello's payout since he'd already gotten his share off top. He knew his nephew would never speak up or admit for trying to get down behind his back; but he still dared him to speak up.

"What up, Unc?" Rello appeared with a lit joint in his hand, coughing and clouding up the room.

"Put that shit out in my house, boy. You know the rules." A perplexed Banko fanned the smoke from his personal space. Selling drugs to his people was one thing God would judge him for on his day but destroying his own temple wasn't an option his educated mind could fathom. He allowed Rello to smoke within the confines of the guest room he stayed in, window open and fan on; but to walk freely around the house, polluting it with weed smoke, was most definitely not allowed.

"My bad, Unc, but you ought to hit this shit." Rello laughed, puffing on it once more before putting it out in the sink.

Banko frowned, hating the disrespect Rello unintentionally showed. He couldn't understand why the young'un couldn't respect the rules, even right in front of his face. Cats in the street were afraid to cross Banko's path but Rello seemed to be too careless or too caught up in being his only sister's only son to give a fuck.

"Yeah, about that, Rell, you can't keep pinching off my crops. It's enough that I feed, clothe, and take care of your mooching ass. But you're starting to bite the hand that feeds you." Banko was ready to sit his blood relation on the streets. He'd only lasted this long off the strength of his sister; but he refused to go broke or in the hole trying to teach Rello the ropes.

"I could work my own shit off if you wouldn't hold out on the work. I'm trying to eat and live just like you," he truthfully responded. Rello admired his uncle's lifestyle, the pretty women, and the amount of respect hustlers gave him upon contact. He would do anything to be the underboss to Banko. All he wanted was his once chance.

"That's supposed to be the plan but I've gotta trust you out here moving behind my name, Rello. You don't take the reputation I've got out here serious. You think it's all glitz and glam but I move weight and deal with demons." Banko took a swig from his beer, staring his nephew up and down.

"I've been around you, Unc. I see how you move in the streets."

Banko stared his worthless nephew up and down wondering if he'd ever amount to anything worth bragging about. "I'm in the perfect position to set you up swell, Rello, but you must prove you're ready. I can't keep nursing you like a little boy."

"Then let me swang my own nuts." Rello threw his hands up. "My momma sent me here to learn how to be a man from you, so teach me."

Banko walked to the fridge, moving Rello from in his path along the way, then handed his nephew a cold beer. Regretting the words before they left his mouth, he couldn't resist the urge to put his family on. Banko knew he was a hated man in the streets and desperately needed a solid and loyal team to roll behind him.

"I've got a package in Chicago that needs to be picked up tomorrow night; and it's dummy proof. All you gotta do is show up at my manz' house with the payout card, collect my product, and make it home. Handle this right and we'll see about more work. Fuck this up, and you're done."

Rello didn't inquire about the driver he was replacing. *Fuck another nigga going broke. It's finally my time and I'm going for mine.* "A'ight bet. I ain't gonna fuck it up, Unc. Rest assured I'm gonna move swift, clean, and just as efficient as you would. When should I be ready to hit the road?"

Enthusiastic to get in the game, Rello wasted no time interrogating Banko for the details. He wanted to make sure he thoroughly understood what was to go down. Banko was surprised; nonetheless, he was finding comfort in Rello taking the task so serious. To Rello though, a lot was on the line and if he played his cards right, he didn't have to stunt throughout town or with Star.

Being a man of all connections, Banko had a chick at Enterprise who would supply the gas-economic sedan. He set everything up in front of Rello's face, including the hotel accommodations; all of was done with prepaid credit cards.

"I don't want to hear another word about being inducted into the game if you fuck up my money or my connection, Rello. This is your starting point; please don't let it be your exiting, too. The game you played with me today won't be tolerated again," Banko spoke with certainty. He knew the route to and from Chicago like the back of his hand and exactly how much payout was in product by sight. He planned to completely cut Rello off if the count or product was short or inaccurate.

"I got you, Unc. You better believe I won't be fucking it up."

The two sat back going over the exact details of Rello's first highway run. Banko would use him in the near future frequently if he proved his status and loyalty. Thus far things had been shaky but all family is worth some love. The plan was for Rello to dip out in a few hours, stay the day riding hoods of the city for potential growth for Banko, and finally picking up the package. If executed successfully, Rello was promised $1,000 upon delivery.

"Here's the prepaid card for my package, gas money, and the car keys. The room has been reserved under your name, completely paid for already. Upon check-in, be sure to use the hotel services and fit in among the other guests. You are not to stand out like by acting all ghetto," Banko warned, handing him an envelope of $1,000 spending cash. He knew that would be more than enough but wanted his nephew to sip some of the good life while out of town on business.

"Cool. I'm about to pack a light bag and be out." Rello jumped up anxious to accept his first mission. There was no apprehension on his end. He was about to stunt extra hard on gullible Star.

Banko dug his phone from out of his pocket as soon as Rello got out of ear distance, hitting send twice. It was time to let his Chi-Town connect know things were in motion.

Bonnie walked into the corner liquor store with her skirt hiked up and her plastic high heels freshly glued back together. She spent as minimal as possible on clothes so she could keep her and Jerome high. "Hey, Hassan, tell ya daddy I'm here and ain't got all day," she rudely spat.

No one in her phone wanted a quick session but Ali; and he tricked with every cheap prostitute from the neighborhood. When Hassan went to the back to get his father, Bonnie darted down one of the aisles for a pack of tampons. She'd been fresh out and using tissue in her panties but knew it wasn't in her best interest to go out with Ali like that. When Ali and Hassan took a minute longer than what she'd expected, she opened the seal of a wine cooler then propped herself up against the counter.

"Bonnie, you know I'm gonna have to work you extra or charge you for that beverage," Ali greeted her with his thick Arabic accent.

"You already know I work for mine, Ali. And in that case, I'll take a bottle of some top-shelf liquor and these snacks for my little ones." Bonnie flipped it on him.

Ali stood by the door with his penis getting hard within his drawers. He knew very well Bonnie worked for hers and wasn't prude when it came to the filthy things he was allowed to do to her. He didn't respect black women and whenever they were down on their luck, he used their disadvantages to his advantage. Ali gave his son the nod to bag up all of the snacks his reoccurring prostitute was stocking up on totaling the bill in his head.

"Yeah, you'll be working, if that's what you wanna call it, for hours." Smoking wasn't allowed in the store but being the owner, he did it anyway. Puffing out the inhaled stream of nicotine smoke, Ali waved for both his son and Bonnie to hurry.

"I'm looking to make your day." She hiked her already too small skirt up, giving him more of a candid view.

"Get in. I ain't got all day." Turning his eyes back toward the store, he hoped his son could hold it down while he was off satisfying his needs with the cheap hooker. Not giving it too much thought, he hopped in the driver's seat headed toward the short stay.

Chapter 4

It was a live night in the hood. Everyone worth mentioning was out getting ready to vamp including hot girl Star and her homegirl Tanisha. The two were known as running buddies, cut from the same cloth, not worried about getting bad reps. Each dressed just as scanty as the other; Star proudly rocked her fresh custom kicks, a denim pair of booty shorts that barely concealed her juicy cheeks, and a baby white tee. Since Rello was obviously on the same tip as last night, Star didn't slow up at her attempts to get on with other boys. Taking walking to the corner liquor store seriously, both girls strutted like skilled prostitutes catching eyes with every wannabe hood star and old washed-up legend. Star loved the attention, and was known to throw ass around from time to time if the price was right.

"Let me get a fifth of Seagram's Gin, cold if you got it." Setting her knockoff Gucci bag onto the counter, she searched for one of the twenty-dollar bills she'd worked for earlier. "And all the snacks this greedy heifer picked up." She pointed to Tanisha.

"Let me see your ID, Star." Behind the Plexiglas counter, the store owner's son Hassan grinned. He knew the young girl hadn't left her teenage years yet, which meant she was easy bait to prey on for his needs.

"Aw, man, are you for real? Are you about to be like that? Where's your father at today?" Star wasn't up to getting harassed by Hassan. She knew what trick bag he was coming up out of since he flirted with her from time to time. She usually made it out of the store without being hassled, though it seemed tonight would be much different.

"He's not here tonight, which means I'm calling the shots. And I need to make sure you're legal."

"Okay, here then." Sliding her state identification card over, proving her to only be nineteen, Hassan held her card up with pride and a grin only a con artist could bear.

"Now tell me why I should risk getting in trouble for your underage ass?" Staring her up and down, fixated on the rounded curves of Star's body, he wanted nothing more than to use what little clout he had to his advantage. Leaning down onto the counter, he made his suggestion more suggestive and clear.

"I'm not asking you to get in trouble, Hassan. What I'm asking for is that bottle. And I've got enough cash to pay my tab."

"Yeah, but you're not old enough to buy liquor out of this store, so it looks like you need a favor. And around here, you already know one hand washes the other." Hassan wanted the same treatment his father had been privileged to many times before.

"Fuck it then, sand nigga. What up? I ain't got all night." Smacking her lips, stepping back out of line, Star knew what was up. She'd gotten down with his dad on the regular for him not turning her in for trying to cash a bad check. So she'd already learned the disrespect his kind had for young black women.

"So you about to get down and dirty with ol' boy? How long are you gonna be? Because I can walk back to the crib," Tanisha questioned Star, annoyed he hadn't tried to get some from her. This was the second time in less than twenty-four hours she'd seen Star pull a man with access to cash.

"Chick, please, not for a bottle of bumpy. By the time you finish popping open a handful of sunflower seeds, I'll be wrapping up."

Familiar with the routine, Star made her way to the rear of the store waiting on Hassan to clear out the other customers in line. Walking past his younger brother, old enough to be Savannah's age, she felt a little shame because he'd seen her go into this same stock room with his dad a few weeks ago. Keeping her face low, she didn't want Savannah to suffer from the same cruel jokes she was bullied with as a child behind Bonnie's promiscuous behavior.

Clutching the bottle of gin like a trophy, Hassan unlocked the stockroom door and allowed her to walk in before him. Smacking her on her plump behind for disrespect, he loved to fool around with the young, misfortunate girls in the hood. His father owned several liquor stores throughout metro Detroit and he harassed females who were short on their tabs, wanted freebies, or looked downright sleazy every chance he got. Like father like son, and soon the little brother would walk the same path.

"Lift that shirt up; let me suck on them fluffy tits and fat-ass nipples my dad be talking about." Grabbing at his tiny pudgy penis, Hassan licked his lips in anticipation. He loved a voluptuous rack, especially a chocolate one.

"Hold up." Star threw her finger up rolling her eyes. "You ain't about to be doing all that for this little-ass bottle. You've got five minutes and not a second longer." Annoyed but not feeling she had a choice, Star lifted her shirt then unfastened her bra.

"Shut up and jack this penis. Women are meant to do as they're told, not as they want. Don't be back here trying to act like your black ass runs something."

Unfastening his brown-colored slacks, Hassan let them fall to the floor then flashed and waved his squishy dick. Cornering her, he ravaged her large breasts suckling like a newborn. Star stared blankly at the large chip boxes and soda pop cradles. Nothing Hassan did sexually turned her hormonal body on. The more Hassan gobbled to make sure his needs were met, the more Star's panties dried up.

After a few minutes of being repulsed, Star pushed him up off her. "All right, time's up, Hassan. You've gotten enough of a taste."

"Hold up, give me a second. Jump up and down, turn around and bounce that booty for me." Jacking his manhood a few times, Hassan was turned on by her willingness to be degraded so much that he released a nut into his own hand. "Now you can go."

"Ugh hell naw, you're disgusting." Star twisted her face up laughing. Picking up the bottle of gin she'd originally come for, she spun to walk out the door but was thrown off when he snatched the bottle from out her hand.

"That was to let you buy the gin. I don't remember discussing anything about letting you have it for free." He smirked, imitating the same laugh she'd just mocked him with. Wiping his cum filled hand across her arm, he then grabbed his crotch to see how far she'd go.

Star was vexed when she realized the trick bag Hassan had stuffed her in. Hawking up a big glob of saliva, she spat on the floor before digging into her purse for the original twenty dollar bill she tried paying with in the first place. "You ain't shit like your daddy, li'l fella." Pointing at his dick, she made sure to let him know he wasn't working with much of anything before tossing the twenty onto the floor. "Give me my shit." Snatching her bottle walking out, Star slammed the door behind her demanding the attention of everyone in the store. "Come on, Tanisha; let's get the fuck up out of here. That Arab-ass clown got me fucked up."

Star didn't slow down marching out of the store, knocking bags of chips and candy bars over on her way out the door. She knew Hassan was too trifling and guilty to call the police, not with Tanisha and the few other straggler customers knowing what was about to go down in the first place as witnesses.

Hassan could've given her the ten dollar bottle of cheap liquor if not something better for leaving his plaque and tarter breath on her body. But to him, Star wasn't nothing but a reoccurring piece of fast black tail to his father who needed a little more downgrading in her life. Their family wasn't about giving freebies.

Before Tanisha could make it out of the store, she turned to see Hassan come from the back room zipping his pants up. Looking up at the two girls, he grinned even wider. "Hey, you can be next."

Star's homegirl, down for the crown as well, smiled and mouthed, "I'll be back."

Bonnie's body shivered as Ali ran his fingers up and down her worked-over body. With welts, cuts, and bruises scattered all over her chest and stomach from beatings by the hand of Jerome, she wondered to herself how the paying customer found her attractive enough to have a hard on. Nonetheless, Ali's penis was hard and poking her in the stomach signaling he was aroused and ready to keep using her body.

Her wrists were sore and handcuffed to the head-board making her arms weak from the strain. She'd been in the same position since they'd gotten to the short stay and had been peed on, been forced to have anal sex, and give head jobs over and over since she was on her menstrual and couldn't have sex. The acts would've been considered rape by the law if Bonnie wasn't an experienced streetwalker with a long track record of not having no pride. Ali knew she could take it, and would come back for more when she needed more cash. Bonnie didn't contest anything Ali wanted because she'd drank the liquor from his store, smoked drugs that he'd purchased from a dealer once they'd gotten to the short stay, and had already spent the few dollars he'd give once they were done. In Bonnie's mind, this was all part of the game of her working.

Breaking the seal on the bottle of bumpy face, Star's mouth started to water knowing she was moments away from getting turned up. After the ordeal with Hassan, she was more than ready to get wasted and on to something else. The neighbors were blasting the local radio station lineup and she, along with partner in crime Tanisha, couldn't wait to start dancing for a few dollars. With barbeque smells flooding the air, the sun going down, and a few firecrackers being sparked up in spirit of the upcoming holiday, everything was all good. Now pitch black on the block, except for the few yards that still had lampposts and the kind neighbors who provided their porch lights, the reoccurring nightly block party really got wild and out of control.

A few drinks and blunts in, the girls were bent back. Even though neither of them was twenty-one,

Tanisha had no parents to dictate rules and Star lived by her own. The two were a terrible match, both reckless and ratchet with all intent. Star and Tanisha twerked, hip rolled, and gave belly dances on the stoop for attention. Too young to work at the strip clubs, they performed on the sidewalk as the crowd of guys circled around them. The more money that was tossed their way for amateur performances was encouragement for them to turn up more.

Jerome watched through the window discreetly with his hand gripped tightly around his stubby yellow dick. Watching Star get loose, allowing a few boys to grab her tits, smack her behind, or outright feel her body up for a few bucks, he regretted not being the father to rip her coochie up. *Damn, step-daughter, g'on and dance for them li'l niggas. Get stepdaddy dick right cause yo' momma been off my radar.* Feeling his meat swell, pedophile Jerome ejaculated to his stepdaughter and friend being true freaks for a crew of dudes.

The crowd died down. Each spectator who watched Tanisha and Star get felt up or took part in the mini freak show was gone their separate ways. Both girls went back to drinking like it was nothing, happy they'd made a few dollars to at least buy another bag of loud fire Kush.

"What happened to ol' boy in the Challenger from earlier?" Tanisha questioned, sipping from the cheap plastic two-for-a-dollar red cups. "Weren't y'all supposed to hook up?" She was being everything including messy.

"Yeah, but he played me again sending me to his voicemail." Shaking her head, Star was disappointed in herself for slipping up. *Get it together. You know better than to tell her your business. That's what happens when you get drunk and the liquor gets to talking.* "But I know he'll be back. I sucked him dry and had him screaming my name."

Tanisha was a good drinking buddy, someone to run the streets with on sack chasing schemes, but she wasn't a confidante to share man problems with. Known for fucking your man for the almighty dollar like Star, they were two sides of the same coin.

"What's his name again?" Tanisha nonchalantly asked, plotting on finding out exactly who the dude was. Her interest was piqued hours ago when Star came back flashing money in her hungry face. After their impromptu bus ride to the mall ending in Star rocking a new pair of sneakers, she was even more green with envy.

Star's street sense kicked in, noticing her friend's sudden interest in him and decided to pipe down on the sob story. Tipsy or not, she couldn't be thrown out her square. "Oh, you ain't slick. You can slow your roll on that one. I'm about to milk that nigga so don't even think about crossing that line." Star got territorial, cutthroat in letting her girl know.

"Whatever. If you haven't locked him down with those lips by now, then he's up for grabs and probably in the streets with the next thirsty girl. You might as well let him hook up with your bestie." Tanisha was honest in a roundabout way.

"Fall back, Tanisha. I don't go for your regulars so take heed and don't come for mine. I'm serious," Star warned.

Tanisha giggled, amused that Star was showing her hand and wrapped tight around a dude who had been shading her. "Okay, chill out, Star. It's not that serious for you to be getting all emotional on me. Did swallowing his nut get you pregnant?"

"Maybe it did," Star sarcastically huffed. "Either way, I'm feeling him and wouldn't mind being wifed up. I can't sack chase and trick with you forever."

"Oh yeah, I know you've lost your mind for sure now. I don't even have a comment for how crazy you sound. You ain't hardly about to play no man's wife when you play the role of his ho better." Laughing uncontrollably, even Star had to give into Tanisha's sense of humor.

Star's phone ringing interrupted their conversation.

"Oh, we must've spoke the devil up." Tanisha rolled her eyes, partially from hate that no one was calling her.

With a smile a mile long across her face, she nodded because it was in fact Rello. She waved Tanisha off so she couldn't ear hustle then ran into the house answering on the third ring.

"Hey what's up, boy? Please don't tell me you're playing games again," Star whined into the phone, caught up in her feelings. Rello was the only person on her mind. She didn't notice the house was quiet from Savannah's and Samantha's laughter and play. Nor did she notice Jerome rushing to pull his dirty sweatpants and underwear up from masturbating earlier.

"Shut up, girl. Ain't nobody got time to be thinking of ways to ignore you, Star. I'm a busy man with a lot going on. You can't be hounding me like that," Rello convincingly spoke.

"Well I don't like being dissed and you've been doing a lot of that lately."

"But I'm calling you now, so be easy." Rello shut her up quickly. "Let me make up everything to you and make you feel better. Can you be gone for a day or two?"

His words made her forget why she was upset in the first place. "Hell yeah! Where are we going? What time do you want me to be ready?" Star was already up packing her clothes into a battered knockoff Coach duffel bag. By the time he answered her questions, she'd already packed lingerie and play toys for their spur-of-the-moment getaway. *After this trip Rello will surely be mine to claim. He won't be getting away and I'll be getting my free ride up out of here.*

"That's more like it, baby. I'll be pulling up in a blue Ford Fusion in about ten minutes. Don't have me waiting either."

"Whoa! What? A Fusion? Why are you rolling in that instead of the Challenger? That car is hella fly." Star was thrown off by his sudden downgrade in cars. What she didn't know was that a bulldozer loaded with surprise would soon be heading her way.

"I see I'm gonna have to take you to school right quick on how the game really goes. True bosses only ride rentals on runs, baby girl, and don't you forget it. It's the best way to stay unnoticed and away from marked cars put in place to tag a runner like myself," a broke-down Rello recited his uncle's knowledge from earlier. He too wanted to floss on the highway, then tear Michigan Avenue up in the yellow bird Challenger.

Fuck it, if this how true bosses roll then I might as well get with the program. "Oh." She giggled. "I'll have my ass on the curb." Feeling like she might've blown her chances she threw in an apology for hounding him hard. *Damn, Star, calm down, you're acting like a dehydrated wolf for his man. Slow up!*

"That's more like it. I'm on my way." Rello hung up, leaving Star beaming from ear to ear.

She hurriedly finished packing and grabbed the remainder of her suck off money before rejoining Tanisha on the porch. Never once did she notice Jerome's watching eye each time her shapely figure passed his path. Bonnie noticed his lurking eye on many occasions, but blamed Star for developing the body she used to have in her heyday before becoming addicted, street trash, and used property in the hood they called home.

"Where are you going? You and ol' boy about to get down?" Tanisha eyed Star's overnight bag.

"Yeah, so let me call you later." Star was short with Tanisha. Since Tanisha was known for being grimy and slick, Star didn't want her around when Rello arrived. Pouring the unfinished cup of liquor out and wiping her hands, Star was clear-cut and direct that their impromptu girls' session had ended.

"Okay, you can be easy, Star. I get it and I'm gone." Tanisha got up with attitude, pulling her shorts from in the crack of her behind. "See you later."

Star didn't care about Tanisha's feelings because if the shoe were on the other foot her emotions wouldn't have been spared. As Tanisha scurried down the street not thinking twice about Star, she couldn't wait to get back to the store to make good on her word to Hassan.

Chapter 5

Rello peeled out of the Enterprise parking lot heading east to pick up Star. Just the thought of her was making him eagerly horny to have her in the passenger seat. He couldn't wait to ultimately live it up with her in the windy city during the summer time. Dressed in his own clothes for a change, which was a pair of Nike gym shorts with a white wife beater, there was no need to floss his uncle's fresh rags for the four-hour road run.

Rello understood Banko's well-kept plan of mice and men. To him it seemed simple enough to pull off in his sleep but he made sure to go over his steps with a fine-tooth comb while making his way to Star's house. Since his uncle loaded the connects money on a prepaid card to avoid possible suspicion if pulled over, he felt a little more at ease about making it to Chicago without a problem.

I hope my execution can be as perfect as Unc's details have been. If all goes well, I'ma be living like his ass instead of living off him. No matter how grateful he was for Banko putting him up and funding his necessities, he knew he was too old to have nothing in name but the want to have it all. There was no other mission on his mind but to make this a successful run and gain respect in the process. Star was just an added bonus for the trip.

Popping a pill, he took a swig of his water then pulled up to the battered bungalow Star called home. With sheets for window coverings, hanging gutters, and a roof almost caving in, it was a clear sign her family was one of the poorest in the financially strapped community. Star slightly ran up to the car and jumped in with one swift movement, a true sign of a go-getter.

"Hey, Rello, I'm sorry about earlier and from now on, I'll be on my best behavior. I be tripping but I know you're important so I'll play my role." Popping her gum, drawing attention to her glossed lips once again, she hoped he'd remember her performance earlier and be cool. The last thing she wanted was for their quality time to start off on the wrong foot.

"It's all good. Just settle back so we can hit the road. I'm on a schedule," Rello lied, knowing he was being timed by his uncle. Instead of being full of cum, dumb, and sprung on the sack chaser in Star, he should've truly been adhering to Banko's rigid instructions.

Sliding back into the seat, Star fell for the bait. "I can't even lie. I'm geeked as hell you're taking me away from here for a few days. I've never been out of Detroit farther than a few miles."

"Oh, well we're about to change all that up. You're with the right one now, baby. And if you play your cards right, I'm gonna be exclusive with you," he gassed her up.

Star was giddy with butterflies flying around her stomach as Rello pulled away from the curb. Waving at her sisters who were looking from the front room window with somber expressions was the only downside of her temporarily leaving for two days. *I can't wait until all three of us pull away from here for good.*

Rello coasted up I-94 West unnerved about the state police flicking him. He was following all of the rules Banko schooled him with: keeping up with traffic, using all the signals appropriately, and staying out of other driver's blind spots. With a valid license in his pocket, no warrants behind his name, and a trunk clean of drugs Rello decided to relax and focus on the conversation Star was trying to have.

"So, I haven't seen you with the fellas I know around the hood. Who's your team?" Star was trying to size Rello up. In just the couple of weeks of them playing phone tag with one another, she didn't know much about him other than he drove a Challenger and had access to bags of cash.

"When you're a boss like me, you don't need a team," Rello lied, then decided to control the conversation before it went the wrong way. He didn't want Star asking questions he couldn't answer.

Star hung on to his every word, hype as hell in the passenger seat thinking she'd scored big. Let Rello tell it, he was the mastermind behind the pill operation, had a deposit box of cash at Chase Bank downtown, and two pit bulls guarding his three-story home in Rosedale Park. Star was dizzy, high in the skies, and couldn't wait to reap all the benefits of being connected to her new boo.

The second half of the ride was more sexually than mentally involved since Star's head was rested in Rello's lap. She sucked ferociously until she got bored with his reaction, then turned the heat up by sliding her shorts all the way off. Rello was surprised but pleased by her whorish ways.

"Damn, girl, that's what I'm talking about. Let me tickle that wet pussy." He pushed his finger inside of her.

Squeezing her pussy lips on his pudgy fingers, she went buck wild like a vulture giving him fellatio until she felt his penis pulsating. Making him cum was just as important as getting her nut off.

Rello temporarily lost control of the vehicle and had to swerve to keep from hitting the minivan he was following. Jumping lanes in the nick of time, he held Star's head down roughly feeling like he was in one of the many pornos he'd watched. *Damn, she gobbling this monster.* He couldn't believe he was tonsil deep in a chick. "Ah! Swallow and keep sucking, I've got some more if you want it!" Rello couldn't stop pounding her throat. The harder he held her face down, the less she resisted.

"I want it." Star barely came up for air.

Neither one of them could wait to get checked-in to experience what they'd been teasing with all day. Each with ulterior motives, it couldn't be denied that in some weird way they were starting to like one another. Star with her hood porn ways and Rello looking to impress, they went together like some broke-down version of Bey and Jay.

By the time he pulled into the valet line of the lakeview Embassy Suites, his ego was more swollen than his dick had ever been. Star had been nothing but a freak and he was already turned out. She'd made sure nothing was left to his imagination and was now lightly snoring with cum crust around her lips.

Rello ran his finger across her moist panties. "Yeah, baby, we're here. Get up and get yo' shit together. I'm about to take that sweetness up out the game." Rello loved calling the shots and being in charge. For once in his life he felt God was smiling down on his existence. *Yeah, I could get used to this type of shit. It's been a good day and with ol' girl willing to bust it wide open, I know it's gonna be an even better night!*

Oh wow, he must have long cash for real. This suite is top of the line. Star took one step into the king-sized Jacuzzi suite Banko always reserved when he made the Chicago run and felt like she'd arrived.

"You like it, baby?" Rello asked, coming up behind Star kissing her neck. "This is all for you. I know I've been busy lately," he lied, knowing nothing consumed his time more than Netflix.

"Yes, of course I do. I've never been in a hotel this nice before." Star leaned in to kiss him.

She was more than grateful for the treatment he was dishing out on her. The bed was enormous, there was a forty-inch plasma flat-screen television mounted onto the wall, and the floor-length windows gave a great view of the windy city. Rello was showing the neighborhood wannabe fly girl more than the east side of Detroit could ever expose her to. Star was impressed.

"I told you earlier to be easy and let Daddy Rello take care of you. Ya manz is gonna take you to the sky, baby. Stick with a real chief." He believed his own lies.

Star felt like she'd won the Mega Millions. All she could do was hug and kiss all over him.

"Slow down, girl. You'll have all night to show me how grateful you are." He smacked Star's round behind. "Let me go make a few phone calls to line up the business meeting for tomorrow; then I'll be back in here to give you all of my attention."

"Okay." Star pouted. "But don't be too long."

"Oh, you don't have to worry about a nigga slow stepping to get back into here to that. That li'l tease in the car got me wide open," he honesty admitted. "Just do me a favor and keep it quiet in here while I make my calls. Matter of fact, whenever I'm taking care of business, stay low-key." Rello closed the door to the two room suite before Star could contest. His first priority was to check in with Banko.

Star quickly sifted through her tattered luggage for a sexy lingerie set she could entice Rello in. She was happy to have the few minutes of alone time to shower and freshen up from the freak session she'd been the star in.

She could tell from giving him two blow jobs that Rello was guaranteed to last for hours, which her young but worked pussy hadn't become accustomed to yet. Even though she was experienced, she'd only dealt with mostly teenagers except for Hassan's dad. Star was slightly nervous but definitely anxious to take a severe beat down to her walls.

Their first few hours into the midnight and early morning were full of raw sex, ones that drove Star up a wall putting her out of commission. Every toy she'd brought for their amusement was used three times over. She'd initially sucked and fucked him off twice, pulling every stunt, trick, and position learned watching pornos with Tanisha. But after riding Rello's dick like a pro until her legs were weak he showed her no mercy ramming her cunt until exploding and jacking it off all over her stomach.

They went for rounds without holding back screams or having discretion. They were fucking on the borderline of lovemaking. When it was all said and done, Star's hair was wild, Rello's cock was semi-hard, and both of their heads were spent. There was nothing left to do but burn a Kush blunt along with two cigarettes to mask the smell.

"Grab the menu so we can order room service." Rello pulled the sheet over his naked body, picking up the remote.

"Can I order whatever I want? I ain't ate shit but some lousy McDonald's earlier." Still naked as the day her whore of a mother birthed her, Star crawled back in bed grabbing a hold of her new best friend: his penis. *I'll suck the skin off this dick if it'll get me a full-course meal.*

"I'll fill that empty stomach up with this thick nut." Rello leaned back, clasping his fingers behind his head. "I can feed you all night."

"C'mon, daddy, can you please buy me some food? I'm starving." Star licked the pre cum from his semi-soft penis until his veins started to bulge. Covering the tip with her mouth making a popping noise, Rello's eyes rolled to the back of his head. "I promise to take care of you, boo."

"Yeah, yeah, yeah; order what you want." Rello couldn't resist his urges. The more she gave him head, the more his ego built up. Never in a million years did he think any woman around the way would be on his nut sac so toughly. "But that throat belongs to me after you eat." Rello tried his luck and wasn't reprimanded for talking brashly.

Star took one last lick of his manhood then came up snatching the menu. "I'll have the steak medium well, loaded baked potato, and steamed broccoli. If I can have my choice of beverage, chilled Moët." She smiled. "By the way, Rello, my throat can belong to you now." Handing him back the menu, Star leaned over and gulped his dick down 'til choking. As slobber and spit dripped from her mouth onto his shaft and balls, he spread his legs wider giving her more access to his testicles.

"Damn, girl, yeah. Work for that." Rello closed his eyes, holding back a massive explosion. Letting her deep throat him a few more times, he realized Star wasn't stopping without a grand finale. "You want that nut huh?" Cocky and arrogant, Rello dared her to say no.

Moving faster, pulling harder, within seconds Star felt his seed shoot down her throat. The bitter taste initially made her want to gag but she continued to swallow until he shivered, pushing her off. "That'll make number three, but I'm not counting." She smiled, leaning back over to light the tail.

Rello gained his composure. He was absolutely sprung off her head game once again. *Yeah, I could get used to this on a daily.* "Yes, I'll have two filet mignons medium well with baked potatoes and veggies."

Star's eyes lit up hearing Rello place the order, which included the bottle of champagne she wanted. She knew she'd probably have to sex him plenty of times more before getting back on the highway tomorrow, but what difference did it make? To Star, she was living the dream. *If I want to live the all-star life, I've gotta earn his ass and my keep. Ain't no hustler checking for a bitch with whack pussy. You better believe I'm about to work for mine.*

"The food is gonna take about an hour. I told them motherfuckas to bring some fresh fruit or some shit like that for the inconvenience," Rello lied. The hotel really offered it complimentary for them being so busy but he couldn't resist the opportunity to stunt. "Now go turn the shower water on hot and high as it can go and leave the door open. We've gotta build some steam up to make sure that Kush smell is killed." He panicked, knowing Banko would go nuclear crazy if he got caught getting high in the hotel messing the plan up.

Ali was long gone and Bonnie was busy counting up the few dollars he'd left by the nightstand. It was enough to go home and get both her and Jerome high, but she couldn't fight the urge to treat herself. She wasn't ready to go home to Star's nagging, Savannah and Samantha being needy, or Jerome going upside her head. Not bothering to slide on her clothes, she covered up in a towel and ran down to one of the dealers lingering by the vending machines of the short stay and grabbed a dime to smoke by herself. The young thug was more than happy to service her and even offered her a freebie if she wanted to service him back. Bonnie never turned down free drugs or sex if it meant getting money or drugs, so she pushed him into the corner and sucked him until his nut touched her tonsils. She did it so good that he gave her the ten back in addition to the bag. Seven minutes past the time she ran from out the room, she was back inside and preparing to get high.

The marijuana wasn't enough for heavy hitter Bonnie. Every time she hit the blunt, all she kept thinking about was how good her body would feel if she popped some pills. She counted her money over to make sure she had enough before making the call, then leaped up to find her phone and saw Jerome calling nonstop. *I wish I would call his ass back. He can't offer me nothing but a hard time right about now.* Since Bonnie had enough money to purchase some top-of-the-line pills to pop, she called directly through to Banko from the hotel phone. He had the best pills Detroit had to offer and would get her higher than a kite.

"Yo, what up?" Banko answered the unknown call, thinking it might've been Rello calling from one of his many minute phones.

"Hey, this is Bonnie. I've got a few dollars. Can I meet up with you for some pills?" She didn't care about talking in code; she was thirsty for a hit.

"Yeah, I'll be down in the projects in thirty minutes. Meet up with me there." He hung up.

Bonnie got dressed and ran to the bus stop barefoot with her plastic pumps in hand. She needed to get to the Sojourner Truth Homes to meet Banko before he left. If he said thirty minutes, he meant just that.

Chapter 6

The two were living it up in Chi-Town blowing through all of the pocket money Banko had given Rello. Star didn't keep it a secret that she'd never seen, legally shopped, or dined at the type of places Rello was breaking cash off at. He however kept his front game high as if being a boss came second nature to him. Seeing Star light up pulling clothes off the rack and ordering the highest priced entrees had him swinging his nuts like a king. Out of the spending money Banko gave him, he'd gone through almost half on a Juicy Couture watch, Michael Kors purse, and a couple pair of Guess Jeans at the Macy's on Michigan Avenue, plus picking up the hefty bill at the Cheesecake Factory.

Shit, this nigga is straight crazy if he thinks he's ever getting rid of me. Nope, I'm here to stay. Star peeked back at her shopping bags with butterflies dancing in her stomach. Although she'd pinched her-self a million times since the first time they took a dip in the Jacuzzi at the room, she still couldn't believe she'd made it out of Detroit, even if it was just for a few days. She could remember watching sitcoms like *The Cosby Show* and *Family Matters* wishing Santa Claus would've delivered a better mother underneath their Salvation Army tree. The deprived, destitute home she was raised in by Bonnie left her always wanting for more; and now it seemed like Rello was that Santa.

Per Banko's orders, Rello had to ride around urban neighborhoods searching for potential spots. He wanted to expand his drug business outside of Detroit, and figured doing that closely to where the pill and lean connect was located at was genius.

"Dang, people act like our hometown is the only place that has ghettos and shit," Star gazed out the window. "They've got just as many abandoned buildings, shanty houses, and streetwalkers posted on skid row as Mack and Bewick." She compared the south side to Detroit's east side.

"And that's exactly why I'm trying to open up shop in these parts. The less these people have, the more reasons they have to get high." Rello recited Banko's reasoning for wanting to expand to the south side like it was his own idea. "Do me a favor and snap a few pictures of houses that look vacant." He passed off one of his responsibilities like a boss.

"I'll do anything to help my man." She smiled seductively snatching the small Polaroid camera.

She snapped feverishly until Rello navigated his way into Hyde Park. With birds chirping, dogs being walked, and families playing at the park, this friendly community was foreign to Rello and Star, which instantly made them feel out of place.

"This is it," Rello felt anxiety pulling up to a two-story brick home. The well-manicured football stadium lawn and appealing landscaping was a far cry from the tumbleweed yard in front of her house she now called a dungeon.

"Oh wow, this is nice as hell. It's like night and day from where we live at." Star couldn't contain herself. She'd never seen a neighborhood so pristine and wealthy looking. *Savannah and Samantha deserve to grow up somewhere like this. I really ain't trying to cut Bonnie no slack and shit but my little sissies deserve better. Just like me, they didn't ask to be born.*

"Chill out, girl. I told you I'd take you places. And those bags in the back seat should be proof enough that I'm good on my word," he tried boasting, though his eyes were bright too. Banko wasn't living like a peasant, but he sure wasn't living like the connect. *Maybe I shouldn't have brought her along trying to front. I didn't think ol' boy was gonna be living like a king. This crib is official.*

Rello rubbed Star's thigh and even though she kept quiet about noticing his anxiety, she could feel him shaking, too. *What the fuck is this nigga nervous for? Let him tell it, he's got this and is showing me something.*

Neither of them said a word as they waited at the front door on someone to answer.

"Yes, may I help you?" Greeting Star and Rello from the other side of the door was a short, plump Mexican lady dressed in a traditional blue and white maid outfit.

"Um, yeah. I'm here to handle some business with Dominik." Rello kept it short and simple.

The maid barely spoke English but she was fluent when it came to keeping a keen eye out for things that seemed odd. And a hip hop–dressed dude in baggy jeans, a loose fitting T-shirt, and laced tight Jordan sneakers wasn't someone her boss typically associated with. Especially when accompanied by a scantily dressed girl. Maria knew if her boss was doing business with the likes of the strangers, the boss's wife would want to know.

"Name please." Maria kept it short and sweet.

"Sure. My name is Rello and this is my friend." He neglected to introduce Star by name.

Star didn't take it personal, nor was she paying close attention to the conversation. She was too busy peeping over the maid's shoulder at how enormous and elaborately decorated the front room was. For the moment, she was minding Rello's rules of staying in her place.

Once Maria received confirmation that Dominik was in fact doing business with Star and Rello, she paged the boss's wife then allowed the two in. "Shoe off please. Then it'll be right this way."

Star gladly followed Maria in complete awe of the connect's home. She'd never walked on marble floors before or been in a home with cathedral ceilings, skylights, and rooms full of plush furniture. *Damn, I've been living deprived my whole life!* Everything seemed larger than life to her. Rello was right; he'd shown her far better than what she'd been exposed to her whole meager existence.

Rello on the other hand was nervous and hoping his cowardly feelings weren't showing. *Damn, I wish I could stand bold and confident like my uncle.* He felt like he was failing miserably at imitating Banko's cutthroat demeanor. Trying not to stand out like a fool, he kept his eyes focused on the goal and kept reciting the game plan in his mind.

"Here are your guests, sir. Is there something you'd like me to bring you all?"

"Thank you, Maria. Bring a bottle of wine and three glasses. Two for us gentlemen and one for the unexpected lady." Dominik looked Star over with a raised eye.

Star immediately picked up on the questioning looks and felt self-conscious. *What the fuck? Check ya manz, Rello. I'm here with you. Why would he be putting me on blast like that?*

Rello stood speechless, wanting the awkward moment to pass. It was then that he knew bringing Star along to meet the connect was biggest mistake of his life. Only having experienced low-level pickups and drop-offs in the hood, Rello didn't understand proper etiquette or the rules to the game Banko and his affiliates played by.

"Okay, sir. I'll be right back." Maria scurried off.

"Have a seat. We've got a little business to take care of, so you might as well get comfortable." With a little annoyance in his voice, Rello was hopeful that his cover wasn't blown, but wasn't getting a good vibe at the current moment.

"I can just go sit in the car until you grown men are done," Star spoke up, knowing her presence was the reason for Dominik's tension.

"I wouldn't have that, young lady. Any connections of Banko's are connections of mine. Have a seat and get comfortable like I said." Star didn't know who Banko was but didn't dare question him. "I'm Dominik as I'm sure you know," he introduced himself, extending his hand for Star to shake.

"LaStar." She smiled, finally feeling more welcomed. "But you can call me Star." Taking a seat, being swallowed by the oversized plush couch, she tried to act interested in the foreign movie playing on the flat screen. *I guess Banko and Rello do business together and this is really one of his boys. Oh well, money is money and it looks like I've hit the jackpot.* Studying Dominik's facial features on the sly, his milk chocolate complexion, strong jaw line, and the intensity in his eyes had her floppin' for him like a fish out of water. She wasn't accustomed to seeing a black man dressed in a linen suit or ordering a maid around. *Wow, it's like I'm living on an episode of reality TV.*

Rello was still uneasy but for good reasons. Dominik had already sent his uncle a text letting him know directions hadn't been followed. When the two amateurs weren't looking, he'd snapped a picture to send Banko and one for his personal gallery too. You couldn't be too safe in today's time. And these two peasants looked suspect to him. Connection to

Banko or not, Dominik didn't fuck around when it came to his home front.

Maria came back right on time, pouring them each a glass of wine. Star guzzled her drink down before Maria could finish serving the guys and sat her glass down for a second fill up.

"Slow down, baby, don't drink the man out of house and home," Rello tried to train the young girl.

"So tell me, Star, are you from Detroit?" Dominik had a long line of questions off the top of his head to quiz her with. Plus he'd picked up on her not-so-subtle stares and wanted to know just how far her curiosity would go.

"Yeah, team East-Side represent." She threw the gang symbol with pride.

So caught up in thinking she was cute, she didn't realize Dominik giving her the side eye.

"What she meant to say was yes, from the east side." Rello cleaned up her more than urban girl slang, shifting in his seat. He might've been from the projects but could imitate Banko with ease. His uncle had been schooling him well.

"Oh, my bad. Let me remember my manners." She giggled flirtatiously. "I guess this wine snuck up on me because I'm already feeling tipsy."

The more Dominik filled her glass up, the more liquor she drank down. "Oh no, don't apologize, just be yourself." He knew a drunk spoke their mind so he wanted her as buzzed as possible.

"Thanks for the invitation." She smiled seductively, opening her legs so Dominik could comfortably peek up her denim skirt. "I don't know what this is exactly, but it's got me hot." Lifting the glass, Star fell into her element of being a ho. She couldn't help herself. The wine was expensive, smooth, and a brand Hassan's family didn't sell. It was way out of her element and it showed.

Star was intrigued by the way Dominik carried himself, far more of a boss than Rello. *Maybe I can get lucky enough to score a little alone time with him. I'll wave good-bye to small-time Rello at the door.*

"Your taste buds have just tasted the best, young lady." Dominik snuck his peek in. "It would be foolish to let my palate experience anything but the absolute finest." To him, she was a no-class girl looking for trouble and wouldn't be caught dead doing anything other than innocent looking.

Rello had no control over the ghetto girl he'd taken so far from the hood. He watched Star desperately flaunt her double-D breasts, bend over to let them hang out of her too small shirt, and Dominik lose his cool zoned in on her thick frame on more than one occasion. *I don't know why I didn't think her thirsty ass wouldn't be on the prowl. I've gotta find a way to get this meeting back on track.*

"Hey, baby, Maria told me you were busy, but I had to let you know I was home." A tall, redbone chick with green eyes walked in, shocking the three of them. "I made dinner reservations for us while I was out shopping."

Dominik stood to greet the woman, embracing her before placing a kiss on her makeup-beat face. "I'm sure she did, sweetheart. I assure you that I won't be long."

The uppity wife acknowledged Star and Rello then turned her nose up in disgust. As a woman, she picked up the greed in Star's eyes in a matter of seconds then summed her up to be nothing more than a cheap thread count hobo who had to be watched. "Oh, well I see you've made them feel comfortable." She picked up one of the wine glasses. "Let me follow your lead by showing my manners. Hi, I'm Nicole," she snobbishly greeted them, but cutting Star an ice-cold glare. *Maria surely deserves a tip for letting me know this filth was in my home.*

"These are friends of Banko's," Dominik responded, before Star could respond.

"Let them introduce themselves, honey." She smiled slyly, never taking her eyes off Star. She knew a virus when she saw one.

Dressed in the best she could afford, which were the tackiest, cheapest clothes on clearance, Star was no comparison to Nicole's elegant appearance and could feel she was being sized up. She felt inferior and for the first time since Rello met Star, she was speechless.

"I'm Rello. This is my girl, Star. We were just handling some business with your husband then we'll be out of both you guys' hair." Rello didn't know what turn the meeting was about to take, but he didn't want it to go left without him getting Banko's product.

"Nice meeting you, Rello." Nicole intentionally left Star out of the greeting. Star had no choice but to feel unwelcomed and intimidated.

The air within the room was stagnant and tense. Star couldn't take being the center of negative attention with the scowl of Nicole burning her alive. *If I don't get up out of here quick, I'm gonna turn into Bonnie on they asses. I feel the walls closing in.* "I've gotta pee; someone lead me to the bathroom in this huge motherfucka before I piss on the couch." Star leaped up from her seat, even making Nicole's head snap back.

"Maria, please accompany her to our private powder room as the guests' washroom is out of order," Nicole yelled for the maid before Star took one foot toward the door then turned to Dominik. "I'm sure you'll be calling the plumber as soon as our company leaves. You already know I don't like common folk, especially within my home." Being hospitable was the last thing Nicole cared about.

Back in Detroit Banko was infuriated and outraged by his nephew's complete disregard for the rules he'd meticulously laid out. After receiving the first text message from Dominik, followed by the picture of Rello and Star, he begged his ally to have pity of the young'uns for any immature behavior or acts of idiocy they pulled off. Banko needed the package of brand name pharmaceutical pills and cough syrup badly.

"Do you want me to stop?" Bonnie came up for air once she felt Banko's manhood going limp in her mouth.

"Naw, fuck that. Suck harder." He slammed her head back down with no remorse. She'd become a second thought to Rello, whoever Star was, and Dominik; but Banko was right back into the groove of getting his dick sucked within a matter of seconds. Getting head always relaxed his nerves, but knowing his money and product were both on the line had his blood pressure rising. He'd just dropped the last of his product of downstairs to head runner of the house, and needed the re-up badly.

Puffing circles in the air, he blamed himself for not sending his regular skilled driver on the run or going himself. *Family or not, this li'l nigga ain't cut from my pedigree. His dumb ass must have his ho-ass father's blood running through him. Rello needs to be broken down and schooled. Until then, he better not fuck up my motherfuckin' product.* Banko took his frustration out on the junkie. When he felt the temptation to release, he gripped the sides of her face with force then shoved himself even farther down her throat. "Yeah, you're gonna swallow each drop out this monster. I've got ya pills all right."

Chapter 7

Nothing perfect lasts forever. Unfortunately for Star, she was born in the struggle and couldn't seem to be reborn from it. The dream Star was living with Rello was abruptly coming to an end as she started to sober up from all the wine she'd guzzled down. She didn't like being out of her element and ultimately thrown off her square.

That bitch Nicole better be happy I'm holding Rello down. Let me catch her on the street, under different circumstances, and I'm gonna cut her fucking bright light face. Star couldn't shake the feeling of being inferior to Nicole. As she stood in the oversized bathroom staring at her cheap attire and basement hairdo, she became overwhelmed with jealousy and green with envy. All of a sudden, the shopping spree Rello gifted her with seemed small time compared to all the Burberry, Chanel, and Gucci fashion bags Nicole had carried in. "I should've at least popped the tags on one of those outfits."

I know something if she doesn't though. Her man couldn't keep his eyes off this fat coochie of mine. Fuck her with a sick dick. Star plopped down onto the toilet then pushed as hard as she could until a big turd plopped into the water. As Star sat scanning the well-designed cherry-oak bathroom of marble sink tops, vanity lights surrounding the mirrors, and Jacuzzi tub that was classier than the one at the hotel, she felt even more disgust for her life. *Since I'll probably never escape the ghetto to something this nice, I might as well take a souvenir.*

With a mind full of devious intentions, Star rushed to finish her business then quickly washed her hands. The one skill she was successful in picking up from Bonnie was rambling, so she put it to use with ease. At first she only came across tampons, cleaning supplies, and a re-up of Quilted Northern; then her eyes zoned in on a gold mine. Nicole kept the jewelry she wore most frequently in the bathroom for quick access. Never did Nicole think a thief would be within her private perimeters and never did Star think the wealthy woman would notice the ugliest pair of earrings were gone missing. Star felt vindicated sliding them into her jeans pocket to either wear or sell once back in the D. *Man, fuck her vain ass. I saw those Tiffany bags in hand; she has the dough to replace whatever I've "accidentally found." I'll be back home to my petty, pitiful lifestyle before she even goes looking for this crap anyway.*

Knocks at the door startled her. "Are you done? You've been in there a long time." Star already recognized Nicole's annoying voice. Not rattled, shook, or caught off-guard, Star made sure to put everything back as found.

Why is she so worried? Am I on her clock? "Damn, am I being timed? I had to take a dump. Is that okay with you?" Star stood still waiting on Nicole's response. "Got some air freshener?" She giggled knowing ol' girl was probably beet red pissed.

Star could hear Nicole's smug disposition through the thick wooden door. "No, you're not being timed; air freshener is underneath the sink. Just hurry up." Seconds later, her Louboutin heels clicked away on the hardwood floors.

Once Star carefully put everything back the way she found it, she swung the door open roughly so it would slam against the wall. When it bounced off the door stopper, Maria giggled because she knew the young girl wasn't familiar with the extraneous object. "Let me take you back to the sitting area." She waved.

"I have all your money loaded on this card. Can I pay you now?" Rello was nervous and it showed. Flashing the prepaid debit card Banko had given him, he'd jumped the gun without seeing the product first. *Oh well, as long as I get this transaction back on track.*

"Of course. But next time, if there's a next time, be sure to come alone. Nicole doesn't like it when females invade her territory. And to be honest, I prefer handling business man to man. That's how real transactions are done. But Banko will get you more background on me I'm assuming." He was stern, knowing he'd hear his wife's bitching later.

"I didn't know. That's my bad," Rello apologized, looking down at his feet. "I see now that I made a mistake, trust me."

"Listen, li'l homie, let me give you some advice to take with you for the rest of your life. Meet your associates on the top. Those who deserve to live like you will either be there waiting or will arrive soon enough."

Dominik was about business and knew Banko's money was good money regardless of Rello's bad judgment. He swiped the card, confirmed the money was transferred, then retrieved the order from what looked like a supply room. "Deliver this to Banko with better judgment, son. It's five dozen bottles of promethazine with codeine syrup and two thousand pure white Molly MDA pills as promised."

Rello glanced inside with wide eyes not expecting such a pricey package then zipped up both sports-equipped duffel bags. *No wonder my uncle laid out a dummy proof plan. He'll never fall off from being a boss in the hood with packages like this.* "Thanks, I'll make sure to deliver them to him, sir." Rello felt compelled to show Dominik the utmost respect.

"Banko has a plan for you, kid. Pussy can always ruin a man's potential if his head ain't in the game," he warned, finally taking a drink of the wine he'd ordered Maria to serve when they first got here. Dominik had no plans on drinking 'til after all monies were exchanged. Young Rello and his sack chaser were set up to get tipsy, so they would be more vulnerable and off their game.

Dominik sized Rello up even more as he spoke to him. It was hard for him to believe he was related to Banko by his disposition. *He's lacking a street eye, hustle skills, and obviously a Mack game to keep broads in line. He's lucky me and his uncle have such a lucrative relationship.* Dominik wasn't a fan of handling business with unskilled men; and though he'd played it cool he didn't want to see Rello or Star back at his doorstep again.

"Maria, show Rello and his company out. I'll have my dinner with Nicole now." Dominik didn't say another word to the wannabe nor did he bid a good-bye to a thieving Star.

Back within the confines of the rental car, Rello began going crazy on Star. He might've secured the package, but he knew Banko wasn't going to be pleased about how the meeting unfolded. "So it was too much for you to sit back and keep your fuckin' mouth closed huh? You ain't nothing more than a ghetto groupie who'll never have shit. I feel foolish as hell for thinking you'd be a quiet piece of eye candy."

"I ain't speak 'til spoken to, damn. You should be happy I ain't check out on that bougie acting bitch Nicole. You know she was acting straight funky toward me. Everything was all good until she pranced in," Star snapped back at him. Although she'd clowned at a complete stranger's house, she wasn't getting ready to back down.

"Naw, you should be happy I ain't slap yo' bottom-feeding ass. I can't have you on my team if you can't get that ratchet behavior under control. That shit was terrible and you could've fucked the whole deal up." He rattled the windows with his screams. Dominik's advice was starting to settle in his membrane and he knew dealing with Banko later was going to be a nightmare within itself.

"I already see you ain't gonna be the one to stick up for a bitch. You should've told her to ease up on your girl and told that nigga to quit questioning me like the Feds. I started to turn and front you off for leaving me hanging, when you brought me there in the first place. I didn't invite myself here. So if you're mad at anyone, be mad at ya damn self." Star was going ham. Reliving being looked down upon by Dominik and Nicole was making her overly emotional.

The more attitude Star popped off at him, the more Rello's anger grew from rage to uncontrollable fury. Star might've been able to give amazing head but her ability to talk recklessly accompanied it and he could do without it. *Her voice is annoying me. I don't think I'm gonna be able to take hearing her much longer.* Rello rocked back and forth in his seat trying to calm himself, then snapped. Open hand smacking an unsuspecting Star across the face, her head bounced off the window then back into an upright position. "I'm tired of your fucking mouth. Don't say shit else until spoken to."

Star sat dumbfounded and completely still. Despite her growing up in the dysfunctional family led by Bonnie, she'd never been struck by a dude. She wanted to break down from the pain throbbing in her head and face. *I ain't ask for none of this. I could've been home getting drunk with Tanisha instead of getting punched on.* Refusing to talk, Star began having flashbacks of her childhood years seeing Bonnie get yoked up. She refused to become a victim of domestic violence.

Rello sped through the streets of Chi-Town on his way back to the hotel. He didn't feel the slightest bit of repentance for knocking some sense into Star. Even though his phone wasn't being rung by Banko yet, he was sure his chances of being the next kingpin were over. All he kept thinking about was the warnings Banko gave him before walking out of the house.

"Look, you've already ruined enough for me; so for the rest of this trip follow every single order I give you without hesitation." Rello barked orders, almost flipping the car over swerving into valet. "When we get to this room with your slip-lip ass, pack your shit and be by the door waiting to go. You better hope I don't leave you stranded at Greyhound."

Star was sunken into a shell. She refused to give Rello any words but she nodded to let him know she understood. Although she had more than half of the money from giving him the head job the other day, she still didn't want to spend it getting home. It was clear to her she'd need that cash to hold her over until another dude took interest in her. The knight in shining armor she thought she'd found in Rello had turned into the devil right before her eyes.

Rello wasn't moved by her inflamed tearstained cheeks or sniffling. In fact it was making him angrier. Getting to the room and swiping his keycard, he went against Banko's direct plan once again because they were about to be out. He couldn't see himself staying with Star another night.

I might be hard up and pressed for attention but Rello has lost his fucking mind. I don't care how Dominik and his uppity bitch Nicole were living or how they judged me; at least I kept it real. That's more than I can say for Rello's punk ass. And putting his hands on me won't be tolerated. Star was semi salty that her mini vacation had come to an end prematurely but was satisfied to at least have some gold earrings to sell once back in the D. Their love bird relationship had turned cold as ice.

It wasn't long before the two were back on the road and unlike last time, Star's mouth stayed empty while Rello's dick remained limp and dry. Rello wasn't concerned about getting a quick nut since they were riding dirty with the promised package. Turning the music up on blast, he set the cruise control and coasted seventy miles per hour up Interstate 94 East. After an hour of Meek Mills blasting through the factory stereo system, Rello noticed the state police hiding out under a bridge in the highway's median.

"You got your seat belt on, girl?" He got uneasy and tried to blend into traffic, but it was inevitable not to pass the speed-clocking man in blue.

"Yeah, I see him." Star low-key shook in her seat hoping if they were stopped the cop didn't run her dirty name. "I've got it on."

As Rello passed the cop, as suspected, he flipped his visor down and quickly pulled out behind the two swooping up like a bat out of hell close to their bumper. "Fuck, this ho-ass nigga about to flick us. Damn!" Hitting the steering wheel, Rello tried to remain cool. No laws had been broken and the car was still staying steady at seventy miles per hour. The cop kept close up on the car running the plates. Seeing a rest stop up ahead, Rello hurriedly threw on his right blinker to signal he was about to exit.

"Please don't tell me he got over too," Star nervously spoke, scared to breathe. "If he did, it's a wrap." Shaking her head not wanting to move, Star felt like the state boys were in the vehicle with her and Rello.

"Shut up, damn. And yes, they got over." Uneasy himself, Rello knew the weight in the trunk would send both him and his hot honey Star in a hellhole for at least ten years. "If they flick us, you better be ready to be down for ya boy."

Star fidgeted in her seat, knowing exactly what Rello was referring to. All men became putty over pussy and a man with a badge wasn't any different.

Oh well, it is what it is. I'm not about to go to jail. She mentally prepared herself for whatever she had to do to get home.

The cop followed behind their rental for almost a quarter mile before coming up on the same exit. Rello's heart was racing and Star's stomach was doing cartwheels. "We're about to be fucked. There's enough pills and syrup in the trunk to have us celebrating our thirtieth birthday behind bars." Seeing that Star was willing made him feel a little better but the cop staying close on his bumper had him close to about peeing his pants. *I ain't cut out for this, real talk!*

"Please don't tell me this is happening. This day has gone from great to horrible too fast and I'm not trying to end it by getting caught up on no drug charges," Star rightfully panicked. She rubbed her nauseated stomach and tried going over an alibi in her head just in case they were flicked and questioned. *I'll suck that cop dry but by no means am I spending any time behind bars for this bullshit. Rello ain't shit for throwing me to the wolves though. And what am I going to do about this stolen jewelry? Please God don't let this cop harass us.*

Getting over into the turning lane to make a left into the Tim Horton's, Rello inconspicuously kept staring into his rearview mirror watching the police with an uneasy feeling. *If they pull me over, this li'l Miss Good Mouth right here better be down for the cause. I know he'll let us go after getting a feel of what she's got!* Waiting on traffic to clear, Rello's dick was mushy soft and his heart was beating rapidly. *Ain't shit going right. Maybe this street life ain't for me.* As tough as he wanted to be, the truth was that Rello wasn't made for pressure. Instead of being in the line of fire, he wished he could be back chilling smoking a blunt at his unc's crib or even in the projects with his boys playing video games. Either way, being a transporter of product may have been too far out of his realm.

The Caucasian state-employed cop stared straight ahead through his Ray-Ban sunglasses knowing the two were watching him back just as hard. Since he couldn't go around the car, he purposely intimidated them and enjoyed doing so. When Rello and Star finally cleared his path, the cop sipped from his own private flask of whiskey then drove along about his merry day. If he wasn't off duty and ready to get home to his loving wife and newborn son, he would've for sure flicked them to see what law they were breaking. On a normal day, the officer harassed black drivers whether they looked suspicious or not.

"Oh my God, thank you." Rello blinked, grateful to see the cop kept going.

"He kept going? Yes! Let's hurry up and get the fuck up out of here before he changes his mind and turns around." Star nervously looked around. "I don't eat no damn Tim Horton's no how; this shit is for white people." Rolling the window down quickly, she tossed the concealed blunt from her purse out the window just in case they got followed by another police officer.

"I feel that but you still ain't calling no shots around this motherfucka. We wouldn't even have been in that situation if I didn't have to pull out early on account of your trifle-life ass not knowing how to act. I'm about to go take a piss then we're getting back on the road. So you can either be cool until then, or walk your ass up 94." Rello went raw on Star like he hadn't just been shaking in is drawers too.

He didn't give Star a chance to respond or defend herself.

Pulling into a parking spot near the rear of the lot, Rello jumped out lightly jogging to the restaurant. His clammy hands, pounding heartbeat, and beads of sweat gathering on his forehead were all signs the cops had shook him; but he refused to confide in Star. He needed the few minutes of alone time to get his mind together for the rest of the ride back to Detroit.

This nigga got us riding with enough work to sit me down for over twenty years? Oh hell naw, that little whack-ass shopping spree, hotel, and food is nothing compared to what he should be breaking me off with. Star couldn't help but play back Rello's words when the cop was following them. "That clown was gonna use me to get off with that cracker cop and probably wasn't gonna give me a penny for it. Oh I will get mine." Star slammed her fist on the dashboard. Unbuckling her seat belt, Star checked to see if Rello was coming out then popped the trunk and slid out. If he came out her lie was going to be that she was using the bathroom, but in reality she was about to get down on Rello and whoever else was associated.

Star unzipped the bags, pulled out a few bottles of promethazine with codeine, and a handful of the infamous Molly pills she'd seen Hassan's father pop a dozen times. "Oh, he was right. We would've went down 'cause he's holding like a boss." Stuffing the pills down in her pocket with the jewelry, she grabbed another handful for the other side just as big. Then she threw a few bottles of codeine cough syrup into her own dusty duffel bag before slamming the trunk back down sliding back into the car.

"The next stop we make will be in Detroit so if you gotta pee, hold it." He jumped into the driver seat ready to go. Rello had taken all the time he needed in the restroom to regain his composure. Overly consumed with making sure his guts were together for the two-hour ride back, he wasn't the least bit concerned with Star. Back on the highway, he couldn't sense her breathing hard out of worry about him checking her bag or pockets.

Chapter 8

"Hey, can I get a ride for a favor?" Bonnie licked her tongue out at a jitney that sat curbside. She was suggesting a head job for a taxi ride.

He hurriedly unbuckled his pants and waved her into the passenger seat. Normally he only took workers back and forth to their homes when they got off the bus route, but he'd figured she was good for the ride until he released his cum. After that, he planned on putting her out to find the rest of her way. That plan didn't include telling her that for her best interest she better had sucked slow. "Where are you heading to? And before you answer, I'm not going far." Despite him wanting a sloppy head job, he still had a job to work and had customers that were counting on him to be on time when they got off the bus.

Bonnie thought about having him run her home or at least halfway, but thought about the extra pill Banko gave her and told him the short stay hotel. The whole time she was selling her mouth for a ride, she kept hoping she could meet back up with the dealer who'd given her a free bag plus the ten back. *My jaws might be tired, but I can take that bullshit weed back to Jerome and pop pills by myself.*

***

"So this is it? You slapped the shit out of me and ain't said two words to me since that ho-ass cop followed us. You're bold for treating me like this." Star pouted, opening her mouth for the first time since being smacked quiet. Now back in Detroit and in front of her poverty-stricken home, she didn't want to part ways with Rello. *I should've at least tried to sex my way back into his good graces.*

Having regretted not trying to fuck her way into his good graces while still in Chicago, now sitting in front of her less than fortunate home, She'd made it back without him hinting toward knowing she'd stolen from up under his nose but Star felt she was losing the biggest jackpot: him. If it ever came up that the package was light, she'd play dumb or suggest Dominik shorted him.

"I told your rat ass up front that this trip was about business. Then I reminded you at the hotel about playing a low-key role whenever matters didn't concern you. But naw, you did what Star wanted to do, and that was put my money at risk. You want me to feel sorry 'cause I put you in your place? The game don't work that way you ain't about to cry on my shoulder." Rello didn't show Star the least bit of sympathy. He was even more vexed and irritated with Star now that Banko was blowing his phone up with calls and text messages.

"Okay, I feel you and I'm sorry if I fucked up money for you or whatever, you've gotta believe me."

Star groveled with her apologies then tried reaching over to hug him. "Let me show you how apologetic I am. Please let me make it better." Star was confident that Rello couldn't say no to a plea of forgiveness when it was accompanied by sex.

"What the fuck can I do with that sorry, tired-ass pussy of yours? Back the hell up off me." Rello roughly shoved Star back, wiping any slob from her kisses off his neck. He wasn't in the mood for beating around the bush or even getting special attention for one last time. The more she apologized, the more he remembered being on the line with Banko. Star had played herself as far as he was concerned.

"Please don't leave like this. At least give me a second chance to redeem myself."

"I tried to turn you onto the finer things in life but I guess yo' typical rat ass wasn't ready. To hell with second chances; you slowing me up with this begging. I gotta make moves. Or do you wanna fuck some more shit up?"

"Naw, I guess not, Rello." All out of moves, tired of being belittled and realizing he wasn't giving her the least bit of sympathy or forgiveness, Star opened the rental car door and climbed out in slow motion. *Please let him have a change of heart after seeing me from the back.*

"Hey, man, you're gonna fuck around and have me out this car on yo' head, Star. Quit holding me up," he yelled, then tossed her tattered overnight bag out to the curb. "Close the door now."

Star was flushed red with embarrassment. She chose to save what little self-esteem she had remaining and pick her bag up off the germ-infested street. There was no point in hoping no one saw. All nosey eyes were focused in on them. After slamming the car door, she barely stepped one foot away from the car before Rello floored the gas pedal leaving her in his dust. *Damn, I fucked up big time. I'm right back to square one.*

"Hey, girl, where have you been at? The block was slapping last night." Tanisha walked up wanting to know Star's gossip but most importantly her business. She couldn't mask the hate in her eyes glaring at shopping bags in Star's hands.

Wow, I just jumped out of the frying pan into the fire. I can't seem to catch a break. Star was too caught up in her emotions about Rello to humor Tanisha or feed into her quests to find out more about her mini-vacation. "My bad if it seems like I'm trying to shade you, but me and ol' boy had a long night. I'll call you once I get up."

"Damn, I know you got some dick from his ass. You shouldn't be still acting all funny." Tanisha took Star's brush-off more personal than she should have. "Haven't you learned about making the money but not letting it make you?" Tanisha rolled her eyes then flicked Star off on her way up the block.

"You're just jealous 'cause you can't never make no money," Star mumbled, glad that Tanisha was out of hearing range. *I swear she better be lucky I'm wore out on arguing and fighting today.*

Star hadn't expected her Chicago trip to end so unexpectedly and definitely not as sour as it had; nonetheless she was back in the bottomless pit she called home. "Where's Momma?" Walking into the destitute house with the same dusty bag she left with, Star found her little sisters sitting on the couch besides their father, one on each side. Seeing Jerome spoiled her mood even more. *Something in the universe must want my life to be ruined.*

"Well hello to your little slutty ass too. Where have you been at? Out in the streets hoeing?" Careless about his choice of colorful language around his daughters, Jerome was always cruel to his step-daughter. She was a spitting image of her mother and just like with Bonnie, he wanted to break her spirits. He couldn't pass up his chance to bully her while Bonnie worked the streets.

"I don't have to answer to you, nigga. You ain't no daddy of mines, remember that." Star didn't bow down to the rule of respecting her elders when it came to her stepfather. He was nothing more than her mother's bad choice; and she wasn't about to honor his ass in no way.

"And you ain't nothing but a little ungrateful bitch. You always have been. Since the day I found your worthless momma hooking I've been dealing with your rude ass and I'm sick of it. Being your daddy is the last thing I've ever wanted to do." His drunken words slurred.

"Fuck you. If it weren't for me, yo' alleged litter wouldn't get the little food they do, have the rags their dressed in now, or know what sobriety is about. You ain't shit but a lowlife bum nigga and would be better off dead!" All of the emotions Star had been holding in for the last twenty-four hours poured out. She was enraged and fuming.

"Hell, if it wasn't for the few dollars ya momma schemes out of you, I would've been kicked you out from around here." His drunken words slurred.

"The day you try it, is the day you die. I can't stand your ass," Star yelled, stomping off to her room. After the emotional rollercoaster ride she'd been on with Rello, arguing with Bonnie's man was the last thing she wanted to do.

Savannah and Samantha looked on terrified with fear in their innocent eyes. Clutching their teddy bears, they wanted nothing more than to run to their big sister's arms for refuge. However, they'd suffered enough leather belt thrashings to know betraying their father was, in toddler's terms, a no-no.

Star thought twice about calling her mom, but hated whenever she and her sisters were alone with Jerome. Sure he was Savannah and Samantha's father and by a court marriage related to her, but she still picked up on his pedophilic vibes. Bonnie wasn't her daughter's savior; she was more of a distraction. After several rings and several attempts, Star left a single voicemail telling her to check in.

Finally alone in her room, she emptied her pockets and duffel bag of everything she'd stolen along the way. Star couldn't think straight for trying to think who she could flip the product to in order to make some cash. She knew without a doubt her time living in the same house with Jerome, her mom, and her sisters was limited.

"Momma ain't been here since right after you left yesterday." Savannah showed up in Star's doorway. "I don't think Mommy and Daddy loves me." With tears covering her brown-skinned face, red lash marks on her arms and legs, Star figured she must've gone against Jerome's wishes to run after her.

"Come here, little sister. I know how you feel." Star held her arms open for Savannah to be comforted in.

Jerome sat on the porch looking up and down the street for Bonnie to come waltzing back. He was furious that she'd left her daughters there for so long when she knew good and damn well he didn't like kids. Not only had he found reasons to neglect them while Star and Bonnie were gone, but he'd emotionally abused them in ways no child should've had to endure. He'd just struck Savannah when she went running after her beloved big sister and was on his way to smack his other daughter for crying. Jerome needed Bonnie home to be their mother and to feed his habit.

Lighting a square because he didn't have cash for hard drugs, he quivered from going through withdrawals. Jerome shook his legs, tapped his right foot, and smoked the cigarette down but his frustration didn't disappear. In fact it grew with every thought about Star. No one knew but him, but he was trifling and perverted and only disliked his stepdaughter simply because he couldn't have sex with her. Every day he watched her prance around in too-tight, revealing clothes; but Star killed his ego every chance she got. Jerome always took his anger out on Bonnie even more when Star acted out.

Shit, that smart mouth kid has worked a nut up in me. I've gotta pound on something. Fuck waiting on Bonnie's good tricking ass. Putting the cigarette out on the pavement, he made a beeline for his bedroom to jack off.

"Daddy, I peed," Samantha called out as best as a toddler could that she'd had an accident.

Jerome ignored the little girl's cries and continued on his quest to relieve himself. He didn't care that little girl he'd helped create sat in urine and scratching at her itching legs. *Hell, if I can walk away from a child, I sure as fuck can ignore one.* He was overly detached from all of his children and couldn't care less if they ate, bathed, or were cared for. In his eyes, that's what mothers were for.

Chapter 9

"So all that discussion and me giving yo' retarded ass the plan step-by-step meant nothing? I oughta pistol whip you for being so fuckin' dumb," Banko roared to his idiot nephew. "I've had the same connect for years and have never had anything go wrong. Like clockwork Dominik and I have been making money, young nigga. What the fuck were you thinking disobeying me on a run I sent you on?" Banko stood over Rello with rage, offended at the young boy's gall to march by the beat of his own drum. He wanted to knock his head off but fought off the urge.

"My bad, Unc. Ol' girl was just a jump-off I had ride with me," Rello tried explaining, but his excuses fell on deaf ears.

"'My bad, Unc'?" Banko mocked him with disgust. "Is that all you've got with your sorry ass? I've had enough of your pathetic-ass apologies, li'l nigga. I gave you a chance, trusted you with my green backs, but your weak ass let me down." Now pacing back and forth bracing his pistol, Banko was trying hard to gain his composure. With Detroit streets needing their fix on schedule, he needed the connection with Dominik to stay immaculate and untarnished. He needed the Chicago native far more than the Chicago native needed him. Rello failing to follow the rules could've put more than his position in the game at risk, but Dominik's future decision to do business with him.

Rello didn't know his circumstances would be this severe. He'd never witnessed his uncle show him this magnitude of cold and hard hate since he'd never been on this side of the game. *How can I tell this old man I've learned my lesson and I won't slip up again? Should I tell him Dominik already put me up on game and I'm ready to work one hundred?* Knowing he'd ruined his first chance at the trust Banko tried to establish with him, Rello sat back and took the verbal beating he had coming. "I don't get no credit for delivering all of the product? At least I didn't fuck that part up."

"Is this nigga serious? Did he just ask me to give him some credit for half ass doing a job and embarrassing me? Tell me this is some type of joke, Lord." With spit flying from his mouth and his heart pounding damn near out of his chest, Banko screamed out loud in the room, with his hands lifted in total disbelief. "I ain't even checked my work yet. It better all be there too since you big lip bragging."

Rello didn't respond but felt brave enough not to flinch. *Shit, I know I ain't stole nothing out that stash, period point blank.* Banko grabbed the scale and the Ziploc bags of Molly pills then dumped them across the glass dining room table. Making sure none fell onto the floor, Rello was already watching closely since his well-being was at stake. "I ain't steal shit from you, Unc," Rello spoke up feeling cocky.

"Yeah, we're about to see right now. I've got a gut feeling that my shit ain't right come to think about it." Usually weighing his pills, Banko felt it necessary to count each one by hand until getting to under 2,000. "1,943 pills. That means I have fifty-seven reasons to whip off into your ass, Rello."

"Naw, Unc! That can't be right. That nigga must've shorted you." Rello backed up with fear in his eyes. Right then and there, he felt like Dominik set him up in a trick bag and wanted him to fail.

Banko was already counting the bottles of promethazine noticing two weren't accounted for. "Shut up, nigga. We're not family and I'm not your uncle. You're dead to me. You've got your father's washed-up, nothing-ass blood running through your blood that ain't got nothing to do with me."

Not only was Rello in shock that his uncle was disowning him; but he was hurt and pissed at Banko comparing him to a man so utterly hated. Sure he'd been guilty of pinching off the weed plants, cash to stunt for Star, and popped a few of the Mollys around the house; but his only fuckup this time around was taking Star for a tagalong. He wasn't anything like the man who abandoned him. "Banko, I promise you I didn't short your package. That's my word. You've gotta believe me."

Tension within the living room grew then the eruption occurred. Banko used the handle of his 9 mm Smith & Wesson and knocked Rello upside his thick but hardheaded skull. Blood gushed from his nephew's temple, but Banko wasn't regretful. If anything, he was fueled to go even harder. "Do I look like I believe your sorry ass? Huh, you little piece of shit? Speak that crybaby shit now."

Rello fell to the floor from the force of Banko's hit. Holding his gashed-open head, he looked up like a weak link in shock that his own family had the audacity to strike him. "Yo, Banko! What the fuck, man? If you were any other nigga in the street . . ." Rello cut himself off before taking it a syllable too far. Even in the heat of the moment, he still couldn't show anything other than loyalty and honor to his uncle.

"You're a bitch, boy. You wouldn't do a mother-fuckin' thang even if I gave you an open invitation. Now g'on and raise the fuck up out of my face before I crack your whole cranium open."

Rello took one look into Banko's eyes and knew speaking another word would be a mistake. He knew he was no match to his uncle's street veteran methods of fighting; therefore he backed down into place. What Rello really wanted to do was run into a corner and cry.

"A'ight, Unc, you can be cool. As soon as I peel myself up off this floor I'll be up and out ya spot. I know when my time is up and when I'm not wanted." After taking a blow to not only his head but his pride, Rello was trying hard to recover.

"You ain't got shit or nowhere to go. Without me, young blood, no one will have mercy on you on the streets," Banko spat. Nonchalant and uncaring, he lit a cigar up and stepped past his kin. "Be like you said: up and out by the time I get back." Banko was fuming at the fact he'd lost his temper, which was ultimately going to drive a wedge between him and his sister. After all she'd done as a child for him, he couldn't return the favor by molding Rello into a man. As the man who was supposed to hold the family together, he ultimately felt like a failure.

Fuck this old nigga. I'm tired of him talking to me like I ain't shit or a force to be reckoned with. Him and his connect were on some disrespectful shit and now damn it, I've got a point to prove. You better believe I'm a man. Once Rello heard Banko's car engine start, reverse down the driveway, and pull off up the street he made his way through his uncle's laid out house gathering his belongings and everything he needed to never return. "Hey, Ma, we need to talk," he spoke into the phone to the one woman who'd always love and accept him unconditionally.

Banko sped down his quiet residential street on his way to the housing projects he'd grown up in. There was too much money up for grabs to let a family dispute slow down his hustle or business transactions. With the cough syrup and pills snuggly hidden underneath the custom back seats of his ride, he was eager to put Detroit city back into a nod.

I've had it with that li'l young nigga testing me. I've bent over backward for him, been carrying him on my back like he's my son, and even tried to put him on to being his own man. He might as well spat in my face. Fuck family right about now, Patrice too if she don't wanna cut me no slack. The more consumed he got with his thoughts, the more animosity filled his heart. He couldn't understand why the boy he'd done so much for stole, lied, and manipulated against him.

Feeling his phone vibrating on his hip, he pulled it from its holster and instantly got aggravated at the audacity of who the private caller might've been. *This ain't the time for no meeting or reconciliation. Back to the old me; fuck that friendly Uncle Banko shit!* "What up?" he rudely spat into the phone, expecting the receiver to be his sister or nephew.

"Bad time, my brother?" Dominik picked up on the hostility in Banko's voice.

Banko was thrown off by the call altogether. *Why is he calling restricted? Something tells me my night is about to get even more interesting. I ain't even getting ready to question him about shorting me; we're better than that. I've gotta tighten my business up before things get messier.* "No, not at all, bro. I'm just out and about tying up some odd loose ends. How can I help you?" Banko knew that Dominik was a stickler when it came to receiving respect from him and anyone else he did business with; therefore, he tried cleaning up his attitude and response.

"Unfortunately I'm not calling to express my pleasure in doing business with you this time." Dominik's words were deliberate and cold.

He knew Dominik was displeased about Rello's decision to bring a random girl to his home, but his tone was downright aggressive and wasn't matching their earlier text conversation. "Whoa, what the fuck? Did some shit happen I don't know about for you to be speaking so recklessly to me?" Dominik had never met Banko's rough side, but it was timeout for the usual reserved approach.

"Ah, I see you are cut from the exact same cloth as your nephew and that trash he drug into my house. Nicole was right; I've been bamboozled by you all these years." Dominik wasn't accustomed to dealing with thugs or gangsters. Living cushy with his squeaky-clean wife, six-figure salary, and maid to do his dirty work, he didn't care if his and Banko's side deal ceased.

"Trash? Bamboozle you for years? You can't call a grown man's phone spitting venom on his reputation. You better start giving some answers, bro." Banko was trying to speak as calmly as he could but rage was overcoming him. If he weren't nearing the entrance to the housing projects, he would've bust a U-turn to catch and confront Rello with Dominik on the phone.

"Let's get one thing straight, Banko." Dominik chuckled. "The only reason I'm giving you answers is because I want justification and consequences served swift for the disrespect of my wife and me in our own home, not because you call yourself demanding me."

He paused waiting to see if Banko wanted to contest him and when the line stayed quiet, he continued. "That girl who accompanied your nephew, 'team East-Side Star,' stole some of my wife's jewelry. If she's affiliated with your camp, you aren't as select or cautious as I thought about the company you keep. Whatever the case, I want Nicole's valuables back nonetheless."

Banko instantly blamed himself for sending Rello and not staying consistent with the original when he heard the discontent and disgruntlement in Dominik's voice. "My bad, damn, bro, I had no idea. Can it be replaced? You can trust I've already handled my nephew though and in light of this news, little Star will be handled too." Banko's nose flared as his breathing deepened, he didn't like having a bad look or leaving a sour taste in people's mouth after dealing with him. However, he understood it was only fair that he gave the prescription connect a pass when it came to venting this one time.

"I appreciate the apology and offer to replace what the trash stole. And the regret for sending your nephew is felt. You can bring me six thousand dollars for the five-karat square diamond tennis bracelet I'd gotten Nicole for our anniversary, but if she can't return the heirloom earrings and ring that bitch lifted that were Nicole's great-grandmother's, she can die. Those items were priceless so I won't be willing to negotiate those terms," Dominik coldly stated before disconnecting the call.

Banko didn't bother getting upset at Dominik for abruptly ending the call or going against the grain when it came to being diplomatic. He'd been utterly disrespected in his home, subjected to bad business, and given a reason to question future dealings with Banko and his camp. The people who needed to fear his direct anger, however, were Star and Rello.

Banko drove through the entrance of the black gated projects he grew up in immediately witnessing chaos and drama unfolding. He might've respected where he came from because it made him value what he's gotten as a drug dealing businessman; but he couldn't fathom himself doing anything more than servicing the common folk of the Sojourner Truth Homes. Dopefiends were bent over in sleep nods, pill heads were wide-eyed on alert, and drug transactions were going on in plain sight. Residents of this poverty-stricken community didn't care about laws, and neither did the cops.

Anyone who made it out of the projects automatically became a hood celebrity. He was that and more. While most people feared getting shot, stabbed, or robbed in the projects, Banko felt safe and comfortable. Out of respect, Banko threw his hand up and nodded a few times to the hustlers he employed as well as a few fiends he kept high. Everyone loved to be acknowledged by the man who had the pharmaceutical game locked up.

"Bingo. Bingo. That's my car," a boy yelled out.

"Naw, that's mine, homeboy. You better quit playing." A group of kids ran up to and admired Banko's custom canary Challenger.

Damn, that used to me out here looking dusty as fuck wishing I was about something. Banko hated his memories of his childhood because he grew up less than poor. Watching the young boys who seemed to be no more than ten, from experience he knew their hunger would eventually turn them into his workers. Banko didn't feel the least bit of remorse for pushing the pills their moms were probably tweeking off of. Playing the role of a boss properly, he slowed down and held a couple of twenties out the window for each of them to grab.

"Dang man, good looking." One of the boys took the bill with a shy nod.

"Yeah, good looking, dude. This right here is what I'm talking about," the other boy spoke up.

Banko took note of the second boy showing more swag and promise than his more sheltered buddy and knew he'd keep him on his radar from here on out. *He'll either be a good recruit or a li'l nigga to watch my back for.* Banko chose to play his role until the time came. "All hard work pays off, young'un. That's for watching my whip while I'm in here. Do a good job and I got both of y'all before I leave."

"Oh shit, we got you. Trust." The outspoken one puffed his chest out.

Banko had to laugh at the youngster's spunk. *Barely ten and tough as nails. If only my nephew could be this go hard.* "G'on and hold it down, li'l nigga. I ain't got a doubt that you got me." He stroked the boy's ego more, which gave him even more courage to go hard.

Banko pulled into the parking spot and jumped out to play street doctor to the underprivileged hood he once called home. Cats from the opposing side were in rare form, eye murking him from head to toe. He was dressed in an official Gucci fit with kicks to match. When he took notice of the hate, he rubbed it even more by knocking the dirt off his soles and adjusting his hat with a grim face as to say niggas better not get stupid enough to test him. Banko was getting bread and didn't hide it. Everyone knew he used to be a straggler collecting bottles for deposits. So he took pride in showboating that he could now afford lavish things and to be legendary walking among them. *Hard work pays off, niggas; ya best bet is to get like me!*

He and his trusty young project runner unloaded the bags of product carrying them into the townhouse that served as the spot. Neighbors watched with an itch, waiting for their fixes to be nourished. Deep into the end of the month, many of them had robbed Peter to pay Paul to pop and swallow one of Banko's guaranteed real deal pills. They had no intentions on paying the debts back come the first of next month, and was using the downtime to plot on future scams.

The trap house was only furnished with a run-down couch with cigarette burns on the cushions, a few IKEA tables, and a high-definition flat screen for video game rotation. It was clear to the obvious eye wasn't nothing family oriented about this subsidized home. Banko didn't care how trifling, nasty, or gritty the place was kept as long as his profit wasn't a penny short. Orders were already on deck to be filled and doughboys were lined up waiting impatiently for their portion of pills to sell. Everyone who ran for Banko ate well, which confused him more to as why Rello couldn't catch on.

His presence was strong and could be felt throughout the cramped space. Clasping, rubbing his fists together, Banko decided it was time to give the boys their work so his return could start being made. "Listen up, ain't no sense in making a long, drawn-out speech to y'all young niggas. You know the rules and what to expect if they are broken."

Collecting the cash from each hustler from their last hookup before handing over the current batch Banko stared each man dead in the eyes to ensure they understood he was firm about the rules. He'd already done the math prior to coming and after getting disrespected by Rello, wanted it to be clear he had a zero tolerance for any shorts.

Patrice never broke her month-to-month ongoing lease with the Sojourner Truth housing projects.

In love with the subsidized rent of only eight-two dollars a month with gas included, she kept her 1,000-square-foot two-bedroom apartment sparkling clean and decked out. She even planted flowers outside with small lights for the pathway when she carelessly came home at night. Banko ran drugs through the "nest," as the neighbors nicknamed it, and begged his sister on numerous occasions to relocate to the suburbs. Nevertheless, she refused time and time again and found other things to spend his cash on like flat screens, plush furniture, high-tech toys, and a wardrobe to shut broads down in mid-step. A lot of people might've felt insecure in the projects known for violent crime, but Patrice felt safe and secure since the young thugs around the way knew her bloodline would murder their family if she was crossed.

Patrice heard her brother banging and yelling her name at the door and immediately thought the worst. Despite Banko being an adult and a boss over the projects, she was still overly protective over him. *Oh my God, please don't let the cops be after him or one of these li'l young niggas turning on him.*

"Are you okay? What's going on?" Seeing speckles of red spots which she knew to be blood, worry flooded throughout her. She instantly went into prayer, truly worried about his well-being along with Rello's. Thoughts of his last words to her before the phone hung up earlier rushed to the forefront of her mind. *Dear Lord, don't let him have my child's blood on his hands. Please don't let my boy be dead!*

Banko ran through the house like a crazed man checking to make sure his nephew wasn't bunked out there yet. He knew Rello had no place to go and no one other than his mother to take refuge with, so the projects would be the first place he'd run to.

"Naw, I ain't fucking good. Your piece of shit-ass son got me into some heat with my connect in Chicago," Banko shouted at Patrice. Out of all the years of their sibling relationship, he'd never raised his voice at his older sister. Yet with his money on the line he only saw red. Banko had saved his sister from Rello, only to get screwed in the end. His anger couldn't be contained.

"Whoa slow down, Banko," she shouted. "Before you barge in here like you own the place calling my son names and shit, you're gonna have to tell me the full story, start to finish."

"Sis, you've got to be fucking kidding me. Straight up, this crib is just as much mine as it is yours. My cash paid for everything up in this place." Speaking the truth, throwing up the way he took care of her every financial desire without question, Banko sat down on the butter smooth leather sofa then kicked his feet up on her granite coffee table. "Get me a bottle of the strongest shit you've got 'cause this is about to take all night. I'm about to tell you why your boy is dead to me."

Chapter 10

He told me to be quiet and I promised to be cool. I'm just gonna keep blaming the reason why I was doing so much on the liquor. But if he don't call me again, it'll be all my fault. With Savannah sitting on a pillow between Star's legs, she beaded the last of her little sister's cornrows with thoughts of Rello heavy on her mind. No matter how much she tried not to think about how much fun they'd had together in Chicago, she couldn't shake the good memories.

"All done, pretty girl. Now go and get ready for bed because we've got a big day tomorrow. I'm going to find a nice school for you and Samantha," Star relayed to her sister while putting up the barrette bucket.

"School? For real, sister? Yay, I can't wait." She jumped in glee. The child who should've been carrying around baby dolls and books had nothing but stress and despair. She couldn't wait to get out of the dungeon of gloom and into school, what she'd seen so many kids on television enjoy. "Is Mommy coming with us, too?"

Star sighed because she dreaded the inevitable conversation she was about to have. She hated talking to her much younger sister about adult reality situations; she knew Savannah was just like her as a kid, which was curious and outspoken. It was something that had to be done in attempt to protect her. Star felt it was her duty to prepare her for what type of family she was up against. "I don't know, pretty girl; however, I think it's time I taught you a few things about the life we were born into. Come sit here next to me so we can talk."

Savannah bounced around the room shaking her beads happily before taking a seat next to the only soul who showed her an ounce of love. "Will me and Sammy be in the same class? Will we have the same teacher?" Like all toddlers adventuring to school for the first time, she had a stomach full of butterflies and a list full of questions for her older sister to answer. Unfortunately she was in store for another blow to her youthful purity.

Star took a deep breath then let it all out. "You're gonna have to find your way, like I'm finding mine and how our baby sis will have to find hers. Your momma ain't shit and probably don't never plan on being shit. Just like me, you're gonna have to grow up before your time, pretty girl." Star was rough but didn't care. Their family wasn't *The Cosby Show* or some spinoff involving a well-balanced caring household.

"What's that mean, Star?"

"It means you shouldn't be like her that's what. Do you see her around here cooking meals for you and Savannah? Combing y'all heads? Or even washing y'all up in the morning? Hell naw! That's what moms are supposed to do; not be gone for days leaving y'all on Jerome or me."

With a face full of tears and ears wide open, Savannah tried her best to listen and comprehend what her older sister was saying. She couldn't remember Bonnie ever reading her a bedtime story, giving her a bubble bath, or even getting kisses of affection.

"And what about my daddy?" Savannah whimpered. "He stays with me and Sammy all the time."

Star took one look at the brown-skinned doe-eyed girl with long, silky locks of hair and could tell she was realizing her parents were monsters. She fought hard to keep her game face on, but was almost in tears surveying her little sister's legs and arms that were full of welt marks and bruises left behind by Jerome. *I've gotta get my baby girl up out of this struggle before it ruins her like it's ruined me.* "Fuck yo' daddy, Savannah. Look at the lash marks on your legs and arms. Don't no daddy do that type of shit to his li'l girl. He ain't shit either."

Bonnie had tricked with the young dealer all night. He brought a fifth of vodka, and that paired up with the pills and marijuana he was letting her smoke on behind him had her mind in a zone that was far from reality. She was loving the stamina of the young'un, unworried and uncaring of Star, Savannah, Samantha, or Jerome. When she awoke with a pounding headache, the room spinning, but more liquor to drink, she took another gulp and passed back out.

Star woke up and took a long, hot shower, curled her hair, and dressed in the items Rello had gifted her with. She even clamped on the gold diamond tennis bracelet like it was hers. *No sense in letting this fly shit sit around collecting dust. He better call me back so I can have the chance to run those pockets some more.* Star was still holding on to hope that Rello would call her back to extend a second chance although the whole night had passed of countless texts and phone calls with no response or answer. Since he hadn't shown up clowning on her head, she figured all things went unnoticed with what she'd stolen. Counting out ten pills and grabbing a bottle of syrup, she banked on selling it to one of the fiends she'd surely encounter on her route to or from school.

Star got her sisters bathed, dressed, and partially fed with cereal and watered-down milk. That was the best nourishment she could come up with so early since Bonnie had disappeared and had yet to return a call. Since she'd researched daycares the night before, she wasn't that worried about them eating because the one she'd chosen served breakfast. They had open spaces according to the Internet, so Star was hopeful everything with enrollment went right.

They managed to make it out without disturbing the house and to the bus stop waiting for the five-mile ride. Savannah had told Samantha about all the great things they'd do in school, so the girls kept Star busy answering questions about everything to expect for their day. Despite Star trying to reach Rello, she found a little peace and joy with the happiness and innocence of her sisters.

The ride was unadventurous for Star since she rode public transportation all the time, but the girls loved it. They seldom went farther than the front porch or maybe to the grocery store for a trip. When they got to the daycare center, Star enrolled them with ease and paid for a week in advance so at least during the day the girls could have security from Jerome. She was starting to feel more like a mother to them than their big sister.

"Come here you two." She pulled them over close to her. "You're going to be safe here until I get back. You'll be here for a while but you can play with all of these cool toys and all of these friendly looking kids; and these nice people will feed you if you're hungry. Make sure you tell them if you need to use the bathroom or want to call me." She'd never left them with anyone and although she felt they were safer at the daycare than at home, Star still had to school them to what was going on. Hugs and kisses were shared between all, but no further words.

Savannah looked at Star with tears in her eyes and wanted nothing more than to make her proud. She remembered the words from last night and tried playing the role of a big girl. She took Samantha's hand and led her to the play area. "Come on, Sammy, let's play with all these dolls until Star comes back." She might've been excited for school, but she was nervous as a child should've been for her big sister to leave.

Star couldn't leave the daycare without letting her know she was proud in every way. She was glad to know Savannah had learned the importance of looking out for her 100 percent blood sister Sammy. Having the same mom and dad, they were cut from the exact same cloth. And since they were coming up stair-step, they'd have a closer relationship. She walked over to them in the playroom. "Keep taking care of Sammy. I see you, sissy, and I'm proud." Smiling, winking, and giving Savannah a kiss on the cheek Star watched her sister light up. "I'll see you two later."

When Star got back to the bus stop to wait, she felt nothing but relief that she'd given Savannah and Samantha safe shelter, definite food, and someone to teach the basic shit Bonnie was dropping the ball on. She held her head high the entire bus ride back to the hood to meet up with Tanisha.

"Where's this bitch at and why isn't she answering? She better come back with a pocket full of money, I know that much." Jerome hung up the phone infuriated at Bonnie not answering. He'd called all night but hadn't got one response back.

He knew the house was empty of his daughters and stepdaughter because he'd heard them scurrying out in the wee hours of the morning. He didn't budge from his bed or care where they were going. He was only happy to have a break from the brats he'd mistakenly put in Bonnie in the first place. He'd gotten out of being a father for eleven years to a son he hadn't seen in that long, to only get trapped by a woman just as cracked out as him in Bonnie.

Lighting another Pall Mall cigarette, he was starting to shake and go through withdrawals from not having his daily dose of pills, crack, and Mary Jane. He'd watched the porno and jacked off his penis to the point of it being sore. Each two minutes he was back and forth looking out the window thinking Bonnie would be walking up. He couldn't believe she'd had the audacity to let the sun beat her home. She'd trick for cash on any given day but at home with her man was where she slept. Between hearing the light laughter, usual gun shots, and sirens of either the police or ambulance, Jerome hadn't slept a wink calling his second baby momma off and on.

Since it was useless to scavenge through the house for bottles to take back for a deposit to possibly get a beer, Jerome chose to gather all the tails in every ashtray he could find so they could be broken down and smoked again. He was desperate, down to no dollars for his craving, and itching for a hit. When he'd broken down enough to fill his personal pipe, he packed it tightly and smoked the burnt, foul-smelling buds. Jerome was accustomed to blowing on recycled weed so he lit it like a pro. *Damn I can't wait 'til that ass gets home so I can run those pockets. I know she's gonna be holding heavy after pulling an all-nighter.* The higher he got, the more times he called Bonnie's cell. His phone eventually ran out of minutes, which sent him into more of a craze. Instead of waiting on her to surface, he flew out the house heading toward the one place he was banned from but where he knew he could get some credit.

Cars and trucks of men sped past honking their horns at Star while she stood at the bus stop, but she wasn't in a sack chasing mood. Her mind was going a mile a minute consumed with thoughts of Savannah and Samantha. She wanted nothing more than to get them somewhere safe to stay twenty-four/seven instead of just eight to ten hours at daycare. She thought about her blemished childhood and what she'd grown into and wanted more for them. *I've gotta start making some grown woman decisions. If I'm not careful, I'm gonna end up just like Bonnie.* Struggling Star took one look at her arm and knew what she had to do.

"What's up, heifer? You done acting all uppity?" Tanisha approached Star standing hood fresh at the bus stop rocking her new kicks, jeans, and tennis bracelet. She instantly started hating and trying to get a reaction from her supposed best friend. *I see that little late-night creep did her good. I've gotta get ol' boy's info somehow so I can benefit too.*

"Whatever, I'm straight. Good morning to you too. Please don't start, girl. I've got a lot of stuff to work out behind Bonnie's neglectful ass." She rolled her eyes, then began filling her girl in about everything Savannah told her. In spite of Star knowing Tanisha wasn't trustworthy when it came to sack chasing, she'd been her only confidante when it came to talking about her family struggles.

"Damn, Star, I would've babysat had I known it was that bad for Savannah and Samantha at home while you and Bonnie were out. I knew Jerome was slime, but I ain't know he was acting up on y'all like that." Tanisha hugged her girl because she saw Star about to cry. As jealous as she got over her friend getting an overnight visit with who she thought was a moneymaker, she felt bad for Star sincerely. Tanisha might've had it hard, but she didn't have any siblings to care for.

"Thanks, girl, I appreciate you even offering to look out. And after this move I'm about to make, I might be taking you up on babysitting." Star hugged her friend back. "Instead of us going to the GED program today, which neither of us wanna go to anyway, let's grab something to eat and open the doors with the pawn shop owners. I need to sell this tennis bracelet in order to afford the apartments we'll go see afterward. I've gotta get my sisters out of that house before they end up dead. Unlike me, they ain't got time to grow into their own."

"Wow, what happened with ol' boy? He can't pay for you a place to stay? That's a nice-ass bracelet." Tanisha wasn't hating. She thought what Star was doing was honorable, so she didn't think it was the right time to gun for her head.

"It is a beautiful bracelet and I'd love to stunt hard with it for sure. But I'm just grateful that I have it to sell." Star knew she'd swiped the fine piece of jewelry and if you got something quick and fast, it's the same way you'd lose it.

"Well, do you, boo. I'll be along for the whole ride, especially if you're treating. With a bracelet like that, you're bound to get some helluva chips." Tanisha winked, then took a sip of her Pepsi.

The bus ride and the rest of the early morning hours went slow for the girls. They grabbed breakfast value meals from McDonald's, blew through a blunt, and looked on Craigslist for cheap one-bedroom apartments with no qualifications that weren't too far from the hood. Star wanted to get away, but not too far from the only thing she knew. Plus she hoped Bonnie would at least want to visit with her youngest daughters.

"It's quite a few apartments that are only four hundred dollars a month with everything included and studios for three hundred dollars. You should be able to swing that if you get on aid and jump on a few dicks when the girls are at daycare," Tanisha advised Star. The more she talked, the more she wanted to move into her own place too.

Star began feeling like she would have good news for Savannah and Samantha when picking them up. Not only was she going to sell the bracelet she'd stolen, but the pills and cough syrup, too. At the thought of having someone to help sponsor her newfound lifestyle came up, she pulled out her phone and called Rello but still didn't get an answer. *When I have my own space to seduce that nigga, I'll get him back for sure.* "Thank you for tagging along with me today, Tanisha. I can't even lie; you made me feel a little bit better."

"Not a problem. I know we bump heads when it comes to these dudes in the streets, but I ain't trying to have nothing bad happen to you or your sisters because of Jerome. If you got a way out, take it. So come on, it's after nine if you still talking about going to the pawn shop."

The girl working behind the counter rolled her eyes out of irritation at Star and Tanisha bouncing in so early. She'd barely sat down and hadn't even checked her Facebook feed for the day and it was time to work. "Yeah, how may I help you? Whatcha got?" Popping her gum, she was rude and ghetto and the reason they say black folks aren't successful when it comes to customer service jobs.

"Let me sit down before I snap on this chick," Tanisha spoke directly to the girl but was talking to Star.

Star giggled then unclamped the tennis bracelet from off her wrist. Dropping it in the metal slot, she wanted to cry watching the sparkling diamonds being weighed up. "How much can I get for selling y'all that? Top dollar, too. Don't try playing me." Star got just as ghetto with the worker.

The worker didn't care about Star's attitude or her wanting top dollar for the bracelet because the Arabic man who owned the pawn shop enforced strict rules to only pay out half of half of whatever that product was worth. That meant Nicole's appraised bracelet for $20,000 would get Star $5,000. The worker knew her manager would have her head for giving away that much cash, so she tried to bamboozle Star herself. "You can get a thousand dollars, but I'll give you fifteen hundred just to look out." The girl smirked. "Take it or leave it."

Star thought she was going to get more, but was too desperate to say no. However, instead of arguing back and forth with the girl she chose to take the cash and go. Having the lump sum would surely be enough for a deposit on an apartment. "Come on, Tanisha, let's go find me and my sisters a new place to call home."

Chapter 11

"So, do you have a job? Any verifiable income? The application fee is twenty dollars," the apartment manager informed Star from across his desk.

"Naw, I don't have a job but I've got cash." Star flashed a few of the crisp hundred-dollar bills she'd gotten for the tennis bracelet in the manager's face. "I can pay you three months of rent right now and I'm good for the other nine months for sure." The one-bedroom apartment she'd seen with Tanisha wasn't close to a gem, but it would definitely serve its purpose as a getaway for her sisters. It was only 800 square feet but would be like a heaven from the hell at Bonnie's. She was willing to spend every dime she'd come up on to get the keys.

The manager tapped his pen on the notepad with a bright idea starting to brew. He saw all types of people managing an apartment building in the ghetto of East Detroit: prostitutes, junkies, and even homeless people looking for a fresh start. He seldom saw young girls looking for refuge unless they tricked at the nearest short stays; but was glad the day had come. "Well, little lady, I see you're quite enthusiastic about being grown and on your own."

"Yes, sir, that's absolutely right. Me and my sisters were born in the struggle and since I'm the oldest it's my responsibility to get us all out," Star spoke with pride, looking him directly in the face.

"Wow, those girls are lucky to have a big sister looking out for them like you." The manager grinned.

Star thought she was impressing him but she was walking right into his trap. He wanted to know exactly why she was desperate and her weakest points so he could use them against her later. Passing Star the application, he questioned her as Tanisha watched on knowing the old man's plot. But since they were both part of the sack chasing game, it was to be expected.

"I think it's admirable what you're trying to do for your sisters, but there's still rules to follow out here in this big ol' world. If you don't have credentials or good credit, you have to have something else to offer up. I think yo' folk call it the barter system. What is it that you've got to offer me for breaking the rules?"

It was then Star realized what was up. She had the cash but he still wanted a piece of what was between her thighs. *There's no way I came this far to not get these keys. Whatever he wants, he gets.* "You already know I've gotta work for mine, Tanisha. So do you mind waiting outside for a few?"

"Not a problem. Holler if you need me." Tanisha high-fived her girl, then closed the door behind her.

Star got to doing what she did best: using her body to get what she needed and wanted. It was something she'd picked up from Bonnie whether she wanted to admit it or not. All it took was for the manager to dangle the keys in front of her face for it to all go down. First she bent over his desk chair and allowed him to tickle her anus with his finger. She was never a fan of being pleased anally, but she squinted her face and mustered up enough strength not to puke. Star was more than willing to take the discomfort in exchange for an apartment. It didn't take long for him to switch their positions with her straddled on his lap. The manager loved watching her busty chest bounce up and down. She pounced on his small pudgy penis until it shot warm cum into the Trojan latex condom that was almost too big. He couldn't keep his loud moans in having the youngness wrapped around his small girth. He was so sprung over Star's sack chasing skills that he waived the whole move-in fee and helped her forge the application as needed. She walked out of the leasing office a proud renter of a one-bedroom slum apartment.

"Let's be out." She disgustingly waved Tanisha toward the main exit. "I've gotta get in touch with ol' boy so I ain't never gotta mess with that man again. His old ass probably got worms."

"Girl, bye. You better test that key to make sure it works before you walk up out of here," Tanisha warned, snatching the key from Star's hand to lead the way. "I might've misjudged that white old fart. He must sex like a stallion and fucked the wires in your brain loose."

***

Rello saw Star calling but couldn't answer with only one minute left on his government-issued phone. Carrying a few shopping bags of his handed-down clothes, he was still trying to act hard like he hadn't hit rock bottom. The more he played the Chicago trip over in his mind, the more he wished it was possible to travel back in time. He missed Star but she was ultimately the reason he was spiraling downward now.

Only a few feet away from the entrance to the Sojourner Truth Homes, he couldn't wait to get to his mother's house but knew her refuge came with a price. Rello knew his mother was going to be disappointed in him to say the least. She wanted nothing more than her son to have the same respect, name reign, and cash flow as Banko did. *Maybe I'm more like my pops than I want to admit.*

Chapter 12

Bonnie's body woke up from the sweet dream she was having about her, Star, Samantha, and Savannah. In the dream they were a normal family living with a dog, matching furniture, and a white picket fence. There wasn't a man beating on her, a drug addiction she was battling, or people who looked down on her. Wiping the sleep crust from her eyes, Bonnie desperately wished she could go back to the innocent nirvana of experiencing pure happiness and joy with her daughters; she wasn't high enough to escape reality. She lay frozen in one spot and stared blankly at the ceiling wondering how she'd gotten so low in life. Bonnie hated coming down from days of being high.

"Time's up in there. Unless you have some more for the front office, you've gotta go," the housekeeper screamed knocking on the door.

"I'll be out in a few. Give me About thirty minutes," Bonnie begged, at least wanting to take a hot shower before having to go. She had a few dollars but wanted to spend it in the projects on a few more pills.

"Unless you've got some money, you've gotta go. You know the rules." The housekeeper was persistent. "And hurry up. I ain't got all day."

Bonnie threw her plastic pump at the door. "Bitch, hold on."

That only made the housekeeper throw her weight. She pulled out her keycard and swiped herself into the room, uncaring that she was invading the woman's space. "You don't have no minutes. I said it's time to go."

Star and Tanisha sat on the back row of the bus in silence on their way back to the hood. Star was lost in thought about how she was going to use the money she got to keep, plus sell the pills and cough syrup to help her, Savannah, and Samantha sustain. Her plan was to get the girls bunk beds and herself a twin bed for the only bedroom, then piece together the rest of the house as money came in. Star knew it wouldn't be much but she couldn't wait to make the place home.

Tanisha wasn't eager about transferring to another route to tag along with Star to the daycare to pick up her sisters, but had vowed to play a friend 'til the end. When the last group of passengers loaded, she nudged Star to make sure she'd seen Bonnie was included within them.

"Lay off, I see her high ass. Let her stay in her lane and I'll stay in mine," Star spoke annoyed with a look of repugnance painted on her face. "I don't need her fucking up my good mood."

"I feel you. Not a problem." Tanisha threw her hands up in defeat. She knew not to do what she wanted with Star when it came to Bonnie. There are some lines that should never be crossed; family being one of them.

Granted, Star didn't want to acknowledge Bonnie or have herself seen either; but she couldn't quit staring at her mother. The woman who'd birthed her looked like pure death from head to toe, which broke Star's heart and churned her stomach. She'd never seen her mother look like a beauty queen, but she'd never seen her look so filthy, high, or washed up. *I'm so embarrassed. Why me? Out of all the buses running in Detroit, why'd she have to get on this one? This ain't nothing but an example of some fucked-up luck.* As Star watched Bonnie attempt to blend in with matted hair, worn clothes, and the reeking smell of a dead rat, she found herself pitying Bonnie more than hating her.

"Excuse me, driver, but this lady stank like trash. She's gotta get off on the next stop," a young girl popped off at the mouth. She was with a clique of girls and was looking to get some attention.

"You want me to get that monkey mouth bitch? You ain't even gotta move out of ya seat, Star. Just give me the word and it's on," Tanisha whispered in her friend's ear, ready to cause trouble.

"Stand down for now. Let me see how far this chick think she's about to go." Star sat up so she could hear the conversation going on in the front of the bus clearer. Gritting her teeth, taking off her earrings, and zipping her phone into one of her purse's compartments, Tanisha noticed Star preparing for war then fell in line doing the same. They might've fought against one another on petty beefs; but they were always riding for one another in the streets.

"Listen here, baby cakes, I'd whip your ass from the back to the front of this bus but I've got places to go and people to see. Don't come for me 'cause you don't want it." Bonnie had no problem holding her own. In fact, she worked best that way. She chewed the young girl up without a worry.

"Well, the least you could do was wash your filthy ass in the McDonald's bathroom before coming around people. So don't be trying to get crackhead crunk with me. Ugh! Driver, please put this riffraff off."

The bus erupted with laughter. Her mom had become the highlight of humor for every passenger's day. When the young girl felt like she had a crowd to perform for, she set Bonnie up on the stage to get clowned even more. Every harsh word or sick joke she could think of slandering Bonnie with, she said it. She was a worthless crackhead, a low-budget ho, and even the scum at the bottom of her shoe. However, Bonnie verbally attacked the girl just as brutally.

Star first contemplated letting Bonnie handle her own battle with the girl as payback for leaving her and her sisters to hold their own against Jerome, but couldn't witness an outsider attacking her own flesh and blood. *Hate or not, these bitches ain't gonna keep popping wrong on my mom.* "Let's beat the breaks off these bitches, Tanisha."

It didn't take the girls two eye blinks before their presence was made known. "Hey, Auntie," Tanisha greeted Bonnie, then punched one of the young girl's friends directly in the nose.

Bonnie didn't have a chance to respond before absolute chaos broke out. Star bum-rushed the mouthiest female, straddled her lap, then began laying haymakers left then right to her face until the girl cried out to call the police. Bonnie watched her neighbor and daughter brutally beat the two girls down as the other passengers cheered, laughed, and videotaped with their phones. No one dared to intervene, not even the other girls of their clique. Tanisha couldn't be contained since she fought for a living anyhow. But Star was taking all her frustrations about everything that had happen over the last two days out on her less than worthy opponent.

"Get her ass, baby. Y'all two fucked with the wrong one today," Bonnie was the loudest promoter, especially since she never had someone have her back. Leaning back in her seat, she noticed her daughter's purse was wide open and found a new interest besides the fight. Her fiend eyes lit up bright when they zoned in on the bottle of promethazine. With all the commotion going on, she was able to snatch it out without been seen and stuffed into her own cheap purse.

"Oh, you've got to be kidding. This foolery won't be going down on my bus," the DDOT bus driver shouted, then swerved over to the curb. "Clear the aisle way. I'll be breaking this fight up damn it. You two girls better get off of them. Do you hear me?" The driver was going hoarse yelling, but it was all in vain.

Star was in the zone beating lumps into the mouthiest girl's face even though Tanisha had dropped the other girl and was posing for pictures. Bonnie smiled with pride when Star bounced the girl's head off the pole like a Ping-Pong ball. The poor girl didn't scream or beg for Star to stop, only because she couldn't get one word out.

Bonnie tried intervening and snatching Star back by the arm but was thrown off by her daughter's reaction.

"Get your fucking hands up off me, Bonnie."

"I have a better idea," the bus driver spoke up over everyone. "Why don't all y'all hooligans get off my bus? I don't have time for this nonsense." Stomping back to her seat to open the door, the bus driver meant business.

Bonnie and Star both ignored the bus driver because they were too caught up in griming each other. Although Star defended her mother against the strangers and anyone else, their relationship was still tainted. Tanisha couldn't understand the unexplained tension between them but knew a move had to be made regardless. She grabbed her and Star's purse then tried pulling her friend to the door.

Star maliciously eyed Bonnie with disgust. *How pitiful is this? She looks and smells like horse shit. Here I am about to catch an assault and battery case over here. Disgraceful ass. I should've let these hoes talk.* Grabbing her Coach purse from Tanisha, she thumped the young girl one last time before walking off the bus.

"Don't think I'm letting none of you troublemakers on my bus again. I don't care if it's pouring down raining, y'all will be drenched and maybe down," the driver barked, then slammed the door. *I've gotta get my ass back to the suburban routes. I wonder if the SMART system hiring 'cause them white people only wanna "park and go."* She shook her head at Star, Tanisha, and Bonnie while pulling off.

"What is your problem, little girl? I'm still your mother and you will respect me as such." Bonnie carried her beef from the bus onto the sidewalk.

"Chill, Ma. I'm telling you to back up off me. I don't have no gray area when it comes to whipping your ass either." Star waved her mother back.

Bonnie fought not to snatch her oldest child bald. "Just because your rough cat ass beat the brakes off ol' girl on the bus don't mean shit to a veteran like myself. Don't get to feeling yourself too much. We're cut from the same cloth and I'll do you in fa'sho." Since Bonnie didn't need Star to feed her little sisters just yet, she felt cocky enough to speak her mind. Matter of fact, she was ready to box Star out if she wanted to keep jumping grown.

"Look, Ma, I'm not trying to take it there with you real talk, but why shouldn't I feel myself? I've been doing me and taking care of your kids for a long damn time per my recollection. I might've came up out of you, but I ain't nothing like you." Star snatched her Coach bag back from Tanisha, who was standing, jaw dropped, watching the two argue.

"You're their older sister. That's your job to be around and mentor them. Momma gotta have a life too." Bonnie smirked, pulling the half-lit cigarette from her plastic purse along with a lighter. "And quit blaming me for your childhood. So what you didn't have Cabbage Patch dolls or fluffy teddy bears? You got life skills, baby, handling yourself like a champ and all. You're everything like me, baby girl." Large clouds of gray smoke filled the air each time Bonnie took a long puff and drag.

"I hope you suffer off some bad rock," Star spat. All the years of her hating her mother was coming out whether she liked it or not.

Catching Star off-guard, Bonnie slapped the gloss off her lips and the spit from her mouth. Then she slapped her two more times. Four swift hits total to the mouth, Star squared up for retaliation feeling her bottom lip swell. "You don't want none of this old head ass kicking I've got for you. I ain't done taking your ass to school." Cracking her neck, jumping up and down, Bonnie was about to let loose on Star. "If I don't teach you shit else today, it will be to respect your elders."

"Well let's go for what we know. Ain't nothing but space and opportunity, Ma." Star invited Bonnie back into her territory but was being snatched back by Tanisha.

"Girl, you ain't about to fight yo' momma!"

"That's right, Tanisha. It won't be a fight because she'll be getting her ass kicked." Bonnie wasn't choking up or backing down.

"Hey, Bonnie, you good? What's up?" Banko swerved up honking in the same yellow Challenger Rello was driving and eyed Star and Tanisha suspiciously. He thought Star looked familiar but he'd been drinking and it never dawned on him she was the same girl Dominik had sent a picture of.

"Banko, my main man." Bonnie let his name roll off her tongue, trying to perp like she had boss status. "You came just in time to see me box this li'l hot thang out." She laughed, with the cigarette hanging from her lip.

"You look like you've already gotten two pieced up. You sure you didn't get the business handed to you? It ain't looking too good on your end." Banko's eyes roamed Bonnie's battered body, noticing she was dressed in the same rags as the day before. He normally didn't care about fiends he served, but Bonnie had given him a grade-A head job.

"I know I look rough, but I'm good. You already know I'm gonna hold my own." Bonnie walked closer to the car. "But anyway, do you think you give me a ride back to my hood?"

"Yeah, but meet me around the corner at the gas station. You're gonna have to get some newspaper to sit on and spray down with a can of air freshener before getting in my whip."

"Bye, niece." Bonnie waved to Tanisha. "I'll see you at home, li'l heifer," she directed venom at her Star then strutted away.

I can't believe I came from that polluted pussy. As much as Star wanted to chase behind her mother and sneak her from behind, she was too caught up in finding out who was driving Rello's whip.

"Are you good?" Tanisha was in total shock of what had just gone down.

"Yeah, I'm one hundred percent good. I swear I'll be sleeping in my apartment tonight even if it's on a cardboard box. That woman is no longer my mother." She snarled her face at Bonnie's back.

Chapter 13

Patrice sat on the porch of her home looking at all the fiends happy that her brother had just supplied them with a fresh batch of pills and syrup. Patrice had a bittersweet emotion when it came to drugs. It was responsible for tearing her family apart with Rello's father, but the reason she was living comfortably. With her son being tied up with some mess that could tear her blood family apart, she panicked with the depressing thought of having to choose between her child and cash. She'd been calling Rello nonstop since Banko relayed to her the connect's message. Since she didn't smoke marijuana but needed a downer, Patrice ran in the house for a drink then dropped it when she got back to the front door. The glass shattered into a million pieces but couldn't be heard over her screaming.

"Calm down, Ma. You act like you've seen a ghost." Rello was shocked by her reaction.

Patrice swung open the screen door and slapped Rello across the face. "Boy, you're gonna be a ghost if you keep fucking with your uncle." She pulled him into the house, locked the door, and then began going off on him about him going against his family. She told him everything Banko told him about Star, what she stole, and the tag on her head if she couldn't give back the jewelry.

He stared at her puzzled like he was confused. "Damn, Ma, what should I do? I promise I wanna get this right as bad as you want me to." Rello only wanted to make his mother proud.

"You are just as dumb as your father." Patrice hung her head, regretting her decision to ever spread her legs to the man who'd given her the only child she'd have. "Call that girl and have her meet you here. I'll call Banko so he can deal with her and y'all two can make amends. You've gotta start thinking, boy." Patrice marched off to make the call to her brother and to give her son privacy to lure Star into the projects.

Rello never wanted to hear his mother compare him to his father, but the words had left her mouth killing his spirit. He felt like nothing he'd done thus far in life had been right. Picking up the house phone to call Star, he refused to continue being the black sheep of the family.

"Hello," Star answered on the first ring.

"Yeah, what up? You've been calling me." Rello kept it cool.

"Don't play with me, boy. You know I've been blowing that damn phone up and you've been ignoring me just the same. I take it you're still pissed about what went down the other night huh?"

"Maybe I am. Maybe I'm not. Why don't you meet me at my crib to do some of those things you were texting me nasty about. I'll see about forgiving you then." He knew Star would jump at the opportunity to meet up with him, especially since he said it was his spot.

"I'm sorry, Tanisha, but that was ol' boy. Thanks for holding me down all day but I've gotta go meet up with him." Star rushed through her words, excited that Rello had finally called. Looking for her compact mirror, she wanted to make sure her face wasn't too bruised to see him. If it was, she was planning on being honest with him about Bonnie and her situation.

"Straight up? He calls and you're just gonna dump me by the wayside? I can't believe you're shading me for a nigga who left you in his dust on the curb. Especially after I helped you beat a bitch down on the bus. I should've gone to school." Tanisha rolled her eyes then plopped down on the bus stop bench. "But I guess it is what it is."

"Are you serious with me right now? First off, how ol' boy did me ain't none of your business. But most importantly, you already know how we play it when it comes to our dudes. I can't understand why you're getting all emotional. I'm not even used to you acting like this." Star was thrown back.

"Whatever, it's nothing." Tanisha shrugged her shoulders. "Do you," she spat, trying to act like she wasn't caught with her heart on her sleeve.

"It's not like I don't appreciate you holding me down and even getting buck with those chicks on the bus; but I've gotta answer to my money regardless, Tanisha. Especially since I've got my own place and gotta take care of Savannah and Sammy on my own."

"I ain't trying to shade your money or how you make a living. You didn't see me flinch back at the leasing office when you got down with that old white man. But right about now, you're wrong as hell for leaving me to catch the bus back to the hood alone."

Star knew Tanisha was right but couldn't see herself passing up the opportunity to see Rello. *If I don't go now, he'll probably never call or answer to my calls again. I can't fuck this up for nobody.* "Look, it's my bad for real. I know I'm wrong for leaving you but I've gotta look out for me. The least I can do is throw you a few dollars toward a cab." Pulling out a twenty, Star hoped the gesture was enough to end the argument.

"You're lucky I don't have any other friends." Tanisha smacked her lips then grabbed the crisp bill. "The first cab that comes is mine. You can wait alone as payback for being so self-absorbed."

"Little heifer thinks she's all high and mighty but let's see how she feels once she realizes that syrup missing," she spoke out loud to no one on the abandoned house block. Bonnie held her purse tightly as she sashayed up the block to meet Banko. She was grinning ear to ear without a care in the world. *I bet Jerome's ass won't have a word to say or a fist to swing when I walk through the door with a full bottle of this stuff. We're gonna be high for days.* All the worries of Jerome being upset at her staying out all night was no longer a thought. *Maybe I can slob Banko down for a few dollars so I don't have to share with Jerome at all. If I didn't have to check in on my bratty-ass daughters I would.*

None of the events or evil words spat by the girl on the bus or her daughter was relevant to the small come up she'd stolen from Star's purse. She couldn't wait to guzzle the prescription down and go into a comatose state. When she saw Banko flashing his lights for her to hurry up, she lightly jogged toward where he was sitting at the gas station. She knew Banko was impatient and would ride out on her without warning. *Damn, I do smell like hot shit on a stick.* The more she ran, the more her atrocious body odor smacked her back in the face.

"Thanks for looking out. That was my daughter and her friend back there giving me a hard time." Bonnie opened the car door ready to jump in.

"Whoa, hold the fuck up. Spray down with this Lysol then air out for a minute. I can't have that funk hitting me in the face or stinking up my car." Banko held the can he'd just purchased out of the gas station out the window toward her. "You're dressed in the same rags I saw you in yesterday but looking even worse."

Although Bonnie's being flushed red with embarrassment, she didn't contest his request. She sprayed down from head to toe then spun around in circles before repeating the same routine. When Banko gave her the okay, she slid in the back seat on top of the newspaper he'd laid out feeling like a maggot. Running her dirty fingers against the plush leather, she understood why he was treating her as such. Nonetheless, she felt good just sitting in such a nice car.

"I'll drop you off near the freeway. I ain't going all the way to ya hood." Banko looked over his shoulder, then threw the car into reverse.

"That's cool but I was looking to cop some pills. If you ain't got none on you, you can drop me off in the projects."

Banko laughed, truly amused by the fiend. "Ay, I have niggas to run errands for me; I don't run them myself. This ain't no damn taxi service. You can either ride to the freeway or jump out now. It makes me no difference." He slammed on the brakes. Before Bonnie had a chance to answer, his phone rang and he answered. "Yo, what up, sis?"

"Dang, Grandma, this chicken is on point." Jerome stuffed his mouth with the greasy fried chicken his grandmother had just served on his plate.

"I don't think you can even taste it. It's going down your throat faster than your taste buds can absorb the flavor." She wiped her hands on her flower-patterned apron. "But by the look of your bones, you needed a good home-cooked meal."

"Yeah, I did. That no-good woman of mine don't cook." He laughed, taking another huge bite.

Jerome hadn't seen his grandmother in eleven years. He kept in contact with her by phone at least once a month when disability checks paid out, which was planned because he knew she'd send a few dollars through Western Union. Jerome always thought he was scheming her with his sweet voice; but Georgia Mae knew her grandson was banned from the Sojourner Truth Homes and chose to help because of her good heart. Georgia Mae might've kept a closed lip, but she always kept her eyes and ears open. Banko wasn't a force to be reckoned with, so she never spoke wiser to her grandson.

"Have you been out to my mother's grave?" Jerome broke the silence in between chews. His intentions weren't good. He knew she always got sentimental when it came to her only daughter who'd lost her battle to drugs already.

"Not this week, but if God allows me to make it after church this Sunday I will. One of the church members will probably take me if I bake them a pound cake." She smiled widely. "You oughta go with me. It would be nice to pay some respects."

"Naw, Grandma, maybe some other time. I'm sure my old lady will have me locked down by then. But I'm glad I was able to come out and see you."

The words sounded good coming out of his mouth and they sounded even better to Georgia Mae. He was the only grandchild she had and since her daughter was gone, she'd never have anymore. She wanted family at her old age and now that Jerome was back in her living room, her heart ached for him to stay.

"Are you sure you can't stay longer? I'd love for us to play bingo, checkers, or even watch some television game shows." She smiled, hoping he'd be warmed enough to change his mind or slow down from gobbling. It didn't work though. "You can even tell me about those beautiful grandbabies of mine I'll never see. I swear I'd spoil 'em rotten." Speaking about Savannah and Samantha, she often wondered if they resembled her daughter and if they even were aware they had a great-grandmother.

"Unfortunately, Grandma, I've gotta go. But I promise to try to come back sooner. Maybe in a few weeks. And I'll try bringing you some pictures of them to put up," Jerome lied through his teeth. Instead of him trying to make Georgia Mae happy in her old age, he was secretly plotting ways in his mind to get over on her. Grandmother or not, he needed his fix.

"I'm sorry to hear that you must go, sweetheart. But hopefully, if it's God's will, you can make it by in those few weeks with pictures of those girls. I pray for all of you all the time, you and all your kids." Her voice drifted off.

"Well maybe you should pray louder. I don't think He hears you," Jerome joked, wiping his mouth. The mood in the room was taking a turn, but it was time for him to steal and run anyhow. His stomach was full, which meant he was hungrier for a high. "I'm gonna take a leak real quick and then I've gotta be heading back home." He wasn't trying to have her flip the emotional script back on him. Jerome didn't have too much of an emotional connect to his mother since she was dead and gone, but Georgia Mae was something different. Although he used her for money, he loved her for having his back.

"Make yourself back at home." She sat back, happy to have life in her home. "It's in the same place you left it eleven years ago."

Jerome flew up the stairs and relieved himself. He hadn't used the bathroom since leaving home, plus he'd gulped down a few glass of fruit punch Kool-Aid that his granny had whipped up. He found himself getting depressed that he couldn't be the grandson Georgia Mae truly wanted and deserved. Staring in the mirror, he was angry at himself for being such a failure. Had he not gotten addicted to drugs eleven years ago, none of this would've ever happened.

Jerome had been running from facing his reality since Banko ran him from out of his first baby momma's house; but all of his pity and guilt came rushing back now that he was back in the projects. He hadn't heard from or seen Patrice in years and when it came to the son they shared, Jerome Jr., he wasn't sure he'd recognize him if they crossed paths. For all he knew, his son could've been the one who tossed him on his ass when he was begging for credit. Of course he'd heard from his grandmother that his son had dropped his name and was only going by Rello. And the more he stared at his deteriorated reflection, the more he wished he could erase his whole existence.

Despite Jerome feeling low, he still was thirsty for a high. Tiptoeing into his grandmother's room, he swiped every piece of jewelry that was in her nightstand along with the few dollars he found in her dresser drawer. Jerome fought the urge to steal the nineteen-inch flat-screen TV that was muted on a movie, but couldn't help himself. After unplugging it and securing the cord so he could make a quick dash, Jerome flew down the stairs and out the door of his grandmother's house with no remorse.

"Jerome! Come back here. Don't you do this to me," Georgia Mae shouted from the couch then jumped up. By the time she made it to her front door, Jerome was halfway across the parking lot. "Please come back here and make this right. I'll forgive you if you just come back. Don't make me disown you, Jerome."

At eighty-two, Georgia Mae was too old to be upset. Her heart was pounding but more so broken that her grandson had done her foul. When she finally walked up the stairs to see what else he'd stolen, her heart sank even further realizing her wedding ring and the watch her job had given her when she retired were gone. Georgia Mae was hurt to say the least. Her husband was dead and gone; and she'd worked long and hard to receive the token of appreciation she'd never see again. Because of that, she never wanted to see Jerome again either.

"Hey, I don't care where you're at; make your way back to the PJ's. Rello is here and I think you two need to talk. Furthermore, he's setting the girl up to meet him here now." Patrice was panting trying to get the words out. She knew if the girl was as thirsty as Rello made her sound she'd be there quick as she could.

"Say word, I'm on the way. Don't let him or that little tramp leave before I get there." Banko made an immediate U-turn uncaring about oncoming traffic. "Good look on trying to make this right, sis. I appreciate you." He hung up.

Bonnie slid to the other side of the back seat but Banko didn't care. His only concern was making sure the drug connection he had in Dominik was fixed and continued to go strong. He floored the Challenger to eighty miles per hour so he could possibly beat the ol' girl there.

"Is everything okay? You're driving like an animal." Bonnie strapped on her seat belt afraid.

"Yeah, it's all good." He swerved through traffic like a beast. "You wanna hop out? You're more than welcome to, but I ain't stopping 'til I reach the projects."

"I thought you said you weren't going there." Bonnie questioned him like she had a position.

"Ay, I've got business to handle but that's none of yours. Again, you can hop out if you wanna but either way shut the fuck up," Banko commanded, continuing to swerve through traffic determined not to be slowed down.

Bonnie kept her mouth closed and her hands gripping the seat belt for dear life. Cars almost collided with them, drivers honked and curse at his recklessness, and Banko shouted back like he had the right.

Chapter 14

"Get ya ass up and onto the porch to wait. Your uncle is on the way." Patrice strutted into the living room. "Ain't no little sack chasing heifer gonna come between the only two men in my life. Banko supports us and is trying to teach you how to do the same. I don't plan on missing a beat with the way I live."

Rello got up and followed his mother onto the porch. Normally he would've been trying to get dressed in the best rags he could find and spraying down with cheap cologne, but none of that mattered now that the truth was about to be exposed. He'd crawled back to his mom with his tail between his legs; therefore, he didn't have a choice but to face the girl he'd blinded with lies.

"Here, you might as well take a sip of Henn Dogg. It's about to get real and you might need the liquid courage to hold your nuts high when that girl arrives." Patrice handed him a cup of Hennessy, then poured herself a cup as well. "Pussy is a powerful thing but you should know that by now. That girl has caused so much trouble just by having your head wide open." Patrice and Banko had been up all night going over Rello's wrongs and how he needed to make them right. She couldn't wait to see the girl her son was so hot over. *I just might smack the shit out of her myself.*

Rello did as her mother told him, but quicker than she'd suggested. He hated the feeling of letting her down, being compared to his father, and not adding up to the man Banko was. The liquor was a welcome respite from the stress and drama on his plate. He guzzled it down quicker and quicker, thinking it would immediately wash away all his self-pity. All he wanted to do was be the boss, call the shots, and delegate his own crew of li'l runners. He'd failed miserably and couldn't stand the feeling of simply being himself.

"Jack me off harder, girl. We'll be pulling up in a few and I need my dick to have spit by then." The cab driver patted Star on her thigh. He might've wanted her to jerk him harder and faster, but he was already having a hard enough time keeping his composure.

"I'm doing the best I can under the circumstances. You better use your imagination." Star rolled her eyes.

"We can always pull into a back alley so you can throw that fat ass on me real quick." He glanced over at Star with lust in his eyes. The cab driver was feeling lucky, especially already having his penis slobbed on earlier in the day.

"Nope, I can't make your dreams come true right now because I'm in a rush. But I'll take your number and maybe if the price is right we can make something happen later." She was repulsed by the taxi driver but attracted by what she could gain by using him. *If a hand job got me a free ride, ain't no telling what else I can get him to do. He can be my personal chauffeur until I come up on a car.* The more she thought about ways to use the cab driver, the harder she gripped his manhood. In a matter of moments, he squirted all over his clothes but Star moved out the way just in time.

When it was all said and done, Star sat in the passenger seat of the cab with butterflies swarming in her stomach over Rello. She could feel the cab driver still staring at her, but she zoned him out and passed him her number for pacification. As a distraction for herself, she pulled out her compact mirror to examine the damage from Bonnie and if the bag of ice she'd used from the gas station helped the swelling. Since there was nothing she could do, she didn't sweat telling Rello the truth and even some of the reasons why she moved. Putting on a thicker coat of makeup than usual, she chose to leave well enough alone.

I know he's gonna be sweating me once I throw this head and pussy game on him. He'll be over me all day and night. I'ma have to beg his ass to go. Star didn't doubt her sack chasing or sex skills. She was assuming Rello was giving her another chance since he'd reached out. She hadn't given the pills or cough syrup another thought. The closer they got to the entrance of the projects, the more her heart started to flutter. Sliding the compact mirror back into her purse, she noticed the bottle of cough syrup was missing and shrieked.

"What the hell? Are you okay?" The cab driver looked over at her with a shocked and weird expression. He didn't know what to think of his passenger's sudden explosion.

"Yes, yes. I'm sorry about that. Keep going please," Star apologized, then waved him back to driving. He'd completely stopped because of her erratic behavior.

Star tore her purse up and even dumped everything from inside out; but still didn't find the cough syrup. She wanted to scream again but couldn't alarm the taxi driver. Star was infuriated. There wasn't a thought that doubted her ability to keep up with things. She knew she hadn't lost it. The first person she called to see if they'd fess up to stealing it was Tanisha though she knew it was Bonnie all along. Once she clarified just that by a pissed Tanisha, Star vowed to be on her mother's head. *I'm jumping on her on sight. I've had enough of her trifling ways. There's just some things you don't do, and that's steal from your child.*

Jerome ran through the front entrance of the Sojourner Truth Homes with the television he'd stolen from his grandmother gripped tightly. In spite of him being desperate for a high, he couldn't chance stopping to sell it to anyone in the projects because he was fearful they'd heard Georgia Mae shouting.

He wanted to turn around and unbreak her heart when he heard her crying out for him not to steal from her; but Jerome was too deep into his addiction.

He was confident, however, that selling it in the hood he'd made his home with Bonnie in had a buyer for sure. Out of breath, he slowed down his pace to gather himself. Usually he wouldn't be sluggish when running from doing a crime, but the fried chicken was weighing heavy on his stomach. Right when he was getting ready to take back off full force, he looked up shocked like he seen a ghost. Losing his grip on the television, it crashed into the pavement and shattered instantly. "Oh shit." He shook, with nothing but fear in his soul for the worst.

Banko didn't want to answer his ringing phone but had no choice. He knew the connect wanted to know what the status was on getting his cash, product, or the girl delivered to his doorstep. "Yo, D, what's good?" He didn't use his full name because Bonnie was riding in the back seat.

"Banko, please tell me you've fixed the problem. Please tell me I can relay the message to my wife that you've found a resolution," Dominik spoke calmly, enunciating every syllable. His patience had run thin. The more he sat in his lavish Chicago home drinking fine wine, the more he felt disrespected and wanted revenge on all parties involved. He had more than enough money coming through the door to be put at risk over a thug from Detroit.

"I'm tying the mess up now. You can expect a call from me within the next hour. Trust my word. I've never failed you before." Banko knew what Dominik was thinking even though he hadn't said the words. They were both criminals in their own way, so silence was sometimes the only way they knew how to communicate.

"One time is always too many in my book. I'll be waiting for your call." Dominik ended the call.

"I swear to God, if I fall, everyone will fall." Banko threw his phone into the windshield. He was on the brink of losing control and couldn't stand it. His whole existence was based on him having complete and utter control. Dominik had already informed him that one false move could end up with him being cut off, so just the mere thought of being downgraded had Banko infuriated.

Bonnie sat in the back seat confused as to what was going on. Whatever the case was, she could tell Banko was scrambling to keep the other person on the line happy. She tried hanging on to his every word, but was too busy trying to hold on to her life. The Challenger was coasting on two wheels. Then it abruptly stopped.

"You've got to be fucking kidding me." Banko slammed on the brakes, making Bonnie's head slam against the back of the passenger's seat. "I swear, this motherfucker and his son gonna drive me into the grave," he roared. "My word must not mean shit to that bloodline."

When Bonnie lifted her head up to catch up with what was going on and her surroundings, her eyes bucked out wide. Jerome was staring back at the car with even wider eyes like he was looking at a ghost or the devil in form. "What in the fuck are you doing over here? You better not be cheating on me with no PJ pussy. Better yet, ya ass better not be trying to sneak no high behind my back."

Jerome dropped the TV but hadn't made a move. With all the open space around him, he felt trapped. He knew what the consequences were if Banko caught him. All of a sudden the high he'd stolen from his grandmother for didn't seem so important.

Despite Bonnie and Banko staring at the same person, they had total different interests in him. Banko had run Jerome out of the projects because he was nothing but bad luck for Patrice eleven years ago, and vowed death would come his way if he ever laid eyes on him again. And Bonnie just wanted answers. Taking off her seat belt, she no longer cared about how crazy Banko was acting or driving. Matter of fact, she didn't care about why he was screaming or what for. She was acting off a one-track mind. Jerome was her man and she wanted to know what he was doing over here. Never once did she wonder where her youngest daughters were. She hopped out the back seat without a second thought and darted toward Jerome.

Banko hadn't paid the slightest attention to Bonnie or the words flying out of her mouth. He was too con-

cerned as to why Jerome was at the Sojourner Truth
Homes in the first place. *This nigga better not be conspiring with that tricky-ass son of his. I swear I'll kill
both of they asses in blood and deal with Patrice later.*
His thoughts were all over the place. All he saw was
red. Reaching over into the glove compartment, he
pulled out his pistol and loaded one up top.

"Didn't I tell yo' cracked-out ass to never step
foot in this hood again? Didn't I tell you to stay
away from my sister? What are you doing over here,
nigga?" Slamming his fist against the steering wheel,
Banko swerved into oncoming traffic and hopped out
ready to make the word he'd huffed into Jerome's face
eleven years ago come true. With his pistol drawn
ready to bust fire, Banko's adrenaline was pumping.

"This is far as I'm taking you. It's obviously some
crazy shit going down up ahead." The taxi driver
pulled over to the side of the road.

Neighbors of Sojourner Truth Homes, those driving by, and even pedestrians walking at their own
risk watched with their phones out as Banko held his
pistol to Jerome's head. The crowd was growing by
the second. No one feared for their life because they
knew where Banko's anger was directed. They all
wanted something to gossip about later.

"Hey, get out or you'll be riding the other way,
girl. I don't tread into the projects when there's beef
brewing." The cab driver nudged Star.

She was too busy caught up in what was unraveling before her eyes to be present in the moment. Upon pulling up, she'd instantly recognized Jerome, her mother, and even the man who was driving the Challenger who was holding the gun to her stepfather's head. Star didn't know who he was, but figured Jerome's territorial ways over her mother had caught up with him. Because Star didn't know who Jerome really was and what he really represented to her, she could only fathom this whole ordeal was in some way because of Bonnie.

"Hey, y'all are about to miss all the action on the porch. Your brother got a gun pulled out on some unfortunate nigga," a boy hollered at Patrice, flying past the porch toward the action himself.

It only took one person to spread a buzz in the projects. The second Banko slammed on his brakes making horns blare out was the second someone peeped out their blinds, windows, and even ran to see what was going on. So far, they'd witness Jerome pee on his pants and beg for his life.

"What? Banko? Oh my God," Patrice sprang up running behind the growing crowd.

Rello was six paces behind her, sluggish because the liquor was weighing him down. Banko having a gun pulled out on someone wasn't new to him. Especially since his uncle had just whipped him up with the same one. He was nonchalant about the whole situation until mother started screaming, crying, and running toward Banko like lightning speed.

"Banko! What are you doing? Calm down and tell me what happened," Patrice pleaded. "Think first and react later."

"What in the hell is this cracked-out coward doing here, Patrice? Was he here to see you or that failure of a son y'all share? I told ya ho-ass baby daddy I'd give him a final blast on the real if he came back to the projects and here he is." Banko was trembling with resentment. No one could talk sense into him if they tried. When he finally noticed Rello over his sister's shoulder, he thought for sure they'd all been conspiring against him. "My word is bond around this motherfucker. I make the final word and y'all best respect it." Banko proved his point to everyone watching.

One gunshot rung out into the air, hushing everyone for a brief second but Jerome indefinitely. He fell to the ground with blood squirting from his throat then Bonnie's shrills broke the silence.

"Oh my God, please no. Please don't take my daughters' father," Bonnie cried and yelled because of the moment. She fell down by Jerome's side; but deep in her heart, she knew she truly wasn't saddened. He'd been nothing but a get high partner, an abuser, and a monster to Savannah and Samantha. For all these years she'd been turning a blind eye but she no longer had to.

Those who stood by didn't know what all the arguing was about; but they did continue to film and take pictures. The few who called the cops left the scene and would beg to differ on the truth if ever questioned by Banko or his soldiers. They even watched the skeptical crying scene Bonnie was putting on by Jerome's side. Her thirst was real and even recorded when she stole the jewelry from his pockets and ran into the projects. She only cared about getting high and locking herself away in the short stay instead of going home to Savannah and Samantha as the only parent they had left.

Karma had caught up with Jerome. In his passing, he left two baby mommas, two daughters, Georgia Mae, who would just shake her head without sympathy and limp away with her cane, and a son he'd abandoned eleven years ago as a young boy.

"Oh my God, Banko, do you know what you've done?" Jumping on her brother's back, Patrice was losing her mind in disbelief. "Why'd you do it? Why'd you kill him? Why? Why? Why?" Patrice was going hysterical smacking her brother upside the head and in his face. She didn't care about the body on the ground; she only cared that her life was about to be over. If Banko went to jail behind murdering Jerome, the life he'd tried protecting her with in the first place would come to an end. "Who is gonna have my back now? Who is gonna hold up our family?" All Patrice saw was the end.

Everyone surrounding them had camera phones. By now, even social media had witnessed her brother kill a man in cold blood. There was no way Banko could deny he was a murderer if he wanted to. Although he was loved by fiends, he was hated by do-gooders of the community. They thrived on sending delinquents away. Banko didn't blink a feeling of remorse or flinch when he heard police sirens from afar. He knew they were coming for him and that's when the final wire in his brain snapped.

"Get the fuck off of me before I shoot ya ass next. I wouldn't be out here going Rambo for a nigga if it weren't for you in the first place." Banko flung Patrice off him. Her body hit the pavement like a rag doll but that only knocked the breath from her lungs momentarily. "I'll kill anybody who goes against me. I told his black ass to stay away from here back in the day or I'd kill him; and I meant just that. Who in the fuck was this nigga to test me? I bet he'll listen now," Banko spat. He was uncontrollable or at least he thought he was.

Patrice looked up from the pavement in total disbelief that her brother had spoken and treated her so foul to her and in front of so many people. The two things that kept their bond tight was trust and love. But now she saw Banko's love was only for control and respect. As the sirens got closer, she turned toward Rello with sorrowful eyes. She was trying to say, "You're all I've got left."

Rello didn't know how to respond. He couldn't believe he was staring at his father bleeding out on the pavement with a gunshot to the neck. He looked around at the crowd, at his mom, at his uncle, then down at his ticking Rolex.

"What the fuck is up, nephew? You got a problem? Some words you wanna get off ya chest about me killing ya pops in cold blood?"

The crowd stood in shock. Banko, Patrice, and Rello had always been the cream of the crop of the projects, but today they were no different from all the other families who were broken apart by dark lies, drugs, and drama.

"Naw, Unc, you call 'em like you see 'em and the coward had to die." Rello shrugged his shoulders.

No one knew his intentions but everyone was in shock when Rello walked over to the dead body of his father and poured a few drops of Hennessy over his face. With the glass bottle of Hennessy clutched tightly, he took it back and guzzled every last drop until the bottle was bone dry. He could barely stand by the time he took the rim from his lips. *If the man I'm growing to represent just got killed by the hand of my uncle, I'm sure my uncle will have no problem killing me.* Seeing the red, white, and blue flashing sirens a few blocks away, Rello geared up to make a coward move. With as much energy as he could muster up, he took six quick steps toward Banko and slammed the bottle against the side of his face.

***

"All right, girl, you can hit me up later or whatever but you've gotta get out. I've witnessed enough and the cops are coming. I'm not trying to be around when they pull up." The driver nudged Star again.

"Do yourself a favor and quit whining. You can pull ya dick back out so I can start jacking it." Star reached over into the taxi driver's pants. "I need to go pick my sisters up from daycare then get dropped off to my apartment. I can guarantee you a few good nuts."

The cab driver hurried to unbuckle his pants. Wherever the girl needed to go, he'd take her as long as her hand was in his lap. He was well aware that she was using him, but he was using her too.

Before they pulled off, Star witnessed Rello slam a bottle against Banko's head then take two bullets to his back when he turned to run. She didn't know if he'd live or not, hustle or not, or if they'd ever reconcile. What she did know was that he was no good to her now and she was on to the next.